Penny Perrick is the author of three works of non-fiction and a first novel, *Malina*, which was hailed by the *Daily Mail* as 'Marvellous . . . a magnificent book' and which was published by Bantam. She has spent much of her life in London, working as a fashion editor for *Vogue*, a columnist on the *Sun* and *The Times*, and a fiction editor and reviewer for *The Sunday Times* Books Section. She now lives in the west of Ireland and has begun work on *Evermore*, her third novel.

IMPOSSIBLE
THINGS

Penny Perrick

BLACK SWAN

IMPOSSIBLE THINGS
A BLACK SWAN BOOK : 0 552 99693 9

Originally published in Great Britain by Bantam Press,
a division of Transworld Publishers Ltd

PRINTING HISTORY
Bantam Press edition published 1995
Black Swan edition published 1996

Set in 11/12pt Linotype Melior by Hewer Text Composition Services, Edinburgh

Black Swan Books are published by Transworld Publishers Ltd,
61–63 Uxbridge Road, London W5 5SA,
in Australia by Transworld Publishers (Australia) Pty Ltd,
15–25 Helles Avenue, Moorebank, NSW 2170
and in New Zealand by Transworld Publishers (NZ) Ltd,
3 William Pickering Drive, Albany, Auckland.

Reproduced, printed and bound in Great Britain by
Cox & Wyman Ltd, Reading, Berks.

To Emmy, my daughter

Acknowledgements

I am grateful to Peter Hennessy and Colin McDowell for writing, respectively, *Never Again. Britain 1945–51* (Cape) and *Hats, Status, Style and Glamour* (Thames and Hudson) and for giving me so much of their time. I should also like to thank Anthony Howard and Stanley Clinton-Davis for sharing their childhood recollections with me, Vanessa Denza, Clive Hirshhorn, Susan Conder and Rose Brooks for information about fashion and popular music, and Dannie and Joan Abse and Sean and Marie Ashe for smoothing my way along the road. My publishers, Bantam Press, have been helpful and encouraging beyond the requirements of contract and courtesy, as has my agent, Caradoc King.

'To a woman, the consciousness of being well-dressed gives a sense of tranquillity that religion fails to bestow.'

Helen Olcott Bell

'I consider that without hats, an intrinsic part of fashion, we would have no civilisation.'

Christian Dior

'Amazed, I clothe myself.'

Gertrude Kolmar

'Nobody after the war wanted ideals. They wanted change and movement and life.'

David Hughes in *Age of Austerity*

PART ONE

1947 − 1952

Chapter One

'You can't beat champagne for washing windows,' Zanna said, 'especially when there's no frigging water. Pardon my French.'

Leonora, who had, a few moments before, walked rather unsteadily through the gleaming pink door of Zanna Modes, looked stunned. Zanna was a dazzling sight. She was wearing what the newspapers had called the New Look: a white silk shantung jacket which pinched her tiny waist and then sprang out over her hips, a navy-blue skirt in fine wool which poured its pleats lavishly over her thin calves. Nobody could buy clothes like these in London; they could have come only from the Paris house of Christian Dior, which had shown them to a delighted audience a month before. Leonora would have loved to know how the pretty milliner had acquired her beautiful clothes.

On that brutish day at the end of the coldest winter of the century, Zanna shone as though enamelled. Pale lavender eyes, their irises ringed with black, glared intensely out of her white face like those of a china doll. Coppery hair was swept back from a round, clear forehead. Zanna's large, square mouth was painted red, the lower lip moist and unfurled; from the corner of one glittering eye, a pale blue vein throbbed towards her left temple. At odds with this tense glamour were Zanna's little squirrel's paws with their chewed fingernails.

Leonora, ashamed of herself for staring, let her eyes drop to her own balding suede boots with their hideous rubber soles and toecaps damp from the slushy pavements outside.

It was the first time she had come down to London since the end of the war, and it was worse than she had imagined. Nearly two years after VE day, destruction still seemed a dry, frightening certainty in the freezing city. The houses, weakened by bombing, seemed to tremble, threateningly, under searing, iron skies, heavy as clay. Leonora had clambered over the rubble of filthy snow at the kerbside, noticing wrecked doorways, wounded stucco, walls that cracked and sifted down. In one bombed house, a fireplace was suspended on one remaining bedroom wall among the cheerful roses of the wallpaper, like a macabre stage set. She had never seen people looking so worn-out, so crushed by fatigue. A film of dust and tiredness dulled their faces; snow seemed permanently gathered in the folds of their clothes. And now all these shortages: no electricity, no water for hours at a time; it was as though the dying hadn't died.

Walking along grimy Bond Street, Leonora had looked across the road and seen something lovely: a shop-window glittering in the icy sunlight and within it, poised on a metal stand, a single hat. Ostrich feathers swirled around its brim, the tip of each black quill spangled with a *diamanté* drop. On the right of the window was a bright pink door and, above it, a fascia of the same colour, 'Zanna Modes' painted across it in a shiny scrawl.

'That hat is inspired.' Leonora spoke aloud without knowing it, and, crabwise, wishing there was something to hold onto, began a tottery climb over the piled-up snow in the gutter so that she could cross the street.

She had thought of buying the hat for Gillian who was looking even more put-upon than usual, her voice a

14

maddening creak of complaint. And who could blame her, married to Gomer who was ruthless and mad with his volcanic temper and dogged, stupid beliefs? Poor Gillian, brought up in South African sunshine, her summer dresses ironed and starched by docile black hands, and now fetched up in Utley Manor, not a place to be happy in. You would think it would be with all those dogs and children, but the dogs always looked so disconsolate and the children scared, or falsely chirpy like underfed sparrows. Leonora sometimes felt that she should apologize to Gillian for Gomer having brought her to the damp, Shropshire house where pompoms of moss spread on the wet, grey window-ledges, although she had had nothing to do with her elder nephew's marriage and, had she been asked, would certainly have advised against it, from everyone's point of view. The only sort of woman who could have coped with Gomer's rage and disillusion would have been someone like her own daughter, Daisy, as big a bully as Gomer in her way. Still, the point was to stop Gillian drooping in that annoying way of hers, her shoulders shivering under her cardigan. That swirling hat in the surprisingly clean window might buck her up. Leonora had continued her slippery progress across the empty street and, disconcerted by the elegance of the young woman who had smiled in greeting and raised one thin arc of an eyebrow, had commented on the window's brightness.

'Champagne,' Leonora repeated now. 'I'd almost forgotten there was such a thing.'

'Well, the Free French never forgot,' Zanna said, in her coarse, low voice. 'Very generous they were with it too.' She looked at the old woman's sodden boots and noticed that her black coat was pre-war but beautifully tailored. 'There's another crate in the back,' she said, 'and you look a bit done in. A glass would do you good. There's a bit of a fire and I was going to close for an hour in any case. No-one else even bothered to open. Sodding shortages. Makes you wonder who won the war.'

The light seemed to brim around her as she opened a door at the back of the shop and steered Leonora through it. Inside, a scant fire of coal and rubbish was burning in a rusted grate.

'It's not much,' Zanna said, 'but that's the last of the coal. I don't notice the cold much. Feel.' She laid a rough little hand on Leonora's cheek. It was almost hot. Zanna hoiked back her skirt – nylon stockings; how had she got *those*? – to get a good grip on the champagne bottle with her knees. 'Here she comes.' Zanna held out a foaming Bakelite mug. 'Sorry. Should have introduced myself. Zanna Gringrich.'

'Leonora Fitzhaven.' The bubbles pricking in her throat brought her back to life. 'I didn't come in just to compliment you on the clean window' – there was a wedding ring on one stumpy finger – 'Mrs Gringrich. It was the hat.'

'Hope Is The Thing With Feathers. S'what I call that one. It's in a poem by Emily Dickinson. Read her stuff a lot during the war, passed the time.' She looked at Leonora hard out of her lilac eyes. 'Dunno that it's your style but try it on if you like, there's a mirror in the corner.'

'It's for my nephew's wife. She's quite young, about your age,' she thought, correctly, that Zanna was about twenty-six, 'with dark eyes, so I think it might suit her. I was planning to return home today, but it looks as though I'll have to spend another night in town.'

She was reluctant to get up from the scarred gilt chair. The back of the shop was fascinating, and almost warm enough, full of hat-blocks and open boxes of different fabrics. There were shelves holding carded ribbon and sequins and, on the walls, studio photographs of film stars – Leonora thought she recognized Ann Todd and Margaret Lockwood – wearing straw picture hats.

Zanna nodded in the direction of the photographs. 'How I started, film work. Someone I met in the war. I loved the war, you know.'

Leonora got up stiffly, offended. 'Thank you for the champagne and the fire, Mrs Gringrich. I think I shall

16

take a chance on the train; the snow seems undecided. What do I owe you for the hat?'

'Nine guineas, but take it on appro. It's always dodgy buying a hat for someone else. Hats are personal, like skin.' It wasn't lost on Zanna that when Leonora had unbuttoned her coat, a star-shaped diamond brooch, undoubtedly real, glinted on the shoulder of her dress.

The train that arrived at Utley station four hours late reeked of soot. Leonora passed most of the journey thinking of Zanna Gringrich: her coarse voice, warm little paws and Dior costume. How *had* she got hold of it? Were Leonora to have asked her, Zanna, usually so frank, would have lied. The truth was that a former lover of hers, a Free French officer now based at the French Embassy, had smuggled several items from the Dior collection in the diplomatic bag. He took this risk because of his sweet memories of Zanna's wartime behaviour. He recalled the way she almost skipped into hotel bedrooms, rented by the hour: being unaccountable and unaccounted for in a strange bed had excited her so much that she would nip the heel of his thumb with her slightly crooked teeth, a habit he found disturbingly erotic.

During all those dangerous days, the officer, whose name was Jean-Louis Mançeur, had kept his nerves steady by flashing pictures of Zanna through his mind: Zanna unscrewing the gilt cap of her lipstick and drawing the scarlet cylinder towards her mouth as though about to eat it; Zanna brushing her dark orange hair with a grubby silk scarf wound around the hairbrush; Zanna's hands flashing white against the shadows in the darkened room, and then the spit of flame from her cigarette lighter; Zanna scowling into her powder compact, wearing a satin petticoat, its lustre sliding along her thighs.

She was a woman sharpened by desire, all edges, without shame. Jean-Louis knew perfectly well that Zanna had sometimes made love to three uniformed

17

men in one day. He knew that it thrilled her to think that she might die with any one of them, crushed by a bomb in an anonymous room. A woman like Zanna deserved beautiful clothes, even though Jean-Louis rarely had the opportunity to see her wearing them, now that her husband had been demobbed. Jean-Louis who, during the war years, had dreamed of taking Zanna to the Paris salons, now reconciled himself, good-humouredly, to bringing the salons to her.

At six o'clock, Raymond Gringrich drove to Bond Street in his Ford Prefect to drive Zanna to their house in Golders Green. He had filled up the car with petrol at a garage in Curzon Street, an arrangement made by Zanna, who had once been on friendly terms with the owner of the garage. Raymond was uneasy about the availability of the petrol and the friendship, but was too weary to question either. He put his head around the pink door of Zanna Modes, shouted, 'I'm here,' towards the room at the back, and returned to the car where he sat, his brown eyes bulgy with tiredness and worry, waiting for his wife.

Zanna took her time leaving. She loathed leaving the West End for the pebble-dash semi in Golders Green, where the ordinariness of her husband and daughter bored and irritated her.

Zanna's parents, Lilian and Sidney Spetner, loved Raymond and were proud of the fact that he was a professional man, a solicitor, although Sidney, who owned a barber-shop in the East End, was far richer. Zanna had been seventeen when she met Raymond in 1937, at her sister Minetta's wedding – a meeting engineered by Minetta, who had sat them at the same table – apprenticed to a wholesale hat-maker in Luton, already able to stroke felt and straw into ingenious shapes. In the beginning, she had loved all the sober things about Raymond which she now disliked. As she got into the car, her big, doll's eyes narrowed at the sight of Raymond's heavy-framed spectacles, but she leaned over and pecked his cheek with her red mouth.

Raymond started the car slowly with lumbering movements. How slowly he does everything, Zanna thought; he can draw out any action interminably, even striking a match.

Before the war she hadn't noticed this, or the way Raymond folded his shirts into fussy squares, or the tiresome glint of his tie-pin, the cautious point of his handkerchief showing above his breast pocket. The war had made her *see* things, sharpened her senses, from the time Raymond had been called up in 1941, just after Aurora was born. When he left, Zanna had felt a sudden, wild surge of freedom. Lilian had taken the baby to Wales to escape the bombing, but Zanna had stayed in London, bought the shop when everything was going cheap in the expectation of annihilation. For the first time in her life she had been free of the oppressiveness of belonging and being belonged to. Not having to think about anyone else, that was the best thing. People thought you were quite a heroine for sticking it out in London, even the fire warden who had tried to stop her returning to a bombed-out flat in Hornsey. 'It's not safe, miss,' he had told her but she had shrugged and said, 'You can beat death by getting to it first. And I've left a box of chocolates in there.'

She had gone home with the warden afterwards, and they had eaten the chocolates, crouched naked in front of a grumbling gas fire. She had loved those wartime encounters: cigarette smoke drifting like oil between expectant faces; Covent Garden Opera House converted into a dancehall; people throwing a party when they managed to get hold of a dozen fresh eggs. Life seemed so limiting now; everyone looked wrung-out by disappointment, Raymond most of all.

'What sort of day did you have?' he asked her, as he did every evening, solicitous and dull.

'An interesting woman came in this morning,' Zanna said. 'Mattli coat, diamonds that have probably been in the family since the Battle of Hastings. She took the ostrich cartwheel on appro for some relative, and I hope

19

to God she likes it because everyone's going to be wearing the New Look before you know it, whatever the bloody Board of Trade blathers on about it, bloody killjoys, and when they do, they'll want something neat and sculpted on their bonces. My cartwheel will be about as correct as a French kiss at a funeral.'

Raymond winced. His shoulders slumped further into his pillowy body. He had come home to a different Zanna, thinner than she used to be, with jutting hipbones and an air of nervy stimulation. Beside her, everyone else looked dowdy and tired. There was a kind of low crookery about his wife that made him feel sad and failed. He thought of his law practice in Hackney and hoped that whatever it was that Zanna had got up to during the war, to get her Bond Street shop and her couture clothes, had been legal.

Every weekday evening, they collected Aurora from her grandparents' house. Lilian and Sidney lived a few streets away in Golders Green. Sidney had bought both houses at a property auction a month after VE day, and planned on staying put after the years of temporary lodgings in Wales and Yorkshire or any other Godforsaken place where he thought Lilian and Aurora would be safe from the bombing. He had moved them back to London before Raymond's demob and while Zanna was working too hard in the shop to claim back her daughter.

Those few months, living with his wife and granddaughter, his 'girlies', in the new house, knowing that all his family was safe, were the happiest of Sidney's life, and ended with Raymond's release from the Army. That had been a terrible time. Raymond had arrived, still in khaki. Aurora had given him one terrified look and run to her grandmother, pushing herself between Lilian's knees. Raymond had taken a banana out of his kitbag and held it out to her. 'It's to eat,' he said. Aurora had tried to bite it, skin and all, and, when she couldn't, had started to cry with bewilderment and humiliation, which appalled Raymond. Aurora had been three months old when he had been called up and the thought of his little girl growing up had been all that had kept him going during his time in the Army which had been spent mainly in military hospitals, trying to recover from frequent bouts of pneumonia. He had thought she would run to him, her dearest Daddy, home from the war; instead, her arms around Lilian's knees, she had shrieked, 'Don't leave me, Nana,' sensing that Raymond meant an end to her living with her grandparents.

Raymond edged the car towards the kerb. Zanna said, 'Let's skedaddle as soon as we can, OK? I've got three designs to finish for Swan & Edgar.' But when Lilian opened the door, they could tell she'd cooked *tsimmes*, Raymond's favourite, by the smell of chicken fat and carrots in the hallway. They would have to stay for supper.

Aurora ran out from behind Lilian and hurled herself at Raymond. He picked her up and rubbed his nose under her chin to make her giggle. It hadn't taken him long to win her round; it was Zanna that Aurora still feared and distrusted. At the sight of her mother taking off her fur coat and shaking out the pleats of her skirt, Aurora's deep-set eyes seemed to shrink further back in her face and her arms tightened around Raymond's neck.

'Did she do the exercises?' Zanna asked Lilian in a demanding way. She did not like Aurora's looks. The child's hair, the same dark orange as her own, was fine and floppy around her plump face, but in everything else she resembled Raymond, even walking in Raymond's lumbering, flat-footed way. Zanna had devised an exercise to raise her arches, in which Aurora was supposed to pick up a pencil between her toes, twenty times each day, but she suspected, rightly, that Lilian never made Aurora do this.

Lilian shrugged. 'Minetta came over with the kids; you know how it is. Sit down, I've made *tsimmes* for my Raymond.'

They ate in the kitchen, next to the round boiler which was barely warm because of the electricity cuts. Sidney came into the room, bow-legged after years of bending towards his clients to trim the hair from the delicate area behind their ears.

'Atta boy, Robbie,' he said to Aurora, pushing in her chair and delighted when Zanna glared at him. She hated him calling Aurora Robbie, even though it was what the little girl called herself. She had been named after Aurora Leigh in the poem by Elizabeth Barrett Browning because, the week before she was born, Zanna had read the lines: 'How dreary 'tis for women to sit still/On winter nights by solitary fires.'

Zanna, always restless, but unable to move much at the end of her pregnancy, understood the dreariness of sitting still. When Sidney had said he thought Aurora was a bit fancy, Zanna had said, 'I almost called her Amapola Tangerine; the man in the flat next door played the saxophone. Played them all bloody day, one after the other.' She had gone to bed with this man and he had composed a song for her called 'Zanna's Serenade', which he was playing in the night-club where he worked when a bomb hit it, killing everyone in the building.

Lilian piled Raymond's plate with *tsimmes*, a delicious mixture of carrots, potatoes and less meat than the recipe demanded because of rationing. Since Raymond had come out of the Army, she had noticed a lostness about him. It was why she queued all morning to get his favourite foods, and spent much of the rest of the day preparing the traditional Jewish dishes he loved: *holishkes*, stuffed cabbage, *lokshen* pudding, hoping that good food would do more than keep him alive, that it would keep him interested in *being* alive.

While Lilian was filling Aurora's plate, Zanna got up, took the plate from her and spooned half of the *tsimmes* back into the saucepan before giving it to the child. Lilian's face took on a pursy expression as it often did when Zanna was in the same room but she stayed silent.

Zanna didn't sit down again. She hated the attention her mother gave to food and the heavy dishes she cooked, always too much, in spite of rationing. During the war, Zanna had got used to living on scraps, and the way Lilian encouraged Raymond and Aurora to guzzle disgusted her. As if Raymond weren't fat enough, the way his belly lumped over his waistband. On Sundays, when Zanna cooked for him, there were never quite enough potatoes to go round, and she never shared the meal but chewed an apple, making Raymond and Aurora feel uncomfortable as they ate the grey, shredding joint which Zanna had pushed into the oven and forgotten to baste.

She prowled around her parents' kitchen, glaring impatiently until the meal was over. Later, when Lilian and Sidney were in their bulgy, soft bed, under the gold, satin coverlet, Lilian said, 'Zanna frightens Robbie. Thank God she hardly sees her.' But Sidney was already asleep.

Chapter Two

Suddenly, the winds were tender and light rinsed the fog from London's plane-trees. After the steely rains that had followed the savage winter, late, green buds emerged on branches, sticky and tightly packed. On a morning of thin sunshine, Harry Welliver came through the pink door of Zanna Modes, rather self-consciously carrying the feathery black hat in its shiny hatbox.

He put it on the glass counter impatiently, his wide shoulders already half-turned towards the door, to dash out of it. 'Lady Fitzhaven says she's sorry to be so long in getting it back to you. The roads were flooded and she didn't want to chance the post.'

'It doesn't matter,' Zanna said. 'I couldn't have sold it anyway. No-one would have worn ostrich feathers in all that sodding rain, not even an ostrich.' She took the hat out of the box and curled one or two of the feathers between her stubby fingers. 'It's not worth two dead flies,' she said decisively.

Harry looked at her sharply. She was wearing another Dior outfit: a dark blue dress, tightly belted, with a full, rustling skirt, obtained, as usual, through the unsuspecting French Embassy. Harry hardly noticed the lovely fluidity of the dress; he was struck by Zanna's dark orange hair, bright as metal, and the immaculate look

24

of her, untouched by disappointment, drabness and fatigue, the tiredness that had struck England like a plague. He decided that there was no need to get to the House of Commons just yet and gave her one of his most calculated, narrow-lipped smiles.

Hats, most of them small and sculpted, covered in blazing velvets, swathed in chiffon or packed with wired flower heads, were arranged prettily on stands amongst hand-stitched gloves and silk scarves, swirled together in bright tangles. Harry began to look around, his eye caught by a silk rose, a taffeta bow, swelling out like a sail, velvet leaves cut like the pastry trimmings on an apple pie.

Zanna jerked her head towards a small, striped sofa against the wall and, when he sat down, rustled out from behind the counter to sit beside him. He offered her a cigarette and lit it for her, liking the sucking noise of satisfaction she made as she inhaled.

'I'm Harry Welliver,' he said. The name meant nothing to Zanna who seldom read the newspapers and didn't notice the slight air of diffidence with which Harry pronounced his name. Since the election of the Labour government two years before, it was a name that was often in the news. At twenty-four, Harry had been the youngest Labour Member of Parliament to take his seat, and he was now the youngest member of the Government, as under-secretary in the Ministry of Fuel and Power.

'Must be fun, working in a place like this,' he said. 'Been here long?'

'Since 'forty-two. I bought it when the whole West End was up for grabs because of the bombing.' Zanna was pleased to see Harry blush. Serve him right for thinking she was a shop-girl. Good-looking though, in a dry, bony way; nice, floppy hair and a big nose with generous, winged nostrils. 'Is Lady Fitzhaven your grandmother?' she asked.

'My aunt, although she's more or less adopted me. My parents were killed in 'forty-one, in the Café de Paris bomb. They were celebrating their twenty-fifth wedding anniversary.'

'Jeez,' Zanna said. 'I wish I had parents who went out dancing. Mine are a pair of old misery guts.'

Her lack of sympathy made Harry smile. 'Mine were like irresponsible children. I tell myself that perhaps it was the best death they could have, dying on the dance floor with Snakehips Johnson playing "Oh, Johnny! Oh, Johnny! Oh!" Old age wouldn't have suited them.'

Zanna stood up and began to dance, very gracefully, her full skirt flicking around her long legs. In her low, throaty voice, she sang:

'Oh, Johnny! oh, Johnny! how you can love!
Oh, Johnny! oh, Johnny! Heavens above!
You make my sad heart jump with joy,
And when you're near I just can't sit still a minute . . .'

It was an entrancing performance. Harry began to sing along with her, until, after a final swirl of her skirt, she sat down again and tilted her face forward, all mouth, for him to light another cigarette.

'I really liked your aunt,' Zanna said. 'A really game old girl, I thought *she* was, chancing the West End on a day like that. Didn't what's-her-name like the hat then?'

Harry rubbed a finger inside the collar of his blue shirt which had faded to whiteness around the cuffs. He was dressed rather oddly, Zanna thought; that very old blue shirt and an equally ancient tweed suit, fitted at the waist in a style that was dandyish at the turn of the century; not at all the sort of thing you wore in London, and a bit short in the leg, as though it had been made for somebody else.

'Gillian,' Harry said. 'My sister-in-law. Yes, she liked the hat all right. Loved it, in fact. Said it made her feel full of juice. It was Gomer. He told her she couldn't carry it off.'

'Could she?'

Harry clasped his arms around his long legs and screwed up his eyes as though against throbbing sunlight. 'Well, perhaps it did overpower her a bit. I mean, Gilly does look absolutely drained most of the time, poor girl. She exhausts herself trying to get the house back into shape. It was requisitioned during the war and the Army more or less left it for dead. But that's not the point. It made Gilly feel good about herself for once, raised her morale. It was really too bad of Gomer to object.'

'Don't talk to *me* about morale,' Zanna said. 'Morale is what the millinery business is all about. That's why they never put hats on points during the war. Even the war cabinet sussed that hats helped you keep your pecker up. Still, talk about make do and mend. You couldn't get the jute and *passementerie* from Czechoslovakia, or blocks, or felts. There wasn't a second-hand clothes shop in the country I didn't rummage in for scraps and pickings, and if I hadn't had this pal in Woollands who sold me all the old stock they'd kept in the basement, Zanna Modes would have gone kaput.' She stroked a little, red-satin toque affectionately. 'Still, it was worth it. Anything to get women out of those horrible turbans and pixie hoods. The war was OK really. You could do what you wanted most of the time. Better than this bunch of busybodies we've got now. Sticking taxes on American films, nationalizing the bloody coalmines. Stupid sods. It's nylons and eyebrow pencils people want, and Fred and Ginger; not bloody state industries.'

Harry, who had had a hand in drafting the legislation to nationalize the mines, blushed again.

'You a socialist then?' Zanna asked in her strange low voice that was almost a growl, primitive and alluring.

'I'm the Labour MP for Chipperton, in the East End,' Harry said uncomfortably.

Zanna frowned slightly, as though Chipperton was somewhere she was having difficulty in placing. In fact, Lilian and Sidney had been born and brought up in its narrow slums, and it was where Sidney had opened his first barber-shop before moving to larger premises in the

27

Whitechapel Road. Zanna, herself, spent quite a bit of time in Chipperton, bringing boxes of straw braid and petersham ribbon to her piece-workers: the near-to-destitute women who lived in dark, red-brick tenements and made up some of Zanna's more simple designs – the models she sold to department stores – at home, stitching in poor light and surrounded by children with dried snot under their noses and dirty ears. Zanna paid them badly, knowing that they couldn't get jobs with decent wages now that all the day nurseries, which had been set up during the war, had closed down.

She was surprised that someone as badly turned out as Harry could be a Member of Parliament, even a socialist one. Shabbiness must run in the family, if he and his aunt were anything to go by. He had a funny kind of elegance though, all bones and angles, like something carved. 'Some of my customers are married to politicians,' she said. 'Leonard Riddick – you must know him. I make all Suzette's hats. She dresses at Hartnell now; Leonard says she has to support the British fashion industry, set an example. He's a bit of a spoilsport in a way.'

Harry hated Leonard Riddick. He was one of the new breed of Tory MPs who had made mysterious fortunes during the war and used them to finance political careers. Riddick was short and thick-set with too much grease on his black hair and strange grey-blue eyelashes, the colour of a Persian cat. Harry suspected him of being a black marketeer and it pained him that Zanna was speaking of him with affection in her low voice, admiring him a bit for laying down the law about his wife's clothing.

'It's a real shame, Suzette having to stop going to Balenciaga,' Zanna was saying. 'You ought to be allowed to buy what you want with your own money.'

Harry said, 'I think it was Disraeli who said, "As a general rule nobody who has money ought to have it." Only he didn't dare take it away from them.'

'Would you?'

'Lord, yes,' said Harry. 'I can't wait.'

He began to feel a reckless urge to prove himself in some way; a soldier's urge. Harry had been in the BEF and the British 6th Airborne Division, where there had been frequent opportunities to put on swaggering displays of bravery during the Allied liberation of France. He had hoped that political life would be thrilling but, after the tensions and dangers of the war, he was bored by the dull conventions of the House of Commons; the corridors and shuffling conspiracies of confined men – there were very few female MPs – reminded him of Eton, whose ancient and complicated routines he had loathed.

Harry had been the smallest boy in his class until he was sixteen, when he had grown twelve inches in twelve months. Ten years later, he still thought of himself as undersized and moved at a small man's speed, alarmingly, striding through cramped rooms with his elastic lope, in danger of crashing into walls. He misjudged the space he took up; stood too close to people, his warm breath shaking their eyelashes, unaware that his big, rushing body forced them to step out of his path.

He had thought that after the war all the old rules would be smashed; but they were still in place: country landowners lording it over tenant farmers, clannish trade barons hoarding up fortunes for their sons. Harry wanted to change the rules so quickly that they would cease to exist.

That was in the future. What he wanted to do that very minute was to convince Zanna, who was rearranging six little saucer-shaped hats in a sort of fan-pattern in the window, of the necessity, the *rightness*, of the cradle-to-grave welfare state that his government had promised to bring about. He decided to take her to lunch.

Zanna's lavender eyes looked at him rather shiftily when he proposed this. She thought of telling him that she couldn't leave the shop but, at that moment,

Mrs Harris, her part-time manageress, arrived to supervise Zanna Modes for the rest of the day, as she did every Wednesday, to allow Zanna time to buy supplies, visit the piece-workers and discuss designs with the department-store buyers of her wholesale line. Zanna did all these things but, as often as she could, lunched with Jean-Louis first, usually at the Ritz, where he booked a room for the night, although he made use of it for only the hour or so that Zanna went to bed with him.

Zanna had been due to meet Jean-Louis that day; he had not yet seen her in the dark blue dress with its wide belt that he had procured for her. But Mrs Harris was all over Harry Welliver, her hand going to the spit-curl on her forehead to make sure that it hadn't frizzed, and introducing herself in a humble way, her eyes lowered, as though to a famous film star. She obviously knew who this man was and thought him of some importance. Mrs Harris was a war widow with three young children and Zanna knew she was planning to ask her for more money, which Zanna had no intention of giving her. She thought she would have lunch with Harry Welliver so that she would be able to tell Mrs Harris about it afterwards; keep her happy for a bit to take her mind off the subject of a raise.

'I'd love to,' she said. 'I'll just telephone the buyer I was meeting and tell her I'll be along a bit later.'

In the back room, Zanna rang the Ritz and left a message for Jean-Louis that she would meet him at three o'clock. Then she put on a hat from her new collection, a doll-sized pillbox in shiny dark blue straw, crowned with a blowy organza rose with petals that grazed Zanna's arched eyebrows. Outside, in the sunlight, Zanna's heavily made-up face looked absurdly glamorous, almost breakable. In spite of her high-heeled shoes, she kept up with Harry as he wheeled towards Oxford Street, wide shoulders swinging inside his too-tight suit. He dived, almost crashed, down a flight of stone steps leading to a basement, each step marked

30

with rust, the traces of the iron stair-rail which had been removed for scrap metal when the war started.

It was not the sort of restaurant that Zanna liked. She regretted not having gone to the Ritz after all. Not because of the food – she always let Jean-Louis order for her and ate only a few mouthfuls of whatever was put on her plate – but because she liked looking at the pretty women lunching there. It excited her to see her own hats nodding and dipping on well-coiffed heads, and to assess the creations of rival modistes, Aage Thaarup, Eric, John Fredericks, Sven and Albouy. Sometimes, she would cross the room, touch a woman gently on the shoulder and tilt her hat to a more becoming angle, whether the hat was one of her own models or somebody else's. Then she would return to her table, pick up her knife and fork and push her food around the plate until Jean-Louis had finished eating and was ready to go upstairs.

In this restaurant, in a Conduit Street basement, there were no pretty women, no couture hats, only a few dusty berets and scarves knotted on top of the head to make an untidy turban. But most of the women were hatless, with small, sullen faces, their hair badly cut and none too clean, or plaited and then pinned up in a straying bun. The men wore stained cardigans under corduroy jackets; here and there a bow-tie or paisley cravat stuck under a chin made a jaunty, unsuccessful attempt to be stylish.

The Dudley, this ugly place she had never even heard of, was a long, narrow room, its tables, set with crinkled paper cloths, lining the two walls, its seating offering a choice between a rexine-covered banquette and unstable-looking bentwood chairs. Harry Welliver was well known here. Plain women gave him pale-lipped smiles; rumpled men raised an arm in greeting. Zanna, her wide skirt spread out on the banquette and the ruched gloves she had just taken off looking unlikely on the paper tablecloth, glared briefly at the indifferent menu and said, 'You choose. Something light; *not* whale steak.'

Harry ordered omelettes and salad and a bottle of white wine from an old waiter, who plucked the menus out of their hands theatrically and returned almost immediately with the wine, which tasted gassy. The omelettes were made from dried eggs. After three mouthfuls Zanna pushed away her plate and stared with her great doll's eyes at the dingy clientele, many of whom continued to smirk at Harry as he ate. 'You seem to know a lot of people here,' she said in a voice which her husband and daughter knew by now to be an accusing one but Harry didn't.

'The Socialist Sunday School crowd, quite a few of them,' he said. 'I do a bit of lecturing there. My brother calls them "that ghastly crew".'

'Your brother sounds like a very critical man.'

'He's a disappointed one. He was turned down by the Army because of his gout and went off to South Africa in a sulk. When he came back to Utley in 'forty-five, everything had changed – house wrecked by the troops, meadows converted to cereals, grasslands gone, stone walls pushed down, and there's still a tussle over death duties, Pa, of course, assuming he was immortal. What with one thing and another, Gomer's inclined to lash out.'

Zanna was only half-listening to Harry. Her attention had strayed to a girl of about her own age, wearing a fawn jumper and an ugly necklace of white china beads. Zanna thought: If she plucked her eyebrows, got a decent perm and brightened herself up a bit, she'd be quite pretty. What a fool she must be to wear fawn with that muddy complexion. Bloody waste of clothing coupons.

Harry wasn't paying much attention to what he was saying either. He was distracted by the rise and fall of Zanna's breasts, two well-defined cones pushing at the taut silk of her dress and quite unlike the squashed and droopy little mounds possessed by other women. That round, white throat, so luscious he wanted to lean across the table and bite it, that moist, bright mouth;

32

he shouldn't have brought her to the Dudley; in that extraordinary hat with its floating rose petals she looked like a bird of paradise that had landed in a hen-coop. Everyone was looking at her and no wonder, he couldn't take his eyes off her; he was straining his ears to catch the sound of her breath.

With an effort, he turned his head slightly, so as not to see the disturbing movements of those pointy breasts. He was sex-starved, that was the trouble. There were women everywhere: making tea and taking the minutes at his constituency meetings; playing tennis on the grass court at Utley, now that Gomer had scythed the grass, put down fresh grass seed on the bare patches, flattened the bumps with a heavy roller, and marked it out; even here at the Dudley, which was as much a meeting-place for Labour politicians and their supporters as a restaurant. Yet none of these women seemed to be sexual beings in the recognizable way that Zanna Gringrich was, sitting there with her chin tilted back, smoking a cigarette as though it were the most delicious thing in the world to do, not caring that from all over the room people were darting looks at her, their eyes hot with suspicious envy. He glanced down at the wedding ring on Zanna's stumpy finger with its gnawed nail, and rubbed the back of his neck thoughtfully. Then, blushing deeply, his stomach trembling, scarcely believing the words that were flying, haltingly, out of his mouth, he heard himself say, 'Shall we have coffee in my flat? It isn't far,' and then scarcely believed the speed with which Zanna scrabbled about for her cigarette lighter, handbag, gloves, and smiled at him to lead her into the next chapter of their lives.

Chapter Three

Zanna threw herself onto a sofa in a graceful swoop, like a dive performed sideways, took off her shoes and, more carefully, her hat. Harry's idea of not very far had been some distance, after all. They had crossed over Regent Street and shouldered their way through the back streets of Soho, past corrugated-iron walls shoring up ruined houses where army deserters were still hiding out, past women in mangled slippers, a few bruised onions at the bottom of their string shopping bags, past spivs wearing ties decorated with painted nudes, propped against doorways.

Harry lived on the top floor of a narrow slice of a house in Great Windmill Street. Its outside walls were thickly plastered and the inscription *Fuller and Richard 1904* was carried out on the front in letters that looked made out of grimy icing.

It was a nasty little flat, scrappily furnished. The edges of the rep curtains strained towards the window-sill but failed to meet it; the jitter and hiss of water pipes could be heard from the bathroom. Copies of Penguin New Writing, *The New Statesman* and *Scrutiny*, long undusted, were piled on an ottoman with a lumpy tapestry cover.

The coffee which Harry brought in on a round tin tray was bottled coffee essence in chipped mugs that were stained brown on the inside. Zanna wondered which would have shocked Lilian most: her daughter preparing to go to bed with a man she had just met, or the unscoured mug she was drinking from.

Sexual tension whirred in the dusty air as obtrusively as the hiss of the water pipes. For Zanna, all that was left of the excitement of wartime was the lure of a stranger's bed; that strange, defiant shame you felt afterwards. There weren't many opportunities now; nearly all the men she used to know were back home with their wives, sucked into dull lives, tussling with the privations that had come in with the peace – whoever would have imagined bread rationing, once the war had been won? – looking, somehow, smaller and mingier in their demob suits than they had in uniform.

The war had got her hooked on danger; the only time feeling returned to her was when she could throw off the numbness of being safe. From the first dangerous nights and fiery skies of the Blitz, she had begun to prefer chanciness to something settled; the only encounters she cherished were futureless. That moment when you undressed in front of a man for the first time; it made you draw in your breath, shake with anticipation, feel the way you used to when you heard the whistle of bombs swinging through the dark skies and war had meant licence.

There had been a time when being with Jean-Louis had made her shiver at the intoxicating uncertainty of life but, to tell the truth, she was getting a bit bored with Jean-Louis's silky technique. The stolen meetings in hotel rooms had become almost a routine, something you did because you had to, like making sure that Lilian didn't stuff Aurora full of *latkes*, the fried potato cakes the child loved.

It was time for a change. Zanna looked at Harry with her unflickering stare. He had the drawn, imprisoned look of an outdoor person made to live indoors: there were shadows under his eyes and little muscles working away tensely at the corners of his long, narrow mouth.

35

While he talked – what *was* he yacking on about? She had lost the thread some time ago, something about the need for a minimum wage, wasn't it? – he pressed the sides of his head with his palms, making his fair hair lie sleek as a seal, and looked at her with an intensity that seemed reckless.

Still he talked on, like a man emptying his pockets, giving everything away – extending public ownership, regional policy, Indian independence.

Well, he would care about that sort of thing; after all, he was a socialist, in spite of having an aunt with a title and heirloom diamonds. He wasn't out for number one, you had to give him the credit for that. If everything he wanted came about, his sort, the ruling classes, would be the first to be out on their ear. It took guts not to be afraid of extinction, that or stupidity.

Nothing in the iron promises of the Labour government appealed to Zanna; they didn't take real life into account. For instance, suppose she, the owner of a thriving millinery business, had to pay a statutory minimum wage to the piece-workers in the Chipperton tenements. It would finish her. Her plan was to keep the price of her hats as low as she could until she'd really established a name for herself, in Paris and New York as well as London, and that meant cutting costs. She'd be put out of business if she had to fork out on higher wages and *then* where would those women be with no money of their own coming in, having to rely on their husbands' pay-packet, which you couldn't rely on in Chipperton, Chipperton men being feckless sods, violent, some of them? Zanna doubted if Lily and Gertie and Doris and the rest of those wretched, weary girls ever saw a penny of what those boozers earnt, if they earnt anything, that is. Cadging and thieving and idling were more in their line. And *they* didn't go short; there was plenty of beer about. Anyway, she hadn't come to this poxy flat to drink what tasted like boiled mud, and set the world to rights.

Zanna stood up, her nyloned legs sliding off the sofa with an alluring rasp. Harry came towards her, standing so close that her breasts were almost touching the worn cloth of his jacket. For one moment, his clear grey eyes looked stricken, then their two bodies seemed to crush the air between them and make it disappear. Zanna looked steadily at Harry out of those huge lavender eyes; he felt as though he were being sucked into them, that they were willing him to push his thighs against Zanna's swaying skirts.

Double doors with glass panes that were frosted into a pattern like thumb-prints led to the bedroom. The handle on one of the doors was a diagonal gilt bar, much fingermarked, held at top and bottom by a gilt hand, each pointing in a different direction. Zanna put her rough little paw on Harry's sleeve and smiled at him. 'It's OK,' she said, 'I'm an easy bitch.' Arms around each other, they went into the bedroom which smelled of shirts which were not quite clean.

That was heaven, Harry thought, late that night in the House of Commons, half-listening to a particularly dreary Labour MP droning on about the need to prohibit the production of the longer skirt to save material. The longer skirt? Was that what Zanna had been wearing? Harry hadn't noticed the length of it, only the way it swished and swayed when she moved. Could there really have been twenty-five yards of fabric in it as the old bore was excitedly complaining that there were? Harry let his mind float backwards through the day, to the moment when Zanna had begun to take off her clothes. She hadn't minded him staring at the wonderful garments she removed; she even explained what they were, like a missionary explaining a system of coinage to a savage. 'This is a waspie, see. It's to nip you in, to give you the right shape. These pads hold the skirt's fullness out like panniers. Monsieur Dior is said to be greatly influenced by the *Belle Epoque*.'

Her hands flitting along a row of hooks and eyes, Zanna had unfastened a wonder of boned and lace-trimmed satin, the like of which Harry had seen only on the seductive dancing girls in the paintings of

Toulouse-Lautrec. Without it, Zanna's breasts were softened, less thrusting. Stiffened petticoats fell to the floor with a crackle and Zanna lay naked on the limp counterpane, light from the hallway dancing on the glistening surface of her skin. How sinuous she had been, a snake-woman, coiling round him in a smother of kisses. How delicious to plunge into her writhing body, so soft and active. Afterwards, his arms around her, each sighing the other's breath, Harry had thought: *This* is peace; not the VE day crowds and the royal family on the balcony, or leaving the Army, but this release from thought, this muzziness, deep, lazy, mindless.

Seeing her reassemble herself had given him as much pleasure as watching the gorgeous performance of her undressing. Her squirrel's paws had whipped her hair back into its tight chignon, pushed at the shiny arcs of her eyebrows, lowered the pretty hat in place. In no time, the snake-woman had been transformed into the fashionplate, with the seductive but aloof air of the beautifully turned-out.

'Where are you off to now?' he had asked, wishing she could take off her clothes again, starting with the glove she was settling over her smooth elbow.

'Squaring things with a buyer.' (She meant Jean-Louis who was fuming angrily at the Ritz.) 'Then back to the shop so that Mrs Harris can get back to her kids. You?'

'The House until God knows when. Then I have to prepare a lecture on equality for the Fabian Society. Any ideas?'

'Well, I'm all for it, naturally. That's why I do a wholesale line for the department stores. You can't tell the difference between a typist and a bleeding débutante when they've got my hats on their heads.'

She had swished her way over to him and flicked him on the cheek with the glove she had not yet put on. 'So don't *you* go putting a spanner in the works.'

'And how would I do that?'

'All your faffy ideas about a minimum wage. I'd have to put my prices up right away. The débutantes would have it all their own way then. Ordinary girls would just have to whistle for a smart hat, and a fat lot you'd care.'

Harry had looked so surprised at this argument that Zanna had shrieked with laughter, her freshly painted mouth stretched as wide as a postbox. 'Oh, come here,' he had said, hugging her and laughing himself. 'You know what you are, you're a socialist.'

'Don't you go calling me names,' she had said happily, the smile still wide on her face. And then she had wriggled out of his clasping hands and out of the door. 'Thanks for the coffee,' she had called back at him, the tip-tap of her shoes already drumming on the linoleum-covered stairs.

Oh Lord, Harry thought, looking wildly around the fluted chamber of the House of Lords where the Commons were uncomfortably housed while their own bombed-out chamber was being rebuilt, how that old bore goes on. How he relishes depriving people of the things they want. The worst kind of socialist, and I don't suppose I'm a better one.

He left the chamber and walked back through the dark, quiet streets to his flat to prepare his lecture. He sat at a roll-top desk that had come from Utley Manor, from the small wedge-shaped room where his father used to struggle with the accounts, digging his knuckles into his forehead as he tried to understand how the family fortune was uncontrollably melting away, a whisky and soda to hand, and a Labrador sitting on his slippered feet to warm them. The desk was ink-stained, marked by rings left by cups and glasses and scorched by the cigarettes that Harry's father had stubbed out on it when all the ashtrays were buried under thumbed folders and piles of bills. 'It's a nice desk, even so,' Harry's cousin Daisy Fitzhaven had said on one of her frequent visits to his flat. 'You should get a French-polisher in. I could send a man round if you like.'

But Harry hadn't liked. The ink stains and cigarette burns were all that remained of his father, that dear, clumsy, irresponsible man who would always push aside his papers when Harry climbed on his knee, and made space among the whisky glasses and account books to set up endless games of noughts and crosses.

A cup of cocoa, a crinkled skin forming on its top, stood on one of the rings left by his father's tumbler, beside it was a corned-beef sandwich made with stale bread and no butter. 'Equality', Harry wrote, 'is not merely a question of access to decent housing, fair employment and good health care. Equality is about pleasure, good times, fun. It is in those areas that we need to redress the balance in favour of the overburdened. That is why we must, as socialists, welcome the growth of holiday camps, support our motion picture industry and ensure that, once the present restrictions can be removed, our clothing industry has the tools to allow typists to dress like débutantes.'

Harry leant back in his chair, which set up a creak. No, really that was going too far for the Fabians, who tended to be snooty about holiday camps and popular entertainment and as dismissive of typists as they were of débutantes. He wondered if any of them knew what a waspie was. Probably not. Harry's occasional forays among socialist females had brought him up against serviceable layers of liberty bodices, rubber suspenders and lisle stockings. In their frazzled dowdiness these women had reminded him of the nursery governesses of his childhood, who had managed, peculiarly, to be both sheepish and haughty.

He thought that he could still smell Zanna's scent, a heady lily of the valley, on the snagged tweed of the sofa. He stopped himself thinking about what she might be doing now, unwilling to confront the fact that she might be in bed with her husband, or even another lover. The way she had come to him in a happy trance of consent; it could hardly have been the first time. And a girl like that, glowing with easygoing mischief when everyone else looked so pinched and defeated, she was as tempting as a honeypot. If he didn't look out for himself, he'd find himself in the grip of a sexual obsession like the poor old Duke of Windsor, and look where it had got *him*.

Harry lifted the skin from the cocoa with his finger-nail and flicked it into the waste-paper basket that was under the desk. No, he must not become embroiled. Perhaps the sensible thing to do would be to try a bit of self-indulgence for once: see Zanna all the time until her novelty value wore off and he stopped wanting her so achingly. Yes, that would be the best thing all round. Harry drank the tepid cocoa and rinsed the cup inadequately before going to bed.

Chapter Four

Aurora did not think that zanna was beautiful and couldn't understand why everyone else did. She thought her mother looked a bit scary: the unflickering stare of her enormous eyes under the eyelashes that she coated thickly with mascara until they looked like spiders' legs, black and crumbly, the heavy mouth that jutted out from her face as though it had been stuck to its rim of white skin.

The mascara came in a little cardboard box with its own brush, clogged at the ends. Zanna spat on the block of eye-black and then rubbed the brush in it. It was disgusting, Aurora thought, and so was the way that Zanna sniffed the crotch of her knickers before putting them on. If Lilian knew the hideous secrets of Zanna's toilette, she might stop calling her 'my beautiful daughter', which implied that Aunt Minetta wasn't. Lilian thought that being clean and tidy was part of being good. What *would* she say if she could see the mess on Zanna's dressing-table – lipsticks without their caps, getting covered in dust; spilt face-powder on the linen runner that could do with a wash? Lilian hated dirt, was even a bit frightened by it. She told Aurora stories about the Gentile women who had been their neighbours when Lilian and Sidney had lived in Chipperton. 'One bowl they used, for mixing the dough, washing the clothes and bathing the baby. It made me sick to my stomach.'

In Lilian's house, there were stacks of bowls in the kitchen cupboards, lined with immaculate chequered oilcloth that smelled of Sunlight soap. Zanna's house smelled of stale scent and cigarettes, in spite of Cath, the cleaning lady, who came in twice a week, although, as far as Aurora could see, only to make telephone calls and sprinkle cockroach powder under the kitchen boiler.

Aurora, at six years old, was an orderly child. She was class monitor at school, in charge of making sure the covers were put on the bowls of powder paint, and the little dumpy milk bottles returned to their crate after morning break. She thought she might try to tidy up her parents' bedroom, since Cath had done nothing the day before except to dab some of Zanna's perfume behind her ears before tiredly rubbing the bottle. She opened the top drawer of the dressing-table where Zanna kept her jewellery. Like everything else Zanna wore, her trinkets were not like anyone else's; she thought Lilian's gold-and-diamond watch 'suburban' and the ruby clips that Minetta's husband, Geoffrey, had given her on their tenth wedding anniversary 'real barrow-boy-made-good junk'. Zanna's jewellery had been scavenged from the second-hand clothes dealers who had kept her supplied with fabrics and trimmings during the war. There was an extraordinary ring in which a very lifelike eye was trapped in crystal; a wide, paste bracelet that shot out tiny sparks, which Zanna wore over long, black satin evening gloves; heavy gold chains more than a hundred years old. Everything was jumbled together. Aurora started to untangle strings of amber beads which had twined themselves around a pearl choker. Suddenly, her mother was in the room, wearing a pink satin dressing-gown which had been part of her trousseau. Without make-up, Zanna looked younger, her skin translucent, her lavender eyes less intense. Yet the huge mouth that pushed out of her face gave her an overwhelming look.

'If you're looking for yesterday, it's already gone,' she said, making Aurora shut the drawer guiltily. It was a Saturday evening and Zanna and Raymond were going to a party given by some people called Leonard and Suzette Riddick, after taking Aurora to spend the night at her Aunt Minetta's house.

Aurora watched her mother get ready for the party in a state of fascinated horror. She knelt on the edge of her parents' bed, her mouth open like a baby bird's, as Zanna began the serious ritual of beautification. She sat on the dressing-table stool, long, pale shins exposed, knees apart, staring at herself in the triple mirror with that look she had, as though she were playing a game she couldn't lose.

'So what have you been up to, sugarplum?' Zanna asked, tilting back her head as she brushed her lashes into a crust, so that Aurora could see the dark red lining of her nostrils reflected in the mirror.

'Daddy took me to the shouting park,' Aurora said. 'We went on a boat and I rowed.'

Aurora called Hyde Park the shouting park because of the soapbox orators at Speakers' Corner who roared hoarsely at the crowd who heckled them, good-naturedly, on the whole. Raymond took his daughter there on most Saturday afternoons while Zanna worked. He was very good in that way, Zanna thought, giving up going to football matches to be with Aurora, although he didn't have to really, Lilian or Minetta were always glad to mind her; she wasn't any trouble.

'Then we saw this film,' Aurora said. 'Me and Daddy. There was this lady, and she went up into the sky on a great big pillar all made of water. Then she wore a gold swimming-costume. Then she held onto a rope made of red spangles. Then she went splash into a swimming-pool which was full of ladies all spread out so that they looked like a daisy made of legs. Then . . .' She stopped as her mother held up her hand for silence. It meant she was going to put on her lipstick, which needed her full attention. Zanna chose a bronzy-red in a gold case from the clutter of make-up on the dressing-table. She applied it carefully, loving the sting of lipstick on her mouth, blotted it on a disgraceful handkerchief, applied another coat, and threw the handkerchief over her shoulder onto the floor. Aurora dared to let out her breath. 'You're an untidy little mummy,' she lectured, picking up the handkerchief and putting it in the wicker laundry-basket. 'The floor isn't a wardrobe, girlie,' she said, in such a perfect imitation of Lilian that Zanna laughed and shrugged her shoulders. 'Sorry, honey-bunch. Don't tell Nana, or she'll be cross with me.'

Aurora smiled back. They both knew that Lilian didn't get cross with Zanna or, at least, never showed that she did. The whole family was in some kind of conspiracy to indulge Zanna and let her do exactly as she wanted, so as to keep her in a mood of cheerful unconcern. Only her sister Minetta dared to argue with her, telling her that she spent too much time away from Aurora and, when she was with the child, fussed too much, pushing her in the back to make her stand up straight. There had been a recent falling-out between the sisters because Zanna had taken Aurora to the showroom of a children's wear manufacturer and let her choose a new coat, a red one, with three bands of rolled black velvet around the hem. When Aurora had opened the parcel later, at home, she had found a navy-blue velour coat with pearl buttons and a stitched collar. She had howled with fury at the deception. 'What was the *point* of doing that?' Minetta had demanded furiously of Zanna. 'You've destroyed Robbie's trust. Why can't you ever let her have what she wants?'

'Because she's inherited your lousy taste,' Zanna said coolly. 'She's got to learn how to dress, and now's as good a time as any.'

But it had gone deeper than that. Zanna had deceived Aurora, as she deceived everyone else, because deception gave her a guilty, addictive thrill. She remained in a mood of biting fury towards Minetta for a whole week but then, restored to her usual state of cunning and high spirits and needing to borrow a hundred pounds from her sister – why not? Geoffrey was always bragging about his wealth – she had brought Minetta round with some French nylons and a big bottle of Bourjois Evening in Paris, Minetta's favourite scent. It wasn't hard because Minetta was so besotted with Aurora, loved her more than her own three sons – the youngest, Tony, still a baby, born that same year, in March, 1947, the peak of the bulge, when more babies had been born in England than ever before and hospitals had run out of cots and nappies.

Zanna went to the big Victorian wardrobe and tugged at the rail on which her evening dresses hung, to slide it forward. Her squirrel's paws scrabbled along the hangers and pulled out one that held a dress shrouded in stiff, shiny blue paper which Zanna ripped off and threw on the bed where Aurora immediately began to smooth it out – just like her father, Zanna thought rather irritably. The dress had a tight, boned bodice encrusted in a prickle of bronze beads which tapered into a series of points over layers of golden-brown organza that swooshed almost to the ground. Raymond came in as Aurora was helping Zanna zip up the back of the iridescent bodice which crushed her breasts forward, creating a shiny looking cleavage, and left her shoulders bare, smooth as cream. 'Like it, sweets?' Zanna asked in her smoky voice, standing with her pelvis thrust forward. In the glittering carapace of bronze beads – glassy sequins and metallic shards patterned into fantastic flowers – she looked like some dangerous insect.

'You look gorgeous, darling,' Raymond said, and then, noticing the paper that Aurora was folding, 'I've never seen that kind of wrapping in England; only in Paris during the war.'

Zanna said, 'Well, I did get this frock under the counter in a sort of way. Someone owed me a favour.'

'Be careful,' Raymond said and laughed, a laugh sounding like helplessness.

46

'Oh, fear is the story of your life,' Zanna said with merciless good humour but shot her husband a look of boundless disappointment.

The sight of Zanna, sparkling and tightly corseted in her contraband dress, the vein in her temple throbbing excitedly, made Raymond feel stale and weakened. The state of the room – clothes everywhere, the wardrobe door open on a welter of shoes – exhausted him further. How could one woman cause such chaos? They should have left at least half an hour ago if they were to drop Robbie at Minetta's first but Zanna was still trying on ear-rings, tilting her head at different angles, and taking them off again. He sat on the bed and Aurora climbed onto his lap. Raymond tucked her floppy hair behind her ears and kissed her round forehead. 'All set to go, little one?' he asked.

She had been ready for hours, the pink plastic suit-case that Sidney had bought for her already packed as neatly as Raymond would have packed it himself, her Beacon Reader laid on top of her nightdress, so that, in the morning, Uncle Geoffrey would be able to give her a spelling test on all the new words she had learnt: rain, reign, sight, site, taught, taut. When she got them right, he would peel back her fingers and fill her palm with threepenny bits.

Uncle Geoffrey thought that people should stand on their own two feet. Aurora had heard him say this and then, more loudly, that he was a self-made man and didn't mind who knew it. It was after Zanna had told Minetta that a duchess had come into Zanna Modes and ordered three hats. After Geoffrey's interruption, she had said, 'Well, of course you are, ducky; no-one else would have made you,' forcing an angry laugh out of her brother-in-law.

Uncle Geoffrey had started out selling fruit from a barrow, and, although he now ran a chain of green-grocer's shops from an office in Covent Garden, the years spent on the street, outside in all weathers, had given him a high colour; the skin covering his pointed cheek-bones was red and tight as a cherry.

47

At last they were away. Raymond edged the Ford Prefect gingerly between the elaborate scrolled gates that were stuck on the end of the cement driveway of Minetta's and Geoffrey's house. It was a larger and more ornamented version of their own, and looked much grander because of the four ribbed pillars outside the front door and the railings, tipped with gold, that protected the front garden from the street, but there was the same red tiling above the bay window on the ground floor and the same stained-glass tulip set into the top of the landing and, in Zanna's opinion, the same air of self-conscious respectability. 'Abandon fun, all ye who enter here,' she muttered, as Raymond, holding Aurora's suitcase, rang the chiming doorbell.

Minetta hadn't got her figure back after Tony's birth but, even before her first pregnancy, she'd been inclined to run to fat – zoftig, Geoffrey called her when he was in a good mood. A head shorter than her younger sister, Minetta had inherited Sidney's lumpy build; she was short in the leg and her large head was set too far forward on her neck, so that she looked a bit like one of those toys that are pulled along on a string. Her mild brown eyes raked over Aurora, who had taken possession of her suitcase, in a searching way that made Zanna feel mutinous.

What's she looking for, she thought crossly. Rickets, impetigo, lash marks on her bum? Some other tell-tale sign to show what a rotten mother I am? Too bad that Aurora's fit as a flea and those cosseted little monsters of *hers* are always having trouble with their adenoids.

Minetta wondered, not for the first time, what kind of God could it be that had shared out the good looks between herself and Zanna. The little sister had been referred to as 'the pretty one' ever since the older sister could remember. The Spetners were a homely looking family on the whole and Zanna's unexpected beauty seemed to hold them in awe, not just Lilian and Sidney, but the whole tribe of aunts and uncles and cousins. They had all of them spoilt Zanna rotten, allowed her to throw her shadow forward however she wanted so that her self-assurance became something monstrous. No wonder she was beginning to make a name for herself; with that amount of cockiness, risks didn't seem like risks, and life became a golden carpet unfurling at your feet. Once, Minetta remembered, when Zanna was about the same age as Robbie was now, Sidney had cut her hair in the style that was commonplace at the time: parted on one side and held back by a bow fixed to a kirby-grip. Zanna hadn't minded sitting on a kitchen chair set on old newspapers while her father's hands flitted at the ends of shiny scissors, playing them like a harmonica, his fingers beating the air. But, when he had finished and had brushed the loose hair from the back of her neck with a silky brush, she had run to the mirror and screamed with fury, 'I *won't* be ordinary, I *won't*,' pulling out her hair in handfuls, while Lilian fixed clutching eyes on her, this beauty who was the troubled pleasure of her life. Minetta herself had submitted to the same haircut uncomplainingly, hoping that it might make her look more like other girls who seemed, even then, prettier than she was.

None of them prettier than Zanna though, no more than they were now. Even though she knew that Zanna was showing off, standing with one foot stuck out like a mannequin, flaunting her glamour, just to pay her back for giving Robbie a rather anxious look – Lilian had told Minetta that she thought Zanna was starving the child to keep her slender. She admired her, just as she had always done, even though Zanna had no business to be gadding about at weekends, when she hardly saw Robbie during the week. And Raymond looked all in; he would surely have preferred to put his feet up, like Geoffrey, who was giving little bubbling snores in front of the radio in the lounge.

'You're a star, Min,' Zanna said, 'the best sister I've got.' She bent down to kiss Aurora goodbye. The bronze beads on her dress, sharp-edged as slivers of glass, scraped the child's neck, drawing blood. Minetta moved towards Aurora, her fat arms wobbling with concern, but Aurora ran to her father, sobbing against his leg. A look of empty desperation shadowed Raymond's face. Zanna didn't move; she began pulling at some of the beads on her dress, testing their sharpness with the tip of her thumb in an interested way. Louder than Aurora's sobs came another cry, the wail of a hungry baby.

Zanna brightened. 'Listen. Tony's woken up. Don't you want to pick him up, Aurora?' The little girl loved babies so much that Minetta gave her outgrown baby clothes for her dolls. She took Minetta's hand and they moved upstairs.

Before getting into the car, Raymond looked up at a first-floor window. Minetta was holding Tony against her shoulder. Aurora leaned against her aunt's solid hip and, when Raymond waved, waved back at him, a child's wave: hand held high, fingers tapping against her palm.

The Riddicks' flat in Grosvenor Square was Zanna's idea of what a home should be like. As though unaware of the damp defeatism that lay outside, the rosy rooms wrapped you in warmth. A uniformed maid opened the door, Suzette immediately behind her, her heels making a clicky sound on the parquet floor. She was already drunk and had the regal vacancy of the sloshed.

'The world and his oyster are here tonight, darlings,' she said, putting one hand on Zanna's elbow and the other around Raymond's waist, and steering them along the hallway, with its glass shelves of Meissen monkeys playing musical instruments, towards the drawing-room, crimson-carpeted with an Érand baby grand at which a well-known nightclub pianist was singing 'Smoke Gets In Your Eyes', letting the melody roll and tumble from his fluid fingers. Women whose evening dresses were tortured with detail – embroidery, flounces, sequins that flared in the shadowy room like fireflies – listened rapturously to dark-suited men.

Zanna sipped a gin and tonic in which the white-green wheel of a sliced lime floated, her eyes flicking around the room. Suzette's social circle consisted of people who serviced her in various ways: her milliner (the dazzling Mrs Gringrich), her couturier, the dapper Mr Hartnell, her gynaecologist, equally dapper and with the same well-tended pink cheeks; he would not have looked out of place in Mr Hartnell's showroom. Suzette invited them to her parties as a kind of support system against her husband's friends, the Tory MPs, who were out in force tonight, since Parliament was in recess and they were free of their constituencies for a few weeks. Suzette was uneasy in their company; their manner towards her, and towards all women, as far as she could see, was almost offensively offhand while, at the same time, making her feel an object of scrutiny who might, by some shaming slip, reveal the background she never admitted to. Suzette was the daughter of a fairground barker from Filey in Yorkshire. Her terror that Leonard's cronies might find this out and somehow hold it against him was the reason she drank. A full glass in her hand and kind friends like Zanna helped her cloak her anxiety that she might let Leonard down in some way and be dumped back in the weed-strewn caravan sites she had grown up in.

Zanna didn't give a toss about what people might think about her, Suzette thought enviously, watching her smile up at the shadow foreign secretary, a man whose hard eyes and wet-looking teeth left Suzette sweating. Zanna was talking as easy as you please and the man was teasing her, calling her 'the she-hatter' and leading her into a smaller room that had been cleared for dancing.

Later, guests were served a buffet supper, which they ate perched on puffy sofas and armchairs, trying not to slide back into the slippery cushions. Suzette joined Zanna and Raymond and the shadow minister, who seemed transfixed by the quiver of Zanna's shoulder-blades. They had plates of sliced pink-orange melon. In the curve of each slice, smoked salmon had been rolled into a rose, decorated with leaves made of cucumber skin. Zanna hardly looked at this delicious arrangement before passing her plate to Raymond who wolfed it down as though worried that someone might take it away from him.

'Listen,' Suzette said to Zanna, 'Leonard's bought a house in the constituency; a big one in a place called Utley.' There was awed wonder in her voice. 'It's stately as hell,' she said. 'Promise me you'll come and stay.'

The shadow minister raised his eyebrows. 'Utley? I know the people at the Manor. Gomer Welliver. A man ajar with his times.' He shook his head weightily.

'How gorgeously sad,' said Suzette, carefully picking her way along the conversation with a drunken dignity. 'In what way?'

'Well, he's written a pamphlet saying that England needs a dictator. He thinks democracy isn't mankind's last word, that it will fall like feudalism, slavery and absolute monarchy and it would be a good move to hasten the day. Of course, some people think he is gorgeously peculiar.'

Raymond, chewing on smoked salmon, could imagine who those people might be: the lunatic right, or the lunatic self-assured, to whom Gomer Welliver was no threat, just battily amusing in a Fascist way. People's memories were repressed, forgotten. Only his own was always present. His head held pictures of the yellow star, perfectly stitched with tiny, silk stitches, that an old woman, a parcel of bones in a hospital bed in Berlin, had shown him, holding it between jerking fingers. A number stuck to his brain: the twenty thousand books burnt in 1933. Better not to think of all that, the cattle trucks slicing through the night, if you wanted to get through life somehow. Better to be like Zanna, buoyant, nonchalant, living in the present. The past would never be able to sink its teeth into her. He stood up and asked Suzette to dance.

'Whoops,' she said, pitching against him as he led her towards the music. Raymond danced well. His feet, slow and flat in daily life, responded to dance rhythms, became forceful, free and orderly. Expertly, he led Suzette around the floor, dancing on the tips of his heels.

Zanna sank deeper into the sofa cushions while the shadow minister brought her a drink and a cigarette from a peach glass box. 'Where do you live?' he asked, hoping that it might be convenient for the House and that she was sometimes there alone, the husband looked a dull sort.

'Chelsea,' Zanna said, guessing that he would view this reply in a favourable light. She had no intention of seeing him again – he had terrible breath and he hadn't made her laugh once – but there was no point in acting unfriendly.

Zanna and Raymond drove back to Golders Green under a silvery midnight sky, Raymond wearied by an evening of social effort, Zanna, not in the least, wishing it were wartime and she could go on to a nightclub and dance some more.

In the bedroom, she stepped out of her clothes and left them on the floor. Raymond hung up his suit and put wooden shoe-trees into his shoes, Zanna watching him from the bed, her arms jutting white triangles behind her bright head.

Raymond lay on top of her while she kissed him indifferently. He had not been able to make love properly since he had come out of the Army. Sometimes, he was impotent, sometimes – the worst times – his semen spurted out while Zanna was still trying to guide him inside her. 'I want to explode inside you,' he whispered into her smoky hair, then moaned in shame and heaved himself off her.

Zanna snapped on the bedside lamp. She scooped Raymond's semen from her stomach and rubbed it on her elbows. During the war, an ATS girl she had met at a dancehall had told her that there was nothing to beat it for keeping your skin smooth. Hearing the rasp of her fingers stroking his seed up and down her thin arms made Raymond feel stained with loss.

His wife finished massaging her elbows. She switched off the lamp and kissed his forehead with her heavy mouth. 'G'night, sweets,' she said, and fell asleep.

Chapter Five

'I've been dying alive for you,' Zanna said. She was lying on top of Harry Welliver in his rust-streaked bath. Harry scratched her wet shoulder affectionately and shifted in the cooling water so that he could kiss the pearly knob at the back of her neck. His desire for her had become almost violent, which made him feel, more than anything else, deeply embarrassed. He spent too much time thinking about her; he knew that. Only when she was there, lying beside him after hectic sex, when his long body was tucked around hers, her backside cool against his stomach, the nut of her nipple in his hand, could he take his mind off her and pay attention to his country's problems, often stimulated by something Zanna had said.

She was always accusing him of denying other people comforts because he had no need of them himself. And she was probably right. He had been brought up austerely; Utley Manor was never warm enough, hot water a rare luxury. Battling ineffectually to keep up the estate, his parents seldom bought new clothes. His mother had given Harry the impression that to be fashionably and expensively dressed was rather vulgar – although her jewellery, hardly ever worn, was magnificent. The food at Utley had been uninspired, at school, much worse than that. Spartan and responsible penny-pinching was what he was used to. It was impossible, Zanna told him, for him to imagine other people's yearnings for perfume and new frocks, televisions, refrigerators, central heating and steaks that lapped over the edges of dinner plates. According to Zanna, most people were materialistic, and why shouldn't they be after all the dangers and anxieties that had gnawed at them during years of war? 'The happiest way to get through life is to want things and get them,' she assured him cheerfully and, somehow, that had led to an attack on the welfare state that Harry insisted on setting in place.

'Money down the lav, cutie, giving people spectacles and false teeth. If you want to play Lord Bountiful, teach the buggers a skill. Once they can do something, they'll be able to earn the dosh to buy their own false teeth.' Zanna had then snipped the peel of an orange (one of a dozen that she had managed to acquire 'under the counter' as she assured him airily) into a row of teeth, which she had stuck in her mouth.

Harry moved his hand concernedly up and down Zanna's soapy back. He felt vaguely that Zanna needed to be saved. Quite from what he wasn't sure, but it excited him to see himself in the role of a stern, moral influence on her.

There wasn't much time available to convince her that happiness had no connection with the things that money can buy. It was October, and Parliament had reassembled – so many bills to pass, so many changes to make before the end of inequality came within reach. His constituency kept him busy too. Chipperton was becoming a place of mutinous rebellion. Its old tenement houses were overcrowded, married couples living with the girl's parents, trying to bring up their own children in the small, damp rooms. Their names were on the housing list but they were being fobbed off with talk about shortages, priorities and bottlenecks. All around them, they could see new bricks stacked on building sites, and nobody to lay them because demobilization was slow and muddled. On other sites, houses stood half-completed because the electrical fittings hadn't been delivered. At one of Harry's weekly surgeries, a woman, whose lipstick was bleeding garishly into the strained lines above her mouth, clutched his arm and pointed to some waste ground, empty except for six new white bath-tubs which had been despatched, inexplicably, before bricks or timber or builders.

'My husband's thinking of leaving me,' she said, staring flatly at the baths lying like strange sculptures among the bindweed and dandelions. 'Says he was better off as a POW. At least he didn't have my mum getting on his tits every evening.' She began to cry. 'You can tell that to Mr Bevan. Him and his national house-building programme. By the time he's found *me* a house, I'll have found one of me own: a wooden one, six foot long, with brass handles.'

'Any more hot water?' Zanna asked, and then, 'Silly me. Might as well ask if you had any caviare in the pantry.' She slid off him, got out of the bath and held out a towel with his father's initials, RHW – Robert Henry Welliver – stitched fatly in one corner. The towel was so threadbare, you could see the light through it. She began to dry him. 'You going to Utley at the weekend?'

'On Saturday, lateish. I've got to open a new play-space in Chipperton in the morning. Just a bit of the square concreted over, but it's somewhere for the children to play. Why?'

'I'm stopping quite near where you are. Suzette's new house – Croston Lacey. Funny that, Leonard being the Member of Parliament where you were brought up. He's come a long way from his scrap-metal yard.'

'Oh, they'll be glad to have him there,' Harry said, spreading his toes so that Zanna could dry between them. 'Some of those landowners would make Genghis Khan look like a dangerous radical. Leonard Riddick is just the man for them.'

'Must think *you're* round the twist then.'

'Absolutely. Even Aunt Leonora says I'm *étoilique* – star-touched.'

'Aunt Leonora is right on the button.' Zanna stood up and put her white arms around Harry's neck. 'Here's the one thing I do know,' she said in her biscuity voice, 'star-touched or not, when it comes to a real trousers-down smasheroonie, *you* are just the man for *me*.'

Later, Zanna said, 'Anyway, what I was going to say was your brother has asked the Riddicks and me to dinner on Saturday. Seems he's got some idea about not paying death duties that he thinks Leonard can help him with. I just wondered whether you would be there. Raymond' – Zanna said the name as quietly and quickly as she could, almost under her breath – 'isn't coming. He's got to sort out someone's estate in Hove. We could see each other.'

As often as he could, Harry went to Shropshire at the weekend. He had moved into Utley Lodge, three miles from Utley Manor, with Leonora, sometimes sharing the driving with his cousin Daisy, Leonora's daughter. During the week, Daisy lived in a service flat in Victoria. She was fifty-four and had never married, having devoted her life to political causes. As a girl, in Ireland, she had been one of the first suffragettes; at the moment, she was running the women's section of the Labour Party from a small office in Transport House.

Harry's father, Robert, had been Leonora's only brother and the youngest child in a family of sisters. Leonora, seventeen years old, and already married to Thesper Fitzhaven and living at Lisnagreve, his Irish estate, had adored him. But, when her own son, Garret, had been killed in the Great War, her love for Robert, only a year older than Garret, had become clouded. He was so like Garret, not just to look at, but in the way that money slid from under his fingers, and his air of energetic disarray. Sometimes, as the world prepared for war for the second time, she had looked at Robert as though she were trying to commit his face to memory, preparing to lose him as she had lost Garret.

Having done her mourning in advance, after Robert's death in the Café de Paris bombing she had moved into Utley Lodge, which had been left to Harry, and prepared it for her nephew's return from active service. She had never doubted that Harry would come back to her; anyone that ambitious was bound to survive.

In her seventies, Leonora still ran a household that was as comforting and sweet with welcome as Lisnagreve had been at the turn of the century. Women from the villages around her old estate sent her their daughters to cook and clean and keep her company, pretty girls who knew how to get a fire blazing, the hens laying and the boiled potatoes fluffed and floury in the Irish way. After more than thirty years in England, Leonora still called Ireland home and swore that everything was better there – softer rain, bluer hills, kinder people.

Harry and Daisy, coming back to Utley Lodge, drained by the privations of London, found a chicken dinner, a good fire and the beautiful smile of the current Briege or Nora, who was uncomplainingly sending back half her wages to her parents in Connemara.

'Gomer won't be inviting *me* to dinner,' Harry said. 'We had a bit of a falling-out last time I was there. He actually pushed me out of the door – heaven knows why, I was leaving anyway – and yelled after me, "You may be the masters now in this country sliding to its downfall. But not in my house." He really is a thug. Did I tell you that he has a portrait of Oliver Cromwell hanging over his desk; just like Hitler and Mussolini did? And probably every other Fascist bully boy.'

'Poor Suzette. She'll be terrified.'

'No. If Gomer wants something from Riddick, he'll be all smiles. He'll do anything to save Utley. It's his obsession, although it's a grim old place. My mother hated it, used to be careless about stubbing out her cigarettes, which I now see was a subconscious desire to see the whole place go up in flames.' Harry shut his eyes in concentration and recited, '*Taceant colloquia. Effugiat risus. Hic locus est ubi mors gaudet succurrere vitae.* I remember that from school. It means, Let conversation cease. Laughter, take flight. This place is where death delights to aid the living. Always reminded me of the Manor. It's the only house I know where the windows seem to let in dark rather than light.'

Harry opened his eyes and watched Zanna furl up her hair, her mouth full of kirby-grips. 'I don't know that I can bear the thought of your being so near to me, and not seeing you. Can you escape on Sunday? I'd like to show you the Lodge. Aunt Leonora's stuffed the attic with all her old stuff. You could say you were going to look for trimmings for your hats.'

'Wouldn't Lady Fitzhaven mind?'

'No. She'd love to see you again. She's always talking about the day you gave her champagne out of a Bakelite beaker. She doesn't see many people; Gomer's more or less banned her from the Manor, too, says she's always criticizing. Pretty rich, coming from him.'

Harry put on his tie, flicking the ends in the air. 'So. Sunday morning then.' He looked at Zanna's delicate shoes with their spindly heels and her black silk blouse with white dots flung all over it. 'Wrap up warm,' he said. 'You've no idea how cold it is at Utley. Even a hot-blooded honey like you would get the shivers in that house.' He took Zanna's hand and held it to his cheek. The touch of her was like sunshine soaking through to his bones.

Zanna and Aurora caught the Ludlow train from Paddington Station. Zanna had asked Lilian and Sidney to look after Aurora that weekend but, for once, they had refused, saying that the country air would do Robbie good, she'd been looking pale lately. Lilian had caught Zanna dabbing rouge on Aurora's cheeks before taking her to a schoolfriend's birthday party, and making her look after her own daughter during the weekend was, Zanna suspected, her way of forcing Zanna to be what Lilian called 'a real mother for once in your life'.

Zanna had never got on with real mothers. She met them at children's birthday parties, or waiting at the school gates on the rare occasions when she collected Aurora herself. How quickly these women had dwindled into what they had been before the war began: tiresome creatures with no go in them, living for the edge of their husbands' smiles. They treated Zanna with a wary disdain, speaking to her in a distant way. 'Did I hear you own a shop, Mrs Gringrich? How I should love to do something like that if I only had the time. Such fun. But, of course, Brian and the girls keep me busy.'

Thinking of their inert, motherly faces, Zanna blew a raspberry, so that Aurora, who was looking out of the train window, wondered if she had done something wrong. She looked at her mother furtively, but Zanna was reading *Vogue*, her legs propped on the seat facing her.

The train lumbered past suburbs. Clothes on a washing-line quivered in the wind. Hoardings advertising powdered milk and tonic wine, drained of their colour, were propped around thistly bomb-sites. Aurora would have liked to have unpacked the picnic that Lilian had made for them. She eyed the oilcloth bag that Zanna had flipped onto the overhead rack. Inside it, wrapped in four layers of greaseproof paper, were egg sandwiches, slices of fruit cake and reconstituted orange juice in a medicine bottle. Aurora waited. Wet streets, filled with sunlight, gave way to sour green fields. Zanna read on, stubbing out her cigarettes in the metal ashtray screwed to the carriage door without looking up. Aurora imagined the soft saltiness of hard-boiled egg on her tongue. 'Are you hungry, Mummy?' she asked.

Zanna threw her magazine onto the seat beside her. 'No. I'm not usually hungry an hour before lunch-time. But you are, aren't you, you little guzzler? Nana spoils you rotten when I'm not around, doesn't she? All that sleep, all that food. How would you make out if there were another war and you had to scrounge and beg?'

'There isn't going to be another war,' Aurora said, terrified.

'Probably not. But it wasn't so bad, once you managed to live without things you'd never really needed.' Zanna swung the oilcloth bag down from the rack. 'Help yourself. I don't want anything.'

Aurora bit self-consciously into a sandwich while Zanna lit another cigarette. The train seemed to be picking up speed, and, even though she was aware of Aurora's stolid munching, Zanna felt the familiar happiness of escape. Freedom fed like a fire inside her, so far and so fast that it made her giddy. She leant her forehead on the vibrating window-pane.

By the time they reached Ludlow, the sky had greyed to smoking clouds and a warm, unexpected rain misted the station platform. Streaming hedgerows fled by the car windows as Suzette, in her new Hartnell tweeds, drove down narrow lanes and then along a drive set in parkland, in which cows stood with their sad, steady gaze, past a lake where swans moved in oblongs of glitter under a pretty stone bridge.

'Why, this is lovely, Suze,' Zanna said, as the house came into sight. It was a plain rectangle of yellow-grey stone with a square porch and large, plain windows. Flattened white pillars rose from a ledge above the ground floor to tuck their curled mouldings under a balustraded roof, cornered with stone urns. Golden yews with rounded tops marched in two rows up to the porch, and a cedar tree threw jagged shadows onto a well-trimmed lawn.

Two fat Jack Russells rushed out, followed by a tall woman wearing the same kind of apron as Lilian: thick flowered cotton, edged in braid and crossed over at the front. Good, Zanna thought, a housekeeper. If I slip her a couple of quid, she'll probably look after Aurora the whole time.

Suzette wafted them inside, Aurora entranced by the dogs whiffling around her Start-Rite shoes. 'Welcome to Croston Lacey,' Suzette said, 'house of instant ancestors.' She giggled as she threw open the door of the dining-room. There was gin on her breath and she was talking too loudly. Always a bad sign.

It was like walking into sunlight. There was yellow silk on the walls and on the seats of the Hepplewhite chairs set around the long, oval table.

'But look,' said Suzette, waving wildly at the many gilt-framed pictures of men in wigs and brocade waist-coats and women with breasts like bubbles, holding rosebuds in their dribbling fingers.

'Oh, Suze, wherever did you get these?' Zanna asked, smiling, as she stood close to the portraits, delighted by them. 'So much prettier than real ancestors. I wish *mine* had been all lace and titties. They were probably pedlars in rags and horrible black shawls.'

Zanna was the only person apart from Leonard who knew about the caravan in Filey and Suzette's painful falling upwards into money and comfort, and some-times Suzette felt wounded by the way Zanna treated it as a joke, as though both of them were a pair of confidence tricksters, when it wasn't like that at all. At least, not for Suzette. All of this was for Leonard; an act she put on that, astonishingly, people took for the real thing, or, at least, pretended to.

'Dominick found them in a sale,' she said sulkily. 'Leonard said to buy as much as I could right away because when his lot got in again, the people who are selling this sort of stuff won't be as ruined as they are now and might want to hang onto it. Dominick works in that antique shop in Dover Street. He could wheedle you into selling him your grandmother if he was in the mood. Queer as a row of tents, of course,' she announced bafflingly.

Over tea – a sponge cake with strawberry jam and real cream layered inside it, to Aurora's joy – Suzette said, as though remembering something unpleasant, 'You know we're dining at Utley Manor tonight?'

'I hadn't forgotten. I packed the Balenciaga – you know, the chequered satin with the stole. Amusingly Arcadian, I thought.'

'Leonard said I should wear the black peau-de-soie to show off his diamonds.'

'They're not Leonard's diamonds; he only paid for them. They're yours. Wear something that isn't so backless. The house is freezing, apparently.'

Suzette looked at Zanna keenly. 'How do you know?'

'Harry Welliver told me.'

'Oho.'

'Oho, yourself. His aunt is one of my clients. I said I'd call in on her tomorrow morning, if that's OK with you. Do you think Mrs Wystan could mind Aurora for a couple of hours?'

'Sure,' Suzette said, and began to whistle 'Don't Fence Me In' in a pointed manner as she rang the bell for more hot water.

'Blimey, what a dreadful pile,' said Leonard Riddick, as Utley Manor swam into the car's headlights. The timbered house, impossibly thin and brittle, seemed only gummed to the ground it stood on. The wind had got up during the afternoon. It slashed their faces like a razor the minute they got out of Leonard's Rolls. Suzette shrank fretfully into her mink coat. The desolation of Utley Manor seemed as thick as fog. It was in the rattle of the poplar leaves, in the howl of a dog chained up somewhere on the other side of the house, in the Michaelmas daisies struggling in the wind.

A door opened grudgingly, rasping against a stone floor. Light from a hallway revealed more ugly sights: a row of pine trees with gnarled and bruised trunks, a neglected garden – nothing but sopping grass and the latticed seed-heads of thistles. Uglier still was the man who stood in the doorway, a threatening smile on his face.

Gomer Welliver was like a tightened version of Harry that had been squashed into the wrong shape. He was smaller than his younger brother and every feature had a condensed look: the almost lipless mouth in a round, hard copy of Harry's spoon-shaped face, the same broad-tipped nose and clear grey eyes, except in Gomer's face they were colder, almost chilled. An outdoor life had buffed his skin to a scaly polish; his dark blond hair, the same colour as Harry's exactly, was cropped close to the sides of his head, revealing neat, small ears. Where Harry looked carved – his jutting shoulders, long thighs – Gomer's heavy frame seemed tightly moulded, rubbery even, his belly pushing a cashmere pullover into a solid curve. On his small feet, Zanna noticed, displeased by them as he scurried down the chipped stone steps to welcome her, were hideous grey shoes.

Gomer led them into a large, squarish room, scarcely lighter than the night outside. Three mullioned windows, lead latticed, meanly trapped the darkness.

'Whisky?' Gomer asked, waving a dusty decanter and then, carrying it to the door, he shouted into the hall, 'Gillian, show a leg, they're here.' Turning back to fill their glasses, his eyes were angry and furtive, despite the tilted smile on his face.

'Just putting Otto to bed,' he explained. 'Boy's a bit chesty for some reason.'

How could any child survive in such cold? Zanna thought. It was seeping into her skin as no cold had ever done before, even during that last freezing winter of grimy snows and the heartless April that followed it. The cold in this house was of a different kind, clammy on the flesh. Zanna felt her face becoming greeny with damp, and saw Suzette's arms – she had put on the skimpy peau-de-soie after all – pimpling in the cross-currents of draughts.

A young woman came into the room, looked around wildly, and ran over to the fireplace, where she began to drop split logs from a basket over the high, rusted fireguard. Gomer watched her with billowing contempt. 'Gillian,' he addressed her thin back, 'come and be introduced. My wife. Mr and Mrs Riddick. Mrs Gringrich.'

They were offered seats: armchairs draped with old blankets speckled with dog hairs. Gillian's long, bulky skirt might have been made from a blanket too. She wore a silk blouse, a modest row of pearls and black velvet ballerina slippers, much scuffed. In high heels, Zanna thought, she would have been taller than Gomer. Gillian was almost pretty, would have been if all the planes of her face – chin, nose, cheek-bones – had not sloped backwards, making her look as though she were struggling against a strong wind. Zanna could see that the ostrich cartwheel wouldn't have suited her at all; the blowy feathers would have emphasized Gillian's receding chin and drawn attention from her lovely eyes, dark as coffee beans beneath strong eyebrows.

'Ever come across my brother, Riddick?' Gomer asked, refilling his glass. Everyone seemed to be drinking a lot, very fast, as a way of stopping the conversation from flaking away.

'Oh, we've crossed swords in our time,' Leonard said. 'He gives a good account of himself. Can even convince *me* that there's something to be said for public ownership, before I come to my senses, that is.'

'It's my opinion that he's mad as a hatter,' Gomer said venomously. Zanna laughed her low, smoky laugh.

'You've just trodden on my corns, Mr Welliver,' she said, 'I *am* a hatter.'

Gomer turned his head towards her, his chin almost scraping his shoulder, which made him look murderous. He gave a cawing, black laugh. 'Just a saying, Mrs Gringrich.'

'Based on fact, all the same. Felting used to be done with mercuric nitrate, so when hat makers inhaled the fumes they came over all woozy and distracted, just like the hatter in *Alice in Wonderland*.'

Gomer gave her a menacing smile. He detested women who knew more than he did. 'Everything oojah-cum-spiff?' he demanded of Gillian, who was looking wonderingly at Zanna, as though she had descended from another planet in her shimmering dress, its stole flung dramatically across her throat. She nodded distractedly and they made their way to the dining-room,

Gomer prodding Suzette's freezing back and gripping Zanna's wrist to hurry them through the icy hall.

Game was unrationed. That must be the reason for this disgusting casserole, Suzette thought, crunching on little bones and odorous mouthfuls of thin, dark bird flesh. Zanna didn't seem to mind. She was just pushing the food around on her plate as she always did, whatever was on it. She probably hadn't noticed that the Brussels sprouts were slug-bitten, although, for once, the cold had got to her. Suzette had noticed her friend rubbing her hands together to warm them.

What a miserable place this was. The dining-room was the worst of the lot. On this side of the house, two draggling monkey-puzzle trees would have blotted out any light that might have been admitted by the mean windows on even the brightest day. Scarred panelling, the colour of a wine stain, ran around the walls. Above it, a reddish wallpaper printed with gold fleur-de-lis showed brighter rectangles where pictures and mirrors had been removed. Under the table, on split floorboards, a dog growled at Suzette's ankles. It emerged, its hind quarters stiff with cold, when Gomer put down his empty plate on the floor. This, Suzette noticed, made Zanna smile.

Dinner was followed by a tour of the house. Following Gomer's hard, square back, they pitched along mouse-nibbled carpet runners, laid treacherously over uneven floorboards, feeling as though they were on board a creaky ship. The Army, requisitioned here, had been brutal. It had sloshed black-out paint on the windows, ripped out doors to use as table tops, partitioned rooms. But years of neglect as well as this later occupation were responsible for the atmosphere of ruin in all of the musty rooms.

Gomer flung open a door to a bedroom in which a carved-oak four-poster bed reached almost to the ceiling. 'Queen Elizabeth slept here. Original hangings,' he said, almost saluting the mothy draperies of the bed's canopy.

'Really, I would have thought they were older,' Zanna drawled, mischief in her coarse, seductive voice. Suzette thought that the brick-red scowl Gomer turned on her could have forced a lock, but Zanna just gave one of her throaty chuckles.

The furniture was dreadful, worse than her parents had had in the caravan in Filey. Groggy wardrobes, listing tables, all chipped or stained or missing handles. Suzette tried her best to look interested as Gomer preened before each dismal object but she was worn out and colder than she had ever been in her life.

At last, they were allowed back into the drawing-room, where Gillian bashed a poker at the fitful fire and filled brandy glasses. 'Well, whaddya think, Riddick?' Gomer asked. Even sitting down he seemed to strut, his arms folded self-importantly across his chest. 'D'ya think I should let the trippers in? Allow the charabancs in? Would that let me off death duties? Seems it's all the go. What's your opinion?'

Leonard's shrewd, narrow eyes with their strange grey-blue lashes swivelled around the room, taking in the shadowy minstrel's gallery, the elaborate but collapsing plasterwork on the high ceiling, the recessed windows. What a hellish evening this has turned out to be, he thought; Zanna wanton and brittle, and Suzette holding out her brandy glass for Mrs Welliver to refill every time he looked at her. 'Well,' he said, 'it's more usual to offer *land* to the Treasury. Hugh Dalton has some bee in his bonnet about handing it over to the National Trust, Youth Hostels Association, that sort of thing. He's keen as mustard on setting up national parks.'

Gomer's face went tight with rage. 'That, never,' he said. 'National parks – democrappiness at its worst. Not on *my* land, the land of my ancestors, men of valour.' He looked broken suddenly. 'What's the point of all this pilfering?' he asked in a pushed, secretive voice. 'Everything's being taken away from me and given to people who've done nothing to deserve it. Holiday camps, rambling associations, public parks. So more stupid people can go to more stupid places and act stupidly together in greater numbers.' He stopped talking as Suzette got up and weaved her way across the room until she was standing in front of him, so close that he had to grip her elbows to stop her toppling into his lap. She gave him a sozzled smile.

'It's a wonderful idea, Mr Welliver, you letting the public into your home. *That'll* teach them not to be so ungrateful with what they've got. They'll soon stop complaining about having to live in prefabs and repairs not being done to their cottages when they see the way *you* have to live and the way you put up with it, the cold and the ceilings all hanging down and . . .' Suzette stopped, sensing someone moving behind her. Turning round, she saw a furious Leonard holding out her mink coat, practically rattling it at her, like a matador in a bullring. She put her arms through the sleeves and let herself be bundled out.

She fell asleep as the car, flaring with light, drove through the silent lanes, awake just long enough to hear Leonard say, 'Well, we'll never be invited there again,' and Zanna answer, 'So what? People like him don't matter. He's history. Just like his faffy house.'

Chapter Six

Leonora looked at Daisy sharply 'Are you sure?' she asked.

'Oh yes. He brings her in to hear his speeches, and she gazes at him, absolutely hot with admiration, though I'd be surprised if she agreed with a word he says. He looks at her all the time he's speaking, as though he's auditioning for her. Then he stays in a gleaming and ardent condition for hours afterwards. Most unlike Harry. Quite sickening.'

'But she's married,' Leonora said. When she was nettled, her eyes went vague. Looking out of the window, she hardly noticed the morning lightening as the sun threw spurry rays around the garden.

'She was married all through the war, all the time that I was working at the Free French mission,' Daisy said tartly. 'That's when I first heard about her. Free French officers, Jean-Louis Mançeur in particular – I've never seen a man so smitten – blowing kisses into the air and talking about this woman they called "La Desirous". I thought she was just one of those lost girls who drifted around London during the war and then melted back into their marriages. Zanna has refused to melt.'

'I certainly didn't mean this to happen,' Leonora said, flustered. 'I feel like a procuress. But who can blame

Harry? The only women he meets are strident drabs in box-shaped suits and darned stockings.'

'Besides,' Daisy said, 'Englishmen have always had a taste for the exotic, used to get it off their chests in the colonies. Harry was born too late for that. Zanna is his dusky enchantress, even though she's pale as an eggshell.'

'Just as long as no harm comes to him.'

'I think it's doing him good, actually,' Daisy said, as though Zanna were some kind of medicine. 'She breathes new life into him. He's more human nowadays, less of the rhetorically heroic tub-thumper. Anyway, it's a hard task to be the same man day in, day out. We have to allow Harry some slippage.'

'I hope he has no illusions,' Leonora said. 'In times like these, illusions are as necessary as food, but damaging too. Harry is so innocent. One might have foreseen he would fall for an initiatrice.'

'My dear, don't think about it because there's absolutely nothing we can do, except protect Harry from Gomer, the way we've always done.'

Zanna propped Mrs Wystan's bicycle against the wall of the village shop, whose window dejectedly displayed a few trusses and brown glass bottles of Owbridges cough mixture. No sign of Harry. She wandered over to a fountain with no water in it that was recessed into the grey stone of a handsome house that might have been the vicarage. Cigarette butts lay soggily in the fountain's damp basin. Set in the curved niche that was ribbed like a sunburst, a chastising verse had been chiselled:

> Lord from thy blessed throne
> The griefs of earth look upon.
> God bless the poor!
> Teach them true liberty.
> Make them from strong drink free.
> Let their homes happy be.
> God bless the poor!

Zanna quickly committed it to memory. It was a knack she had, learning things by heart. Quite useful to be able to recite something inside your head so as to keep awake when someone was boring the daylights out of you. She went through reams of poetry during Harry's speeches in the House of Commons, being careful to keep her lips slightly parted, which made her look enraptured by all the tosh he was talking about the need to nationalize the steel industry.

Turning around, she saw Harry coming towards her with his pitching walk, wide shoulders swinging, a smile on his narrow, witty mouth. He was wearing a muzzy tweed jacket and corduroy trousers worn at the knees to the soft paleness of peeled mushrooms. Zanna herself looked like a Hollywood film producer's idea of a land-girl: cream gabardine trousers with wide turn-ups, a matching jumper knitted in a cable pattern that wiggled around her jumping bosoms, the sleeves of a cream cardigan tied artfully around her neck. On her feet were a pair of glossy, laced shoes, handmade in Italy, of a kind which had never been issued to the Woman's Land Army.

'You look nice,' Harry said. 'Unusually wholesome.' In her flattish shoes, he towered over her. Without her high heels and extravagant skirts, Zanna felt like an uniced cake. She batted at her trousers.

'I don't feel right in comfortable clothes. Flat shoes make the backs of my legs ache,' she said with un-characteristic petulance. Less sexual, less sleek, was what she really meant.

'Let's get you in the car then,' Harry offered gently. He drove uphill along a rutted road. On each side, dark wedges of trees separated listless fields, a thin sun turning the grass into long slants.

'God, my head,' Zanna said, kneading her forehead with her knuckles as a tractor emerged in front of the car, lopping off the view. 'I would've sworn you couldn't have a worse evening than one of my sister Minetta's Seder nights – the way Geoffrey sits there with his belly curving over the table, and Minetta looking as though you're killing her by not tasting her *gefüllte* fish, it makes me want to yank the tablecloth and send the chicken soup crashing to the floor. But she's way behind your brother in knowing how to give people a rotten time. I mean, he's *deranged*, isn't he?'

Harry flinched. 'Damaged is the word we prefer to use. Mother got puerperal fever after he was born, went completely off her rocker for months afterwards, couldn't stand the sight of the baby. He was looked after by father's old nanny, who'd become a bit of a secret drinker. Gomer got diphtheria and then they discovered she'd been jabbing nappy-pins into him.'

Zanna made a clucking noise. 'What happened after that?'

'Worse things. Mother eventually got better but Gomer always reminded her of the bad times. They sent him to boarding-school when he was four, a dreadful place where they locked him in a cupboard to punish him for being left-handed. And then Mother adored *me* from the word go – easy birth, a complete recovery and her sitting up in bed with a ribbon in her hair for the *Tatler*. Gomer always felt that he was the child of darkness and I was the child of light. He was murderously jealous – they stopped leaving us in a room by ourselves after he tried to blind me with a red-hot poker; inspired by Shakespeare, I think. By the time I was sixteen, I was taller than he was, which he took as a terrible slight, as though I'd been given more air to breathe than he had. And then the Army turned the poor sap down and I had what they call a good war. You can imagine how he feels about me now, serving as a minister under Mr Attlee, Gomer's bogeyman *du jour*. The only thing he's got that I haven't is the house. That's why he's so obsessed with it.'

'And a wife and kids,' Zanna said. 'You haven't got any of those. Yet.' A frown flickered a moment on Harry's narrow face, and was gone, although his eyes took on a shuttered look.

'I don't think Gillian and the children mean all that much to him. When he's with them, he looks as though he's annoyed at having to squander time that could be put to better use. My released life is another thing he's jealous of.'

As the car began to bump downhill, Zanna groaned. She was shockingly hungover, the vein in her temple throbbing frantically, the ruthless, glittering gold of the stubbly fields scratching her eyes. Harry was driving much too fast. The road plummeted downwards, the trees descending on either side of it sifting the shade. She could see what must be Utley Lodge held in the cup of the valley, its tall, thin chimneys streaming smoke. The road became smoother as they approached it, the sun flittering gently along an avenue of trees with trunks like slicked, grey pelts.

Two beige Labradors looked up hopefully from the fireside as Harry led Zanna into a room that was a comfortable clutter of wide sofas piled with cushions, jugs of flowers, photographs of people smiling, tight-eyed, into the sun. The room had a strange, sleepy atmosphere, the sort of place where it would be easy to fall into a light, delicious sleep at any time of day. Apart from the dogs, the house seemed to be empty.

'Everyone's at church. I wanted to have you for myself for a bit, that's why I was driving so fast,' Harry said. 'Come here, and let me love you up.'

Harry's bedroom at Utley Lodge was a replica of the one at Great Windmill Street; the same kicked-in furniture, the same piles of yellowing magazines, their covers fading under a film of dust. 'You live like a grubby monk,' Zanna complained fondly, pushing herself against him under the lumpy eiderdown. 'I like this. Come closer, closer than pages in a book.' Harry's lips moved in her perfumed hair. 'Kiss me all over,' she said, kicking back the quilt, and he took her hands and lifted her long white arms above her head, nuzzled their silky undersides, began to lick her nipples.

74

'Does your aunt ride a horse to church?' Zanna asked suddenly. 'I can hear hooves.'

They were out of bed, into their clothes, Harry loping down the stairs ahead of Zanna, who was busy with her lipstick, just in time to see Gillian dismounting from a stubby-looking horse.

Harry was annoyed. That morning he had woken up with such an extreme need to hold Zanna in his arms that all his senses seemed peeled. But now, need satisfied, he had been rather looking forward to the return of his aunt and cousin. They could be relied upon to entertain Zanna while he attended to his red boxes. Gillian's arrival meant that something was up; the poor girl was as unstable as water. Her dark eyes flicked from him to Zanna as though they were some fantastic apparition, then she flung herself on a sofa and began to howl, making the dogs whimper uselessly.

'What is it, Gilly? What's he done?' Harry asked, not unkindly. It was unthinkable that anyone besides Gomer could be the cause of the howling.

Gillian's voice was muffled by the cascade of cushions in which she had buried her face. 'Sending Otto to boarding-school,' they could just make out.

'Which one?' Harry asked with foreboding.

'Bridforks. Where he went, where he was beaten, where he kept on running away.'

'This is damnable,' Harry said. 'Otto's only six.'

Zanna thought that anywhere must be better than Utley Manor and the raving lunatic who lived in it, but she knew how much children hated change. Aurora had screamed the place down when she'd taken her away from Lilian after Raymond had been demobbed. She would gladly have left her where she was but Raymond had put his foot down for once. He wanted his daughter home, he said, just like any father would. Bloody inconvenient it was too, sometimes, having to keep on the sweet side of Lilian and Minetta so she could park Aurora with one or the other of them and not be stuck inside like a ninny, although she was thinking

75

of sending the kid to Roedean later on. What a fool she had been not to have got rid of the baby as soon as she knew she was pregnant. But she'd been so surprised, she'd told Raymond and then there was no way out of it. He'd been overjoyed, even though the chances were that he would be called up, and Britain seemed likely to lose the war then, not to mention the unbelievable things you were beginning to hear about what was happening to Jews in Germany. Gillian's boy was the same age as Aurora. Had he been a mistake too? More than likely. No woman in her right mind would have deliberately conceived a child in the mangled place the world had become in 1940.

'That poisonous system,' Harry was saying. 'It will never stop destroying children until we destroy it. Private education must be made illegal. The public schools particularly must be abolished. Sending children away from home is barbaric and perpetuates class distinctions—'

'Do belt up, cutie-pie, we're not a public meeting,' Zanna interrupted. She walked across the room to Gillian. Even without her full skirts and petticoats, she seemed to whisk across the rugs on the floor, making their edges flutter. She put her squirrel's paw on Gillian's shaking shoulder and forced her to sit up. She patted Gillian's face with her scented handkerchief until her tears were dry, lit a cigarette and gave it to her. 'This Bridforks,' she said. 'Fee-paying, is it?'

Gillian nodded miserably. She had a soft little bosom, like a bird's, Zanna noticed. Good figure altogether, could have done better for herself, definitely. 'Your husband was crying poverty last night,' she said. 'How's he going to pay school fees, hock the fishknives?'

'He says he's going to raise the money by opening the house to the public. You know, he was talking to Mr Riddick about it after dinner.'

Zanna's smile glinted like the edge of an axe. In a perfect imitation of Gomer's contemptuous voice she said, 'And now, ladies and gentlemen, we come to a *very* important piece, a very important piece indeed: a commode that has remained in the Welliver family for six million years. Legend has it that Queen Victoria herself pissed in it. Chin up, Mrs Welliver,' Zanna said, in her own gravelly voice. 'The punters won't be interested in Utley Manor. Not unless you stick a fairground at the front and a roller-skating rink at the back. If your husband thinks he's going to make any money that way, he's a tit – pardon my French. Forget it. Your boy will still be at home with you when he starts shaving.'

Gillian's startled face softened into a slack smile. What a gift Zanna has, Harry thought. She glides along on oceans of delight and refuses to allow anyone else to gloom about. Gillian was giggling now; it sounded almost indecent coming from her, she was usually so muted by Gomer's suffocating demands and their life of dreary indebtedness. She was preparing to leave, bracing her shoulders.

'Aren't you going to wait for Aunt Leonora?' he asked. 'She's been complaining that she hasn't seen you for ages, wondered if you were OK.'

'I'd better go. You know what Gomer's like.' Gillian sounded as though whatever Gomer was like, she was more than a match for him.

'Better make sure that everything's oojah-cum-spiff then,' Zanna said, impersonating Gomer. It was uncanny, Harry thought. She only saw him for a few hours, yet you'd have thought she'd been studying him for years.

'Be careful,' he said, when they could hear Gillian's horse clip-clopping on the road. 'Gomer has more corns than toes. Don't ridicule him; he's dangerous.'

'I've a gift for danger,' Zanna said. 'It's ordinary life I don't have the talent for. Anyway, you're pretty dangerous yourself.'

'Meaning what?' Harry asked. He had taken over the sofa that Gillian had howled on. It seemed to have shrunk in size, hopelessly trying to accommodate the knobbly sprawl of his arms and legs.

'You think everything is fixed, that people aren't just themselves, only cogs in a system. The way you talked to that poor cow just now, you sounded as though you just wanted to hear the words that came out of your mouth.'

'That's a bit rich, considering how committed I am to change,' Harry protested.

'I know you want to change *things*. But you think that everyone's ticketed the minute they're born and can't become someone else. You don't see that people create themselves, it's not something you inherit. That's why all your remedies are booby-trapped. You don't leave any room for people to become whatever they want.'

They were glaring at each other when Leonora and Daisy bustled into the room, pulling off their gloves, finger by finger. Good heavens, Leonora thought, watching the rapid rise and fall of Zanna's breasts and Harry's mouth pulled into a snarl, as though he were about to rape her. This isn't a love affair. It's a battle.

She pulled herself together. 'My dears, how lovely to see you,' she said in her bone-china voice. 'Mrs Gringrich, I don't think you know my daughter, Daisy.'

'I've noticed you in the House of Commons,' Daisy said. She wasn't surprised when Zanna showed no signs of recognition. Daisy, once a heart-breaker, had grown unremarkable in middle-age, a large-waisted woman with sloping eyes and a sturdy chin. She understood Harry's moods perfectly and, when she saw him glance rather wistfully at the two official red boxes on the window table, she said at once, 'Harry thought you might like to go through all our old finery in the attic, Mrs Gringrich. You're welcome to salvage anything the moths have spared.'

The attic made Zanna's lilac eyes shine. Leonora seemed to have kept every item of clothing she had ever worn, preserved it too. Satin evening gloves were ranged like sardines under sheets of tissue-paper in cardboard boxes; there were chests full of neatly folded dresses, hatboxes keeping the dust off wilted boaters and collapsed cloches pierced with *diamanté* arrows.

Zanna's squirrel's paws flitted through lace, silk, artificial flowers, feather fans. She lives through her fingertips, Leonora thought, fascinated. She looks almost ecstatic as she touches things with those ragpicker's fingers; her eyes are almost closed in rapture.

Zanna picked up a pair of black lace gloves, much torn. 'Extraordinary,' she said. 'Where from?'

'Ireland,' Leonora said. 'From the lace school in Roundstone, long gone. Someone told me that my arms looked like netted salmon in them – I was plumper then. Ridiculous not to have chucked them out, they're practically rags.'

In a sewing-box beside a tailor's dummy, Zanna found needle, thread and scissors. She snipped away at a black linen cloche and then reshaped what was left of it, using her knee as a block – 'I did this often enough during the war, believe me.' She cut the gloves into strips and resewed them so that they winged into a short veil.

'How fast you work,' said Daisy, spellbound.

'Immigrant fingers,' Zanna said. 'When my grandparents landed in England, they couldn't speak the language, had to work with their hands. It's been a lucky inheritance. You should just see the way my father cuts hair. His hands bounce through the air like butterflies. Now then, Miss Fitzhaven, let's see if this works.'

She put the hat tenderly on Daisy's head. It had a jubilant precision. Daisy picked up a looking-glass with a tortoiseshell handle and peered delightedly at herself. 'It's the balance that's the important thing,' Zanna said. 'Precision of scale is what it's all about.' She gave Daisy a little push. 'Walk across the room.'

She watched as Daisy did so, pinching her lips in concentration, then lifted the hat off Daisy's head, adjusted the set of the veil and made a few stitches on the underside.

'When you wear it,' she ordered, 'make sure that these stitches are aligned with the tip of your nose.'

'I can't think when I *would* wear it,' Daisy said. She was holding the mirror again, tipping her head backwards and forwards, admiring herself. What has come over her? Leonora thought. Daisy has always despised frippery; she'd bite your head off if you were to suggest she combed her hair. Yet here she is, tossing her head, winsome as a circus pony, and letting Zanna pin up her hair at the back. What an improvement; my rumpled daughter looks almost *soignée*, her frumpiness magicked away by Zanna's clever, scrabbling fingers. What an extraordinary woman Zanna is, so lustrous with energy that she leaves you feeling quite jolted. A sheer pagan, unencumbered by morals, the way I used to be once. Pure delight. But a bad hat all the same. Leonora could sense it in Zanna's shameless smile. Harry could get out of step with the world over her. Deeply troubled, Leonora smiled at her daughter's smirking reflection in the mirror.

Chapter Seven

In the early summer of 1949, Zanna Gringrich had her long marmalade hair cut into the new urchin style. The wispy fronds of hair, framing her face, hid the interesting vein that throbbed in her temple and made her strange lilac eyes look even larger, swimming with light.

'I miss watching you unfurl your hair before coming to bed,' Harry told her.

'Don't cry for things that can't cry for you,' Zanna said. 'Just think of the time we'll save now that I don't have to fix my chignon,' and she gave him a suggestive poke in the ribs and ran her stubby fingers through her hair, which fell back into place immediately.

'It's about time I left,' Harry said, regretfully, stroking Zanna's sleek buttocks. 'Promised to go to a ward meeting in the constituency.'

'I'm going that way too,' Zanna said. 'One of my piece-workers is ill – dying, I think. A bloody genius at making silk roses, and just before Ascot. You can give me a lift.'

'No Sunbeam today then?' Zanna had learnt to drive, and bought a custom-made black coupé with a dash-board of bird's-eye maple and cushiony seats made of vanilla-coloured leather that gave off a delicious, nutty smell. The car, as Sidney had pointed out, was useless for family outings, which was why Zanna had chosen it. She scorned Harry's car, a pre-war Morris Oxford with several puzzling defects. When you shut one door, the other flew open, something Harry always forgot to get fixed.

'In for a service,' Zanna lied.

Outside in Great Windmill Street, showgirls in bright summer dresses were trying to slither past a white Rolls-Royce which was parked on the pavement. A uniformed chauffeur, red-faced and breathy, called out to Zanna, 'I can't stay here. I'll be nicked.'

Zanna tucked a ten-pound note into the top pocket of his buttoned tunic. 'Skedaddle for now, then. Nine sharp tomorrow at the shop.' She reached inside the Rolls for a bright pink Zanna Modes hatbox, which she laid carefully on the ripped upholstery of the Morris.

To Harry, she explained, 'People don't seem to be buying so many hats since clothes came off rations. I owe a bit here and there, so I hired the Rolls to give the creditors a bit of schmooze. They see me arrive looking like royalty, so when I promise to pay up by the end of the summer, they believe me. Mugs.'

Harry nosed his old car through the hot, wilted city and turned off into the narrow streets behind White-chapel. Smells poured through the Morris's rattling, open windows: smells of drains, an escaping dribble of gas, rotting vegetables noisy with flies. He thought: What the bombs missed could be killed off by slumdom and disease.

'What's the meeting about?' Zanna asked, not really interested. She rubbed her scented wrist under Harry's nose to blot out the worst of the street smells.

'About how best to teach people how to use the health service. They're so used to having nothing, they can't grasp that there's help at hand. Do you know, when I first got this seat, someone sold me a raffle ticket – some chap's leg had been crushed by falling masonry and his neighbours were trying to raise the money to get him a peg-leg.'

'Shows enterprise, that,' Zanna said. 'Whew, this place stinks.' She wound up the window, having difficulty with the loose handle, although the inside of the car was stifling. 'Of course now, with your wonderful health service, the poor blighter would have to sign a hundred forms and wait years. He'd probably peg out before he got his peg-leg. Give me a raffle any day.' She stroked Harry's thigh. 'I know you mean well, sweetheart. It's just that you like to draw people's breath for them. Drop me here.'

She got out in front of a liver-coloured tenement block. The geraniums in a ground-floor window-box were covered in smuts.

Harry drove on. Zanna was right, he admitted to himself. Enterprise was being ferociously stifled by the bureaucracy that seemed to be growing as fast as fireweed on bomb-sites. There had been a case recently of a greengrocer being fined for selling potatoes out of his own garden. If the Government didn't put a stop to things like that, it would be clearing a path for Leonard Riddick's lot to sweep to power at the next election. Funny how Zanna never let go of his mind; maybe it was the trace of her lily of the valley scent still under his nostrils. She was the person he talked to when he talked to himself. Must remember to tell her that; his reward would be one of her wide, lipsticked smiles.

Zanna jiggled the flap of Rachel Rubinstein's letter-box. As usual, the doorbell wasn't working; Leon Rubinstein had probably spent the electricity money on books. Leon let her in, scuffling along the corridor in cracked shoes. Zanna went into the dark kitchen with her hatbox and took out of it a side of smoked salmon, a jar of calves-foot jelly and a bunch of grapes.

'So how is she?'

Leon shrugged his scholar's bent shoulders. 'How can she be? So hot, if you cracked eggs on her they'd fry. Go in. She's been asking for you.'

Rachel's eyes were closed, her eyelids gauzy, the wig, which Orthodox married women were required to wear

83

all the time, a little askew. Apart from the bed, the room was Rachel's workspace, piled high with boxes of silk and the coils of thin, cloth-covered wire that she used to make artificial flowers. She woke up, her eyes gummy. 'Did you bring me more work?' she asked Zanna, wheezing terribly.

'Not today. It seemed to me that you and Leon could do with a bit of a holiday before the autumn rush starts. You'd be doing me a favour, coming back to town all refreshed and ready to work the clock round. Here's your holiday pay.' She pushed a wad of notes among the useless medicine bottles.

Rachel smiled. 'Leon leave the shul and his books? Don't make me laugh.'

It had been accepted from the day they married that Rachel would support Leon, a scholar, as well as, as time went on, their six children. Rachel had not thrived on this arrangement; aged only thirty-six, she was dying of overwork and worry. 'I'll be on my feet again soon,' she said and closed her eyes.

'Sure you will, Rachel. Who else could I get to make such beautiful trimmings? Meanwhile, how about Leon getting a job for a change?'

Rachel's dry lips quivered like a rabbit's. 'Leon's a scholar. You know how things are, Zanna. Every morning he prays, "Blessed are you, Lord our God, King of the Universe, who has not made me a woman." '

'You mean he thanks God for making him a man so that he doesn't have to earn his living?'

'Nah. Because women are inferior; that's why we're the ones who have to work.'

Zanna burst out laughing and her throaty chuckle brought Leon into the room, angry at being disturbed. Zanna thought of the various kept men she knew: the gigolos that some of her more desperate customers brought into the shop to help them choose a hat, and to show off their latest catch to the salesgirls. At least, those mindless women got their money's worth, Zanna thought. For a besotted month or so, they had a pretty boy's attention, his charming little gallantries, and, Zanna would put money on it, fun in bed too, before the pretty boy walked off with a diamond bracelet in his pocket, or towards a more generous *patronne*. How different those boys were to Leon with his pallid, stubbly face and dingy skullcap. Still, all those children . . . maybe there was something there. She kissed Rachel's forehead. It boiled under her lips. 'There's smoked salmon in the kitchen, cutie. Get well soon.'

'You're so kind, Zanna. Leon will enjoy it.'

Zanna flicked her fingers deliberately through her shiny hair as Leon, glaring disapproval, opened the door for her. 'I know you hate me, buster,' she said, 'but I'm your meal-ticket right now. *Me*,' she rolled her eyes upwards, 'not some higher authority. Remember to let me know when the funeral is.'

The Spetners and the Fadges had rented a house in Cliftonville for the whole of August and were taking Aurora. 'You go too, for a fortnight at any rate,' Zanna urged Raymond. 'I'm a bit tied up but I'll come down at weekends.'

She had no intention of doing this. Zanna couldn't see the point of holidays; they were intermissions, and she hated life to have intermissions. Minetta, excited about the purchase of a sarong-style bathing-costume in a harsh peacock blue, shook her head at Zanna's lack of enthusiasm for golden sands and ice-cream cornets on the prom. 'You and your career,' she said.

'I'm not just making a career, I'm making a life,' Zanna snapped, and Minetta flinched as she folded clothes into a suitcase. Zanna at once began to make amends – after all, Min was going to be looking after Aurora for more than half the school holidays. She took the garish bathing-costume and snipped off the bow on one hip. 'Really nice now, Min, without that bit of tat. Decoration betrays.' The costume was cruelly boned down the sides; Zanna could imagine the weals it would leave on Minetta's podgy flesh.

'Well, you're the expert,' Minetta said, snatching it from Zanna's exploring fingers. She could see already that it was a mistake.

Another reason for Zanna not going to Cliftonville was that Leonora and Daisy had gone to Connemara with their Irish maids and she and Harry would have Utley Lodge all to themselves, for the first time.

Zanna had begun to find Leonora's welcomes a bit overwhelming. She was as insistent as Lilian when it came to food, lapsing unconsciously into an Irish brogue – 'Ah, you will take a little, you will so,' until Daisy checked her with a reproving, 'Mother.' Zanna knew that she was fussed over so strenuously at Utley Lodge because Leonora so adored Harry that she needed to prove to him that her devotion could withstand anything, even to the point of accepting the *louche* married milliner who was his mistress.

They drove to Shropshire in Zanna's Sunbeam. 'Might as well arrive in style, rather than looking as though we picked up something in the scrap-metal yard,' Zanna said, filling the Sunbeam's boot with bottles of champagne, tinned white peaches, a whole roast chicken and the cold, fried halibut steaks that Lilian had cooked for her and which Zanna, to her mother's surprise, had accepted.

Harry seemed distracted. According to Leonard Riddick, who had told Suzette, who had repeated it to Zanna, Harry was beginning to be seen as a bit of an eccentric by some members of the Labour Party; a bit of a lofty nob who was rooted in an unhealthy kind of nostalgia. 'Someone put it about', Leonard had said, 'that he calls the working-class Labour MPs "the illiterates". Probably not true but doesn't do his reputation any good. In my view' – Leonard had recently started to use expressions like 'in my view' – 'the real problem with young Welliver is that he has the romantic's dislike of power. Not that he'd ever admit to it if you made him dance on broken glass, but there's something tamed and tired about him. I can't see him ever getting the leadership now. As it is, he could drop out of the parade with nothing but a lifetime of anticlimax to look forward to.'

Who knows? Zanna thought. Life writes new songs every day. Who knows what the world's got up its sleeves? Right now, the catalpa trees in the Members' Yard had come into flower, the signal that Parliament should rise. Time for politicians to retire into their private lives, something they dreaded and disliked. Harry, too, if it came to that. Politics appealed to men who liked life to be drained of clutter. I'm just about the only bit of emotional untidiness in Harry's life, she thought. If it weren't for me, how magnificently simple everything would be for him.

She began to sing as she drove through the leafy suburbs of mock-Tudor semis and grass-edged pavements. 'I've got you under my skin,' she sang and went through the whole song from beginning to end, word perfect, Harry thought admiringly, floundering in the complex lyric as he tried to sing along, the beat almost too fast to fit the words. 'I would sacrifice anything come what might for the sake of having you near. In spite of a warning voice that comes in the night and repeats and repeats in my ear . . .' He loved watching Zanna drive; she seemed to sail the car through the streets, her squirrel's paws, jabbed all over with pinpricks, kept low on the wheel, her strange eyes blithe. She had no guilt, that was her secret. The gentle plink-plink of the champagne bottles in the boot didn't make her remember people who could scarcely afford their tea ration and who put the used tea-leaves to dry on the windowsill, to be used again. Although, if she were to see such a sight, she would be touched to the point of giving away all the 'oodles of goodies' she acquired so effortlessly. Leonora had once said to him, 'Zanna has *la bonté* – kindness and generosity, although I suspect she withholds both from those who would most appreciate such a gift.' She had meant Raymond, of course, but Harry refused to think about Raymond, after all, Zanna never did. He looked at her hair, fluttered by the breeze. Like everything about her, her bright hair seemed predisposed towards hope and the expectation that, somehow or other, whatever happened to her, she would always be delivered back into the sunlight.

They followed the road that wound around the back of Utley Manor. In the warm evening, the house seemed lightly toasted, serene, the tennis nets softly blowing, the rooks tidied away in their nests. From an upstairs window, Gomer saw the car snoozling along the brow of the hill, sunlight bouncing off its bonnet. Even from a distance, he recognized the marmalade hair of the driver. 'It's that woman with the mauve eyes. Probably on her way to see Riddick, that diddler, that wormy character.' Gomer's bristling hair was turned silvery by the sun as Zanna's Sunbeam slid around a corner, out of sight.

'My Tom Thumb, my angel,' Zanna murmured in her low voice that sounded like an engine running in her throat. Tom Thumb was what Harry had been called by his classmates when he was an undersized schoolboy, and Zanna had resurrected this long-ago nickname as an endearment. 'Tom Thumb,' Leonora had said, when she first heard Zanna address her nephew this way. 'What an inappropriate name. Harry is of excessive appearance. I love him dearly but find so much of him tiresome. Those wild good looks, those dangerous shoulders. He moves like an out-of-control donkey.' She had looked fondly at a photograph of Harry as a baby, sitting on a sheepskin rug and wearing a vest that slipped off one tiny shoulder. 'Everything about him was so little,' Leonora said. 'Corkscrew curls like fine wires, a button of a nose with perfect, round nostrils like pinholes. What a love he was. We all thought it would be Gomer who'd grow up to be the unruly giant; he had such huge ways with him as a child.'

Zanna and Harry were eating the cold roast chicken in bed. When she had finished, Zanna wiped the grease from her hands by letting her fingers dart like lizards in the fair hair that spread across Harry's chest in the shape of a shamrock. Earlier, they had wandered through the fullness of the empty rooms, walked in the garden among the waggling flowers, Zanna wandering dreamily among the dollopy heads of hydrangeas. They had watched the evening sharpen into stars before going back to the house for supper in bed.

Reaching across Harry for the champagne bottle, Zanna saw his face cloud. Champagne was a mistake, she thought. Why do I always forget he's allergic to treats? What a fool I am.

'Do you miss your family at all?' Harry asked unexpectedly.

So that's it, Zanna thought. He's come over guilty. She smiled at Harry and pulled down the sheets to display her naked breasts. 'To tell you the truth, my darling, no-one means much to me unless I happen to be in love with them at the time. And anyway they'll have a much better time without me. I won't be there to scoff at my father tying knots in his handkerchief to use as a sunhat, or to scold Aurora for eating too much. They'll all be able to make what my mother calls "nice-nice" without any chorus of disapproval from me. Does that reassure you?'

'I'm not sure that reassurance is what I want.'

'Really? Is there something else you want then? If you'd just put down that glass for a moment . . .'

Grating birdsong woke Zanna in time to see a flat red disk of sun float in the sky. She dozed for a while, to be woken again by the sound of rain booming into the gutters. Edging herself stealthily out of bed, so as not to wake Harry, she looked out of the window. In the small, untended patch of grass at the back of the house, the yellow of the dandelions made her dizzy. Pearls of rain glistened on a clothes-line, wobbled on the rose-leaves. Silvery trails shone on a path; rain had brought out the snails.

Damn, Zanna thought. She had been hoping to wear her gingham dress and a straw hat that Rachel had trimmed with starched daisies and silk butterflies just before she became ill.

Zanna went downstairs and opened the kitchen door. She held out her long white arms and the rain hit them like spiteful pinpricks.

A car was driving towards the back of the house, sending up a wake of water.

'I saw the lights on last night,' Gillian explained, gazing longingly at Zanna's cream satin négligé with its froths of lace falling back from her elbows. She looked even more longingly at the pile of tins on the kitchen table.

'Come in,' Zanna said. 'Take anything you like; there's plenty.'

'I was on my way to the WVS,' Gillian said. 'They're collecting clothes for some refugee families who are stuck in the village, heaven knows why, they were supposed to be sent to Manitoba yonks ago. Some trouble with papers, it seems. Strange how everyone's ended up in the wrong place after the war.' Her wonderful eyes went dreamy. She was thinking of the *right* place: her parents' bungalow in Port Elizabeth, its gleaming verandas tilted towards the blue ocean.

Their voices brought Harry ambling down the stairs in the stiff woollen dressing-gown that had once been his father's. He looked sheepish, but Gillian thought of Harry and Zanna with their success and power and exotic London lives as though they were characters in a play, beyond the rules that confined real, drab people.

'Seeing that you're here,' she began doubtfully, 'would you mind taking the stuff into the village for me? Only I'd rather like to try and get hold of the vet. Crackle has a sore that isn't healing and we'll lose money if she stays out of action.'

Crackle was one of the Connemara ponies from the famous McCalla stables that Gomer had had sent over from Ireland. Turning Utley Manor into what he referred to as an 'Equestrian Centre' was his latest plan to hang onto it. So far, it had not been a success. The ponies stood darkly in their boxes, lonely for the mountains and rough scrubland of home, getting sick on the rich grazing and costing more to groom and stable than Gomer could earn from giving riding-lessons to the scared, whiny children of Shropshire's professional classes: architects and bank managers and dentists, who thought that horsemanship was an asset, like the trust funds they set up for their children's future.

Gillian did most of the work in the sour stable yard, mucking out, and getting in the hay. It left her no time to tend the disordered garden with its wind-scoured borders of lavender and poppies brushed sideways against the verges. Moss spread in damp patches over the unraked gravel, making the Manor look more comfortless than ever; a place of mean, tight-fisted buds, where it seemed always to be raining; where the fierce west winds swept in from the Bristol Channel, bitterly cold, and a slimy twist of river sagged its way across churned, muddy fields.

Zanna wrested the bundle from Gillian's arms. Its contents were wrapped in a blanket that reeked of mothballs and old dogs. She took a shopping basket from a ceiling hook and tossed some tins of fruit in it. 'Off you go, Red Riding Hood. I was going to go to the village anyway – see the sights.'

She had a jumpy, excited look in her eyes that made Harry suspicious. What was she up to? He shaved himself in a hapless way, pulling his face out of shape as he drew the razor down his narrow cheeks. From the bedroom, he thought he could hear Zanna laughing to herself as she dressed.

The parcel that she flung into the boot seemed a neater shape than the one that Gillian had handed over. 'I'll drive,' he said, and, two miles along the road, stopped the car at the edge of a field and opened the boot.

On top of the pile of clothing was a pair of Zanna's ivory silk camiknickers, beautifully folded. Harry rubbed his chin hard with his knuckled fist and looked despairingly at the peaceful road edged with pale headed grasses.

'What the hell is going on?' he asked.

Zanna twisted around on the passenger seat. 'Doing a swap,' she shouted back at him. She had fished out an old tweed suit of Gillian's and substituted the cami-knickers. 'Wish I'd brought some nylons, they could have had those too,' she said.

'What are you going to do with the suit?'

'Keeping it for something.'

'You realize that makes you a thief.' Harry's face flamed at his own pomposity but Zanna only beamed at him.

'Only if you get arrested and I never am. Anyway, it's an insult to those poor sodding refugees to give them that shabby old suit; it reeks of cat's piss. A bit of gaiety is what they need. My undies are guaranteed fun – you should know that.'

A few weeks later, Zanna came through the customs at Dover. She had been to Italy, supposedly to look around for ideas worth copying, but, really, to buy Italian leather goods for Zanna Modes, which she was planning to expand on the accessories side.

'Anything to declare?' asked the customs officer, rubbing a stick of blue chalk between his thumb and forefinger.

'These, I'm afraid.' She held up a creased paper bag. Inside it were a cluster of purple grapes and six crusty white rolls. 'I forgot you weren't allowed to bring in food.'

The man took the bag, concentrating on keeping his face frosty. His wife would be delighted with the grapes. Neither of them had tasted those little seedless ones in years.

Harry was waiting at the barrier. It took him a full minute to recognize Zanna. She was wearing one of Mrs Harris's cheap felt hats, wire-rimmed spectacles and Gillian's hairy tweed suit. Her right shoulder dipped from the weight of the suitcase which the customs officer had neglected to open.

'Are you going to explain?' he asked.

Zanna took off the spectacles, the ugly hat and scratched her head vigorously. 'Home first.'

He drove to Great Windmill Street. She had told Raymond that she was arriving in London on the following day, so that she could spend the night with Harry. He had missed her dreadfully and snuffled his nose in the back of her neck like an affectionate dog. Inside the suitcase were two dozen envelope-shaped handbags, soft as butter, several pairs of elbow-length gloves and a pigskin wallet for Harry. He groaned. 'Oh Zanna, darling, darling, you shouldn't do things like this.'

'Course I should, Tom Thumb. Nye Bevan says so. "The religion of socialism is the language of priorities." You read that to me once, remember? Well, the priority is to make Zanna Modes really exclusive. You won't see stuff like this anywhere else in London.' She held one of the handbags against her cheek, stroking its softness as though it were a kitten.

'Is that why you nicked Gilly's suit?'

'Exactly, my dear Watson. I reckoned the customs men would think anyone stupid enough to dress like this would never see an opportunity to go on the fiddle.'

Chapter Eight

Harry Welliver was in the news. Reporters skulked outside his frowsty flat in Great Windmill Street, distracted by the tall showgirls in their pancake make-up and black-seamed nylons picking their way among the bits of torn newspaper and old bus tickets on the pavement on their way to the Windmill Theatre.

Harry had resigned as a junior minister after Hugh Gaitskell, the Chancellor of the Exchequer, had imposed charges on false teeth and spectacles in his April Budget. 'What's the point', Harry had asked Zanna wearily, his narrow mouth drooping with misery, 'of setting up something and then pulling it to pieces five years later? Teeth and spectacles are just the beginning; the whole principle of a free health service is at stake.'

'You're right, sweetie,' Zanna said. 'It should never have been set up in the first place, then there wouldn't be all this trouble now.' She looked out of the window at the one reporter who was still hanging around, waiting for his shift to end and eating a salt-beef sandwich out of a damp paper bag. 'Still, it got your picture in the paper. Nice one too.' She smoothed out the late edition of *The Star*, which showed Harry in his complicated old raincoat, all tabs, flaps and buckles, leaving Downing Street, smouldering handsomely.

'I know the girl who does the fashion sketches; I'll get a print off her for Leonora to stick in a silver frame.'

Daisy was chairing a meeting of the Labour Party Women's Section. She sat on an uncomfortable stacking chair, made of tubular steel with a canvas seat and back, on the platform of Kilburn Town Hall, listening to a woman from the Council of Industrial Design talking about her work for the forthcoming Festival of Britain. Daisy longed to telephone Harry. She found it hard to concentrate on the attractions of the Festival which the speaker was describing: the Dome of Discovery and the Skylon, which sounded like objects from Mars in the stories in Otto's comics – childish and unnecessary. Daisy felt absolutely worn out and infuriated by both the self-assured guest speaker and the messy, unpredictable way that Harry had resigned. He had become such an unlikely person, leading this double life of public conscience of the nation and private adulterer.

When the meeting was over, she walked to a telephone kiosk, which smelled of tobacco and urine, and dialled Harry's flat. Engaged. Daisy suspected, rightly, that Zanna was with him and had taken the telephone off the hook. She went back to her own flat and called Leonora. 'I heard the news on the wireless,' Leonora said. 'What a surprise. Harry is so unsystematic and hard to put together but, where politics are concerned, deeply right. In the other thing' – Leonora always referred to her nephew's adultery as "the other thing" – 'he is just the opposite: madly driven, unreasoned and deeply wrong. Perhaps it is all part of the same urge: he is unequivocal in his socialism, unequivocal in his rapture. I don't suppose anyone can go into politics unless they have a passionate nature but it is extraordinary for a man to have such a *ceaseless* desire.'

'Strange, isn't it, Mother,' Daisy said, 'that whenever we start talking about Harry, we always end up talking about Zanna.'

'Yes, I know, dear,' Leonora said. 'But she is so luridly exotic.'

'Oh, sexy enough to damn a saint,' Daisy agreed crossly. 'Why are we so fond of her when she rumples up our lives so disastrously?'

'Because', Leonora said, 'it's so outrageous that someone like her can cause people like us such unease.' She looked out of the window at a leaf fretting on a twig. 'It's going to be a cold night, I think. How gloomy things are still, worse than the war in some ways. I hope Harry brings Zanna this weekend. When all's said and done, she is sunshine in a dark world.'

The lone reporter in Great Windmill Street had gone away at last, Harry told Zanna as he drew the skimpy curtains. He and Zanna had listened to the news, and he had heard himself described as a man of uncompromising left-wing views. Only that wasn't the whole story. The truth was that he'd lost his taste for the messy scrimmaging of politics, hated the feeling of collapse in the air. All the old socialist warriors were fading away; Orwell and Bevin dead, Cripps ill, said to be dying. Maybe it was time to let Leonard Riddick and his friends have a turn at trying to govern this ungovernable country. No. None of this defeatist thinking. It would be unbearable to blunder about in the wilderness, watching those sleek, cocky men dismantle the welfare state, privatize the coalmines again, lower safety standards in the name of free enterprise.

How tired he was. He rubbed his eyes to bring them back into focus. He would have liked to sleep for hours, but he sensed that Zanna, who was happily snapping the black lace suspenders of her waspie and peeling down her stockings, would be hurt if he didn't make love to her first. To ignore the lure of that light body, that fox-red bush, would be the sort of thing that Raymond did, the act of an exhausted, powerless man. Harry pushed Zanna down onto the dusty bedspread and dug his whole self into her.

An hour later, he was woken from deep sleep by the upward scratch of a zip, the snap of a clasp. He clicked on a lamp; under its hard wedge of light, his face looked like something carved on a tomb.

'Odd,' Zanna said. 'I rang my parents to check that Raymond had collected Aurora; no reply. He's not at home, neither is Minetta. So I'd better go, something might have happened to Dad. His blood pressure is a bit dodgy.' Her eyes had darkened to violet, spiky fronds of hair lay flat on her cheeks. It was the first time that Harry had seen her look worried.

'Go back to sleep, Tom Thumb,' she said. 'See ya.'

Raymond had rung Zanna Modes from Edgware General Hospital. Zanna's new modiste, Natalie Bertoud, had told him, 'Madame is not here, I regret. Today, I think she has many, many affairs. It is now the time when many ladies want new hats. It is the springtime.'

Natalie Bertoud was a refugee from Czechoslovakia. Had had a bad time in the war, Raymond had gathered from Zanna; lost everyone and everything. She spoke English so carefully, she sounded as though she were tiptoeing across a tightrope.

'Thanks, Natalie. If Madame rings, tell her Robbie has appendicitis, Edgware General. The doctor says there's nothing to worry about.' Raymond guessed that Zanna was with Harry; he couldn't ring her there. He left Lilian, Sidney and Minetta at Aurora's bedside, drove home to Golders Green, scribbled a note for his wife, put Aurora's favourite doll, which Zanna had dressed in a miniature copy of a red velvet Balenciaga ballgown, in the child's pink plastic suitcase, and drove back to the hospital.

Aurora had been sick when she had come to her grandparents' house straight from school. Lilian had taken her temperature and telephoned Minetta, who had driven her mother and a whimpering Aurora to the hospital, while Sidney waited for Raymond. 'Could have been a stomach upset,' Sidney said as he and

Raymond made their way to Edgware, 'but we weren't taking any chances with our girlie. Turns out it's appendicitis. Soon as she's better, it's off to Brighton. Mum and I will see to everything – the Metropole, or maybe the Grand, why not? It's not that we don't love Min's boys; course we do. But Robbie means the world to us, we brought her up, didn't we? No sign of her ladyship, I suppose? So what? Long as Lil's there to kiss her troubles away, Robbie won't miss her mother. You don't miss what you never had.'

Raymond hadn't replied, although he knew Sidney would take his silence as another sign of his weakness, his failure to stop Zanna treating him with bruising indifference. When they reached the hospital, Sidney was out of the car and running towards the swing-doored entrance before Raymond had finished parking the car.

Zanna swung the Sunbeam around a corner, her bumper clanging against some galvanized-iron pig bins, proclaiming PIG FOOD in painted black capitals, that had been grouped underneath a lime tree since the early days of the war. In the hospital waiting-room, her family waited fretfully. Raymond leaned against a wall, jiggling the loose change in his pocket. Lilian put one side of her spectacles in her mouth, breathed on the lens and polished it with a spotless handkerchief. Minetta looked at Zanna accusingly out of eyes that had become slatted with fat. She really should stop eating the children's leftovers, Zanna thought, you can hardly see her eyes in that pudding face. She became aware that Raymond was looking at her in wordless pain.

'I saved you a chopped-liver sandwich,' Lilian said, rootling in her oilcloth bag, a gesture that always annoyed Zanna.

'Dr Tallantire is with her now,' Minetta said in a stone-cold voice. 'Matron wouldn't let us stay in the ward.'

Zanna was out of the room, running down the corridor, hobbled by her tight skirt that cut into the back of her calves. A door of a small office stood open. She went in, flipped a sheet of headed hospital paper from a filing-tray, scrawled on it: 'Sparterie to be ordered for Friday. Tell Nat' in letters illegible enough to be a doctor's. She clattered on, picking up speed as she heard footsteps around the corner, so as to be sure of colliding with the nurse who soon emerged. 'Sorry, Sister,' Zanna said breathlessly. She waved the piece of paper not quite close enough for the nurse to be able to read it. 'I'm Aurora Gringrich's mother. Note from Dr Tallantire, wanting me. Nothing serious, I hope.' The sheet of paper was in her leather portfolio and the clasp snapped to before the nurse's hand had reached out for it.

'He's with your little girl – the ward at the end of the corridor.' The nurse went on her way, her shoes squeaking on the grey lino, wondering what Dr Tallantire could be thinking of. The child had no complications that she knew of. Dear little moppet, she was. Hadn't made any fuss about having her temperature taken or the coldness of the stethoscope on her skin. Unlike most of the kids in the wards. Spoilt mothers' darlings, thanks to Mr Hitler. It had taken a whole generation of young dads to see him off, when they should have been at home, providing a bit of discipline. It wasn't right for kids to be brought up by women alone. Women were too soft, especially the grans. You could always tell a child who's been raised by his gran: mollycoddled, mulish and tantrums you wouldn't believe. Anything out of the way could set them hollering – the doctor's white coat, a tray of surgical instruments, pilchards for lunch. Healthy enough though, thanks to the Vitamin Welfare Scheme, she hadn't seen a case of rickets in years. Lovely straight limbs they had on them, shame they were such cry-babies.

The ward had grim white tiles to dado height. Above them, cut-outs of Mickey and Minnie Mouse, Donald Duck and Pluto suggested someone's cheery effort to make the children feel more at home. Three of the four beds contained small, sleeping bodies; blue cretonne curtains were drawn around the fourth. One side was agape. Zanna slinked up soundlessly and stuck her head through the gap. Aurora was facing her. The sight of her red-and-white bow-shaped hairslide on the pillow made Zanna's heart swerve. The doctor and matron had their backs to her, sitting on hard chairs, heads close together, examining a chart on a clipboard.

Aurora looked up and saw her mother but Zanna put her finger to her red lips and drew a hand across her throat. Aurora pretended to examine the ceiling. The matron lifted her pencil like a baton. 'How long since you did your jobbies, dear?' she asked. Zanna, behind her chair, held her nose and pulled an imaginary lavatory chain. Aurora swallowed hard to stop herself from laughing and said politely, 'After breakfast, Matron, like I always do.' She felt better now. If Mummy was larking about, making funny faces, she couldn't really be ill, even though her tummy hurt and the inside of her mouth tasted of sick. When Dr Tallantire had said 'acute appendicitis' in a toneless sort of voice, Daddy's face had gone grey and Nana Lilian had clenched her lips together as though, if she didn't, she might begin to wail dreadfully. Aurora had thought that acute appendicitis must be something you could die from. She had wanted to cry but knew that if she did it would start Nana Lilian off and Daddy too, probably, and she couldn't bear it if he started blubbing in front of Dr Tallantire, if he made her feel ashamed of him. She was glad when Matron said they had to go.

Zanna gave a polite little cough and when the doctor turned round it was to face her lovely wide smile. In her narrow-skirted suit with its stand-up collar lined with white piqué, she had an easygoing dash which made him think that here was a woman who was serious fun.

'I'm sorry, Matron, Doctor,' Zanna said, 'I know how busy you are – can't thank you enough for caring for my little chickadee. Could I have a word?'

The matron frowned and stayed where she was but the doctor held the curtain aside for Zanna to step back into the ward with an exaggerated gallantry that made the matron fume.

'I can assure you there is nothing to worry about, Mrs Gringrich,' the doctor said urbanely.

'Of course not.' Zanna beamed at him. 'Not as long as she's in your hands. Just one thing though.' She tilted her hips back and drew a finger across her pelvis, low down. Dr Tallantire followed the direction of the finger, fascinated.

'I'd like you to make the cut just here, a horizontal one,' Zanna lowered her eyes, 'that will be covered up when she's a bit older.' She slid her portfolio from under her arm and shook out some pages cut from a fashion magazine. 'Look at these – from the American sportswear collections. Two-piece swimming-costumes. I'd like to think that, in a few years' time, Aurora could be sunning herself on the Riviera, baring her belly button with the best of them. Can you do it?'

'I'll do my best, my dear, I used to enjoy the Riviera before the war.' He ogled the pictures of the model girls with their sleek, taut flesh, wearing nothing but triangular scraps of fabric and ridiculous sandals with high platform heels made of cork. 'By the way, your daughter is a great hit with the day nurse. She said it was a pleasure to see a nine-year-old child with such beautiful manners.'

'Yes. Aurora's very considerate, takes after her father in that. I'll just go and kiss her good-night, if I may.'

Zanna knelt down beside the bed and blew softly into the child's ear. 'Tell you what I'm going to do tomorrow, sunshine, bring in all the comics – *Bunty, Girls' Crystal, School Friend*, the whole bang shoot. We can read them together when you come out of the anaesthetic. So *there*'s something to look forward to. Sleep tight, darling. See you in the morning.'

She'd have to send Natalie round to see the buyers but Natalie was well up to that by now. Her English was almost perfect and she was always beautifully turned out in Suzette's cast-offs, her blue-black hair in a long page-boy, curled under at the ends.

What a stroke of luck to have found Nat. She'd been working as Suzette's personal maid. 'I'm in fifty minds about what to do for the girl,' Suzette had said. 'She's the best maid I've ever had, a genius with accessories, but she deserves better. Before the war, she was a student at the Academy of Fine Arts in Prague, ended up in a concentration camp called Terezin, and then somewhere even worse. Leonard pulled some strings to get her to England. Don't ask me how, you know what a smoothie that varmint can be when he tries. It gives me a guilty conscience to see someone with a good education and loads of talent ironing my panties.'

So Zanna had agreed to train the girl as a modiste and couldn't be more pleased with her. The way Natalie lifted the hats gently off their stands and presented them to the customers; it was a real performance, you'd have thought she was giving them a bouquet of rare flowers. With Natalie in the shop, Zanna had been able to spend more time with Harry too. She walked back to the waiting-room where Geoffrey had joined the rest of the family. They were talking in strained, uncomfortable voices as though they had no right to be taking up so much floor space.

'Aurora's going to be fine, let's call it a day,' Zanna said, and Raymond took her portfolio from her and kissed her gently on the cheek. He's so reliable, Zanna thought, so painstaking. But painstaking was a virtue of the last resort really, something you could praise someone for when you couldn't find anything else to admire. She patted Raymond's cheek. It was grey with five o'clock shadow. The stubble scratched her fingers, made furred furrows in the slackness of his chin. The skin underneath felt wasted.

Raymond would lay down his life for her and Aurora, she knew that. Not that it made any difference, could make her love him. The trouble with their marriage was that there ought to be a thing that wasn't there.

'I'm taking the day off tomorrow anyway,' she said. Minetta turned on her.

'What's this then?' she spat out sourly. 'Are you entering for the mother of the year award?' She thrust her massive arm through the loops of her handbag and clomped out of the room.

Chapter Nine

Everything was conspiring to drive Suzette Riddick to drink: the maddening, delicate whine of mosquitoes in the landscaped gardens of Croston Lacey, the elm trees that in the heat of the day had a flaky look, like sawdust.

How I hate all these views, Suzette thought, retreating into her bedroom that smelled of gin and the acetone she used to remove her nail varnish. She spent a lot of time doing her nails, between drinks.

She was terrified that the Tories would regain power. The Labour Party was hanging on by a thread that any fool could see was about to snap. In the 1950 general election they'd got in with a majority of five, and since then the trade unions had got out of hand, the meat ration had been reduced to a squeeny-weeny scrap and that man with the undertaker's mouth, Hugh Gaitskell, had clobbered the country with more taxes.

You couldn't go on punishing people for ever, not when they'd won a war. Labour would be kicked out in the autumn, you could bet one of Zanna's hats on it. And Leonard saw himself as a future minister. Suzette curled her hands into fists at the thought of it. He was quivering with excited anticipation, sniffed conspiracies and counter-conspiracies in the bars and tea-rooms of the House of Commons. When a fellow backbencher and possible rival for office died unexpectedly, Leonard had mumbled petulantly, 'What can have been his motive in doing *that*?' sure of trickery somewhere along the line.

He had turned Croston Lacey into the weekend head-quarters for a group of MPs known as the Reserves, who came to the house for elaborately informal house parties. Some of them were Tory grandees, bloated with bland self-satisfaction, who would pick up a Georgian wine-coaster or a Waterford goblet from Suzette's dining table and examine it bemusedly, wondering how it had got into the hands of people like Leonard Riddick and his unsound wife.

Others were more like Leonard himself, 'The Bryl-creem Brigade', Zanna called them; former wide boys who bragged about being educated at the school of hard knocks. Suzette, who'd been to that school, couldn't remember learning anything there, apart from how to dodge the next bruising that was coming her way. She'd never learnt anything until she'd got enough dosh to chum up with Zanna Gringrich, who explained to her what fashion and style were all about, and Dominick Byrde, who showed her how to furnish a house properly. Dominick took her to the V. & A. and the National Gallery and made her read books on Georgian architecture and artefacts, so that she appeared less of a tit when Leonard's friends asked her about the painting above the mantelpiece or the unusual *bonheur-du-jour* in one of the bedrooms. But, underneath her skin-deep gaiety, she *was* a tit. And Leonard wasn't. Not any more.

That's why it was hard not to hate him, sometimes; the smug, confident way he patted his cheeks with cologne, his tolerance towards her. He let her dress at Dior now, said the Tories would get in whatever they did, so there was no need to stint herself. She'd gone to the Paris collections with Zanna and found just what she wanted: a dress with a skirt so full – layer upon layer of ash-grey tulle – that it wouldn't fit into the Rolls, and she'd gone to a ball at one of the neighbouring stately homes in a horsebox.

Still, Leonard condescended to her in a way he never did in the old days, not when he'd relied on her to get hold of a few forged petrol coupons or dispose of a hot lorryload of car spares. Remembering some patronizing remarks of her husband's, Suzette would pour her gin into the rice pudding that Mrs Wystan had made for her lunch, so that the delicious aroma of juniper berries steamed out of the Pyrex dish, and burble hazily, 'I am not going to leave Leonard, I am going to flee Leonard.'

Instead, she drank more. Gin straight from the bottle before facing the Reserves and their wives, all of them women who, unlike Suzette, gleamed loyally towards their husbands' ambition, over pre-dinner cocktails. Intending to sip her brandy Alexander, Suzette couldn't stop herself from slurping it down; glass always in hand, she was all fluttery surface and scarcely hidden terrors. At table, the terrors worsened, showed themselves in a deathly liveliness as course followed course and conversation turned to the Korean ceasefire talks and whether Iain Macleod, the ambitious MP for Enfield West, was pulling above his weight.

After three glasses of wine, Suzette's behaviour became wild and shocking. She would shout across the long oval of mahogany to Leonard, 'Soon be time for Mr Wobbly, Len. Wanna sink the sausage, presh?' Leonard ignored her, although she knew he would like to clap his hands over her mouth and frogmarch her out of the room. The atmosphere around the table remained stiff with politeness until one of the more forthright wives gripped Suzette by the arm and signalled to the other women that it was time to leave the gentlemen to their port and dirty stories.

It had got to the point where Raymond and Aurora hated staying at Croston Lacey, although Zanna said it would be wicked to desert poor Suze in her hour of need; her real friends ought to protect her from all those fishy-eyed politicos that Leonard was so busy cultivating. The nerve-ragging process of waiting for the Election to be called was an agony for Suzette, Zanna said.

Raymond should sympathize with that if anyone should; he who found any kind of change disturbing and made a fuss if she put the toothpaste back on a different shelf.

Raymond was being rather tiresome. Harry was on a Labour Party delegation to Yugoslavia, so this was a very convenient time for Zanna to spend more time with her husband and daughter, as Minetta always nagged her to do. She'd much rather be *en famille* at Croston Lacey, being waited on hand and foot, than in the neglected house in Golders Green, where Raymond and Aurora seemed to expect her to cook regular meals.

'Suzette's crocked half the time,' Raymond muttered resentfully as they set off for Shropshire on a Saturday morning.

'And her eyelashes look all funny,' Aurora, who had overheard him, complained from the back seat of the Ford. 'They've got blobs on the ends, like matches.'

'Well, you need a steady hand for mascara,' Zanna said, 'as you'll find out in due course, miss.'

'I'm never going to wear make-up,' Aurora said. She was disgusted by the sticky, scarlet lip-prints that Zanna left on teacups and cigarette butts and the clogged mascara brushes on her messy dressing-table.

'Never is a long time,' Zanna said. 'But you won't need much – you're turning out to be a real looker. All those fights I had with your grandmother to stop her stuffing you and make sure you did your exercises really paid off.'

She had never expected Aurora to have grown into such a pretty child. The fine auburn hair of babyhood had deepened to chestnut, shiny as cellophane. Her eyes were deep-set but a clear, light brown and she'd been blessed with a double ration of eyelashes and good straight eyebrows that would only need a lick of Vaseline later. A nice olive complexion and a small beak of a nose, pert yet rather formidable. Only her mouth was a reminder whose daughter she was – full and wide. Zanna noticed she'd got into the habit of pressing her lips together, as though trying to narrow them. Aurora's teeth were a little widely spaced and she'd inherited Raymond's long, useless fingers. She'd never make a milliner but she was a clever kid, all the same, bound to do all right for herself.

Pity she wasn't interested in clothes the way most little girls were. Aurora would as soon put on one of the jumpers Lilian knitted for her in strange, marbled patterns, made from odds and ends of wool, than the cashmeres Zanna got her from Harrods. Sometimes, Zanna thought that Aurora was paying her back for that earlier deception, years ago now, when she'd changed the coat Aurora had wanted – dreadful vulgar red thing – for a more correct navy blue. Perhaps she shouldn't have done it, but deception was second nature to her, she couldn't help herself.

Suzette stumbled towards them, between the rows of rounded yew trees, glass in hand. 'Well refreshed as always, darlings,' she screamed, and Zanna jumped out of the car and rushed her into the house, out of earshot of any house guest who might be playing croquet. Raymond and Aurora immediately offered to take the Jack Russells for a walk.

They crossed the bridge, stopped to watch a gliding vee of ducks on the river, became aware of the stillness of nettles, the noise of bees in the limes, the wheat coming into ear. It wasn't so bad here after all, so long as it didn't rain and you could keep out of Suzette's way.

The dogs bounded ahead, rabbits in mind, but suddenly began to yelp. 'Winston, Randolph,' Aurora called them back and ran towards the yaps and snarls. She rounded the corner to find the stumpy dogs being quietened by a middle-aged woman wearing neat, tough clothes – a sailcloth skirt, a man's poplin shirt with the sleeves rolled up and a Jacqmar scarf folded inside the collar. In her arms, a very young whippet snuffled. Swan-necked, the puppy was creamy-white with a golden blur on its coat like a perfect meringue.

'Your dogs aren't to blame,' Daisy Fitzhaven said. Aurora thought she had the sort of voice that made words click inside her mouth, but her face was reassuring with kind, drooping eyes under an untended straggle of eyebrows. 'This is just about the most timorous pup ever born,' Daisy said. 'Jumps at her own shadow. Can't blame your boys for teasing her – they can sense the fear.'

'They're not ours,' Aurora said. 'I wish this one was.' Daisy let the puppy tumble into the child's arms. It seemed frightened by its own survival and continued to whimper against Aurora's thin chest.

What a beautiful child, Daisy thought. She couldn't be more than ten years old but was already handsome in an adult way. There was something familiar about her straight back and the tilt of her chin, but she couldn't think what it was. The Jack Russells, noses out of joint, began to pant theatrically.

'My house is just around the corner if you'd like to give them a drink,' Daisy offered. She wanted to find out more about this poised little girl. She held out her hand to the child's father, a tall man, quite attractive, but with sloping, soft-looking shoulders, which spoilt the effect. 'Daisy Fitzhaven,' she said, smiling.

'Raymond Gringrich,' the man said quietly. 'And this is Aurora. We wouldn't want to put you to any trouble.'

Daisy concentrated on putting on the whippet's lead. This was an encounter she had never once imagined. 'Aurora,' she said, savouring the vowels like an olive, 'one of my favourite names. It's no trouble at all. Stay for tea.' Thank heavens Leonora was in the South of France with her old friend from Connemara, Rose Erris Trewin a.k.a. The Merry Widow, and the hat that Zanna had started on during her last visit to Utley Lodge, for Daisy to wear at a Buckingham Palace garden party, had been tidied away that same morning.

Aurora. The way Miss Fitzhaven said it, pulling the word slowly out of her mouth, made the child feel as though some privilege had been bestowed on her. She decided, from that moment, that she didn't want people to call her Robbie any more.

'We call her Robbie at home,' Raymond said, 'except for her mother, that is,' and was surprised to see his daughter knit her brows.

He thought what a lovely old place Utley Lodge was. Drifts of flowers everywhere, rambling over the edges of the flower-beds, left to grow their own way instead of being staked and cut back and arranged in sharp patterns the way they were at Croston Lacey. So peaceful here, in this garden. He leant back in his deck-chair and closed his eyes while Aurora and Daisy threw chewed, pitted rubber balls, sopping with saliva, to the dogs.

'So when do you think you'll see Harry again?' Suzette demanded.

'It's hard for us to make too many plans, Suze,' Zanna said. They were at the far end of the garden, shielded by a showy display of roses, and were wearing new bikinis, Zanna's black with *café au lait* ribbing, and Suzette's poppy red, knotted between her small breasts, emphasizing them. They wore sunglasses with wide white frames; their thighs were waxy under lavish amounts of suntan oil. A pitcher of Pimm's was on the rug they lay on.

'Improvise and dare,' Zanna said, 'that's me and my Tom Thumb, the way Mr Churchill told us to during the war. How I built up the business too. I'm useless at strategy. Do it now, do it all, is what I say.' She sat up and began to peel rinds of hard skin from the balls of her feet, pushed the sunglasses to the top of her head so that Suzette could see the throbbing vein above her eyebrow.

'How does Raymond fit into all this?' Suzette persisted. Sometimes, Zanna made her sick with envy. She had everything: beauty, success, talent, a man she loved and a husband who let her do whatever she liked. She was like someone in a film.

Zanna frowned. 'He doesn't, not very often. The thing I do well is to love Harry, not much room left for Raymond. I'm a worry to him, I can see that; he suspects I'm on the fiddle in more ways than one.

110

Every morning, when I leave for work, he says, "Be careful." Drives me nuts. I mean, I know how to protect myself if anyone does. I got hold of a consignment of jute last week. It was meant to go to the Ministry of Agriculture for sacking, but there's this chap I know in charge of despatch and he made it fall off a lorry for me. The way Raymond looked at me, you'd think I'd done something criminal.'

'Well, Harry would certainly think that,' Suzette said. She wagged a finger at Zanna who was lying on her front, head resting on thin white arms. 'He'll never marry you if you carry on like that.'

'I know that, sweets. But I can't change myself into somebody different,' Zanna mumbled into the rug.

'You're probably better off the way you are, in any case. Keeps the rapture on the boil.'

'We conjure wildfire up from common earth,' Zanna said, her voice sleepy and muffled.

'Come again, Zan?'

'It's a poem by Robert Graves. "Seldom Yet Now". About how you stay splashy with desire as long as you don't see each other much. Like me and Harry.'

'Desire?' Suzette probed. 'After all this time?'

Zanna sat up again and lit cigarettes for both of them. 'You'd have to call it that, I think. Always satisfied and still unquenched, so what else can it be?' The Pimm's was making her recklessly self-revealing. She put her hand over her glass as Suzette reached for the jug but went on talking. 'You know what it was like when the war was on, Suze. You'd be dancing with a bloke, having a drink, and you *knew* what was going to happen later. The anticipation was the best part; nothing to beat that moment when you went up in the lift to the hotel bedroom and he put the key in the lock. But it's different with Harry. I get what I want and go on wanting it, more than before. And it's the same for him. It's like we give each other permission for boundless love.'

They could hear Leonard calling them from the terrace. 'I'll bet his cock to a kipper he's invited twelve

111

more people to dinner,' Suzette said. She hitched up the top of her bikini and walked carefully towards the house, almost sober. 'What's it matter? He can have the whole stinking swamp of them over if he wants. Just means the gardener will have to bring in more asparagus. Funny it's considered such a treat. I always think it tastes of cat's piss.'

The sun glittered on Leonard's stiff, wavy hair. He looked at the two women approach from under his strange, grey-blue eyelashes. How thin Suzette had become: hollows down the length of her thighs, chipped looking knees. It didn't suit her. Caught in a noose of light as she walked out of the shade of a cedar tree, she looked slack and caved-in. When he'd first met her, she'd been a chubby kid, black roots showing through peroxide curls, which were now an expensively tended silver-blond. Yet underneath the Mayfair hairdo, she was still the same old Suze. That was the trouble. Well, she'd just have to buck up. The world wasn't going to stand still for her, and neither was he.

When Raymond and Aurora left, Daisy, unusually for her, felt lonely. She thought she might take some of the early strawberries up to the Manor, see how Gillian was. And Otto too. He was such a worrying child, so thin that his clothes looked empty and with a bare blue gaze that seemed uncomfortable with life. Daisy much preferred this awkward boy to his little sisters, Georgina and Katherine, who, at the ages of six and four, already showed signs of slyness with their slithery, deceitful eyes.

Gillian and the three children had gone to the pony show in Kidderminster, Gomer informed her. He was in the garden, pinching greenfly off the roses with his fingers, and greeted Daisy with a cold smile. She thought: Poor old chap, he has never been taught how to engage upon a conspiracy to please, or realized how ill-mannered it is to bore and perplex other people. She went up close and kissed the tight skin of Gomer's cheek.

'What are you after, Daisy?' he asked. 'Have you come to sell me a subscription to the *Morning Star*? Are you going to take away all my coupons' – he pronounced it 'coupongs' – 'and give them to some toiling widow-woman whose husband fell down a mineshaft before the Labour government made mineshafts safe as houses? Face facts, old thing. Your lot have had it. This country's going to hell in a handcart.'

'There are no facts, Gomer, only interpretations,' Daisy said, and instantly regretted it. It was just the sort of remark that got Gomer overheated. Gomer wiped green smears from his fingers onto his trousers. Daisy sighed. There would be no escaping one of Gomer's acid-hearted lectures now.

Gomer looked up to the flat blue sky and began. 'In the depths of my heart I can't help being convinced that my fellow-men, with a few exceptions, are worthless.' He caught hold of Daisy's arm as she was about to protest. 'Not my words, my dear,' he said nastily, 'but Freud's. Perceptive old Yid. No illusions about the people, unlike you and my little brother, who should know better. The people! How you parlour pinks revere them, refusing to admit that they are dishonourable, foolish and vicious. This democracy of yours, what is it but a ridiculous notion to raise the proletariat to the level of stupidity attained by the bourgeoisie?'

Daisy had willed herself, years ago, never to respond to Gomer's taunts. It would only encourage him in his obscene views. But it was hot, and she was tired after her walk. 'I don't believe you really believe any of that Fascist tosh,' she said angrily. 'You talk all this nonsense because you're jealous of Harry, jealous of everything he's got, although he went out in the world and worked for it, while you buried yourself away here, clinging onto everything that doesn't matter.' She couldn't stop herself now. She was flame-eyed with indignation. 'You're jealous of his fame, his freedom, you're probably even jealous of his thing with Zanna.' She spat out the words as though they were burning her mouth. She had gone too far. She could see understanding gleam in Gomer's cold eyes, his thoughts go round in ever-tighter circles, until they caught the truth.

'Zanna?' Gomer said, genuinely surprised. 'But I thought she was a Yid?'

They were interrupted by the arrival of Gillian and the children in a chauffeur-driven Daimler. Her car, horse-box in tow, had broken down. Some guests of Leonard Riddick's had stopped to help. One of them had driven off to fetch a mechanic while another had insisted on sending her home in his own car as the little girls were getting sleepy. As if on cue, Georgie nudged Kate and they yawned widely and, sensing trouble to come, skipped into the house.

Otto hung about in a misery in the dimming garden while Gomer's eyes squished up in anger as he looked at his wife. 'Clearly, none of you covered yourself in glory. Not one rosette between the lot of you, as far as I can see, and then to accept favours from Riddick's crooked cronies.' There were whole fistfuls of contempt in his throat, his sharp teeth could have stripped the skin from Gillian's bones; it was like watching fingers close around a neck.

Daisy's blood stopped for a moment at the violence in Gomer's voice but Gillian had a faraway expression in her eyes as she picked at some mud on her riding-boot. 'We did our best, dear,' she said mildly, and put an arm around Otto's trembling shoulder. She was a woman used to catastrophe, used to the pity and cruelty that Gomer showered on her, although you could tell her sad little wish to be loved in the droop of her chin. Daisy put down the basket of strawberries on the unravelled wickerwork garden table.

Some women enjoy sacrificing themselves to impossible men, she thought, even though they complain about how miserable they are. I've been noticing that for a long time now. Gillian likes people to think of her as a poor girl married to a monster. It's a trick for sympathy.

114

She pushed half a crown into Otto's fist as she left, and was glad to be back at Utley Lodge, the whippet rubbing its lovely neck against her skirt. But she couldn't sleep that night, even after a brandy and soda and the comfort of all three dogs lying heavily at the foot of her bed.

Chapter Ten

Hiss. Float. Hiss. Float. Fireworks hissed up towards the evening sky, floated down in sparkles onto the shaved lawns of Croston Lacey, where lanterns on poles flickered along the rows of golden yew trees, guiding guests towards the riotous house.

The Riddicks had decided to celebrate the Tories' election triumph early. Leonard's own victory in his constituency was, he said smugly, a racing certainty, although, in such a large rural seat, the final count might not be known until the following afternoon. As early results began to come in over the radio, a Conservative government seemed as sure as Leonard's own re-election.

The Reserves and their ostentatiously dutiful wives were in their own constituencies, so this election-night party of the Riddicks was less gruesome than most of their shindigs, Zanna thought; a mixture of Leonard's constituency workers, mainly decent, elderly women on fixed incomes, and Suzette's crowd of campy hair-dressers, model girls and antique-shop owners, plus some local businessmen who were eyeing up the model girls with enthusiasm. Natalie Bertoud was there too, as gorgeous as any of the professional beauties in a silk jersey dress that yelled the details of the body it clothed, and opal ear-rings which Suzette insisted on lending her, that brightened the gleam in her large, light eyes.

'Phwooaahrr,' said a property developer with a fat chin as Natalie passed by. He had been helping himself to the buffet; a hunk of game paté as big as a kitten weighed down his plate.

Dominick Byrde and his friends brought the elderly constituency workers glasses of champagne and plates of salmon in aspic. The old dears deserved a treat after weeks of licking envelopes and stuffing Leonard's election manifesto through streets of letter-boxes. Besides, you never knew but that they might have something of value in their shabby houses, something that Dominick might be able to persuade them to sell at well below its value. His smile stretched with insincere charm as he refilled the champagne flute of an old lady who was wearing a rather nicely set amethyst on her shaky finger.

Suzette was in black velvet, designed by the Rahvis Sisters in Berkeley Square; strapless, to show off an antique necklace of graduated diamonds, invisibly mounted so that each flashing solitaire seemed suspended like a star against the strained tendons of her neck.

One of the antique dealers, a young man with glittery teeth and buffed fingernails, slung his hands on the piano keys and began to play 'Some Day I'll Find You'. People drifted in from the garden and reached towards each other to dance.

Only Zanna didn't seem to be having a good time. While Raymond and Aurora watched the fireworks, Aurora's mouth wide open like a nestling's, Zanna prowled through Croston Lacey's gilded rooms, smoking endlessly, leaving her red-tipped stubs in dessert-plates, Sèvres ashtrays and Chinese cache-pots as she stalked past them in her restless wanderings.

At last, she fetched her mink coat from Suzette's dressing-room and crossed the darkened grass to where her newest car, a wine-red MG TD, glinted under the cedar tree. She drove to Chipperton without stopping.

As she parked outside the town hall with its sooty, stone garlands, she arranged a serious, almost sorrowing expression on her face. It would never do to arrive in Chipperton with a smile on her face although, of course, she was delighted that the Tories seemed to have won. Her ideal world was one that was loose and uncharted, with everyone scrabbling for what they could get. She had not said that to Harry, not in so many words; he would think it tasteless of her, as vulgar as Churchill's Montecristo cigars.

Inside the town hall, the decaying grandeur of cracked stone and filthy marble steps gave way to cement floors, peeling, blistered walls and a smell of drains. Harry stood on the platform with the Conservative candidate. A funereal-looking official read out the result. Harry, not surprisingly in a working-class Labour stronghold like Chipperton, had won, his majority increased by five thousand and fourteen votes in a straight fight. He and the defeated Tory shook hands with clipped courtesy, listened to each other thank their party helpers with smiling attention, their minds elsewhere. Harry's supporters raised a few muted cheers but rumours of a Tory landslide had already rumbled around the room, their hearts weren't in it.

Harry, scooping papers into his father's old briefcase, looked up and saw Zanna walk towards him down the length of the shabby hall, the glimmering pelt of her mink coat making the other women in their matted jumpers and wrinkled stockings stare at her in tired envy. Zanna's strange lavender eyes locked into Harry's, making his heart bump. 'My shoes are killing me,' she said. 'Any chance of a little lie-down?'

She drove him to Great Windmill Street in her stockinged feet, Harry cradling her black satin shoes in his arms, neither of them speaking until they were in his grimy flat, gulping whisky from cloudy glasses.

Then, at last, Harry let himself rail against the coming times, tapping his fingers against his high forehead as he listened to the radio drone, 'Conservative gain,

Conservative gain,' endlessly, it seemed. He had long ago acquired the politician's habit of keeping a long smile on his face at all times, but now his narrow lips drooped. 'Why do you think we lost?' he asked Zanna bleakly.

'Well, you didn't get enough votes, wasn't that it?' she said, standing behind his chair and dropping kisses onto the top of his head. 'Then there's the fact that everyone's pissed off with good behaviour. They could have torn old Austerity Cripps limb from limb that time he said he lived off mashed carrots and orange juice.'

She gave her low, throaty laugh as Harry looked astonished. 'Jeez, your innocence can be quite dangerous sometimes, Tom Thumb. You think that just because *you* don't give a toss whether you're eating a spam fritter or a crown roast of lamb, nobody else does either. You don't understand *greed*.'

'Start teaching me then,' Harry said in such a bleak voice that the air around him seemed to harden. 'God, how I loathe what Marx called "the primitive accumulation of capital". Nothing left now but the altar of profit,' he said, even more bitterly.

'We should all say our prayers at *that* altar,' Zanna said, beginning to unbutton Harry's shirt and wondering whether the Conservatives' campaign slogan 'Set the people free' would mean fewer import controls; she'd been having a real sod of a time trying to bring in Italian velvets.

Harry was fumbling with the small silver screws of her ear-rings. She pulled them off herself, tugging at the grey pearl droplets, and threw them on the table beside the radio, which she turned off. Harry hardly noticed.

'What we in the Labour Party must never lose sight of', he said, as he slid into Zanna's long white arms, 'is the most vital thing of all – social ownership of the means of production. If we ignore that, we shall become no more than listless, kindly social reformers.'

Zanna laid the thick smear of her lips on his mouth to shut him up. She opened her fisted hand at him. In her palm was a pair of cuff-links, each one a soulful head with a beard suggested by lines etched in the thick gold.

'These are lovely,' Harry said.

'Too good for you, really,' Zanna said cheerfully, 'but I thought it might make you chuck out those ratty old shirts with bits of thread unwinding from the cuffs. The head is St Jude, the patron saint of lost causes. How could I resist?'

She threw herself on top of Harry, nipped his long cheeks with her slightly crooked teeth, buried her nose in the familiar, bitter smell of his armpits. Harry held her close, moved his fingers beneath her thighs until her lily of the valley scent was lost in the reek of her body, that feral reek of redheaded women. How Zanna fed his darker instincts; perhaps, on strange nights like this one, threatened by harsh changes, the only instincts worth having.

They fell asleep, cupped against each other like spoons in a cutlery drawer. By the time they woke, late the next morning, Winston Churchill was Prime Minister again. 'Nuts to that,' said Zanna, yawning and stroking her red bush. 'No matter who's in power, pussy rules the world, right?'

PART TWO

1953 — 1959

Chapter Eleven

Hats were walking out of the door again. Zanna was charging roaring prices for them in her expanded salon that had a uniformed commissionaire to open and shut the bright pink doors, a cockade of the same pink in his black peaked cap. Inside the salon, the oily scent of Madonna lilies flew up the nostrils of Zanna's pampered customers. Hats were displayed on the heads of marble cupids, or on china mannequins whose glazed hands supported their chins. Life-sized ceramic tigers prowled the thick white carpet.

When she left the shop at lunch-time, moving among the crowds of shoppers in Oxford Street, girls with new Eugene perms arm in arm with hopeful-looking young men, Zanna felt that a breezy sanity had swept in with Mr Churchill's return to power, blowing away social-ism's solemn good intentions for ever.

These days Zanna was more than a society milliner. She was a personality, always in the public eye, the subject of newspaper interviews. She had become famous for persuading the beautiful Princess Margaret to throw away her girlish picture hats in favour of brimless caps that crowned her heart-shaped face with a cluster of velvet loops, closely wound tendrils of silk ivy or organza lilac blossom that clung tightly to her head. Journalists liked Zanna's gimmick of giving her hats poetic names – The Darling Buds of May, Song for the Head, The Garden of Love – which made millinery seem less frivolous than it had been during the war years.

When asked to explain her success, Zanna smiled her wide red smile and said, 'I made lemonade out of my lemons, I suppose, used what I'd got.' Tales about the she-hatter flittered about London. Zanna had scowled at a diplomat's wife who was wearing a hat by Paulette which, although lovely, was out of proportion with the woman's Jacques Fath dress. She had taken the hat off her own head and insisted that the diplomat's wife wear it – 'There's no charge, I just want every woman to look the best she can. I insist,' she had added, her smile wide and encouraging but her violet eyes sparkling icily.

Another story, murmured in Fleet Street, was that, during the war, Zanna Gringrich had earned herself the name 'La Desirous' because of her passionate friendships with Allied officers stationed in London. But, well, during those dark years, plenty of girls had whooped it up. Who could blame them? Live and let live; more than enough of them had died. Journalists rarely asked Zanna about her private life. Although she was so vividly beautiful that she seemed to make the world spin faster, it was difficult to imagine her living a life outside the salon. She looked as permanent a fixture as the china mannequins and marble cupids. Besides, all she talked about was hats. 'My hats are myself, my flesh, my blood, my head, my heart, my soul,' she told a young woman reporter from the *Daily Express* who had dared to ask her whether her success had caused any problems. She was the sort of person, Zanna suspected, who might start mentioning things like working mothers, and whether it was difficult to leave her family when she had to spend so much time abroad, establishing herself in the States. The only way to forestall her was to wave her arms around and come over all dramatic. In the face of Zanna's dedication to her craft, the reporter put away her notebook; it would be shabby to bother this obvious artist with mundane questions like how she coped during the school holidays.

'I really ripped the piss out of her,' Zanna reported to Suzette later. 'She got her bam well boozled that time. Well, see a mug, use a mug.'

Harry was doing well too. Even though he was out of office, sneering at the victorious Tory Party, calling it an organized hypocrisy, sickened by the way it picked and pared away at the edges of the welfare state, Harry was more famous in opposition than he had ever been as a government minister because he was regularly seen on television.

He was, everyone agreed, a natural; a man with a recognizable image that verged on a caricature of himself. Where did he get those extraordinary gestures from? Flicking the fat end of his tie while he waited impatiently for someone to finish speaking, pulling at the air with his hands and then kneading it between his fists. His ancient tweeds and the complicated raincoat with its fraying tabs and scuffed buckles were at once reassuring and distinctive. Even the dried blood on his chin after one of his inept shaves made interesting lines on Harry's handsome, bony face. He had given up cigarettes and taken to fiddling around with a pipe, distracting fellow panellists by tamping and puffing. Zanna called his television manner the country-house Marxist approach. 'It gives the punters a tiny thrill to see someone as dashing and dangerous as Tom Thumb invade their pissy little lounges with their cross-over net curtains,' she said adoringly.

Success always pleased her and she began watching the television regularly, honking with laughter whenever Leonard Riddick was interviewed in his new post at the Ministry of Distribution and Supplies. 'Giving Leonard that job is like putting the rabbits in charge of the lettuces,' she said. 'What a lark.'

Leonard, like Harry, had created a new image for himself. He dressed in neo-Edwardian suits: curved jackets with turned-back cuffs and double pocket-flaps, worn with a lapelled waistcoat, tapered trousers and a bowler hat, fashionable again now that you could get the imported shellac that hadn't been available during the war. Sleekly packed into his Savile Row suits, Leonard still seemed to have the shine of rotten mackerel on him. Still, Zanna was fond of him; he'd dragged himself up from nothing and nowhere, brazened things out, even though the newspapers were always criticizing the lushness of his life.

'Can't see what they're on about,' Leonard complained testily. 'It's a well-known fact that Engels said that what he wanted most in life was a bottle of Château-Lafite 1820, so why the hell should the *Daily Mirror* get so shirty about my new yacht? British-made as well, demonstrates how much faith I have in our shipyards when nobody else seems to. And the only reason for using gold plate for the portholes is that it doesn't *rust*. I hardly think that warrants the miserable rag to refer to me constantly as Luxury Len.'

Coronation Day dawned cool for early June, the sky hardly less grey than the gurgling pigeons in the street. Along the route, in St James's Park, the waiting crowds shivered in their summer clothes and leaves flapped in the trees like wings.

The Riddicks would be in Westminster Abbey, eye-witnesses to the young Queen's crowning. Harry would be there too, then he'd dash to the BBC to take part in a discussion on the New Elizabethans. Since Geoffrey Fadge had moved into a new suite of offices in Oxford Street, its windows only a few feet from where the procession would pass, he and Minetta were going to entertain the whole family there. Aurora had asked if she could invite someone she knew from her weekends in the country, a woman called Daisy Fitzhaven, referred to affectionately by Zanna as 'Old Ironknickers'. Minetta telephoned Daisy at her office and, when it

126

turned out that Daisy had invited a young cousin of hers, Otto Welliver, to come up to London for the day, the simplest thing, Minetta told her, would be to bring him too, he'd be company for her own boys. She'd also invited one of Zanna's assistants, Natalie Bertoud, because otherwise, Zanna said, the poor kid would be on her own all day in her poky bedsit.

Zanna had misgivings about the hat she had sold to Suzette. A spiky plume of osprey, dyed a vivid orange, sprang from each side of a grosgrain crescent.

'It's more of a cocktail hat, really, Suze,' Zanna said doubtfully as Suzette tried it on, jerking her head from side to side so that the stiff feathers spliced the air. 'It's a bit strident for the Abbey, and besides, those feathers could give someone a clip in the eye.'

'That's the whole idea,' Suzette said. 'I'll take it.'

The Fadges had been busy for days, bringing carloads of food and drink to Geoffrey's office, and rolls of red, white and blue crêpe paper, which the boys, Ivan, Jonathan and Tony, inexpertly twisted into streamers to drape over the filing cabinets. Cotton Union Jacks on sticks were jammed into tin waste-paper baskets and umbrella stands; in one room, chairs were grouped around a hired television set, while in another, desks had been nudged together and covered in a Coronation paper tablecloth, printed with medallions of the young Queen in profile, crowned with an olive wreath. Minetta had prepared enough food for fifty people rather than the dozen who were expected. She beamed welcomes, her head poking forward on her short neck, urging food and drink on everyone, encouraged by Geoffrey, who was smoking a cigar, pleased with life. His profits had zoomed, along with rising food prices. Sidney rubbed his hands together briskly when he saw the bowls of chopped liver, the cold turkey, the champagne bottles nestling in ice buckets. 'This is it, girlie,' he said to Aurora, pinching her cheek. 'This is the life de luxe.'

Expecting the party to be a family affair, he was a bit put out at the sight of Daisy and Otto, until he saw the love in Daisy's eyes when Aurora greeted her with a hug. 'Nobody ever tells me anything,' he grumbled when Minetta introduced him to this woman he'd never heard of, but then, in a loud aside to Aurora, he said, 'That's a fine person.'

Otto was another matter. Daisy had done the best she could with the boy but he looked scabby and unnurtured next to the three Fadge children in their grey flannel suits, whose short trousers displayed their fat knees, scrubbed to pinkness. Ivan, Jonathan and Tony had dark, side-parted hair, slick with Brylcreem. Their shirts were white, their black Oxfords so new that the soles were still slippery. Otto's bare blue gaze travelled up and down the boys' well-cut clothes and Daisy cursed herself for trusting Gillian to see that the child was properly turned-out.

Clearly, he wasn't. That he was the victim of Gomer's vicious little economies showed in his stubbly hair, which Gomer cut himself, with a hair-clipper, nipping it so close to Otto's skull that you could see the bones move under it; in the serge trousers, two sizes too big, that flapped against his skinny hips, in the outgrown Viyella shirt that exposed the boy's scrappy, brown wrists.

At least those wrists were clean now. When Daisy had met Otto off the train the day before, the child had been filmed over with grime; old black dirt under his fingernails. There was never any hot water at Utley Manor; Gomer, like his father, thought it a shameful luxury. And, when you considered how much coke had to be shovelled into the rusting boiler to provide even a tepid bath, it was hard to argue with him. Otto had had two baths in the few hours he had spent in her flat, assured by Daisy that Londoners bathed at least twice a day, and had asked if he could take home the rest of the bar of Floris soap for his mother. 'Of course you can,' Daisy said. 'When my boat comes in, I'll buy her an immersion heater to go with it.'

Sidney put an arm around Otto's shoulders. 'Noo, boychick? How about some grub? I only wish Her

Majesty could have a taste of Minetta's chopped herring. Robbie, doll-face, look after this young man, see that he eats.'

Otto thought that the girl called Aurora looked like one of the paintings at Utley Manor. It hadn't been cleaned for years and was treacly with damp dust, but you could just make out a girl with shiny hair and straight dark eyebrows leaning against a tree. Aurora was wearing a dress that Zanna had made for her. It was rose pink with a full skirt over layers of petticoats. Into the lace edging of the topmost petticoat, Zanna had sewn six tiny silver bells that tinkled as Aurora moved. She had intended to make her daughter a dress in autumn-leaf brown moiré, to bring out the chestnut glints in her hair, had, in fact, already bought the material. It was Natalie Bertoud who had persuaded her to make Aurora a pink dress. 'When I was in the camp,' Natalie said, 'the worst thing was not having my own clothes. I minded that more than being hungry, more than being frightened. You get used to fear when you face it day in, day out. I kept myself sane by remembering all the clothes that had ever hung in my wardrobe at home in Prague: the little fur coat and bonnet I wore when I was two years old, my first evening dress, white satin with a halter neck, that my parents gave me for my seventeenth birthday. But always I thought of the pink taffeta dress with the bells sewn in the petticoats. For little girls, pink is the colour of happiness.'

Natalie wrinkled her nose at the bolt of brown-gold moiré. '*Très* chic,' she said, 'but a chic twelve year old? A little bit ridiculous, I think.' Tears shone in Natalie's light eyes. 'I think I could grip life with more certainty if you could re-create my pink dress, the dress of my dreams.'

Zanna held up her pin-scratched hands in submission. 'Okey-dokey, Natalie. Pink it is, with bells on. To make *you* happy, not Aurora. That child couldn't tell the difference between a bath-towel and a Balenciaga; at least, she pretends she can't, just to get my goat.'

Natalie hardly ever talked about her life at Terezin, the old military barracks outside Prague, where she had been imprisoned before being transported to Auschwitz. But, in the weeks leading up to the Coronation, she was woozy with tiredness and overwork – she and Zanna had worked through a week of nights to complete all the orders, there couldn't have been a woman in England who was prepared to celebrate the occasion unhatted – and fatigue had loosened her tongue to speak the unspeakable. 'In the camp, those who were not gassed or shot tended to die at two in the morning,' she said, one night, busy braiding a straw coolie hat. 'I wondered why this should be, those dark hours held no more terrors than any others, and then I thought: Those small hours of the morning, they are such an age away from the last time you heard a human voice, maybe silence kills. So I struggled to keep myself awake so that I could talk to the dying. Stories, hopes, plans, the pink frock of my childhood, anything to keep them connected to life. And some of them did live, but who knows the reason?'

'Poor Natalie,' Zanna said. 'The holocaust was one of history's bad turns, wasn't it? Over now, though. Nothing but blue skies from now on, just like the song. Don't let the past smother you, popsie. Enjoy the future, you've earned it more than most.'

When Natalie arrived at Geoffrey's office, Aurora spun around for her so that she could hear the bells tinkle. Otto was entranced by their jingling.

'Mummy made it,' Aurora said, 'the first dress she's made for me that I've really liked.'

Aurora's mother was the pretty woman that he'd seen in the village sometimes with his Uncle Harry. They hadn't seen him though, he'd made sure of that. At the moment, the pretty woman's fork was fluttering over her food, hardly touching it, although Otto had never tasted anything so delicious. Yellow plaited bread with a shiny crust sprinkled with poppy seeds, fried fish balls that Lilian kept on spooning onto his plate. This wonderful food had strange names: *challah, gefüllte* fish, strudel.

Otto wondered what they would be having for lunch at Utley Manor; tinned tongue, probably, and a salad with beetroot juice leaking over mustard and cress. He thought he could sneak some of those almond-flavoured pastries back for Georgie and Kate. He could scoop them into a red, white and blue paper napkin without anyone noticing. While working out his strategy, he absent-mindedly scratched his stubbly head with his fork.

The goyim, thought Lilian, shocked. The way they bring up their children, you wouldn't treat a stray dog. Look at that poor boy, he can't take his eyes off the food, or Geoffrey helping the kids make a banner for the window or Robbie with her arms round Sidney's neck. Lilian wondered if, without giving offence, she could replace Otto's fork and put the one he'd scratched his head with into a bowl of Dettol to soak off the germs. No, better to leave him be, he was uncomfortable enough as it was.

Otto's narrow face looked starved of more than food. Natalie, catching the boy's hungry eye, flinched and turned away, reminded of things she had told herself not to think about. She found Geoffrey Fadge at her side, a new cigar in his mouth, his hair sleek on his round head, looking as established as the sky. 'Everything all right?' he asked her.

'Everything is perfect. It was so kind of you and Mrs Fadge to include me.'

Geoffrey waved his cigar around the room. 'Could be a once-in-a-lifetime chance. Seriously, though, if she lives as long as Queen Vic, God bless her soul, there might not be another Coronation in our lifetime. Well, mine at any rate,' he amended, taking a closer look at Natalie. She was younger than he'd thought at first. It was her stiff way of talking, her sophisticated page-boy hairstyle and the strict cut of her linen suit that made her seem older. The suit was the exact blue-grey of the smoke curling out of his cigar and the way Natalie moved her head on her long neck had the same delicate sway.

There was something sad in Natalie's large, light eyes, something needy, even when she smiled. Aghast, Geoffrey found himself slithering into love. He squeezed Natalie's elbow and resumed his role of host with noisy energy, calling out to Lilian, who was collecting plates and glasses before people had quite finished with them, 'Give it a rest, Mum. There's a girl coming in later to do the clearing-up. Stop wearing yourself out.'

'Better to wear out than rust out,' Lilian said, but she went and sat down; people usually did what Geoffrey told them.

They drifted between the two rooms, the children watching less of the televised service in Westminster Abbey than the grown-ups, not really interested in the tiny black-and-white figure of Elizabeth II on the screen, inside its elaborate casing like a cocktail cabinet. They were waiting for the real thing: the gold coach with painted panels, carrying the flesh-and-blood monarch who might, if they cheered loudly enough, look up at the windows of G. Fadge and Associates and wave to them.

The Fadge boys were starting to bicker quite meanly about who was going to sit just behind the window-boxes with their patriotic display of geraniums, forget-me-nots and white Canterbury bells, when Zanna, ignoring them, notebook grasped in her squirrel's paw, passed into the room where the television flickered, to sketch any noteworthy hat that might be caught on camera. Ivan and Jonathan, both solid in the shoulder, began to jostle for the centre of the window. Aurora slid in front of them. She planted her white kid shoes with their cut-out petal design on the instep firmly in the middle window-box and spread out her arms, blocking the view.

'Get on out of it, Robbie,' Ivan warned.

'Not until you let Otto and Tony sit in the front, and don't call me Robbie,' Aurora said. The railings in front of the window-boxes were quite low. Otto was terrified that Aurora might fall backwards into the festooned street in a flutter of petticoats and jangling bells, especially when she began to make backward circles with her arms, lurching and wheeling like someone about to topple over.

'I'll tell Mum on you,' Ivan said, uncertainly.

'Go on then. You know she'll tell you to behave like a nice little gentleman and let the younger ones sit at the front, so you might as well save her the bother.' Seeing sullen resignation on her cousin's wodgy face, Aurora jumped down into the room and riffled through a bunch of flags until she found the biggest one, which she gave to Otto. 'Sit in the middle with Tony,' she instructed. Ivan gave her a hard pinch on the arm but, without even looking round, she kicked him on his fat, bare leg and, as the grown-ups, all except Zanna, came to take their places behind the children, she ran to Raymond's side, so that they could watch everything together.

The royal coach was already in sight when Zanna emerged. Now that's what I call a complexion, she thought admiringly, as the Queen, to the children's delight, waved up at them. The pink and whiteness of the Queen's cheeks seemed lit from within, glowing against the grey skies and sopping shop-fronts. Nice to have a woman on the throne, good for the fashion industry, although that hairdo was a disaster, those solid, unassailable curls would have to go. Well, God bless her, anyway. Zanna raised her glass as Geoffrey proposed the loyal toast. He was looking particularly smug today. Strange how Geoffrey always managed to have his bum in the butter, while poor Raymond, a more intelligent man in so many ways, was always struggling, the grim smell of want at the end of his nose, his eyes bulging with unspoken troubles. Zanna drained her glass impatiently.

How restless Zanna is today, Daisy thought, half-listening to Lilian recalling her early life in Chipperton. Zanna was wearing a dress in a swirling black-and-white print, the pattern swerving in different directions as she moved. It had very short sleeves and Daisy, noting that Zanna's elbows were smooth as a boiled egg, plucked at the sleeves of her own dress, pulling them down over her roughened elbows that were getting grey and scaly because she never remembered to take Zanna's advice and push them into the cut halves of lemons for an hour once a week.

Lilian was dabbing at her eyes with a spotless handkerchief. 'Is anything wrong, Mrs Spetner?' Daisy asked in her kind way.

'Such happiness,' Lilian moaned into the handkerchief. 'The family all together, a beautiful young Queen, may God pour blessings on her head.' She blew her nose and then powdered it from an ugly gold compact, an L studded in diamonds in one corner. 'Mustn't let Zanna see me like this,' she said. 'She's always criticizing me for wearing my heart on my sleeve. But,' she gave Daisy a damp smile over her powder puff, 'our feelings, isn't that all we have?'

'I think Zanna and I are rather alike in that respect,' Daisy said, more coldly than she had intended. 'We do not like and do not traffic in emotion.' She felt an absurd loyalty towards Zanna who, she could see, was an exotic misfit in this stifling family. Zanna had been trembling with boredom when she'd crossed the room a moment ago; the flowers in the window-boxes had vibrated from the force of it. Really, the way she smouldered was rather terrifying. What must it be like for Raymond and Aurora to live with her? More than once that day, she'd caught Zanna staring at her husband and child as though they'd wandered in from the street and had nothing to do with her. 'It's hard for ambitious women to lead rich, emotional lives, perhaps that's the problem,' Daisy told Lilian gently. 'But you must be so proud of Zanna; she's achieved so much.'

'Much wants more,' Lilian said, giving Daisy a jolt; surely she didn't know about Harry? Lilian patted her arm. 'God forbid I should complain about my own daughter, Miss Fitzhaven. But, believe me, ambition is a rope that twists around the heart.' Lilian pressed her lips together and Daisy realized that, far from being proud of her daughter's success, she was puzzled and embarrassed by it.

Zanna was alone in front of the television set. Against the soundtrack of Ronald Binge's 'Elizabethan Serenade', the title of the next programme, *The New Elizabethans*, appeared on the screen, and then the camera roamed purposefully over the signs and symbols of the new era, the visual proofs that optimism was, at last, groaning into place as England emerged from its post-war doldrums. It lingered over a serious little boy putting together the first Airfix kit, a replica of Sir Francis Drake's ship, *The Golden Hind*. It followed two laughing girls as they treated themselves to half a pound of toffees at a well-stocked branch of Lavelle's sweet shops, a reminder that sweets had come off ration the previous February. It showed the expression of delighted surprise on the face of a well-made-up housewife as she brewed a pot of tea using the latest novelty – a tea-bag. A group of expectant tourists boarded a BEA plane, car-workers admired their handiwork: a Jaguar XK120, a Silver Wraith, a Land Rover. 'Do get on with it,' Zanna muttered crossly.

At last, the camera settled on the television studio. Three men sat in three impressive but uncomfortable chromium and leather armchairs. In between the philosopher, A. J. Ayer, and the playwright, Terence Rattigan, Harry sat, flicking his tie and looking out of sorts. He immediately challenged the idea that there could be anything new about the age when Coronation Day itself was a pathetic demonstration of how Great Britain as a nation fêted its past. 'What we have just witnessed at Westminster Abbey was the worst kind of ancestor worship,' he said testily, 'completely out of touch with the lives of ordinary people, although', he conceded with one of his narrow smiles, 'a superb show of pageantry.'

Oh, Tom Thumb, what a killjoy you are, or pretend to be, Zanna thought. She felt vividly in love with Harry at that moment, so happy to see his face, his large nose with its horsy nostrils almost filling up the screen, that she could have leant forward in her chair and kissed the glass. She was concentrating so rapturously on Harry's hard, driven opinions that she didn't see Aurora come in with a plate of smoked-salmon sandwiches which Lilian had insisted she bring in to Zanna who had eaten nothing during the day.

Aurora knew the man who was talking on the television. His name was Harry Welliver. She had met him once, during the school holidays, when her mother had taken her to work with her. He seemed to be a favourite of Mrs Harris. When he came through the door that led to the workroom, pitching through it as though he had not expected it to open when it did, Mrs Harris had clapped her hands with their flaking nail-polish and congratulated him on a television debate he'd taken part in. 'That was a real argy-bargy last night, wasn't it, sir? That Anthony Eden really got the hump.'

Aurora hadn't liked Harry. He seemed the sort of person who put himself on display, the way Zanna did. She was glad when they both left the shop at lunch-time and Mrs Harris could make one of her fry-ups. Bacon, pork sausages, things Nana Lilian would never have allowed, and Mrs Harris ate as greedily as Aurora did, her pencilled eyebrows swooping down over her exhausted eyes, wiggling her stockinged feet.

Zanna's lavender eyes were sucking in the sight of Harry Welliver now. Her red lips were slightly parted and her breaths were heavy. He means more to her than anyone else, Aurora understood instantly, and went out again, still holding the plate of sandwiches. She wished she could lock the door behind her, imprisoning her mother like a wicked witch in a fairy story before she could do any harm, leave her sitting in front of the

136

television for ever, out of everyone's way. That Zanna was capable of doing harm was something that Aurora had never doubted.

In the front office, Raymond was padding heavily about on his flat feet, distributing the cups of tea that Minetta was pouring.

'What's Mummy up to?' he asked.

'Watching Harry Welliver jawing.'

Daisy, at the far end of the room, heard Harry's name and smiled at Aurora. 'That's Otto's uncle,' she said.

Aurora looked stricken by this news. Otto was half-way through a slice of fruit cake iced in red, white and blue. He was shovelling it into his mouth, licking his fingers to lift loose crumbs from the plate. Aurora looked as though she might be going to cry. He wished that Uncle Harry wasn't related to him if it was something that made Aurora unhappy. The day had turned out so well; for ever after, to the end of his life, the word 'celebration' would bring back that Coronation Day, when one meal slid into the next, his boy's hunger recognized, satisfied.

Yet, even as people were gathering up their souvenirs and mementoes, the Coronation silver sovereigns in satin-lined boxes, the flags, china mugs and dishtowels that Geoffrey had given them, Otto could feel a sadness in the air, caused, in some way, by Uncle Harry. He pushed his plate away, a gesture of sympathy that Aurora was meant to notice, and did.

Bloody hell, Raymond thought. Robbie's guessed that something's up. The stolid innocence children have always leads them to the truth. Pointless to suppose he could have gone on protecting his daughter for ever, or himself, which was, perhaps, the same thing. He felt boneless with grief. He could imagine the lascivious look in Zanna's eyes, giving the whole sordid game away, crumbling to pieces her daughter's safe, warm world.

Daisy and Otto were going; the boy's ears were on fire as he subjected himself to Minetta's and Lilian's hugs and pawings. Zanna, who had just come into the room, waved at him, a flick of her hand, and blew Daisy a kiss.

At the door, Lilian hurried forward again. 'Keep us in your heart,' she said strangely, pressing Daisy's hand.

Chapter Twelve

Geoffrey Fadge drummed his fingers on his desk and stared blankly at the photograph of his wife and three sons which stood on it. They stared back at him, heavy-shouldered and serene. His deadly, happy family.

Minetta was a wonderful girl, no denying it. Wonderful homemaker. Wonderful mother. Now that the boys were growing up, she was going to be a Justice of the Peace, putting herself at the service of the community. Wonderful. The only place she was not wonderful was in bed. There had been no sex since Tony was born, six years ago. Minetta always turned away from him when Geoffrey put his hand on her hip, pretending that she was sliding into sleep. Right from the start, she had disliked sex. Every time Geoffrey unbuttoned his pyjamas, she gave him a reproachful look and reached for the tube of vaginal jelly in her bedside cabinet.

Geoffrey sighed. You can't have everything, he thought, but, a few minutes later, he put on his hat and crossed Hanover Square on his way to Bond Street.

'Zanna is in New York,' Natalie told him.

'I know. I came to see you. When do you finish here?'

Natalie pushed back her hair with delicate fingers. On the inside of her arm, a row of blue numbers bumped against a blue vein. 'Mr Fadge, I think no,' she said.

'Please,' Geoffrey insisted. Emotionally evasive all his life, at that moment he would have knelt before her on the white carpet, pleaded with her to let him lift the weight of her blue-black hair and see it fall back over her shoulders.

'OK,' Natalie said. 'Six o'clock. A quiet drink only.'

'The worst room you've got, provided that it's also the cheapest,' Zanna told the receptionist at the Plaza Hotel in New York. It made sense to stay in the worst room of the best hotel so that you could say, 'Call me at the Plaza.' New York was where the hot money was after the war. Women there spent money on clothes in an intense way that she'd never seen in Europe, planning their wardrobes twice a year, down to the last hairpin and then, the following season, giving the lot to their maid and starting over, rather than have anything altered to make it more up to date.

In London and Paris, when Zanna complimented an elegant woman on her dress, she might respond, with no feeling of shame, 'Oh, this old thing, I've had it for years.' In New York, it was social death to be seen in the same outfit twice in front of the same people. It could even send shares in your husband's company plummeting.

The swanky department stores, Saks Fifth Avenue, Henri Bendel, Bergdorf Goodman, had the same air of reverential hush as a Paris couture house. High-spending clients were 'protected'; once they'd chosen a particular model, it was pulled from the racks so they wouldn't bump into other women wearing the same suit or frock. Zanna loved department stores. They'd started in France, a hundred years ago, and Zola had said that they represented the democratization of luxury. Maybe not at New York prices, but they certainly turned shopping into a social event.

Harry would hate it here, Zanna thought as she sipped pale tea in the Palm Court of the Plaza, surrounded by women in mink coats and flamboyant diamond ear-rings. Harry thought that Americans were crude, and half-believed that the White House had a plan to dominate the world by infiltrating it with American films and show tunes and glossy consumer goods. The pianist was playing a selection from *Guys and Dolls*. Zanna hummed along with 'Luck Be A Lady Tonight'. She wouldn't mind being dominated by this kind of thing one bit.

'Excuse me, ma'am,' someone said in a pleasing drawl, 'would you mind telling me where that great hat of yours came from?'

Zanna was wearing Giddy Heaven, a severe black satin cockade, intricately folded over her forehead and pierced with a *diamanté* star. 'My own design.' She shook a dry, slightly puffy hand and put one of her bright pink business cards into it.

The hand belonged to a shortish, sandy-haired man wearing an expensive suit and a Cartier watch. He put on gold-rimmed spectacles in order to read her name. 'You thinking of doing any business while you're over here, Mrs Gringrich?' he asked.

American buyers hardly ever set foot in London. They went to the Paris collections and came right home again, complaining about French plumbing and how impossible it was to get iced water. That's why Zanna had come to New York, with a trunkload of samples from her last collection. It was the only way she had a hope of breaking into the American market like the French modistes, Agnès, Suzy, Georgette, Rose Descat and, of course, the genius who designed hats for Christobal Balenciaga, Vladzio D'Attainville.

'I hope so,' she said. 'I have appointments all over town.'

'Save one for me.' The sandy-haired man extracted his own card from a crocodile case. Rhodes T. Calderone III, Zanna read, President, Calderone Park Avenue. A woman who looked as though she might be Mrs Calderone glowered from a tapestry armchair some distance away.

Zanna riffled through the blank pages of her diary. 'Let's have a look. You know, I've been so rushed, I haven't got around to calling your buyer yet.'

'Forget the buyer. Where are you showing?'

'Right here. In my suite,' Zanna lied.

'I'll be there at eight-thirty tomorrow morning.' He walked back to his fretful wife.

Elizabeth Taylor had booked the best suite in the hotel and would be arriving the next afternoon. It was already filled with flowers. 'Let me have it for a couple of hours in the morning and I'll give you a hat for your wife,' Zanna pleaded with the hotel manager. He'd been stationed in London during the war and had a soft spot for Limeys. Although he didn't have a wife, and lived with a male companion in Washington Square, he unlocked the suite and had Zanna's trunkful of hats sent up.

Rhodes T. Calderone sat perfectly still while Zanna modelled tip-tilted boaters, embroidered berets, wide-brimmed hats as romantic as a summer afternoon.

'Ever heard of a man called Zadoc Benedict?' he asked, when the last hat had been returned to the trunk. 'He set up the first hat factory in America, in Danbury, Connecticut, as a matter of fact. I'm a descendant of his on my mother's side of the family, which might explain why I'm mad about hats. Yours are really something. Elegant. Witty. They create their own world, as all great fashion does. I'd no idea stuff like this was coming out of London. Last time I was over there, back in 'forty-five, everything was the colour of gravy. Overcoats, the paint on the walls, even the skies, or so it seemed.'

'Everything changes,' Zanna said.

'You've said it.' He stood up and put his hands on her shoulders. 'Time to cut a deal,' he said and kissed the tip of her nose. 'Exclusive licensing,' he murmured, starting to unfasten the small hooks and eyes at the back of her dress. 'Reproduction rights. Full prior consultation.' He lifted the dress over her head. 'Sixty–forty in your favour.' He tossed his trousers over a chair.

Zanna felt bouncy with glee. She looked into Rhodes T. Calderone's merry little eyes and saw dollar signs twinkling in them. Quickly, she pulled him onto the floor. The bed had already been made up for Miss Taylor with piles of lace-edged pillows and it wouldn't do to muss it up.

He was a spry, energetic lover. Zanna's stumpy fingers pulled the wiry hair that covered his back and shoulders; she faked an orgasm as soon as she credibly could, so as to be out of the suite in time. Afterwards, he said, 'You're a poet of the appetites, Zanna. Not many women are. I take off my hat to you.'

'Thank you,' Zanna said. 'Still, I wonder what got into us. What made us behave like that?'

'Can do, must do,' he said, and lifted his chin to knot his tie.

'It seems heartless, somehow.'

'In New York, you can't have a heart. My attorney will call you in the next hour to draw up a contract. Take care of yourself, sugar.'

'Promise me never to cut it,' Geoffrey said, lifting up Natalie Bertoud's blue-black hair and skeining it around his hand. Nowadays, he was allowed to help Natalie perform her evening ritual of hair-washing. First, she grated some flakes of Sunlight soap and shook them into suds in a bowl of hot water to which she added some drops of glycerine. She rinsed the lather off her hair in many changes of water, putting vinegar in the final rinse to make her hair shine.

'No, I shall never cut it,' she assured him. 'It was cut only in the camp. The guards sold women's hair to textile companies – it is ideal for making felt, rope, carpets even. Maybe I owe my life to my thick hair. It grows quickly and they could earn money from it every few weeks.'

At first Natalie had refused to talk about her past but now, resting in Geoffrey's arms, filled with the gentle hopes of love, she discovered that she could unfold herself to him, without being seized by the old terrors.

143

She told him how she was taken from her parents' house and driven through the empty, corrupting beauty of Prague's streets where the rain, glinting in the spaces between the cobbles, framed each space in water. Geoffrey held her closer, comforted her with kisses so long his lips might have been sewn to hers. And then they were gasping, writhing, clutching, tangling on Natalie's narrow bed, stirred by the tenderest moods of the soul.

'Got something for you,' Geoffrey said, disentangling himself from Natalie's arms. He had to get home; Min had asked their next-door neighbours round for dinner and a game of bridge. Natalie opened the small, velvet box. A tiny gold envelope swung from a gold chain. 'Look,' Geoffrey said. He slid open one side of the envelope and revealed a gold tablet inscribed, 'Everything leads me to you.'

'It's true and all,' he said guiltily. His shoulders slumped as he put on his shoes and tied the laces. Natalie hated to see him leave. 'I expect you're busy with Zanna away,' he said, 'must have a lot of work to be getting on with.'

Natalie shook her head wildly. 'I am your lover. That is my job in life,' she said.

Geoffrey wished she wouldn't say things like that; it reminded him how burdened their love affair was, how startling Natalie's ravening needs were. He moved towards her but Natalie stopped him by holding up her hand like a policeman halting a car. 'It must be understood, I am lorn for love,' she said.

'I know, my darling. I know. We'll work something out soon.'

Natalie flung her arms around Geoffrey's neck. 'We will be more and more never apart,' she said, smiling at last.

Earlier in the day, he had bought Tony a cowboy outfit at Hamley's, uncomfortable about buying Natalie a present without also getting something for his family. Tony put on the fringed waistcoat and chaps and buckled on the holster. 'Bang, bang, you're dead,' he said, aiming the silver pistols at his father. Geoffrey rumpled his son's hair.

'No I'm not, sunshine. Your old man is very much alive.'

Gomer was in the village pub, The Rising Sun, lunching off a slab of cracked, sweating cheese and three pickled onions, and boring his solicitor with stories about his hero, Oliver Cromwell.

'His name wasn't really Cromwell at all,' he said. 'It was Williams. But the great man's grandfather, Richard Williams, took the surname of his patron who was Thomas Cromwell, Earl of Essex.'

The solicitor, who wanted to get back to his office, yawned rudely, keeping his arms folded across his chest. He was usually polite and a good listener but Gomer annoyed him intensely, sitting there with his hands on his fat, somehow obscene thighs, while his two smelly dogs dribbled on the floor at his feet.

He got up to leave and Gomer, only halfway through his pint, looked around for somebody else to talk to. The lunch-time drinkers had nearly all gone back to their shops or farms. In a dark corner, a woman in a mink coat was sipping a gin and tonic. She wore a brightly patterned silk headscarf, the ends crossed around her throat and knotted at the back of her neck, and dark glasses, but Gomer recognized her wide, jutting red mouth. Carrying his pint, he walked heavily across the room, followed by his disagreeable dogs.

From the way the beer swung inside the glass as Gomer lurched towards her, Zanna knew he was drunk. He took one of her soft, leather gloves from the beer-stained table and squashed it in his fist. 'A bit of a soiled dove, aren't you?' he hissed out of his lipless mouth. 'A demirep. A doxy.'

'You're drunk, Gomer. Give me back my glove.'

'Harry's as much to blame,' Gomer slurred pompously. 'He's poohed in our nest. *That* won't be forgiven.' He

145

stared at Zanna out of his chilled, pale eyes, and she had to sit on her hands to stop herself from drawing her coat more closely around her.

Gomer began to twist the fingers of Zanna's glove. 'I'll tell you something about Harry,' he said. 'He thinks that getting mixed up with your sort of people shows how egalitarian he is, how tolerant, how *democratic*. Probably thinks you're worth a grind too. But that doesn't mean he takes you seriously. As far as Harry's concerned, you're a throw-away woman. You're a fool if you think he will hang onto you after he's had enough of your vulgarity.' Gomer leant across the small table. He held Zanna by the chin and, with his free hand, touched her lips and smeared the greasy, scarlet lipstick over her cheeks. Then he left, banging into chairs, to return to Utley Manor with its lumpy ceilings and tall, rook-loud chimneys, where he and Gillian lived in their shared, brooding isolation.

Zanna had come to Utley by car and had taken shelter in The Rising Sun until it was time for her to meet Harry's train. They were going to spend a long weekend by themselves at Utley Lodge, their first meeting since Zanna's return from New York.

The tops of the stone pillars that supported the station's roof had been painted in rings of red, white and blue for the Coronation. Already, in the cold September air, the paint was beginning to flake. The train stopped and Harry scudded towards her, shoulders swinging, and gave her a bone-cracking hug. He released her and they stood close; he slid his arms inside the sleeves of her coat and gently scratched her elbows. The flop of his hair stirred in her a familiar, fanatical depth of passion. She tucked her arm into his and led him towards the car.

How comforting this house is, Zanna thought, later that afternoon, sitting on the fireside rug at Utley Lodge. Daisy's whippet circled a spot on the rug and lay down on it, beside her. The fire wobbled brightly and together they listened to the glup glup of the flames being pulled up the chimney, while rain slapped on the windows. Harry was upstairs, having a bath; you could tell that by the way the water tanks in the attic gurgled and hummed. In the kitchen, the latest Connemara girl, known always as Mary Mac to distinguish her from the six other Marys in the village, was singing 'Carrickfergus' as she held a cloth over the pan of boiled potatoes to encourage them to fluff up.

After supper, Harry expounded on the current state of the nation, pulling at the air with his hands, the way he did when he appeared on television. 'The Tory back-benchers are a tremendously unformidable lot, while the Labour Party now practises the politics of prudential acquiescence. These are tainted and dangerous times, my love.' He thought that Zanna was even paler than usual, so pale that the vein in her temple gleamed a vivid blue.

'Is anything wrong?' he asked. Zanna broke into loud sobs. Harry glanced towards the door to make sure it was closed; he didn't want Mary Mac to hear this strange, ugly sound. Then he wiped Zanna's tears with a torn handkerchief.

'Tell me,' he said.

'I'm a soiled dove,' Zanna said.

'You're being melodramatic, Zanna.'

'In New York, I had sex with a man called Rhodes T. Calderone III because he bought my entire collection.'

'Rhodes T. Calderone III,' Harry marvelled. 'Oh darling, you are quite preposterous.'

'Don't you mind, Tom Thumb?'

'My darling girl, of all the things that you and I have in common, the most remarkable is our refusal to contemplate failure as a respectable destiny. You want to leave your mark on the world. So do I. My greatest ambition is to return this country to socialism; yours is to become the most successful hat-maker in the world. To get what I want, I befriend idiotic and greedy trade union leaders whom I despise. To get what *you* want, you sleep with Rhodes T. Calderone III. That is the way of the world.'

147

'Fancy you teaching me the way of the world, Tom Thumb. Once upon a time, it was the other way round. You're right. I want to win everything. It's a habit with me.'

'It's a habit with me, too.' He took both her wrists in his hand. 'I claim the winner's prize,' he said.

In bed, feeling Harry's heart beating over hers, Zanna was tempted to tell him about her meeting with Gomer but thought better of it, there had been enough disclosures for one day. She felt quite calm now. Outside the house, the night was safe and quiet and it was a long time before she and Harry parted in two to sleep.

Chapter Thirteen

'Lawdie–Gawdie, not you as well,' Zanna growled down the telephone to Suzette Riddick. 'I thought I could rely on you at least not to mention the word S–U–E–Z. I've never seen Harry so thunderously angry; his lips are *mauve* with rage.' She impersonated Harry's hard, driving voice: ' "An insane enterprise. Imperialism's last stand. Eden will never survive this débâcle. Blah. Blah. Blah." As well as that, Mum and Dad are worried about the cousins in Tel Aviv; they think Nasser might bomb Israel. And *I'm* in a complete crisis over the new flat. Should I knock down the inside walls and do something Californian with exposed brickwork and next to no furniture, or have a very English Regency décor with delicious taffeta bows over the picture frames? Oh, one more thing, Suze. This will interest you. My brother-in-law has buggered off. Left Minetta for another woman. And here's the extraordinary thing: it's Natalie Bertoud. Well, that's gone down as pleasantly as a rat sandwich, as far as Mum and Dad are concerned. I don't know who they want to murder first, President Abdul Nasser, or Geoffrey Fadge.'

Zanna could hear a bottle chime against a glass. She looked at her watch. 9.15 a.m. 'Anyway, enough grumbling. How are things with you, toots?'

149

'Peachy creamy,' Suzette said, her voice slurred and boozy. 'Peachy creamy. Leonard is quite impossible. He's wasted years sucking up to Eden, buzzing about, pissing himself to earn a little hoard of smiles. And now that the PM's in the doo-doo, Leonard doesn't know where to launch the next charm offensive. Butler? Macmillan? He just can't decide which one is the goose who's going to lay the golden beanstalk.'

'Egg, Suze. The beanstalk was what the goose was on top of. Oh, I see what you mean. Are you having a drink?'

'Only cooking sherry. Leonard keeps everything else locked up. He wants me to be a political asset.' Suzette giggled wildly. 'Fancy Natalie having a winky-wanky-woo. Well, she's always been quite a glamourpussy in a serious sort of way. Must go now, Zanna. Tory wives' coffee-morning.'

'Keep it cookin', Suze. Bye.'

Zanna was taking her sister Minetta to lunch at the Mirabelle, and wasn't looking forward to it. For some reason, Minetta blamed her for Geoffrey's desertion, as though the proximity of Zanna Modes to his own office made betrayal easier. Zanna remembered the first time Harry had come into the shop, tossing Leonora's hatbox on the counter, in a hurry to be on his way. They'd ended up in bed that same afternoon. She smiled to herself. Quite a trysting place, Zanna Modes. If the millinery business starts to fall off, I could turn the place into a knocking shop.

It was Aurora she was concerned about, Minetta said. She sat opposite Zanna, wearing a fawn wool dress with pink flecks and a horseshoe-shaped pocket on each bosom. A half-moon shaped hat, pasted with flat, pink feathers, was clamped on her coarse hair.

'Robbie's not happy about moving to Chelsea. It's a long way from her school, and she's got O levels next year.'

'What rubbish. Raymond is going to take her to school in the morning and there's a bus that is almost door to door to get her home. You're putting her up to this, Min, or Mum is. Neither of you thinks I'm capable of bringing up my own daughter, do you? Well, if I'm such a terrible mother, how come she's top of the class every term? Form prefect, netball captain and . . .' Zanna tried to remember what was inscribed on the other enamel badges that clinked on Aurora's school pullover, but failed.

'Because she's scared of failing,' Minetta said. 'You *numb* her, Zanna. She works much too hard, so you won't look down on her. She'd be much better off living with Mum and Dad till she finishes school. There'd be less pressure.'

'No,' Zanna said. 'And when I say no, don't ask again.'

'Raymond agrees with me.'

'You've talked to Raymond? I don't believe you. Aurora is his whole life. He'd hate her to leave home. It was him who insisted on having her to live with us when he came out of the Army, when I wouldn't have minded leaving her with Mum and Dad. It wasn't easy trying to bring up a kid while I was building up the business.'

'Aurora needs family life,' Minetta persisted. 'She needs a routine, a proper tea when she comes home from school, and someone to talk to. She likes ritual, candles on Friday night. You can't give her any of that, Zanna.'

'No,' Zanna agreed cheerfully. 'She can whistle out of her arse for all that tedious serenity, as far as I'm concerned.' She was outraged, though, that Raymond had agreed to Aurora leaving home without telling her. He must be really scandalized by the way his wife lived if he was prepared to let his daughter go. Now she thought about it, he'd been looking at her with a sort of baleful disapproval for some time, and, a few days ago, he'd said there was something he wanted to discuss. They'd been getting ready for bed, and Raymond had stood there, naked except for his socks and horn-rimmed spectacles, the most

151

ridiculous sight imaginable. She'd sniggered a bit, and he'd clammed up.

Minetta said, 'I could see how difficult it was for Raymond to broach the subject, so I decided to mention it myself.'

Zanna knew that she was waiting for her to lose her temper, so she kept her voice silky. 'Tell you what, Min, Aurora can stay in Golders Green during the week, just as long as she turns up at Chelsea at the weekends. Well, some weekends, anyway,' she amended, remembering that she would be absent from Chelsea herself, whenever there was a chance of a weekend with Harry. 'That way, I can keep an eye on her clothes, see she isn't eating too much.' She looked pointedly out of her lavender eyes at Minetta's drab dress. 'Now, much more important. How are you?' She touched Minetta's wrist with her warm squirrel's paw, but her eyes gleamed malice.

'How could I be? Like any other woman whose husband has abandoned her, I suppose. Betrayed, angry, hurt, trying not to let the boys see how upset I am.' Zanna patted her sister's hammy arm; the expression in her hard eyes softened. Minetta was encouraged to pour out her resentment. 'He's bought a flat for her now, paid a fortune for it. Throwing his money about.'

'Men don't look for bargains when it comes to sex,' Zanna said, gratified when Minetta's neck flushed red. She flapped a hand at a waiter for the bill. 'We're a pair, aren't we, Min? You can't hang onto a husband, I can't hold onto a daughter. Must be something wrong somewhere.'

Leonard Riddick frowned at the empty bottle of bay rum which had been full the day before. Suzette drank everything that he didn't lock away – cooking sherry, his aftershave, and now hair tonic. He had stopped taking her to fund-raising dinners in his constituency, since the time she had plucked one of the gladioli from the elaborate centrepiece on the top table and started to nibble it. He had reminded her time and time again that the role of the political wife was to be nice and smile and say the right things. Suzette was nice all right, the kindest woman in the world, and, as long as she was tanked up, which was nearly always, she beamed blindly at everybody, but, every time she opened her mouth, Leonard feared political ruin. She looked all wrong too. Too fashionable, too raddled. Her current style was inspired by Brigitte Bardot. Her hair was piled up at the back and tumbled over her eyes in an elaborate arrangement of curls and fronds, and her eyes were darkly outlined, with pencilled flicks at the corners. Maybe she would have gone down a treat in St Tropez, but she looked all wrong in Utley, a place where women weren't supposed to look like fun.

What really alarmed Leonard was that that dreadful piece of work Gomer Welliver had joined the Utley Conservative Party and sometimes turned up at ward meetings with his wife, who was almost as unsettling as Gomer with her jumpy eyes and extraordinary view of the world. She'd come to Leonard's Friday-night surgery a few weeks ago, to complain about over-crowding in her younger daughter's class at the village primary school. Same thing all over the country, due to 'the Bulge', everyone at it like rabbits after the war, although Gomer hadn't been in the Army; the child was probably a mistake. Plenty of those around. 'Why not get up a petition for increased teaching staff, Mrs Welliver?' Leonard had suggested in a hearty, encouraging way.

Gillian had given him a startled look. 'But none of them would listen to *me*. They're jealous of me because I live in a big house and keep ponies.'

Leonard, remembering the newspapers under the doors of Utley Manor, put there to absorb puddles from the tilting floors, had thought that Gillian was joking, until he looked into her flickering dark eyes and realized that she truly believed her unpopularity was caused by envy of her privileged lot.

153

No doubt about it, Gomer's presence was cause for concern. His neat, small ears were sharp as a dog's to any gossip, as he sat at the bar of the Conservative Club, looking like a man who was familiar with all the world's dirty devices. What could Gomer have on him? Leonard had covered his traces pretty thoroughly; he'd sold all the crummy little companies that connected him to his black-marketeering past, all the slum properties, whose combined rents had enabled him to furnish Croston Lacey. It couldn't be political incompetence either. Leonard was a success in office, a nimble speaker who could disguise his nasty intent in a fog of eloquence.

It had to be Suze and the scandal she caused. The time had come to trade her in for a starchier model. He'd miss her though. They'd had fun in the early days, thieving and bluffing their way out of the dead-end poverty they'd been born into. He would make every provision for her, let her keep the Grosvenor Square flat and everything in it, including the Annigoni portrait of them both that he'd commissioned for their tenth wedding anniversary. Suze would understand. She knew what his career meant to him, how essential it was for him to grab all the apples before the tree fell down.

The smell of school hadn't changed at all. Chalk, dust, furniture polish and sweaty plimsolls; the smell of tedium. The rows of schoolgirls in front of Zanna had soft, expectant smiles on their faces, tolerant of the restrictions of timetables and routines. At their age, she'd been as restless as a colt, always in trouble for skipping lessons; hiding in the library all day, reading poetry and books on the history of fashion. The only sanctioned activity she'd enjoyed had been designing the costumes for school plays, when informality broke out and the drab English mistress, the play's producer, had grasped Zanna's hand when they took their bow together at the final curtain.

Funny that she, of all people, should have been asked to give a talk at Aurora's posh school on being a businesswoman. Zanna had left school when she was fourteen, without any qualifications, desperate to learn a trade, earn some money and find out what real life was all about. 'I'm disappointed with you, Zanna,' her old bag of a headmistress had said. 'You could easily get into Oxford if you wanted to.' Zanna had shaken her bright head. 'Sounds like school over again. I want to do something glamorous. I hate the taste of the usual.'

How right she'd been. With one bound she'd escaped from that dowdy, dusty world and never looked back. I've got dollars and dreams. Who could ask for anything more? she thought as she smiled her wide smile into the sea of pink-and-white faces in front of her.

'The Industrial Revolution has a lot to answer for,' she began in her coarse, low voice. 'It made a lot of men rich – a good thing, obviously. But it was a setback for women. I'll tell you why. It meant division of labour, division of the sexes. Work: men. Emotions: women. The idle wife, imprisoned at home, the angel in the house, became the status symbol that all successful men craved. The industrial society took a lot of women out of the labour market who might have become sublime milliners instead of fettered wives. And it put obstacles in the way of women who wanted to design and manufacture hats, or follow any other trade or profession. Always the feeling that they'd trespassed into a forbidden area, were in the wrong place. Only comparatively recently have milliners, most of whom are female, been considered of equal importance to couturiers, most of whom are male.'

Zanna paused and rested her elbows on the podium, the way Harry had told her to. He'd helped her write this speech, suggesting that she didn't just talk about her own life but those of generations of women who had gone before. And it was going down a treat; the kids were almost panting for her next words. When it came to a touch of drama, Harry was the business. He reminded her of Churchill sometimes, although he'd be insulted if she said as much. She took a deep breath and continued.

'Hats have always represented something crucial in our culture. Our very language recognizes that. Old hat, to throw your hat in the ring, to lose your hat, a bad hat, all these sayings underline the hat's importance as a possession, or a symbol of possession.

'November is the hatters' month, perhaps because the hat's primary and primitive purpose was to provide warmth, and November heralds the winter. November 23rd is St Clement's Day, the hatters' holiday. St Clement is our patron saint because, inadvertently, he invented felt, the staple of the hat industry. To keep his feet warm he stuffed straw inside his sandals. As he walked, the straw got kneaded to a sort of woolly pulp, and very useful it has been ever since.

'Two days later, milliners celebrate St Catherine's Day; in France, single women who work in the hat trade are called Catherinettes when they reach the age of twenty-five – a mark of their dedication to their craft. Two feast days in the same wintry week. Two saints with names beginning with C. I've often wondered whether Clement and Catherine were one and the same. If there are any theologians among you, perhaps you could find out, and let me know.'

Zanna made millinery into a kind of fairy story. The schoolgirls in their ugly gymslips and jerseys hooked fascinated eyes on her as she recounted the life of Rose Bertin, Marie Antoinette's conspiratorial milliner, and Betsy Metcalfe of Providence, Rhode Island, who launched the American straw hat industry with a pink-lined bonnet with inserts of bobbin lace. Extraordinary woman, and Zanna, with her huge eyes and marmalade hair, seemed as strange and glamorous as these legendary hat-makers. Although she must be quite old, the girls reckoned, probably in her thirties, she showed no signs of sliding drearily into middle-age the way their own mothers were. Thin as a rake, she stood behind the podium like a mannequin, one foot at right angles to the other, hips thrust forward, emphasizing the lean cut of the tightly belted dress, its severe neckline covered in rows of oddly shaped blue glass beads. From time to time, one of the girls would turn in her chair and smile at Aurora but the smile went unrecognized. Aurora looked straight ahead, her satiny lips sullen.

'Mrs Gringrich has kindly agreed to answer a few questions,' the headmistress announced nervously, when Zanna had sat down to a long burst of applause. She had not realized that Mrs Gringrich would be quite so strident. She had almost given the idea that a career was the most important thing in life. Some of the other mothers in the audience were looking quite dismayed.

'Is running your own business something you can combine with marriage?' a sixth-former asked priggishly. You should be so lucky, my old sweets, Zanna thought. The girl had acne as lumpy as cottage cheese, and mousy hair swept off her spotty forehead by a grubby hairband.

'It's my firm belief that you can do anything by the sheer power of your intention,' she answered rather snappily.

The afternoon ended with some of the girls modelling Zanna's hats. Aurora had flatly refused to be one of them. Her mood towards her mother had become self-destructively defiant. It dismayed her that she had inherited Zanna's narrow frame and full, deep bosom. She hunched her shoulders to hide her breasts and walked with her feet turned inwards so as not to develop that seductive twitch of the hips that was part of her mother's chaotic allure. To demonstrate the importance of accessories, Zanna dressed her schoolgirl models in potato sacks which, once hats, gloves, shoes and costume jewellery from Zanna Modes had been added, looked as chic as couture dresses. This has really gone much too far, the headmistress thought, as her pupils swayed along the platform in Italian court shoes and gilt ear-rings. It will lead to another outbreak of turned-up blouse collars, tinted lipsalves and other infringements of the rules regarding uniform and appearance. One girl in the audience was already tightening the sash of her tunic around her waist in a way she knew to be forbidden.

Some of the other mothers helped Zanna pack up her stock, fingering the bright Italian scarves distrustfully as they folded them into boxes. Most of them wore Gor-ray skirts with permanent pleats, and low-heeled shoes. A frumpy lot, these mousewives. She hoped their bright-faced daughters wouldn't grow into them.

'Aurora's a splendid girl,' a woman whom Zanna knew slightly said. What was her name? Angela something. Chambers, that was it, married to a solicitor. They'd met at some boring party Raymond had dragged her to, full of lawyers reminding each other of cases they had won and lost. Angela was a handsome woman who knew how to dress. Today she was wearing a silk shirt, straight flannel skirt and Ferragamo pumps. Her husband must be doing well, unlike poor old Raymond.

'Oxbridge material,' Angela went on. 'Not like my Jenny, who'll need extra coaching if she's going to crack her A levels.' She slipped a gilt cuff bracelet over her wrist. 'Can I buy this now, or do you have to take it back to the shop?'

'Consider it a gift,' Zanna said. 'It was your Jenny who did all the make-up for me this afternoon, showed a real flair. Has she thought about working in films at all? They're crying out for good make-up artists.'

Angela Chambers smiled with bitter eyes. 'Her father would never agree to that; he wouldn't want her mixing with actors. No. I'm afraid if she doesn't get into university, it will have to be a secretarial course. My husband's a bit hard on her. He missed out on her childhood, doesn't seem to understand what it was like here at home while he was away fighting. Poor little lambs. They look normal enough, but you can't help worrying if those terrible early years might harm them for ever, can you?' She stopped sorting through the jewellery and turned a worried face to Zanna, deep lines cutting the sides of her chin. 'I asked Jenny once what her first memory was. "A mouse of light," she said. Turns out it was the light from an air-raid warden's torch bobbing along a wall. Well, thank God it was only that, not the scream of a siren or that terrible slow whistle followed by a bang, or the stretchers on the roofs of cars.'

'Do you know, I'd forgotten all about things like that,' Zanna said, surprised. 'It *was* scary, wasn't it, the way the air swelled and vibrated with planes, and the fires, and chimneys trembling for a moment before they fell? But it's like a bad dream, or something that happened to somebody else.' She lit a cigarette and inhaled greedily. 'I'm sure there's nothing to worry about, Angela. If *I've* forgotten all those horrors, the girls can't possibly remember; they were practically babies then.' She waved her hand to where Aurora and Jenny and their friends were stacking up the rows of canvas chairs. 'Just look at them. Innocent as grass, my dear, although the way they're shaping up, perhaps not for much longer.'

'You need a haircut, son,' Sidney said, when Raymond walked into the hall carrying Aurora's cases. Sidney didn't like retirement. He missed the low camaraderie of the barber-shop, the smutty jokes and swapped stories. He missed the smells of lather, pomade of violets, freshly ironed linen capes, the weight of sharp scissors in his hand. Missing these, he insisted on cutting the hair of all the men in the family, although his eldest grandson, Ivan Fadge, said that as soon as he was sixteen he was going down Dean Street for a Tony Curtis.

Sidney arranged Raymond on a kitchen chair, happily whistling 'Underneath the Arches' as he put newspaper on the floor. Soon the smell of singed hair was everywhere. Sidney held that singeing the ends encouraged thicker growth and he didn't like the look of Raymond's

159

head. Definitely thinning at the crown; he could see the pinkish shine of scalp. Sidney snipped and massaged and singed with his beautiful old barbering tools that he'd had since he'd been apprenticed to a long-dead uncle.

'My Robbie, come and see the new bedroom suite,' Lilian called to her granddaughter.

Now that the plate-glass windows of John Barnes, in the Finchley Road, displayed sofas, refrigerators, rolls of carpeting, Lilian was on an unstoppable spending spree. She bought and bought, haunted by a conviction that Austerity Cripps would rise from his grave and say again those dreadful words 'personal extravagance must be eliminated altogether', whereupon everything would disappear from the shops all over again.

She had covered the ground floor of the house with a new ruby-red carpet on which yellow primroses, the size of dinner plates, dazzled. In the kitchen, the old tin cupboards had been replaced by white fitted units with plastic handles, and a refrigerator as big as a wardrobe held joints of salt beef, boiling fowls and roasting chickens, cold fried fish and sliced pineapples. To compensate for so much reckless spending, Lilian practised mad little economies. She spooned minute portions of leftovers into lidded Pyrex dishes until mould coated them; she cut old nylon nightdresses into strips which she knitted into lumpy 'sockettes', which even Aurora refused to wear.

Now the soft old bed with its satin coverlet had gone. There was a new fully sprung divan covered in something pale and thickly quilted.

'You see, you see,' Lilian said, 'everything matching.' She flicked back the pale pink skirts of a new dressing-table and patted the matching stool for Aurora to sit on it. 'Ouch,' Aurora said. The fabric against her thighs was cold as ice. She touched it and discovered cellophane, stretched over the pale satin. 'How else to keep it clean?' Lilian shrugged. She pointed out the button-backed and flounced chair, the bed's padded headboard, the sliding doors of the new, built-in wardrobes. 'All made by Lipki's. We used to know the family, years ago, in Chipperton. The father hardly off the onion boat, and now millionaires. Millionaires.'

Aurora flinched. Everyone in this family thought that money was everything, even Nana, although she'd never admit it. She and Papa thought that not being rich was something horrible, even though they said that nothing mattered as long as you had your health. They loved Daddy, said he was like a son to them, but their eyes raked over him in concern and embarrassment. Unease always hung in the air when they were with him. They didn't really like being with someone who was doing badly.

Lilian opened her jewellery drawer and picked up several ugly diamond rings and brooches in the shape of flower sprays. 'These are your *knipl*, your nestegg,' she said. 'Whatever your mother does, you'll be all right.'

From the front-room, they heard Raymond's shout of 'Oh God!', and rushed in. Sidney, his palms smeared with brilliantine, had collapsed on the floor.

Chapter Fourteen

'Aurora must spend the summer at Utley Lodge,' Daisy insisted. 'The poor child's shaken to the heart by all this. I'm devoted to Lilian as you know, Zanna, but she is rather a *clutcher.*' Daisy's gentle, effusive face took on a stern expression.

'You're telling me,' Zanna said. 'I was dying to do the season in Deauville, but it's out of the question. My mother won't let any of us out of her sight for a minute. She can only cope with the truth as long as she's bolstered by the family.'

The truth was that Sidney had leukaemia and was going to die in a matter of months. 'Don't let him know, the news will kill him,' Lilian implored her daughters, and was outraged by Zanna's low chuckle. When two of Sidney's fingers had to be cut off, Lilian assured him that he was suffering from septicaemia and would get better now that the infected fingers had been removed. The doctors had assured her he'd be out of hospital by July, she told him; they'd be able to go to Cliftonville as usual.

Sidney looked doubtfully at his hand lying on the thin hospital coverlet. His whole working life had existed in that hand; shaping men's hair so that they walked out of his barber-shop feeling taller than when they walked in.

It was useless now; a stump where his expressive forefinger had been, the back covered by a cobweb of wrinkles under glazed skin. He smiled at Lilian. 'Cliftonville? I should think we bloody will and all,' he said. Then he closed his eyes, pretending to sleep, so that he and Lilian could have some relief from telling lies to each other, which exhausted them both.

Daisy had never seen Zanna look so tired. Her glistening pallor was quite frightening; the face that Daisy had always thought so beautiful because it was so unclouded – not surprisingly, since Zanna was immune to the everyday emotions of ordinary people – sagged with fatigue; the wonderful eyes were a dull, dark violet and the skin under them bruised and pulpy. It was astonishing, Daisy thought, that Zanna felt Sidney's approaching death so keenly. She had never shown any fondness towards him; in fact, she was rather repulsively cold towards her parents, who were thoroughly decent types.

'Well, thank you, Daisy, Aurora would love to stay with you,' Zanna said. 'It's hitting her hard, seeing her entire family going to pieces. Minetta's no bloody use at all; slops around in her dressing-gown all day, moaning that everything's being taken away from her. Pathetic.'

Harry found Zanna waiting for him in his flat, writing something in a notebook, a full ashtray beside her, the stubs in it stamped down hard. She put the notebook in her handbag rather furtively as he came into the room. He began to take off his evening clothes; the old-fashioned dinner-jacket with its pointed lapels; patent shoes, cracked across the instep; the St Jude cuff-links that Zanna had given him after the Labour Party's defeat. 'I've had a perfectly ghastly evening,' he said, 'giving a speech at a dinner hosted by the Independent Television Authority. What a toshy lot of people. It's obvious that commercial television is going to be an industry run by thugs in shiny blue tuxedos and frilly shirts.'

'Did you tell them that?' Zanna wished that Harry had taken her along. She loved listening to him harangue people who disagreed with him. He was wrong about everything, yet while he talked, his listeners changed, in spite of themselves. You could tell by the way they moved their backsides on the chairs.

'I certainly pointed out that, since the Government had been misguided enough to allow them to invade the nation's drawing-rooms, they had a responsibility to provide acceptable programmes, that is, if the idea ever catches on. Personally, I find it impossible to believe that people are going to want their viewing interrupted by advertisements for toothpaste and cornflakes.'

'Darling Harry. They couldn't possibly know what a drawing-room is. Men who dress like Cuban band-leaders always have *lounges*. What were their wives wearing?'

Harry blinked stupidly. He didn't notice women except for Zanna, hadn't done for ten years. He could remember every detail of the dress she'd worn the first time he'd met her, the way its full skirt swayed when she started to dance. 'I only have eyes for you,' he said, rather pleased with himself for quoting the title of one of Zanna's favourite songs, and was shocked at her mirthless laugh.

'Zanna, dearest girl, what's the matter? You're not . . . ?'

'Don't be daft. I wouldn't make that mistake twice. No, it's the business, Tom Thumb. I've just been working out the figures. I'm on a losing streak and I don't like it. The American line has gone belly up. Looks like American women have stopped wearing hats, except at weddings and funerals. And, of course, on the strength of the deal with Calderone's, I expanded over here, not to mention spending a fortune on the new flat. Then there were one or two other things which were meant to come shining through, which didn't,' she added, not meeting Harry's eyes.

He wanted to say, 'If you get involved in grubby profiteering, what can you expect?' but she looked so

164

tired, so frightened, that his heart reached out to her. 'Are you in debt, Zanna?' he asked gravely.

'I owe what the French call *une somme sérieuse*.' She gave her coarse, low chuckle. 'It's no joke.'

Harry was at her side, folding himself carefully beside her on the precarious sofa. 'Zanna, I can lend you any amount. I haven't touched a penny of my television earnings.'

Zanna looked around the comfortless flat with its stingy gas fire and disintegrating furniture, Harry's shabby evening clothes heaped on the balding carpet.

'I believe you, Tom Thumb. No-one could ever accuse you of going on reckless spending sprees. But the money's not a problem. It won't take me long to recoup. It's the failure. I've never had a flop until now. Getting everything right, the way I've always done, is a way of making people take you seriously. Not that the home market isn't holding up well, but I was set on making a name for myself in New York. The trouble with American women is that they're suspicious of anything sophisticated. They want to be girls for ever. It's a real youth culture over there; middle-aged harridans with ribbons in their hair, and having to sleep with their eyes open because they've had so many face-lifts, their skin is stretched tight as a drum. Thank heavens it will never happen here.'

Harry held her squirrel's paw. It felt cold, limp, not like Zanna's hand at all, that raspy, ugly little hand that gave off a fizz of energy when you touched it. She slumped against him listlessly. This was worrying. He rubbed the bridge of her nose as gently as he could.

'That's nice, Tom Thumb.'

'Well, you see, Rhodes T. Calderone may have proved a bad 'un, but you've still got me.'

Zanna sat up. 'And what does that mean exactly?' she asked angrily.

Harry was alarmed by her awful pallor and the harshness in her voice. It was not like Zanna to be so prickly; she had a rather galling good humour.

165

'You know what it means, Zanna,' he said. 'Whatever I am, whatever I do belongs to you. It's you I talk to when I talk to myself.'

Zanna gave him a smile like granite. 'I ought to walk away and see how you get on without me.'

'But you're part of me and everything I'm doing. Come to bed instead.'

'Yes. Yes, I will.' She got up and walked towards the bedroom, shedding her clothes along the way. If only Harry would marry her, she might throw in the sponge, stop trying to prove herself. But this messy flat with its unwashed mugs and piles of old Hansards was proof of Harry's self-absorption; he didn't need anybody else. And he disapproved of her really, and what he called her bright, bubble world. That brute Gomer might be right; maybe she was disposable, although not yet, not from the way Harry was lifting her onto the bed. 'I wish I weren't so hooked on you, Harry,' she said. 'I wish you weren't so essential to me.'

'I thought I'd take Aurora up to the Manor,' Leonora said. 'Gomer's put up a new tennis net. His latest idea is to offer bed and breakfast to rich Americans. Since none has arrived, Aurora will be able to play a few sets with Otto.'

'I'll drive you, Mother,' Daisy said, getting up from her deck-chair, where she has been reading Anthony Crosland's *The Future of Socialism*, the whippet's muzzle companionably nudging her palm. 'I was thinking of going up to see if Gillian needed a hand with the beds, anyway,' she lied.

Daisy was anxious about Leonora driving. Her eyesight was excellent for a woman in her eighties, but she had become very deaf, unable to hear other drivers tooting their horns in warning as they came round the bends of the narrow lanes. Old age had struck her suddenly. She had shrivelled and grown thin, her face so lined that face powder settled in orange blobs in her grooved chin. Her deafness isolated her horribly, since she refused to acknowledge it and watched people's faces with an attentive expression, hearing only silence. 'How tragic,' she would say inappropriately as someone finished a joke. 'Will it hold up fine, d'ye think?' she would interrupt, unaware of a tense, serious conversation taking place. Mother's hardy enough though, Daisy comforted herself. Leonora worked in the garden in the coldest weather, her bare legs red and shiny and, when she made the effort, could still look elegant, apart from the ladders, that she hadn't noticed, ripping up from the heels of her stockings. If her step was less steady these days, she refused to admit it, and gathered the crockery off the table defiantly, tottering into the kitchen with a sliding pile of plates.

It was so hot, the fields seemed glazed, but the garden at Utley Manor was deserted when they drove up to the house. They blinked in the sudden darkness of the hall and eventually made out Gomer polishing the bronze bust of Oliver Cromwell that glimmered in an alcove. There was the sound of something being bumped down the stairs, and, in a moment, Gillian and Otto appeared, heaving a collapsed *chaise-longue*.

Gomer looked at his wife with eyes like knives. 'Where are you going with that, Gillian, Silly-yun?' he asked threateningly.

Gillian faced him with an impenetrable serenity. She and Otto dropped the *chaise-longue* on the hall's cracked tiling. 'Throwing it out,' she said. 'Come and look.'

Even from a few feet away, Daisy could see small white worms wriggling in the ratty velvet. Next to her, she could hear Aurora draw in her breath in disgust.

'Throwing it out?' Gomer roared. 'You'll do no such thing. A bit of sprucing up is all it needs. It's a fine piece, been in the family for years.'

'It's Edwardian junk, Gomer,' Leonora said. 'And it's got woodworm as well as the other kind.'

Gomer glared at her. 'To what do I owe the pleasure of this visit, Aunt Leonora? Harry not around for you to slobber over? Off somewhere with the mauve-eyed trollop, is he? Well, he may be under your thumb, but I'm not.' He thumped upstairs, and soon they could hear him slamming doors and stomping in and out of rooms in a mood of menacing disorder.

Horrified by Gomer's indiscretion, Leonora and Daisy both turned towards Aurora. She smiled at their concerned faces. 'It's OK. I've known about it for years,' she said, and followed Otto out of the house.

Gillian sat down on the stairs and put her head in her hands. When she looked up, Daisy was crouched beside her, her eyes blue and damp-looking, like sky reflected in water. 'No, no, I'm all right, Daisy, really. Just a bit giddy. Fine now. Sorry about that, Aunt Leonora. Let's have tea in the garden, shall we?'

Gillian is an admirable woman, Daisy thought, following her into the kitchen to help her with the tea things. She senses how fragile and artificial social forms are and has willed herself to believe in them above everything, knowing that it is the only way she will be able to keep going. They settled themselves in the flaking wicker chairs on the terrace, Daisy smoking a cigarette to banish the tangle of gnats hovering unpleasantly above their heads.

'It's hopeless trying to get Gomer to throw anything away,' Gillian said. 'He had to sell so much of the really good stuff: the lovely little Fragonard, the Pauly Venetian glass and the Fabergé photograph frame that King Edward gave to his grandmother. So he hangs onto everything that's left, even pieces of wrapping paper that are too torn to reuse. I'm trying to clear out some of the bedrooms, so we can do bed and breakfasts, but as soon as I move something out, Gomer moves it back in again.'

'Even so, I'd get rid of the *chaise-longue* if you can, Gilly,' Daisy said. 'Paying guests prefer the furniture not to be swarming with life, and I've heard that Americans are particularly choosy.'

Daisy had seen the Fabergé piece – silver gilt frames that revolved cleverly on a crystal base, she had recognized it at once – at Croston Lacey, when Zanna had taken her on a visit. Suzette Riddick's antiques dealer friend, Dominick, had bought it for her at an auction and she was delighted with it, twirling the frames around with her taloned hands. Daisy lit another cigarette and hoped that Gomer never discovered the present whereabouts of his heirloom.

Aurora found Otto in the stables, leaning his cheek against the creamy flank of a Connemara pony. In the four years since she'd seen him last, he'd grown taller than his father. Still lanky though, so thin that he seemed to be rattling around inside his clothes. His hair was long now, thick and dark, curling over the collar of his shirt. His deep-set, dark blue eyes were wary in his tanned face. He looked like the gypsy boys who came to her grandparents' house from time to time to sharpen the knives and Sidney's scissors.

She sat on a low wall, looking up at the slipping slates on the stable roof and, after a while, Otto came and sat beside her. 'Things bad at home?' Aurora asked gently.

'Bad? Oh no. Everything's normal here, as long as you turn a blind eye to what's really happening. Such as my father being raving mad, and getting madder.'

'Daisy said he's worried that he might have to sell the house.'

'I hate the house,' Otto said violently.

'I know how you feel. Whatever your parents love, ruins it for you.' She looked at Otto with her clear, light brown eyes and the boy thought how beautiful her lips were, so wide and generous.

Aurora jumped off the wall. 'The best revenge is not to be like them,' she said, with such venom in her voice that Otto flinched. By tacit consent, they turned away from the house and made for the river bank, Otto whistling for Daisy's whippet, which came running, its torso at full stretch. The sticky air was cooling at last, the shiny grass at the water's edge smooth and delicious under their bare feet. Otto, stopping for a moment to watch two swans gliding towards each other until, bills touching, their necks shaped a feathered heart, noticed the touching blue veins behind Aurora's knees as she walked ahead, and felt suddenly alight with happiness.

Gomer hadn't reappeared. He skulked around the upstairs rooms, pushing pieces of furniture around, trying to make the bedrooms, with their water-stained ceilings and shifting floorboards, more appealing. He was standing in his favourite spot by the window that overlooked the river when he saw his son and the chestnut-haired girl walk across the grass to where the three women were still sitting gossiping on the terrace. The girl sat on the arm of Daisy's chair and Daisy reached up and stroked her shiny brown hair. A strangely affectionate gesture, Gomer thought, from a woman who didn't bless many people with her affection.

Who *was* this girl? She reminded him of someone; the smooth, inscrutable sheen of her. A good looker, no doubt about that, and Otto obviously agreed. Gomer watched, amused, as his son's eyes fixed themselves on the girl's cone-shaped breasts, and then slid off, while his cheeks burned. Lovely breasts they were too. Glad the boy was turning out normal. When he'd been younger, Gomer had caught him dressing up dolls with his sisters. He'd thrashed some sense into him immediately, and it seemed to have done lasting good.

'The chicken without any sauce and just some rice, boiled, without salt,' Raymond told the waiter, who raised expressive Hungarian eyebrows. Raymond's current ailment was a nervous stomach and he was anxiously protective of it. He'd always been a bit of a hypochondriac, his brother-in-law, Geoffrey Fadge, thought, as he tucked into a bowl of goulash, fiery with paprika, its juices glinting and winking like freshly spilt blood. Poor old Raymond, a timid prisoner of respectability, married to a handful like Zanna, who was disreputable enough to give Al Capone a nervous stomach. Poor old Raymond, Geoffrey thought again, mopping goulash from his chin with a starched napkin. The poor nebbish suffered from bad luck combined with bad judgement, a lethal combination, far more likely to ruin his health than his protesting stomach. The latest story was that one of Raymond's partners had absconded with twenty thousand pounds belonging to one of his clients. That was probably why Raymond had requested this rather awkward meeting, to ask for a loan. Geoffrey would give it to him, of course. The least he could do, even though he'd probably be kissing the money goodbye. You couldn't expect anyone as feeble and hopeless as Raymond to stir his stumps and get on top of life. His plans were always as wispy as prayers. Geoffrey sat back in his chair and waited for his brother-in-law to get to the point.

'I think it's time you came home,' Raymond said.

Geoffrey flushed with anger. 'You can think what the hell you like, but I'm staying put. Do you honestly think I'd give up a girl like Natalie for what I had before? Correction: what I didn't have before.' He bit into a slice of poppyseed strudel, liking the smoky stickiness of it on his tongue. 'And don't tell me that Minetta will never get over it. Minetta can get over anything, same as Zanna, same as Lilian. Born survivors, the lot of them. We married into a nest of matriarchs, old son. They're like those women in the Bible, always tripping men up by sheer will-power. Tricking them into marriage or getting hold of their dosh, or making them kill some poor fella who'd been stupid enough to give them the brush-off.'

To Geoffrey's surprise, Raymond nodded his head in agreement. 'That's the way things used to be, certainly, Geoffrey,' he said, rather regretfully, it seemed to Geoffrey. 'But everything's changed now.' He told Geoffrey that Sidney was dying, described how their father-in-law lay in a hill of rugs and blankets, his eyes filmy.

Woozy from pain-killing drugs, Sidney had begun to speak a mongrel language that none of them could understand: the Russian of his Lithuanian parents, the Hebrew of the synagogue, the Yiddish of his boyhood, all incomprehensibly mixed together. Memories, long forgotten, stumbled out of his mouth. He talked about a river called the Wistula, a city called Lotz, or Plotz, it was hard to tell which, Raymond said.

'The girls are doing all they can but they have troubles of their own,' he said, keeping his eye on the spoon he was stirring his coffee with, trying to keep an accusing note out of his voice. He did not tell Geoffrey about the feverish sparkle in Zanna's darkened eyes, or that Minetta spent long hours in her dressing-gown, shapeless and puffy and irritable with her sons. 'It's Ivan who's getting the worst of this,' Raymond said.

Geoffrey looked uncomfortable. Since he had left home, his eldest boy had refused to see him. When Geoffrey called at the house on Saturday afternoons, Tony and Jonathan would be waiting for him, beautifully dressed in double-breasted blazers with gold buttons. But never Ivan, his firstborn, his pride. Minetta, too, always managed to make herself scarce.

She had written to Geoffrey that, naturally, he could see the boys whenever he wished, as long as he didn't take them to what she referred to as his love-nest. On no account were her sons to be mixed up with 'all that', she had informed him.

He had telephoned her once to ask plaintively why Ivan wouldn't see him. 'He's ashamed of you, and for you,' Minetta had said, and added, 'And so am I.'

Oh, those terrible Saturday afternoons with Jonathan and Tony, hurtling between Madame Tussauds, the zoo, newsreel cinemas. Lunch at Wheeler's, tea at a Lyons Corner House, the three of them boisterous, pretending to be happy. And then, after driving the boys back to Hampstead Garden suburb, returning to the flat behind Kensington High Street, to find Natalie muted and slightly reproachful. He would almost rather not see his sons again than under these tense conditions; a terrible thing for a father to admit, he knew that.

'Ivan's got in with a bad crowd,' Raymond persisted gloomily. He picked off the foil covering from two indigestion pills and swallowed them. 'He spent the summer hanging around a coffee bar in Leicester Square; now he says he's thinking of not going back to school when term starts. You wouldn't recognize him, Geoffrey. He's got his hair in a greased quiff and wears shoes with pointed toes. There was some trouble about a motor scooter. The police came round.'

Geoffrey was mortified. Not on account of Ivan's behaviour – probably just a bit of boyish wildness – but because so much had been going on without him. Sidney getting ill, Zanna obviously in some sort of mess, and nobody had even told him. He felt as though he had been dissolved. Wearily, he signed the bill. He would have to go back, back to the suffocating house, smug inside its gold-tipped railings, back to the overstuffed brocade armchairs, the trivial socializing, Minetta's solid shoulder turned away from him in the double bed.

As though reading his thoughts, Raymond, eyes on his coffee spoon once again, mumbled, 'Minetta wants you to know that she realizes that some of the fault for', he halted, quite clearly racked with embarrassment, and then went on, even more quietly, '*all this* lies with her.'

Geoffrey patted him on the shoulder. 'No need to go on, old man; I'll come quietly. You can tell Min that.' Already, his love for Natalie had taken on the precious quality of something that was going away. How could he live without her? The answer was, he couldn't. Raymond, with his agonized delicacy, had just persuaded him to throw away his life and settle for the clamp of existence. Moving heavily between the tables, Geoffrey left the restaurant, looking like a man in mourning.

Otto and Aurora were dancing to the record of Elvis Presley singing 'Heartbreak Hotel'. They bawled along with Elvis as they jived around the pretty sitting-room at

Utley Lodge, making so much noise that even Leonora could hear them. She pushed her thin legs further down the bed, although it was a warm night, and tried, unsuccessfully, to sleep. It's as well Aurora is going home tomorrow, she thought. This business with Otto could lead to silliness.

Leonora knew a great deal about the foolish nature of sexual love. Married to a kind but uninteresting man, she had taken many lovers, one of them, most regrettably, she thought now, a brooding Sinn Feiner called Damian Dashwood. Leonora considered herself to be a rational woman, but, more than thirty years after Garret's death, she was still haunted by the idea that her son was killed to punish her for her immorality. She strained her deaf ears for the click of the front door closing behind Otto, to be followed by Aurora's light step on the stair. She heard neither, but the effort tired her, and she slept at last.

It had been a golden October day but, just as Sidney's coffin was being edged into the grave at the Hoop Lane cemetery, an unexpected wind blew up the hill and lifted the sides of the men's dark jackets. After the funeral, prayers were held at the Fadges' house in Hampstead Garden suburb. Sidney's widow and his two daughters sat on low stools, wearing slippers, according to Orthodox Jewish custom. Friends and relations brought in covered dishes of food and murmured empty sympathies, while their eyes flicked around the room to see who else was there.

Surprisingly, when everyone had left, Lilian decided to go to Chelsea with her younger daughter, although Minetta had already made up the bed for her in the guest bedroom. 'I want to be with my Robbie,' Lilian said, and held onto Aurora tearfully. Zanna shot Minetta a triumphant smile. It said, 'You see how I am still the favourite, how *my* daughter is the best beloved.' Lilian saw the smile and felt guilty. The truth was that she found being with Minetta and Geoffrey unbearable. A canopy of sadness hung over them, and Lilian craved laughter. She had done all her mourning while Sidney was still alive; had started to grieve for him the day she had seen his hand missing two of its nimble, fluttering fingers. Now she'd run out of grief and wanted to be cheered up. And Zanna, although her mood was sometimes black these days, could still be relied upon for a display of defiant lightheartedness that Lilian turned towards gratefully.

It was time to get Lilian to bed. Her face was exhausted behind her heavy make-up which ended at her chin, leaving her white, crêpey neck vulnerable and exposed. Lilian's hat lay on the hall chair; black angora steamed and moulded into a peaked dome. An ugly thing. Lilian had always refused to wear any hat designed by Zanna. 'Too fancy-schmancy for me,' she said, and would add maliciously, 'I can always find something I like in John Barnes. They make a fuss of me there.' Zanna sighed, picked up the black dome and twiddled it around her finger before going back into the room.

Minetta and Geoffrey went into the bedroom. Minetta slid her hand under the pillow for her nightdress, and was about to go into the adjoining bathroom to undress. Then she remembered. She began to take off her clothes with Geoffrey watching her.

This was the unspoken bargain between them. Geoffrey had come back home. He never spoke about his affair with Natalie Bertoud and was quiet and chastened, as though, as Zanna put it to her friend, Suzette Riddick, he was being house-trained for something. And, in return for all this, Minetta had to allow her husband to make love to her.

Chapter Fifteen

Zanna loped down Bond Street in her cream Chanel cardigan suit; her skin glowing milky white, like the long rows of fake pearls that swung almost to her waist.

Coco Chanel's comeback four years before, on 5 February 1954, had filled Zanna with a leaping delight, although nearly all the buyers in the audience had greeted that first post-war collection with icy silence. They had thought that women would refuse to give up the feminine restrictions imposed on them by Christian Dior. After years of wartime drabness, everyone loved transforming themselves into the tiny-waisted creatures of Dior's imagination, teetering on high heels, their knees pushing against the tide of their full skirts. But now Dior was dead, and Chanel reigned over the Paris catwalks and far beyond them; her soft little suits with their braid-edged jackets were a universal uniform. Women began to move in a different way in Chanel's shorter skirts: leading with their shoulders instead of their hips, taking longer, bolder steps, lifting their feet off the ground.

Zanna liked to compare herself to Chanel. The great couturier, now well into her seventies, had started out as a milliner, making the enchanting boaters that were once again the height of chic. Once, in Paris, where both women had been choosing ribbons at a supplier in the rue du Cherche-Midi, Gabrielle Chanel had put her old, roughened hand in Zanna Gringrich's pin-pricked squirrel's paw and said, 'There is nothing to worry about, my dear. I can tell at once that you are a real *femme d'enterprise*. You are a businesswoman because you know how to survive, as I do.' Then she had kissed Zanna on both cheeks with her heavy mouth, as wide and brilliantly red as Zanna's own.

Another likeness: Chanel had had an aristocratic lover. But, when Zanna started to compare the Duke of Westminster with Harry Welliver, she collapsed with laughter. Chanel's duke had been so fastidious that he demanded that his valet iron his shoelaces. Harry's shoelaces were beyond ironing. They were frayed to breaking point and the torn ends tied together in hard, tight knots. Perhaps the greatest similarity between herself and Chanel, Zanna thought, was that they shared the dark delight of being considered rather strange.

Zanna was passing Dominick's antiques shop. She stopped to admire a carved Minoan princess, wearing a straight skirt of narrow stone pleats. Would it look well in her Chelsea flat with its vast, sliding windows and chromed steel chairs whose seats were slings of black leather? No, Zanna decided. As Chanel had said, luxury has no other purpose than to make simplicity appear remarkable, and the carving would make everything else look a little *done*. She was heading towards Zanna Modes when Dominick tapped on the window and jerked his head at her. Zanna turned back and went into his shop. Dominick's mouth was puckered with annoyance. 'Have you any idea where Natalie is?' he asked crossly. 'She's two hours late.'

When Geoffrey had left home, Natalie had gone to work for Dominick. 'It is adding to Minetta's misery too much if I stay with you,' she had explained to Zanna, hanging her head.

Zanna had exploded. 'Minetta's misery is less than crucial to me right now,' she had stormed. 'Does anyone ever think about *my* inconvenience?' Sometimes she felt as though her business were suspended from the tips of her stubby fingers; its success or failure of no concern to anyone else. 'Oh, all right, Nat,' she had said, calming down. The girl was trembling and wrecked; you could hardly expect anyone in that state to take an interest in bucket crowns and flipped-back brims. 'Tell Dominick he owes me a *big* favour for letting you go. He'd better let me have the next piece I buy from him at cost, or he'll be for it.'

Zanna pushed past Dominick and dialled Natalie's number. Engaged, but that could mean she'd taken the phone off the hook. She was out of the shop and into a taxi. She gave the driver the address of G. Fadge and Associates and told him to wait. Geoffrey was dictating something to a secretary in a pale pink twinset. 'Keys, quick,' Zanna said, holding out her squirrel's paw. Geoffrey read her face instantly, took the keys to the Kensington flat out of a tin box and made no protest when Zanna ripped them out of his hand.

'Up you get, kid,' Zanna said, heaving Natalie from the bed. She made her walk up and down the hallway, the girl's limp arm hung around Zanna's shoulder. Whenever Natalie started to slide to the floor, Zanna bumped her side with her sharp hipbone. Zanna had turned off the gas, opened the windows, noticed with relief that the whisky bottle was still half-full, and quite a few aspirin tablets were scattered on the carpet. She had pocketed a note addressed to Geoffrey. It said, 'I told you that being your lover was my job in life. Now I have no lover and so no life.' Zanna had shuddered when she read it. Natalie had obviously crashed into sleep before she'd had time to do herself serious damage, and luckily, the windows were loose enough in their frames to let most of the gas escape.

When Natalie started to blink and shift her weight off Zanna's shoulders, Zanna pushed her into a chair, slapped her hard on both cheeks and made her drink a potful of strong black coffee. 'What's the idea, Nat, ruining everyone's fun like this?' She put her hands on Natalie's white wet face and let her weep into their warmth.

'She doesn't love him,' Natalie moaned into Zanna's hands. 'It was that I couldn't bear. That he went back to where love wasn't.'

'Geoffrey's a prize boob,' Zanna agreed impatiently. She could throttle her brother-in-law for all the warm, ill-fated promises he'd made to Natalie, after everything the girl had been through during the war. 'But, honestly, Nat, love isn't the point with Minetta. Even if she couldn't stand the sight of him, she'd fight to the death to stay married. In our family, staying married for a long time conveys some kind of moral distinction. You've no idea of the clan's devouring grip. None of us can really get away.'

'So that is why you stay married to Raymond?' Natalie asked, interested.

Zanna smiled at her; the coffee had obviously perked her up. 'Possibly. I never felt I loved him. But it was out of the question for me not to be married. If she hadn't managed to fix me up with Raymond, Minetta would have gone on and on matchmaking until I gave in. And I could have done worse. It's not Raymond's fault I feel nothing for him. He does his best. It's just that the war opened my eyes, that's all.' She fell silent, remembering the ways in which the war had enriched her. Jean-Louis. He most of all.

'I feel ashamed,' Natalie said. 'I survive the Nazis and then try to do their job for them.' She began to sweep up the scattered aspirins, which were fuzzed with pile from the new carpet Geoffrey had had installed.

'Don't be,' Zanna said. 'I've never been of the opinion that a good life has to be a long one. A good life involves taking risks that could kill you. Even so, Nat, it's a wicked waste to try and top yourself over Geoffrey. What an unlikely Romeo.' She inspected the half-full whisky bottle. 'I don't think you meant to do it though. Seems to me that you didn't really want to die; you were just pissed off with having to live.'

'Yes,' Natalie said. 'That was it. I felt too tired to live.'

Zanna took a slug from the bottle. 'There's a saying: what doesn't kill you, makes you strong. Anyway, the thing is, there's nothing to stop you from coming back to Zanna Modes now. Don't I always say that every cloud has a silver lining? You can't believe how busy we are. I thought that once they'd stopped having débutantes presented at Court, it would be the end of the London season. I couldn't have been more wrong. Curtseying to the Queen was never the point; it's all about meeting Mr Right, or, at the very least, Mr Wrong. So there are more goings-on than ever. All the debs' mums trying to outdo each other with the coming-out balls. Bags of fun, I must say. Swagged marquees with stuffed deerheads on the walls with strands of pink pearls looped through their antlers. Enchanting.'

Zanna lit a cigarette and frowned through the white drift of smoke. 'Something I've noticed though: the debs are dressing in a different way. Skimpy little frocks, tight at the armhole; hair puffed up at the crown and flicked up at the ends; loads of eye make-up – makes them look like Italian film starlets. The mums aren't too happy about *that*. The girls rave about some shop in the King's Road called Bazaar. We ought to go and check it out. Things could be changing in a big way.'

'Harry's getting very peevish,' Leonora complained to Daisy. She wrinkled her nose as they went into the kitchen for their mid-morning cup of tea. It smelled of Harry's breakfast: burnt toast and endless cigarettes. He had upset a china ashtray and the kitchen table was smeared with greyish threads of ash. 'You and Harry always smoke more when you're out of sorts,' Leonora said, carrying the ashtray to the waste-bin at arm's length. 'I'd almost rather you took to booze, I much prefer the smell. What *is* the matter with you both?'

'Butskellism,' said Daisy curtly. 'That's what the *Economist* christened it. It means that whatever party you vote for, you'll get the same thing: a watered-down capitalism, or a compromised, muddy socialism. Both parties are standing in the middle of the road, and I don't give a damn if they get run over. Everything we fought for in 'forty-five is considered dangerously extremist now.' She lit a cigarette. 'Oh, do stop glaring at me, Mother. Cigarette smoking is the only pleasure the modern world has that the ancient world didn't know about; it's certainly the only pleasure I have.'

'Harry must be feeling a bit out of things; that is regrettable,' Leonora said. She loved her nephew and despaired of his arid ambition. He had gone for a walk, and she hoped he would be less surly when he came back. Standing at the kitchen sink, rattling the dishes, she looked out of the window and saw a fat brown bird on the lawn and, in the field beyond it, a horse, asleep, surrounded by cows. Comforting sights, if Harry would allow himself to be comforted. 'Thank heavens he has Zanna,' she said.

'Why do you say that, Mother?' Daisy asked, surprised. 'You've always insisted that she is only a twisted desire of his.'

'Ah yes, but she has a merry mind. That is what he really loves in her. There are very few merry minds in a man's life.'

Harry stomped across the fields, his trousers tucked into Wellington boots. It had begun to rain quite hard and the swirly grass of summer was mashed down in the wet. He didn't mind the rain punching through the skies or the squelchy grass under his feet. He walked on, twitching his long nose to shake off the droplets of rain, trying to shake off the things that worried him.

The day before, Harry had been eating beans on toast at a tucked-away table in the House of Commons canteen. He had almost finished when he heard his name mentioned by someone sitting on the other side of one of the supporting pillars. The voice belonged to a Labour MP called Charlie Belling, a fierce anti-Bevanite. 'If Welliver gets in as Treasurer, we've had it,' Belling was saying. 'We can kiss the Election goodbye right now. The voters can't take that ghastly moral nostalgia of his. We've gotta make sure he falls out of the procession. Can we get anything on him, d'you think?'

There was some embarrassed clearing of throats. Harry couldn't see Belling's companions but he could guess who they were: a group of younger MPs who'd come into the House in 1955, members of the new white-collar proletariat from the redbrick universities, inclined to boils on the back of the neck, nylon shirts, and no manners. Harry knew that they called him 'The Soothsayer' behind his back because he was always railing against the politics of the comfortable, a one-man awkward squad. They found his nostalgia for the immediate post-war years incomprehensible. A man whose best memories were of the dark age of ration books, fuel cuts and queues was obviously bonkers. Embarrassed by Harry's muddled fire, they kept out of his way, hiding the froth of their ill-will towards him in public.

Not knowing that he had overheard them, the group of MPs produced calculating smiles as Harry left the canteen, in his strange old suit which, like its owner, had seen better days.

They'll have a hard time finding anything corrupt in my life, Harry thought, as he walked back to Utley Lodge in the nipping rain. I don't hobnob with press barons and I pay half my parliamentary salary to the Chipperton Labour Party, much to Zanna's disgust.

The thought of Zanna eased Harry's heart. She was her old self again, her business thriving by all accounts. And she gave him the best thing on earth: love without care.

Harry, about to rinse the mud off his Wellingtons in the scullery sink, stopped with his hand hovering above the tap. In his head, he heard Zanna's coarse, low voice as she let herself be wrapped tightly in his arms. 'We're a pair of nesting sinners, that's what we are,' she had said happily. Harry frowned at his muddy boots; then his face cleared. He couldn't see how that delicious sin could ever become public knowledge.

What Suzette didn't like about Zanna's flat on the Chelsea Embankment was that there wasn't enough in it. No carpets on the highly polished oak floors, no curtains on the floor-to-ceiling sliding windows from which grey clouds, lined with apricot, hung over the Battersea Pleasure Gardens across the river.

'You need a few knicky-knackys, blossom,' Suzette said, tapping her nails on the chrome arm of the Eames chair in which she was uncomfortably perched, her legs stuck out in front of her, brittle as matchsticks. She turned away from the cruel sunlight that was stabbing at the sparkling windows, probing every line on her neck.

'No thanks,' Zanna said. 'I grew up with too much clutter ever to want any more. Shelves of cutesy-poo Dresden shepherdesses, and every bit of furniture fringed and bobbled to within an inch of its life. At the first sign of sunshine, my mother drew the curtains together so that it wouldn't fade the carpet. It was like growing up in a very overcrowded womb.'

She was standing in front of an alcove lined with mirror-glass which reflected a bay tree in a terracotta urn. Zanna peered over the top of the tree and plucked at the grey hairs which had started to dull her coppery hair. She'd have to start dyeing it soon, she thought, maybe go a shade lighter. She threw the hairs into the coke fire that was set, heartless, in the brick wall, where they fizzed briefly.

'Leonard sloping off like that is a real disgrace,' she said. 'A mean return for your pains after all you did for him.'

Suzette leant back in the low-slung chair – she had finally got the hang of it. 'I don't mind really. It's Dominick I can't live without.' Zanna snorted derisively.

'You can laugh if you like,' Suzette said. 'I don't give a flying fuck that he's a poof. Suits me down to the ground. Bodies have had their day as far as I'm concerned. Makes a nice change not to have to take my clothes off for anyone, especially since I spend a fortune on them.' She sighed with pleasure, thinking about her new hostess gown: a tightly fitting top and toreador pants worn under a sweepingly dramatic overskirt. 'When I try on a new frock, I can feel a smile on my bottom. And now that Leonard's slung his hook, I can entertain who I like; add a slug of Benzedrine to the cocktails to get things whizzing without a lot of politicians in five-piece suits glaring at me. Anyone you'd like me to invite to the next bash, Zanna?'

'Yes please, Suze. An old flame of mine called Jean-Louis Mançeur. You'll love him. He has this way of kissing you all the way up your arm as though he'd like to make a snack of it. And don't forget to invite Natalie. I've got plans for that girl.'

Aurora took the bus back to Golders Green from the Union of Jewish Students in Bloomsbury, where she'd been attending her weekly Hebrew class. She lived with Lilian all the time now, hardly ever setting foot inside the Chelsea flat, although Raymond pleaded with her to visit more often. She hated the place; all that glass, it was like living in a shop-window. She could tell that her father hated it too; he slumped in the fashionable chairs and couldn't find his milk of magnesia in the wall of hinged and strangely angled cupboards in the bathroom. Dad would never say anything, Aurora thought, clutching her furred pink bus ticket. He would never change; always doggishly tender towards his wife, but in a slightly obvious way, to let Aurora know that such tenderness made him suffer a little. Zanna hadn't changed either. She looked at Aurora out of her strange lilac eyes, as though wondering how she could possibly be related to someone who didn't pluck her eyebrows, and then scrabbled for a cigarette out of the red du Maurier packet that was always within reach.

Zanna had reacted crossly to the Hebrew lessons and Aurora's intention of reading Sociology at London University. 'Sociobloodyology? Trust you to choose the least glamorous subject you could find. Oxford not good enough for you then? Too many rich, handsome men knocking around the place, are there? And they might even expect you to have some *fun*. Lawdie-Gawdie, how could I have given birth to such a prig?'

And how could I have been mothered by a bothersome bag of tricks like Zanna? thought Aurora, but left the thought silent.

She liked going back to her grandmother's house in Golders Green where she had spent the happy years of her early childhood. She could spend hours rummaging through camphor-smelling drawers for reminders of that untroubled infancy: embroidered tablecloths with faceless ladies in crinolines and poke bonnets standing beside hollyhocks as round as fried eggs; her own baby clothes, the clover-pink leggings and matinée jackets that Lilian had haphazardly knitted; table-mats of mirrored-glass squares stuck to a felt base, which had turned out not to be heatproof. All these treasures belonged to the days when she and Lilian and Sidney had lived in unexceptional contentment, before Zanna came to reclaim her. Zanna, that alarming stranger with her hard doll's eyes and restless energy, who lived off scraps wolfed from the larder at odd times, pacing the room, her teeth cracking an apple, never sitting down to a meal.

The bus chugged along Baker Street, smelling of peppermints and wet wool and of the hot, copper coins in the conductor's hand. When Aurora got home, Lilian was watching a programme with Philip Harben, the TV chef. She switched off the set as he was about to sprinkle parsley on a chicken fricassee.

'Who needs all that hajmahala?' Lilian shrugged. 'You have left-over chicken, you make a sandwich.'

Aurora loved the way her grandmother invented her own words: hajmahala, zuzzery, slomdich – words that had no meaning except to Lilian, frustrated by the English language, whose cool intricacies she couldn't quite master. Lilian showered advice on her granddaughter which Aurora never challenged and never followed. 'Don't wash your hair when it is that time,' Lilian warned her repeatedly. 'When people ask you over for six o'clock, they like you to be there five minutes before. When you go out with a boy, don't order ravioli, it will make him think of pillows.'

Lilian shuffled around the house warbling, 'You'll look a little lovelier each day, with Fabulous Pink Camay.' She remembered the words of the advertising jingles perfectly, although she instantly forgot the contents of the programmes sandwiched between them. She had aged since Sidney died. The irises of her brown eyes were milky, webbed grey pouches under them like trapped dust. The loose flesh on her upper arms flapped; folds of skin slipped over the collar of her blouse. She could no longer see the dirt she had warred against all her life; fingermarks on the glass-fronted cabinets, grime on the chair-covers, brown rings inside the teacups. Even her cardigans had a dingy film on their pile. When Aurora brought Lilian a cup of early-morning tea, the girl held her breath and didn't let it out again until she was outside the door, hating the rotted smell of old age in the bedroom.

Zanna was far less patient towards Lilian's fading mind and body. It exasperated her, the grumpy way that Lilian puttered down the corridor saying, 'All right, all right, all right,' when the doorbell rang. And she said such peculiar things. Once, when Zanna was buttering a creamcracker for her, Lilian had complained that she was spreading the wrong side. 'You just don't like Nana getting old,' Aurora told her mother, 'because you know that you're next in line.'

'Good-evening, my shameless one,' Jean-Louis Mançeur greeted Zanna Gringrich in the crowded drawing-room of Suzette Riddick's Grosvenor Square flat. 'Let me see if you have changed.' He stood back to admire the white pleated tunic by Mme Grès, which was moulded to Zanna's narrow body, leaving one shoulder bare. 'Not in the slightest,' he said. He pushed at Zanna's waist with his firm hand to make her spin round, so that the silky pleats shivered and rippled over her long flanks. 'You are madness, you are light, as you have always been.

'Ah, my dear, who could forget the way you gleamed in the thick, dense dark of the blackout. How I miss that, Zanna, and the dangerous sounds of war: the rattlings and tremors of pictures on the walls, that noise like wind-chimes when they swept up the broken glass. You too, I think. You were a woman who loved to be always at the edge of arrival, and this peace does not seem to have a destination.'

Zanna stretched her mouth for a kiss. What a dear Jean-Louis was, although he had lost all his hair and his hard shiny head was tinged pink by the rosy lighting in Suzette's plushy drawing-room. Years of good food had fattened his belly too. Zanna recalled with regretful pleasure a younger Jean-Louis's taut, hairy stomach, so flat that he could balance a full cup of coffee on it as he lay on a hotel bed watching her undress, oblivious to the bombs outside, winnowing the darkness. Time he got married before he got stuck fast in the pathetic role of an elderly roué. He didn't have the figure for it any longer. She linked her arm through his. 'There's someone I'd like you to meet,' she said.

At the far end of the room, Suzette, quite drunk, had become rapidly self-revealing. 'The latest I've heard from

Leonard is that he has to wear a truss, carry his balls around in a bag. So there's no danger of him losing them. And the places he's been seen in. My *dears*. He's starting to find his way through life by keeping a compass in his trousers. Canoodling with the waitresses at Esmerelda's Barn, spending weekends at Cliveden with a man called Stephen Ward who lays on wall-to-wall tottie for the entire Cabinet, and every High Court judge who wants to be shagged senseless.'

Dessert was being served. One of the hired waiters offered Suzette a small, gold-rimmed plate, almost hidden by a large slice of gâteau Esterhazy, raspberries embedded in the dark chocolate. Suzette stubbed out her cigarette in the glossy icing and waved the plate away. 'No thanks. My body is a temple. I wouldn't say no to a double brandy though.'

Zanna introduced Jean-Louis to Natalie Bertoud. The week before she had taken Natalie to Paris and bought her one of the plainest of Chanel's little black dresses, which she was wearing tonight. She had made Natalie cut her hair. 'What's over is over,' she had said. 'The Nazis who sold your hair in the concentration camp have all been topped. Geoffrey's gone back to his wife – probably wishes *he'd* been topped when he sees Minetta on one of her off-days: a symphony in puce Acrilan. So come on, girl, get with it. We'll both have a do-over while we're in Paris. I've booked appointments at Alexandre.'

They had emerged from the hairdresser with glossy bobs that curved around their cheek-bones and hid their foreheads under thick, straight fringes. Men sipping their digestif in the glass-walled cafés along the Champs-Elysées followed the two women with craving eyes. 'Satisfied now?' Natalie asked, liking the feel of the warm, Parisian breeze on the back of her neck, where her new haircut ended.

'Of course I am,' Zanna said. 'You know how easy I am to get along with, as long as I get exactly what I want.'

Tonight, in her black dress, Natalie was a dark angel, sombre yet luminous. Jean-Paul's eyes glistened with pleasure.

'This is your future, Natalie,' Zanna whispered in her ear. 'Now go and knock his socks off.' And when Natalie hesitated, she said roughly, 'Oh come *on*, sweetheart. You're tired, and he's rich.'

Chapter Sixteen

'They don't know what they're talking about,' Zanna said. She slithered her narrow body underneath Harry's. 'Come on, Tom Thumb, I'm wet for it.'

Afterwards, she said, 'Take it from me, life is absolutely divine under a socialist.'

Zanna was doing her best to make Harry smile again. The Tories had just won their third election victory in a row with the campaign slogan, 'Life is Better Under the Conservatives.'

'I can't imagine *which* Conservatives,' Suzette Riddick said. 'Being under most of them would be like being under the sod.'

'Or the sodomite,' Dominick said. He had some experience in these matters. He and Suzette cackled maliciously together as they sipped delicious ice-blue diaquiris at tea-time.

'I wouldn't count it as any kind of a victory if you became a socialist out of pity for me,' Harry told Zanna, as they were getting dressed. He felt better now, as he always did when she was with him. She was so full of joy and energy, never having second thoughts about anything. When he touched her, it was like reaching out and touching the world. As though to reassure himself of her presence, he touched her necklace that she'd taken off an hour before and tipped onto a stack of books. The pearls were still warm from her neck.

'Pity for *you*,' Zanna snorted. 'I should say not. You'll be in government again some day; nothing ever stays the same. And as for becoming a socialist, spare me, please. Who needs socialism today? You heard what Macmillan said, "The class war is obsolete." You should get out of politics for a while and concentrate on the telly. That last series of lectures you did on the Industrial Revolution was terrific. I mean it, Harry, you really know how to make history breathe. Put yourself above politics for once.'

'There is nowhere above politics,' Harry said pompously. But when Zanna lay down on the bed again, and put her slender, erotic feet on his shoulders, he found that he wasn't in the mood to convince her of this. 'What would you like now?' he asked.

'A bit of blind adoration,' Zanna said.

London was changing. Glassy towers jabbed at the city skyline: Bowater House in Knightsbridge, the Thorn building in Upper St Martin's Lane; shining symbols of what was being referred to as the Boom. Just before the October general election, *Queen* magazine had published a Boom issue, its glossy pages showing every kind of lavish living. Zanna had appeared in it as 'the she-hatter extraordinaire', photographed in her salon by Terence Donovan as she adjusted a baker-boy beret over the curls of a pretty socialite called Mrs Gerald Legge. Dominick was in there too. He had given up the antiques shop to become an interior decorator to the wives of property developers and washing-machine manufacturers.

Macmillan had got it just about right, Zanna thought, when he'd said, in 1957, 'Let's be frank about it; most of our people have never had it so good.' What a showman he was. Supermac, or Macwonder, as Nye Bevan called him scornfully, was leading the country into a new golden age. Luck had a lot to do with it. Even the weather had been Macmillan's smiling accomplice that past summer; months of sunshine that brightened everyone's hopes and made them think that all was right with the world.

Aurora didn't agree. She had started university and was doing voluntary social work in her spare time, mostly in Chipperton. People certainly weren't sun-blessed there. Wet clothes steamed on clothes-horses in front of weak fires. People lost their jobs, fell behind with the hire-purchase repayments and watched, powerless, as the television set and the washing-machine were repossessed by men it wouldn't do you any good to argue with.

In the same dark tenement block where one of Zanna's piece-workers, Rachel Rubinstein, had died of tiredness more than ten years ago, a young Irish girl, pregnant and alone, had taken Aurora's hand and pressed it against the wall to show her how damp it was.

'Well, what do you suppose can be done about it?' Zanna asked her daughter crossly. 'Nothing, that's what. It's just the way life is, Aurora. You're just like Harry Welliver, always wanting to get hold of people and save them.'

Aurora flinched, as her mother had intended her to. 'They don't need saving, Mummy. All they need is more money.'

'Now you're talking,' Zanna said. 'I've been saying that for years. Only I expect them to earn it.'

'This is extremely delicious,' Leonora said, tasting the apricot jam that Zanna had bought her in Paris. She propped *The Times* against the jam jar. 'Minister found dead in office,' she read. 'Good gracious, it's Leonard Riddick.'

Zanna telephoned Suzette who sounded mysterious and urgent. 'It could have been worse than just bad,' she said, and Zanna could hear her suck in her breath.

'Would that have something to do with Leonard being in the House of Commons on a Friday night?' Zanna asked. 'Perhaps you'd like to tell me what he was doing there.'

'Oh God, Zanna,' Suzette began to sob down the phone. 'Of course he wasn't in his office. You know as well as I do that they all leave for their constituencies on Fridays, or pretend that they do. Leonard was in this club in Soho; it's members only, but it's not like the Garrick, you can buy membership at the door as you go in. And the films they show. I thought nothing in the world could shock me, but when Dominick told me about the Coca-cola bottles and the donkey—'

'*Dominick*. What was he doing there?'

'His friend Marty is the projectionist. Dominick had gone to meet him. Talk about a piece of luck. He was in the projection booth, and the first thing he sees is Leonard. The next thing he sees is Leonard dead. Heart attack, poor angel, and no wonder. Anyway, between the three of us, we got him into the House.'

'How on earth . . . ?'

'Easier done than said, darling.' Suzette had stopped snuffling now; she was quite enjoying herself. 'Nobody else had noticed; all eyes on the screen and all hands on the sausage, I suppose. So I raced round to Dean Street in the Rolls, and Dominick and Marty came out with Leonard between them, and it just looked like they were escorting a drunk from the premises. And, as you've probably found out, Zan, the Palace of Westminster has one hundred and fifty-seven entrances, and I'd discovered one that was never locked; I'd used it for years when I'd needed to nip in and out. We just drove into the courtyard with Leonard in the passenger seat. The policeman hardly looked at him. Even though he was dead as a herring, Leonard looked perkier than most of the MPs who pass that way. Besides which, it was quite dark. The boys dragged him through the unlocked door and then down the stairs and into his office. Talk about Guy Fawkes. But it was worth it. Couldn't have old Len found somewhere he shouldn't, dropping dead while watching two slags getting up to no good with half a cucumber. He'd never have lived it down.' She began to giggle.

'It was really decent of you, Suze, after the way he'd treated you.'

'No point in being twitter and bisted.' Suzette giggled again. 'Did I really say that? I'd better pull myself together. Someone from the PM's office is coming to pay me a condolence visit and all I'm wearing is my nail polish.'

'How is poor Mrs Riddick?' Leonora asked, when Zanna returned to the breakfast table. 'I must write to her. Leonard was an excellent constituency MP; Croston Lacey was available every summer for the hospital fête. Although I couldn't approve of his taste in roses; he favoured the blobbiest varieties. And then, his separation made the situation rather awkward.' It seemed to Zanna that Leonora was looking at her rather keenly.

Zanna had been surprised when Daisy had asked her to Utley Lodge for the weekend – by herself, since Harry was on an all-party delegation to some miserable East European country. Romania was it, or Bulgaria? Somewhere, anyway, where the millinery business was lamentably underdeveloped, and so of little interest to her.

Harry and Daisy had had a bit of a falling-out lately and Zanna thought that perhaps Daisy wanted her to try and patch up things between them. Daisy had finally been seduced by the modernizers in the Labour Party, especially the charismatic and dashing Anthony Crosland. Harry had accused Daisy of being panicked into changing courses by Labour's defeat at the polls, of being as much of an opportunist as Charlie Belling (who Daisy detested as much as Harry did). Daisy accused Harry of being blimpish, parochial, obsessed with the dilapidated issue of nationalization. She yelled at him the way she had yelled at the policeman who tried to arrest her when, aged sixteen, she had marched with the Irish suffragettes more than forty years before. Her voice was so strident, it could have rearranged the furniture. 'The trouble with you, Harry, is that you're too bloody fastidious for political life,' she yelled. 'You think adapting your ideas is vulgar. At heart, you're a damn Conservative.'

Daisy had gone too far and she knew it; Harry had left England without saying goodbye to her. But that wasn't why she had invited Zanna to Utley Lodge.

'It's like this, Zanna,' she said, when they were sitting either side of the fire, drinking brandy, after Leonora had gone to bed. 'You're such a success now.'

Zanna shrugged. 'Success is whatever you can get away with,' she said, her eyes as hard and clear as the glass she held.

Zanna is quite untouched by guilt, Daisy thought. That is the key to her. It makes what I have to say very hard. 'The newspapers are becoming more intrusive, don't you think, Zanna? Nobody's private life is safe. A journalist was seen snooping around Pamela Mountbatten's dressmaker, trying to find sketches of her wedding-dress. Acton Fordyce, the editor of *The Summit*, told me that he knew about Pamela's engagement to David Hicks before the Queen did.'

'What are you getting at, Daisy? You should just hear yourself, you're bleating with embarrassment.'

'I think it's time you ended this business with Harry,' Daisy said quickly. 'It would be disastrous for all of us if your infidelity became known. You and your family as much as Harry. And the end of his career, that goes without saying.'

Zanna stood up. 'My infidelity, as you call it, is sleeping with Raymond, although, as it happens, it's been a very piddling infidelity ever since he came out of the Army. I never think of Harry as adultery; I think of him as my husband, only I'm married to someone else.' She gave Daisy one of her wide, lazy smiles. 'Do stop worrying about this. It *screams* with unimportance. I'm going to bed.'

Daisy held her back by taking a fold of Zanna's jacket in her hand. 'Sit down again, Zanna. I'm sorry, but there's something else. Gomer is a bit put out.'

'Gomer. That creep. He belongs in a nut-house.' Zanna flung herself back in the armchair, her white face suddenly rosy with anger.

'It doesn't do to get on the wrong side of him. You know the old saying – Keep your friends close but your enemies closer.'

'Heaven forbid, in Gomer's case. He smells of dead dogs and blocked sinks. What's he on about?'

It was Daisy's turn to flush. 'He's found out about Otto and Aurora.'

'Daisy, have you gone mad too? God knows, Aurora's got no taste, but even she would draw the line at Otto. He's a complete savage.'

'You haven't seen him in years,' Daisy reproved her. She loved Otto so much, she could have wept at Zanna's harsh contempt for him. 'Otto has left agricultural college to be near Aurora. He's got a job managing a coffee bar called the Two Is. Gomer's furious about it.'

Zanna looked at her curiously, and guessed at once why Daisy's face and neck were covered in red splotches and why her voice sounded whimperingly apologetic. 'Oh, I see,' she said. 'Gomer is worried about his son and heir associating with a Yid. That's what all this is about, isn't it? Gomer's the kind of chap who can't stand Jews. He probably thinks we're to blame for his house falling to bits and his riding-school losing money and American visitors walking out without paying the bill because they don't understand what an honour it is for them to be allowed to sleep on damp mattresses and be served lukewarm coffee essence for breakfast. It can't be Gomer's fault. He's a fine, upstanding specimen of English manhood with centuries of ancestors pushing up the daisies in the churchyard to prove it. It's so unfair to bastards like him that bloody immigrants come over here and do quite well for themselves because they've got a few brains in their heads and work their balls off.'

Imitating Gomer's cold, yelping voice so brilliantly that it made Daisy shudder, Zanna said, 'How perfectly frightful that one's son has fallen for one of *those* people.'

'Oh Zanna, do stop talking like that,' Daisy pleaded, absolutely mortified. She covered her blotchy face with her hands.

'Hey, Daisy. No-one's blaming you. We can't choose our relatives, or we'd both have made a different selection. Just tell Gomer that if I catch his son hanging around my daughter, I'll have him horse-whipped in the good old English tradition. Not that Otto will get anywhere with Aurora. She's become so bleeding pious that even her grandmother is uneasy about it. Aurora won't answer the telephone on the Sabbath, or the doorbell either; seems there's some religious restriction against it. Makes her rather a difficult girl to court, especially if you happen to be an uncircumcised male who hasn't been bar mitz-vahed. Otto is definitely a no-no. Go to bed now, Daisy, you look done in. Sleep tight.'

The next morning, Zanna slept late. Leonora and Daisy walked to the far end of the garden, watching two blackbirds feeding on fallen apples in the small orchard beyond.

'Zanna's strengths could be our undoing,' Daisy said miserably, shouting into Leonora's deaf ear. 'She won't ever give up what she wants. She's so relentlessly hopeful. And why shouldn't she be? Look where she's come from and where she is now. A smash-and-grabber. Of course she thinks Harry is there for the grabbing.'

'Harry's as bad,' Leonora said. 'Strong to the verge of weakness, just like his poor father.'

Daisy kicked at a clump of moss on the flagstone path. 'The two of them are like destructive children, the way they relish thrills. Zanna's so used to being chancy; having her name linked publicly with Harry's is just one more risk she's prepared to take.'

Leonora said, 'Zanna has no sense of sin, and that is to have no taste, in spite of all her stylishness.' She turned towards the house, the bones in her ankles clicking as she walked.

'I'd cut myself in four for you, Aurora.'

'Otto, I would never want you to do that.'

It was the middle of December and the Christmas lights strung across Oxford Street were trembling in the rain. Otto and Aurora had been to a Wednesday matinée of *Fings Ain't Wot They Used T'Be*, which Aurora had thought rather crude but Otto had enjoyed. He had danced in the rain and sung 'They've *turned* our local palais in*to* a *bowl*ing alley.' But now, inside the Kardomah Café, eating a poached egg on toast, he had reverted to his usual state of gloomy anxiety. He hunched further inside his duffel-coat and Aurora pushed herself closer to him on the leather banquette. Otto was comforted by her warm, nutty smell. Like her mother, Aurora never felt cold. Even though it was nearly Christmas and the moon stayed in a cold sky all morning, she had come out without a coat, perfectly warm in her long, loose red jumper and a shapeless tweed skirt. Her chestnut hair hung down her back in a thick, shiny plait, its ends held together with an elastic band. Otto's voice was parched and throbbing. 'You know I want to marry you, Aurora.'

'I couldn't take a risk like that, Otto.'

The boy was stung, and Aurora put her warm hand on his. 'Sorry. That's not what I meant. You're a wonderful person, Otto, my best friend. But I want to put things back together, the way they used to be.' She poured them both another cup of tea. 'My grandmother talks to me a lot about the old days,' she explained gently. 'Ritual kept everything in place then. People were poor but they knew they were part of a pattern; that's how they survived. All those rules: don't carry an umbrella on the Sabbath, don't eat milk and meat products at the same meal, they seem ridiculous to outsiders, even to me. But rules keep you safe; they let you know who you are. I need to feel safe, Otto. I have this feeling that if I could only go back to the past, it would give me a sense of self.' Otto was staring at her as though she were some dotty stranger, a cause of mild concern. She hated to see that look on his face but she couldn't stop talking now, she had to explain. 'My family used to be like a jigsaw puzzle, every piece in place. Now it's getting picked to pieces. Something's happened to my aunt and uncle; there's a space between them that's bristling and shivery. My father seems dragged to the point of collapse by bad luck. Then there's my mother.' Aurora smiled, showing her white, gappy teeth, a smile that broke Otto's heart. 'Well, at least *she* hasn't changed, but she was never part of the jigsaw in the first place, never wanted to be.'

'So you're putting the jigsaw back together, is that it?'

'Trying to. I invite all the family to my grandmother's house every Friday night to celebrate the Sabbath. Naturally, my mother always has an excuse why she has to be somewhere else. Nana's taught me how to cook. I can make my own *challah, gefüllte helzel, tsimmes* with dumpling.'

'And has this made fings wot they used t'be?' Otto knew he sounded facetious but he made the silly joke because he felt embarrassed at hearing Aurora use all those foreign-sounding words that he didn't understand.

'Not exactly. Uncle Geoffrey looks as though he'd give anything to be tucking into a lobster at Prunier's. Dad's always on some sort of diet because his ulcer is giving him gyp, and my cousin Ivan sticks out his lower lip to let me know how mutinous he feels about these weekly get-togethers. I'm not going to give up though.'

'Suppose I turned myself into somebody who wasn't a risk?' Otto suggested. Aurora's glossy eyebrows flew up her forehead. 'You can't, Otto. That would be an impossible thing.' She gulped down the rest of her tea. 'If you're going back to Utley, we'd better make a move or you'll miss the train.'

199

He saw her onto the Northern Line tube to Golders Green before making his way to Paddington. Before the tube's hissing doors had closed behind her, he had made up his mind.

Utley Manor was muffled in a doleful mist. It had snowed earlier; large flakes that softened into nothingness as they met the winter grass. Inside the house, it was so cold that Georgie and Kate, making paper-chains out of gummed strips of coloured paper, felt their fingers grow brittle, and gave out clouds of breath as they bickered with each other. They wetted the gum too enthusiastically with their tongues and the colour came off the paper and made rainbows on their cold fingertips.

Gillian appeared with mugs of watery Marmite. 'Daddy's making a bit of a racket,' Georgie said, warming her fingers on her mug. 'Is Otto in for it?' From the room directly overhead, Gomer's study, they could hear their father crazily smashing around.

'Christmas can be a stressful time for all concerned,' Gillian said in a rather papery voice, ignoring the shouts and thumps upstairs. 'Have you finished all the paper-chains? Well done, you. I thought we'd make a start on the tree while the fire's still going.'

'You want to do what?' Gomer yelled. In the tight, scaly flesh of his face, his eyes were cold enough to stir the devil.

'Convert to Judaism,' Otto said. 'Aurora will never marry me otherwise. She might not, even then. But if I get circumcised, at least she'll realize how much I love her.'

Gomer leaned forward in his chair and dug his fingers into his fat thighs. 'If you do this disgraceful thing, I shall cut you off. You will never inherit this house. Never.'

Otto shrugged. Strange how his father didn't frighten him any more. He was all bluster, powerless against Otto himself, who felt as strong and righteous as an

Arthurian knight. ' "Inheritance is the fatty degener-
ation of property." Uncle Harry quoted that on the
programme he did on H. G. Wells.' He was enjoying
taunting his father; it was something he should have
done from the beginning, instead of always trying to
please him. As though you could ever please a man who
was darkly determined not to be pleased.

Harry, he was the cause of all this. Gomer closed his
eyes. A sense of fatality soared over him. Otto would
never have met Aurora Gringrich if Harry hadn't been
carrying on with her mauve-eyed mother. Leonora and
Daisy had set out to ruin him too. They had always
hated him and everything he stood for. They thought
Cromwell was an evil butcher who tried to wipe out the
Irish race. What they didn't understand was that everywhere and for all time, an Englishman's first duty was to
keep native populations down before they plunged a
knife into the heart of the British Empire. Where were
such Englishmen now? Nowhere to be found. Every
jewel in the Empire's crown had been burgled, while
its rightful owners looked on. India had gone, so had
Ghana. Kenya, Malaya and Cyprus kicking up a fuss and
no-one prepared to put a stop to it.

Nobody listened to Gomer when he explained that the
only way to save the Empire was at the point of a
bayonet. Pinkoes. Bleeding hearts. Jews. Niggers. Peace-
niks. Bringing the country to its knees. He thought about
the photograph of Harry that Gillian had torn out of the
Daily Telegraph to give to Leonora (who took *The
Times*) but which had stayed on the kitchen dresser
for the best part of a year, annoying Gomer every time it
caught his eye. It showed Harry shambling along on the
first Aldermaston March, in that ludicrous raincoat of
his, arms linked with some loathsome leftie cleric and a
doddery Cambridge philosopher. Harry was a traitor to
his country and would destroy it given the chance, just
as his birth had destroyed Gomer's childhood. It was
because of Harry that Gomer had been sent to boarding-
school when he was only four years old. His mother had

doted on her new baby son so completely that there was no love left to give her older one. All these years later, Gomer could remember how he felt when his housemaster had taken away Phibbs, his beloved teddy bear, his only connection to home. 'We're all big boys here, Welliver. Can't bring the nursery into the dormitory; there'd be no end of teasing.' Gomer had been teased anyway. It had been so easy for the other boys to get a rise out of him. However hard he tried not to scream with fury, a howl would rise up from under his ribs and pierce the air. And then he would be locked in the cupboard under the stairs to make him quieten down, although the dark and the smell of mice and old floorcloths made him scream louder than ever.

Harry had always been encouraged to cut a dash. 'Harry looks exactly the way Robert did at his age,' Gomer had overheard Leonora say to his mother on Harry's twentieth birthday. And his mother had answered, 'Yes, he does. You can see why I fell in love with his father at first sight, can't you?'

Nobody had ever fallen in love with Gomer at first sight, or even when they had taken a longer look. Gillian had only married him because, in South Africa, he had enticed her with stories about Utley Manor: its ancestors and ghosts, its high windows and tall chimneys. In the Shropshire of her imagination, she saw soft green fields and opal skies, rose gardens and log fires, snow-covered hills and bluebell woods and, set among them, Utley Manor, Gomer's glorious birthright, waiting in the aftermath of war for him to come home to claim it.

Gillian was a sheltered girl who demanded further sheltering. Gomer would look after her, he had made that clear; she would never have to do as much as even think for herself. He had got on well with Gillian's father, a hard, round bullet of a man, not unlike Gomer himself, loudly dismissive of kaffir-loving liberals. Gillian had felt comfortable with Gomer because his type of man, full of noisy, unshifting opinions, was one she was familiar with.

Trouble began the moment they came back to England. The Army had left the house in a filthy mess: broken plasterwork, partitioned rooms, the lingering stink of men's unwashed feet, and some sergeant's false teeth discovered in a drawer by Gillian who gave a mousy little cry of disgust. And what a time for a homecoming: food rationing, fuel shortages, no trains, no servants, no treats of any kind, and death duties so biting that the only way Gomer could keep his home was to sell everything in it. Gillian had soon begun to hate Utley Manor as much as his mother had done. At least his mother, in spite of her husband's bad management of the estate, had been able to afford trips to London, a show and a nightclub and a suite at the Savoy every few weeks with the husband she adored. 'Our little honeymoons,' his mother had called their escapes from Utley. Out of the question, these days. Gomer doubted whether Gillian would have wanted any more honeymoons with him; neither of them had enjoyed the first one.

'If you'd just apply your tiny lady-brain for once and tell me just what *would* make you happy,' Gomer had snarled at Gillian one day, when she seemed to have shrunk into her cardigan even more woefully than usual. And she had answered, 'Only the impossible – to go home.' Gomer had understood then that, for Gillian, Utley Manor was not her children's priceless heritage but just an uncomfortable house where she didn't belong. She worked hard for its survival, gave riding-lessons, cooked breakfast for the infrequent paying guests, out of nothing more than duty. For some reason, this saddened Gomer so much that he didn't speak to Gillian for three days.

And here was Otto, standing in front of him with amused contempt in his dark blue eyes, a look that might have been Harry's.

'Get out,' Gomer screamed. 'Get out. Become a Jew with a mutilated prong, an outcast. But you know what happens to Jews, don't you? Sometimes they get a bit above themselves, think they're better than the rest of us, and then they find they're not wanted. Some people still think Hitler had the right idea, you know.'

'Are you one of them?' Otto's gypsy face had gone quite white.

'Let's say I wouldn't want a Yid hanging around my daughters, or around my house. Get out of my sight. I never want to see you here again.'

Kate and Georgie were asleep, their heads hanging half off the pillows. Otto straightened the covers over them. From the kitchen he could hear a thin trickle of water run into a tin bowl – Gillian washing the Marmite mugs. He left without saying goodbye to her.

Gomer shut his eyes again, squeezing the lids. It did no good. He could still see Otto standing in front of him, insolent, contemptuous, the corners of his long mouth twitching into a smile just like Harry's. It was Harry that Gomer must ruin. He got up and stood by the study window for a while, watching the dark. He would have to give some thought about what he could do that would hurt Harry most.

Chapter Seventeen

When the telephone rang, Zanna, glad of the diversion, said, 'I'll take it in the bedroom,' and was gone, leaving her family standing around awkwardly. Raymond had been about to propose a birthday toast and shifted the weight on his flat feet, looking blue-chinned and haggard, not knowing what to do next, feeling foolish.

'I'm going to ask Clemency to start serving supper,' Aurora said. 'No point waiting for Mummy, she won't want any.'

It was 21 December, Zanna's thirty-eighth birthday. Aurora thought it a good joke of fate that her mother shared a birthday with Stalin.

'So you think I'm a tyrant, is that it?' Zanna asked good-humouredly. 'That shows how wrong you are. Joe Stalin could always get his daughter to do anything he wanted.'

'He wouldn't have if he'd asked her whether she thought *Vogue*'s fashion choice for spring should be deep burgundy or coffee and cream,' Aurora had told her. 'Poor Mummy, what a tragedy it must be for you to have a daughter who isn't interested in the fashion trade.'

'On the contrary, my girl. It spurs me on in blind fury.'

Raymond had organized this family birthday party as a surprise for Zanna. Suzette had found a cordon bleu graduate whose name, Suzette insisted, was 'Clemency Double-Barrelled' to prepare a buffet supper, and, to keep Zanna in the dark until the last moment, had lured her over to Grosvenor Square to see Suzette's latest acquisition, a painting by Vincent van Gogh of a vase of irises. 'If I'd been your mum, Zanna, I'd have called you Iris on account of your eyes,' Suzette burbled. 'Or Violet, or Lavender, or maybe Lilac.'

'Glad you weren't then. Imagine: Iris Modes. Sounds like a corsetière in Purley.'

Geoffrey drove Minetta, Lilian and his two younger sons to Chelsea through a peasouper fog, worried about Ivan making the journey on his motorbike. These days, Ivan modelled himself on James Dean; he wore a black, leather jacket even in summer, was lazily rude to his parents and drove too fast as a matter of principle.

They were all there when Zanna arrived back with Suzette, shouting 'Sur*pri*-ise. Hap-pee *Bir*-irth-day.' Zanna quickly fixed a delighted smile on her face to hide the sensation of glumness that always came over her when her entire family was gathered together in one room. They bored her to tears, that was the problem. They were so ordinary, so satisfied with their own drab concerns that the sight of them shook the glitter off life. They exasperated her with their cautious, watchful eyes.

Minetta especially. She had pulled herself together, and the result was disastrous. She had had her coarse hair restyled into a stiffened, sticky helmet, turned up at the ends in a hard, unyielding ruff. It's to show us all how plucky she is, Zanna thought, that frightful hairdo and her new acid, untrue smile. It's to show us that the past is past and she, for one, has no intention of wilting. Zanna was surprised by Minetta's steely winter-heartedness. What a demanding woman her sister had become, trying to compete with Zanna by redecorating her hideous house in the modern style: built-in leather sofas that made the sitting-room look like an airport departure lounge and a kitchen flashy with appliances including, Zanna assured Suzette, a pastry board standing on fake Corinthian pillars.

'That's amazing,' Suzette said. 'It's something to do with Minetta being proud of being a housewife. I can hardly find the way to my kitchen, even when I'm sober.'

'Please, please, let it be Harry.' Zanna spoke the words out loud as she picked up the white telephone. In the twelve years since she'd known him, Harry had never remembered her birthday but, to be fair, he never remembered his own. He was always surprised when Zanna turned up with a present he would never have thought of buying for himself – a Russell Hobbs automatic electric kettle, a Roberts portable wireless with red leatherette cladding – but which, after a week, left him wondering how he could have lived without it.

Ask Harry what he had eaten for lunch that day and he would grind his knuckles into his forehead trying to remember. His mind was stuffed with the past and Labour's glory days. He could remember to the minute – a quarter past four in the afternoon of 22 May 1946 – when Ernest Bevin clapped his hands like a boy as the House of Commons passed the Trade Disputes and Trades Unions Bill, which repealed the anti-union measures of 1927, and changed the nation's moral stance. Compared to that thrilling moment, the banal present, with its weaselly little compromises, was something to slip out of your mind, if you could.

It wasn't Harry. Zanna recognized Gomer's hard, yelping voice at once.

'You've been very careless, Mrs Gringrich,' it was saying, sounding choked with fury, 'very careless indeed. Disclosure is imminent.'

Zanna's mind was jumping like a flea. She'd taken every precaution. She'd brought in the diamonds from Paris a stone at a time, taking delivery of each one at a different place: the Luxembourg Gardens, Fontainebleau,

207

Versailles, the jewels always handed to her discreetly by a fence she had not met before and would not see again. She was certain that she had not been followed. Late at night, in her hotel bedroom, she had removed a fake stone from a piece of costume jewellery that she had bought from the wholesale showrooms and substituted the diamond.

She put the fake stone in the cellophane wrapping of a Fox's glacier mint, ate the mint, and put the wrapped stone in the packet of sweets in her hand-bag. At the customs desk, she produced the receipts for all the artificial jewellery she'd bought in Paris for her London boutique and paid the correct amount of duty, far below the level of the exchange controls on real gemstones. She had completed this manoeuvre six times. In London she passed on the diamonds to the man who used to own the garage in Curzon Street which had supplied her with black-market petrol during the post-war years of austerity. She slipped her commission into her account book disguised as payment for non-existent crocodile handbags and fashion consultancy fees. She couldn't begin to im-agine how Gomer had found out. If he meant what he said, she'd be hunted down like a dog. They'd suck on her bones.

'My brilliant brother made a mistake leaving your billets-doux at Utley Lodge,' Gomer gloated. 'He knows that Leonora has the Irish habit of leaving her front door unlocked.'

Zanna felt a delicious relief. He hadn't rumbled her; he was only threatening to reveal her affair with Harry. It could have been so much worse.

'Adultery used to be called criminal conversation,' Gomer said menacingly.

'Blackmail used to be called a criminal offence, and still is.' Zanna's low, coarse voice was steady.

'Blackmail is not what I have in mind, Mrs Gringrich. Rather a season in hell than accept your tainted money.'

'Then what is the point of all this? What good can it possibly do?'

'Good? It's my brother who claims to be the do-gooder, not I. My intention is to ruin him, an act of revenge if you like.'

'For turning out better than you did?'

Gomer's voice was so loud that she held the telephone away from her ear, and still felt deafened by it. 'Between you, you have contaminated my son,' he shouted. 'My former son, I should say. He is nothing to me now, as good as dead, a name I have forbidden my wife to mention. But stealing Christian youths, that's nothing new for you people. It shouldn't have taken me by surprise.'

'Steal Otto? I wouldn't accept him as a gift. He's thick as a pudding, a complete chump.'

'It will be Harry the hypocrite who will be made to seem foolish when I've said my say. I have already told Acton Fordyce of *The Summit* that I have something of national importance to discuss with him. The only reason for this telephone call is to give you the opportunity to tell my brother to resign immediately. It's up to him whether he decides to flee the country to avoid the inevitable disgrace. Your laughter doesn't disturb me, Mrs Gringrich. As I told you once, you are a disposable woman, unlikely to cause any problems for me.'

'Look in the mirror sometime, Gomer, you'll see the cause of your problem.' Zanna slammed the receiver into its cradle.

She lay on the bed, rubbing the furrowed space between her arched brows. Had taunting Gomer been a mistake? It might make him more eager to blab. But look at it this way, could it do her any harm? Perhaps Harry would have to resign, but she'd been telling him for ages that he ought to get out of politics; no point in fretting away on the Opposition benches, watching the other side have all the fun that power brings. Her own name would be front-page news, of course, but what harm could that do? Might even be good for business, which could do with a boost. Minetta wasn't the only idiot to have adopted that ugly hairdo. If it continued to catch on, women would spend less on hats; they wouldn't want to cover up the lacquered hair-helmets that had taken hours to style and shape.

Britain was loosening up. Aristocratic heiresses were putting on black stockings and eloping with dodgy, long-haired men from the Chelsea set. In the Sunday news-papers, busty starlets revealed that they had mirrors on their bedroom ceiling as casually as they might have mentioned hanging gingham curtains in the kitchen.

The way things were changing, once Harry was out of politics, there'd be no fuss about him marrying a div-orced woman – in view of the publicity, he'd probably feel that it was his *duty* to marry her. Raymond would let her go; he was a decent old cove, and he'd got in the habit of letting her have anything she wanted. Zanna swung her legs off the bed and reached for her lipstick. Let it happen, let it unfurl, she thought. That creep Gomer had got it wrong if he thought she was going to come crawling to him, begging him to keep quiet.

Suzette came into the bedroom. 'I'm the search party. They're all dying to bring in the birthday cake. You look pleased about something and I bet it's not about being thirty-eight.'

Zanna told her what had happened. 'Harry's not going to like it,' Suzette said. 'Shouldn't you have pleaded with Gomer to give your letters back?'

'You have to put publicity before everything.' Zanna blotted her lips. 'Think if it had been the other business. I could have ended up in jail, and that's happened. And smuggling is something Harry would *not* have forgiven. I'd never have convinced him that it was only a lark.'

Suzette stumbled in the doorway. 'Maybe you should stop wearing high heels,' Zanna suggested.

'Never,' Suzette said. 'They put your bum on a pedestal. I think I'll just concentrate on drinking until it's time to go home. This party is turning out to be a rather unnerving event.'

Lilian eyed the supper table beadily. Raymond had forgotten to tell Clemency that none of them ate shellfish and she had created a centre-piece of oozy oysters layered on a bed of crushed ice, which drew exclamations of dismay. The other food looked just as suspicious, everything in the shape of something else: a pâté of some kind in the shape of a fish, with cucumber scales, potatoes halved and latticed to make baskets for minced lamb that Lilian didn't like the look of. And everything excessively garnished. Fried parsley, chopped nuts, tomato peel shaped into roses. A lot of nourishment you'd get from that. Lilian blamed Suzette for this catastrophe. You couldn't expect Raymond to get anything right, but Suzette Riddick was London's most powerful hostess, Lilian had read that in the *Daily Express*.

'I've never taken to Suzette,' she said to Raymond, lifting a slice of cucumber with her fork and taking a good sniff at the salmon pâté under it, to check that it was fresh.

'She's a good sort, Mum,' Raymond said. He knew about the removal of Leonard's body from the Soho club and had been touched by Suzette's loyalty. 'She's got nerves of steel.'

'Easy to have nerves of steel when you have money of gold. This fish paste isn't as terrible as it looks,' she told Clemency, and held out her plate for a second helping.

Seeing his grandmother's baleful eye on him, Ivan helped himself to an oyster. It was like having a mouthful of snot, but Lilian looked so shocked that he ate another one. He felt that he'd joined the ranks of the Big Sinners. He took a pair of dark glasses from the pocket of his leather jacket and put them on. He pressed his palms against the sides of his head to smooth his greased-back hair and sauntered towards the kitchen from where he could hear the faint, snuffly sounds of a cordon bleu cook trying not to cry.

'Happy birthday, darling,' Raymond said. He lumbered over to the light-switch with his heavy, flat-footed tread and snapped off the light. Minetta carried in a pink cake with a single candle. She had been tempted to top the glazed icing with the full thirty-eight but knew that Zanna would have found some horrid way to pay her back. Her arms shook with fat as she struck a match.

Zanna made an exaggerated show of blowing out the flame. She closed her eyes, rounded her red lips and wished, silently, to be in the arms of Harry Welliver. Raymond switched the light back on and Zanna opened her eyes. Her family stared at her, chewing at her, their eyes showing a slightly disapproving curiosity. Lilian broke the awkward silence. She raised her glass and gave the old Yiddish toast, 'Here's to an even better time next year.'

Such energy Zanna has, Lilian thought. Even when she's still, she's moving, the way a cat is still.

Aurora raised her glass to her mother. Her shiny smile offers the illusion of a harmless world, she thought. It's why everyone calls her a beauty, although I don't think anything as worthless and destructive as that smile could ever be beautiful. I hate the way she behaves in front of the family, as though she were in a film, starring her, with the rest of us in small, unmemorable roles. She is up there, aloft in the world, beyond us and our dreary lives. I should have talked Dad out of giving this party. Everyone looks ill at ease, except for Mummy and Suzette. I wonder what they're giggling about.

Cake crumbs fell on Geoffrey's expensively tailored chest. Minetta reached out to brush them off; Geoffrey scowled but didn't move away from her hand. Zanna came up to them, her twitching lips suggesting suppleness and availability. No wonder I am known as 'the other daughter', Minetta thought enviously. Glamour's an attitude that Zanna has and I haven't.

Guessing her thoughts, Geoffrey whispered. 'Zanna's too skinny to be sexy; it would be like going to bed with a hatstand,' and made his wife blush. That's the way to do it, he said to himself, I should criticize Zanna more often; it would make things better between Min and me.

212

'I hope you like the jumper,' Minetta said. She had gone all the way to the Scotch House in Knightsbridge to choose Zanna's birthday present, and bought the most expensive cashmere sweater in the shop.

'It's divine, sugarpie. Just the thing for slobbing about in at weekends. What a nice birthday this is turning out to be.'

'We must be getting along though; Tony's got school tomorrow,' Geoffrey said. He smacked Raymond gently on the lapel, and noticed how frantic and worn out his brother-in-law looked. Someone should make him see a doctor; indigestion pills weren't doing the trick. Geoffrey looked around for Ivan, but he wasn't there, probably slunk off to Soho.

In the kitchen, Ivan helped Clemency scrape dressed crab from untouched platters into the bin. Her tears dripped into the bin too. 'How were you to know?' Ivan comforted her. 'You couldn't suss that people in the twentieth century would still be following dietary laws given to an ancient tribe wandering around in the desert a dillion years ago.' He pressed Clemency's blond head against his leather jacket. Her hair smelled newly washed and lemony. This was a classy doll, all right. Gorgeous legs and nothing doing in the tits department. He thought of what Jimmy Dean might have said if he'd still been alive. 'You seen *East of Eden*?' he asked tenderly, holding her tighter, so that the smell of her hair mingled with the leathery smell of his jacket.

Zanna brushed her hair with a brush wound with a rather dirty silk scarf, her heart pounding. She felt a mixture of fear, excitement and sexual thrill. Far from unpleasant; it was the way she had felt during the war, when every dangerous day moved her towards the destined future and life was bright with surprises.

She flicked her wide smile in place and turned towards Raymond, who was swallowing some bright yellow capsules. What were they supposed to do for him? Settle his stomach? Shrink his ulcer? Help him sleep? Zanna couldn't remember.

213

Raymond drained a glass of water and stroked his neck to help the pills on their downward journey. 'I'm sorry about the food, I should have thought . . .' he began.

'I thought it was a bit of a lark. You should have seen Mum's face when Ivan sampled the oysters. That boy had better shit pearls tonight, or he'll be for it. Lucky that you were the one in charge though. If it had been me, they would have thought I'd done it for a tease.'

Which you would have been quite capable of doing, Raymond thought, buttoning his pyjamas.

'It was a bit hard on Clemency, though,' Zanna said. 'When she was taking away all that uneaten food, she looked like a little girl who'd been disqualified at a gymkhana. What a well-turned-out girl she is, even when she's wearing that daft organza pinny.' Zanna sighed. 'If you can manage to be well born, it saves you thirty years.'

She was trying to keep Raymond from dwelling miserably on the oysters and crabs – the Forbidden Foods Fiasco, as she and Suzette had dubbed it. The evening had been a disaster. Raymond had a natural gift for failure, she'd known that for years. He could do with a bit of reassurance tonight. Zanna slid her hand under the elastic of Raymond's pyjama trousers, and tried to stroke his soft penis into life. Hopeless, as usual. It was a good thing that sex had never gone right for them; there would be nothing for Raymond to miss when she left.

Gillian was terrified by the gale. It swept over the garden in an uninterrupted rush, shaking the window-panes loose in their rotting frames. It blew soot down the drawing-room chimney and sent it puffing into the cold room, settling on the paper-chains that Kate and Georgie had gummed together, their fingers shaking with cold.

The trouble-laden winds knocked against the stiff monkey-puzzle trees in the derelict garden, made the whole house moan and rattle. In strange contrast, Gomer was jarringly quiet, padding about in his ugly grey shoes, singing 'Land of Hope and Glory' under his breath, almost hissing it.

There was something secretive and forbidding about him that made Gillian long for a row. There were certainly grounds for one: Otto gone, no-one knew where, Kate and Georgie refusing to lend a hand in the stables, huddling round the sooty fire reading Monica Dickens, and every sign of the coal running out. No use trying to order any more with the coal merchant's bill six months overdue.

Well before supper-time, Gomer had started to drink. 'A bit early for Christmas cheer, isn't it?' Gillian reproved him. She had a pile of Christmas presents beside her, most of them bought at jumble sales, and was smoothing out pieces of used wrapping paper to put them in, trying to ignore the sinister sound of the creaking trees outside.

'It's not Christmas I'm celebrating,' Gomer said in a quiet, controlled voice that was so unlike him that Gillian stopped wrapping up a knitted hot-water bottle cover, a present for Leonora, and looked at him anxiously. 'Wait and see, Gilly-yun, Silly-yun, wait and see.' His lipless mouth curved into a smile that was as thin as a needle.

With his earnings from the Two Is, Otto had bought his younger sisters a second-hand television set with a nine-inch screen. They watched it in the kitchen, the only room at Utley Manor where it was warm enough to sit down for any length of time.

Although it was nearly supper-time, Georgie and Kate made themselves a stack of jam sandwiches and switched on the set. It was a while before jumpy white lines gave way to a flickering image. 'Drat,' Georgie said, 'it's Uncle Harry. Yak, yak, yak. I was expecting Cliff Richard.' Gomer never bought newspapers or the *Radio Times*, so the girls had to guess when their favourites might appear.

They chewed their sandwiches and watched the programme which was about a family who would be spending Christmas in the prefab they'd lived in for the last twelve years. From the television studio, Harry said it was shameful that, more than a decade after the end of the war, there were still people in Britain who were not properly housed. The camera swung around the prefab again and Kate and Georgie noticed that it contained a deep-freeze, a gramophone and a television set with a much larger screen than theirs. The young woman who lived in the prefab was wearing a wide circular skirt with an appliquéd poodle on it and hoop ear-rings. Even though her blouse had short sleeves, she didn't look cold. 'I wish I lived in a prefab,' Kate complained, looking with distaste at a line of silverfish flitting over the cracked stone floor of Utley Manor's kitchen.

Gomer and Gillian could hear the rumble of Harry's voice through the wall. Gomer lifted his head, pointing his small ears towards the sound the way a dog does. 'There he goes again, Harry Welliver, champion of the oppressed, always letting us know he's there. He won't be spouting his devilish drivel much longer. It's not the right season of the year, but the time has come to crucify.'

'Gomer, what a rotten thing to say. What do you mean?'

'Chastisement, going in for the kill, wiping him out, him and his mauve-eyed tart. Not that she's worried. Laughed in my face. Thinks nobody can destroy her. How I long to kick that hussy into the ditch.' Gomer snapped his lipless mouth tight shut.

The thing to do is to stay calm, Gillian told herself. Gomer's gone mad. He's going to murder Harry and Zanna. I must get help. 'Just going to see how the macaroni cheese is getting along,' she said.

Georgie switched off the Minister of Housing who was talking about record levels of construction all over the country. They hadn't been able to see or hear him properly; the unreliable old set had started to buzz and fling white dots all over the screen. 'I hope the reception improves over Christmas,' Georgie said, 'otherwise we'll have to make polite conversation.'

Kate put her hand to her throat and made the sound of someone vomiting to show what she thought of that idea.'Maybe it's just the wind. Just listen to it; I expect the powerlines are down.'

'Get your coats,' Gillian said, coming into the kitchen with some lumpy parcels. 'We're going to take the presents over to the Lodge. Do as I say now.'

They were about to protest: it was too windy, it was nearly supper-time, Kate had a cold; but Gillian's dark eyes snapped them into obedience. They unhooked their coats from the peg on the back door and followed their mother out to the car.

The trees bordering the roadside looked flat, sharp-edged as metal, ready to tear their roots from the ground. The thunder came just as they arrived at Utley Lodge; looking back they could see the Manor caught in a birdcage of lightning.

'My dears, my dears,' Leonora said. 'What a night to be out. Surely the presents could have waited? Daisy is still in London, in any case.'

She was wearing her new hearing-aid and had been listening to a concert on the wireless. As she herded them into the sitting-room, the woodwind chattered, and then there was the sound of applause. Leonora's silk embroidery and her spectacles were on the arm of her chair, whose cushiony seat was dented to the shape of her body. The thick damask curtains muffled the sounds of the raging night and the calm of the room made Gillian feel foolish.

'You gels, off to the kitchen and ask Mary Mac to be kind enough to make some coffee,' Leonora ordered. 'What's wrong?' she said to Gillian. 'Is it the storm making you so jittery? What *would* you have done in the bombing, which was *much* worse?'

'You must stop Gomer,' Gillian began, and then her words were drowned out by the sound of something crashing onto the road.

217

'We'll be able to see better from the half-landing,' Leonora said, and made for the stairs, snapping on lights as she went.

A tree had fallen to the ground, blocking the road, the wind pushing at its branches. 'You will have to stay the night,' Leonora said. 'For myself, I'm delighted. I was looking for an occasion to open the foie gras and some other interesting-looking delicacies that Zanna brought back from Paris on her last trip. Tell me about Gomer tomorrow, Gillian. You are too unsettled tonight and would only jabber pointlessly. Better to wait until Harry and Daisy arrive; they'll know what to do, if anything needs to be done. Bath and bed for you, my dear. Mary Mac will bring you some supper on a tray. I'll telephone the Manor to let Gomer know where you are.'

'Not that he'd care,' she muttered under her breath as she went downstairs, but Gillian wasn't listening. She was walking happily towards the bathroom, Gomer's deadly agenda forgotten in her desire to soak her tired, cold body in water hot enough to haze the world over in whorls of steam.

Gomer didn't hear the telephone, neither had he noticed that his wife and daughters hadn't returned. Some time before, he had gone upstairs to his study – a long way from Utley Manor's single telephone, which was in a draughty corner of the downstairs hall – and shut the door. He had taken the brandy bottle with him and, at frequent intervals, poured a measure into the one remaining Georgian goblet from a set of twelve, swung the liquid around, then tilted back his head and flung the brandy inside his mouth. Writing had never come easily to him, but he had promised Acton Fordyce to let him have a few notes about the story he proposed telling him. Gomer rubbed his palms on his thighs and began to write about his brother's hidden life. He thought of Harry under a pitiless spotlight, and wrote more fervently, splashing brandy onto Zanna's letters, which lay on the desk beside him. Whenever they caught his eye,

Gomer pressed his almost invisible lips together and pulled at the bristly hair on his cropped head. That lascivious, mauve-eyed bitch; her wanton scribblings made Gomer writhe with envy and disgust. Zanna was part of that world of love where Harry had always been allowed to nestle. No wonder that the patronizing, hypocritical bastard looked as though he were rolling in feathers. Harry had never known what it was like to feel that people, even your own children, were repulsed by your presence, and flung themselves from your path. God rot him; God rot all of them. Gomer shook the dregs of the brandy straight into his mouth.

He lit another cigarette from the case that some rich Edwardian magnate had given to a prankish Welliver great-aunt. It was a trinket that Gomer was greatly attached to: blackened steel with a compartment for matches and tinder and a gold thumbpiece set with a cabochon sapphire. He would have to sell it in the spring, if he was going to repair the worst parts of the hunched roof and do something about the dry rot. The house was like an old animal, almost at the point of death and hardly recoverable, however much time you spent ministering to its moaning carcass. Just thinking about its upkeep exhausted him. Gomer's head slumped onto the desk, he shut his eyes and slept, the cigarette between his fingers slipping, unheeded, onto the wormy floorboards.

Gomer's evil-tempered dogs, who had been nosing the back door, waiting to be let in for the night, yowled helplessly as the rotted timbers crackled and spurted flames. As the outside walls toppled, they ran towards the river.

Towards morning, the rain began, black and whispery, and the only sound you could hear was the thin twitter of the wrens nesting in the ivy on the side of the stables.

Chapter Eighteen

The hymns stuck in their throats. How could they mourn Gomer when his death was like the lightening of a burden? The vicar gave a hasty sermon, scarcely concealing his displeasure. This funeral could not have come at a less convenient time. The nativity was already in place in the side chapel: a porcelain baby Jesus sleeping in his straw-filled manger watched over by assorted wooden shepherds, kings and farmyard animals, freshly painted by the ladies of the parish, everything suggesting hope and renewal.

The vicar had never got on with Gomer; by dying so near to the Christmas festivities, the vicar felt that Gomer had scored a cheap point against him. He asked God's forgiveness for such an unchristian thought.

He had asked Lady Fitzhaven if one of the family would like to add some tribute to her nephew at the end of the sermon. 'That makes a difficulty,' Leonora had said drily. 'Any word about Gomer is too much. I think we should prefer to mourn him in silence.'

Otto had come home, his gypsy face sallow, like someone who had spent too much time indoors. He stood beside his mother and sisters in the front pew, all of them keeping their arms close to their sides, taking care not to touch each other.

How emotionally secluded we are, Harry thought. We train ourselves to be indifferent to one another, convinced that the best thing possible is to withhold the whole of oneself. The vicar was murmuring some thin inexpressive words of comfort to Gillian, to which she responded with her automatic good manners: 'Thank you so much for all your help. I think the whole thing went awfully well.'

Our voices are refined and dowdy as chintz, Harry thought. He imagined Zanna's languid, husky growl and ached for her. He wouldn't have put it past Zanna to have marked Gomer's death in some way, perhaps by sending a dozen long-stemmed thorny roses with their heads cut off, that would be her idea of a good joke. But, so far, she had shown uncharacteristic restraint. Harry trailed out to the graveyard with the rest of his family, their shoes making a sad chush-chush on the gravel.

'It's a wonderful feeling when fate settles your scores for you,' Zanna said. 'My faith in the universe is restored.'

'The poor man's dead, petal,' Suzette reproved her. 'I'd say fate went a bit too far this time, leaving three kids fatherless just to do you a favour. Honestly, the way you behave; there's more elastic in your conscience than in your knickers. Gomer was Harry's brother, after all.'

'And overflowing with brotherly love, I should think *not*. Gomer hated Harry for being so gorgeous and brilliant. As though Harry could help being the way he was, but hatred isn't amenable to logic, never has been.'

'All the same, you were looking forward to Gomer spilling the beans.'

'To tell the truth, Suze, I'd rather changed my mind about that.' She told Suzette about her encounter with Gomer in The Rising Sun, all those years ago. 'He sneered at me for being a vulgar doxy. That rankled, it really did. I've been thinking things over, and I'd more or less decided to put some money into the Utley Manor Restoration Fund in return for my letters. The one thing stronger than his loathing for Harry was his obsession with his poxy house. Well, no need to haggle with the blighter now, that's what I mean about fate settling the score for me.'

The Fabergé cigarette case had survived the fire. Slightly misshapen, it rested in Otto's hand. He and Gillian were inspecting what remained of Utley Manor: a scorched stone fireplace standing among burned and broken bricks, scatterings of glass, an old tin lemon-squeezer, the carved canopy from the Elizabethan four-poster, quite untouched, although the rest of the bed had crackled up like firewood.

It was Christmas Day, and Otto and Gillian had walked from the Lodge, and Leonora's rather over-powering hospitality, to take a last look at the rubble of the home they had hated. It was raining again; they passed through the dripping shrubbery, hardly aware of the watery cold and the bird shapes dissolving in the thick, muddied skies. They talked, their heads bursting with plans. Otto had, as Gillian put it, come to his senses. Gomer's death had proved to him the pointlessness of striving for impossible things. Otto took the view that Gomer had wasted his life trying to restore the past, instead of shaking off the unceasing demands of Utley Manor and enjoying the present. And he had behaved just as stubbornly as his father, entangling himself in a hopeless passion that had no future. He'd been a fool to have hoped against hope for so long.

Otto had tried to explain this to Daisy and she had kissed him and quoted Pericles: 'Happiness is freedom and freedom is courage.' He repeated the words out loud as he and Gillian walked back to the Lodge and Leonora's mince pies, and felt a glorious sense of release. This would be his last Christmas in England. Gillian's father had suggested that she and the three children come back to South Africa. Looking at his mother, her dark eyes watering from the cold and her head wrapped in an ugly nylon fur beret with scarf ends that tied under her chin, Otto knew that this was the right thing to do. He would take her away from the shivering bullrushes, away from the slimy twist of river that sagged its way across the churned fields, away from the mud that slipped over her shoes. He'd get a job in Cape Town, something in the music business. His grandfather wanted him to take over the farm, but he'd had enough of the countryside, the months in London had taught him that he liked the feel of pavements under his feet.

Gillian wiped her streaming eyes and turned a radiant face towards her son. 'Do you know what I'm looking forward to most? Picking a peach straight from the wall and feeling its warmth in my hand, like the throb of a cat's purr. That would be so awfully nice.' She put her arm through his, as the Lodge's lighted windows came in sight.

Acton Fordyce suggested that Daisy pick him up at *The Summit*, rather than the Savoy, where they were to lunch. They had known each other for years, since the time when Acton, then a cub reporter on the *Barnsley Courier*, had been sent to interview Daisy, who had come up to Yorkshire from the Labour Party's London headquarters, to give advice to women textile workers during the General Strike of 1926.

Acton, expecting some dour old scrub-heap, had been surprised to find that Miss Fitzhaven was a young, untidy blonde with delighted blue eyes and a trace of an Irish accent. They had been friends ever since, their friendship based on a shared fascination with the ways of the world and a need to direct those ways, although Acton was, in Daisy's view, regrettably right wing and Acton regarded her, fondly, as a Marxist firebrand.

Although they were the same age, Daisy had always treated Acton as though he were a rather amusing schoolboy, and that's how she treated him still, for all his power. He spent a lot of time trying to convince her how important and influential he was, and Daisy indulged him in this, which was why she agreed to meet him at his office, so that he could show her what an impressive figure he cut.

He was in his shirtsleeves, sitting at his desk that looked like a battleship, snapping orders down the telephone in his loose, honking voice, while a cigarette bounced in the corner of his mouth. Acton had not aged well. His face was puffy and his crafty little eyes looked as though they had been slotted between the swollen bulges of flesh above and beneath them. His Jermyn Street shirt and Italian tie, stuck through with a pearl-knobbed pin, did not prevent him from looking badly cared for. He tucked the telephone receiver between his chin and shoulder (a feat that *did* impress Daisy, despite herself) and clasped his hands behind his head, showing ovals of dried sweat under his arms. He pushed back his chair and swung his legs onto the desk, and Daisy noticed that his silk socks had ladders in them.

At last, Acton wound up the telephone conversation with a cheery, 'See you later, son, we'll have a few gargles.' Even then, he did not greet Daisy immediately, but seized a pen, let it hover above a galley proof on his desk, made circles in the air over it before, finally, swooping on the paper.

'Magnificent, Acton,' Daisy said, laughing, as he put on his jacket. 'If you're auditioning for the part of a power-crazed newspaper editor, the role's yours.'

He smiled at her with his curved yellow teeth and came round the side of his battleship of a desk to give her a hug. 'Don't ever stop scoffing at me, Daisy. My doctor said I was to avoid surprises at any cost.'

Acton expanded in the restaurant's hum and buzz. 'Get your snoot into this,' he ordered Daisy as wine slid into a goblet. She took a delicate sip. It was sunshine on her tongue, like swallowing warmth. 'Château Lafite-Rothschild,' Acton smirked. 'Nothing but the best for socialists.' He cut into a vaporous steak-and-kidney pie,

224

hissing and sizzling inside its crust, and speared a lump of meat onto the heated plate, where it seethed.

'The stately home quite gutted then, is it? Everything gone?' Acton spoke with his mouth full.

'Thankfully, yes,' Daisy said, cutting her veal escalope into small pieces. She looked hard at her old friend: his finger was twanging thoughtfully at his lower lip. She guessed that there had been something at Utley Manor that he had wanted to get his hands on.

'Nice hat, Daisy.' Acton deftly changed the subject.

'It's by Zanna Modes. The designer has rather taken me in hand. She was determined to smarten me up, and smartened up I am, as you see.'

Daisy smoothed the sleeve of the Harry B. Popper jacket that Zanna had persuaded her to buy. It was long and loose, worn over a matching dress. Useful enough, but Daisy missed her old cardigans.

Acton's slatted eyes glinted. 'You talking about the rapturously lovely Mrs Gringrich? Didn't see eye to eye with old Gomer, did she? Last time I spoke to him, he seemed to think he had something on her. Told her as much, apparently, and then went ballistic when she laughed in his face.'

'Poor Gomer was not the most rational of men. This escalope is exquisite, Acton. How you do spoil me.'

As he was handing her into a taxi, Acton poked his head and shoulders inside the cab.

'Do not adultery commit, Advantage rarely comes of it,' he intoned. 'Eh? Eh, Daisy?' He brought his face close to hers.

'Quite so, Acton. Arthur Hugh Clough, rather an amusing poet. Thank you for a superb lunch. Goodbye.'

'I'll catch you out one of these days, Daisy.' Acton backed out of the taxi and shut the door hard.

'I don't like to think of Zanna being so underhand,' Daisy said to Harry, 'it's such bad manners. Harry, if you don't stop flicking the ends of your tie, I shall go mad.'

Harry started to pull at his thin cheeks instead, which irritated Daisy just as much. His long face had become rather slack and leathery. He was losing his looks; this annoyed Daisy too.

'But why didn't she tell us?' Harry threw the question into the air quite pointlessly. 'We could have knocked some sense into Gomer. We would have only to have mentioned that any bad publicity about me might have had an adverse effect on his plans for Utley Manor, and he'd have had second thoughts, surely.'

Daisy looked at him curiously. 'You have very untidy morals, Harry. Like all politicians, I suppose. Zanna, at least, is defiantly immoral, and has never made a secret of it.' Daisy's kind blue eyes looked regretful. 'Her lunatic honesty was what I liked best about her,' she said.

Daisy's use of the past tense made Harry pull at his face more savagely. His eloquent nose twitched and he rubbed it furiously. 'You're suggesting that I give her up?'

'You have no choice. Gomer's death won't stop Acton rootling around, he told me as much. Like all newspaper men, he believes that men in public life have no right to a private one. You must put an end to it. You've said often enough that there is nothing above politics. How will you feel when Labour wins the next election, as we are certain to, and you are kept out of the Cabinet solely on account of your association with another man's wife?' Tears sprang into Daisy's moist, troubled eyes. 'I won't have Charlie Belling baying for your blood, and getting it,' she said.

Harry ground his knuckles into his forehead. 'I've never heard you sound so harsh, Daisy.'

'No, you haven't. Mother and I always indulged you in everything. We stood aside while you and Zanna behaved like two people in flight from the everyday world. But it's caught up with you now, Harry; face up to it.'

Harry said wanly, 'She's the only woman I've ever loved.'

226

'I'm not surprised.' Daisy blew her nose gracelessly. 'You were perfectly suited, both of you so self-centred that you understood each other's selfishness, as less single-minded people would never have been able to do.'

Harry smiled for the first time in days. 'That's what Zanna said. She called it giving each other permission.'

'And so you did. The only things central to you were your careers and each other. Everything else was just a blur around the edges of your lives. Not a thought for Raymond or Aurora. And did Zanna ever consider Lilian's feelings? Suppose Gomer had given Acton whatever it was he needed to go ahead with the story? Pictures of her scandalous daughter splashed all over *The Summit*; she would have been too ashamed to show her face in John Barnes.'

Harry smiled again, he couldn't help it. Every time Zanna saw her photograph in the newspapers she behaved like an excited child. Mrs Harris kept up a scrapbook in which every bit of publicity Zanna had received since the opening of her shop was lumpily pasted. Harry had once caught Zanna, late at night, turning the pages of the scrapbook, practically crooning with happiness. She was furious when any of her rivals hogged the limelight, and miffed that the Queen ordered her hats from Simone Mirman and Rose Vernier rather than Zanna Gringrich. 'I expect Her Majesty likes to have some say in the matter,' Aurora had said once. 'Perhaps she wouldn't appreciate a milliner telling her that she wasn't making the most of her eyes or that the Order of the Garter didn't do a thing for her figure.'

'I don't seem to be getting through to you, Harry,' Daisy said. 'Don't you see that what Zanna did simply isn't done? She had the choice of alerting us to Gomer's devilry so that we could have acted, or keeping quiet and ruining your career and her family's privacy. For heaven's sake, Harry, for a moment all our lives were in her hands, and she decided they were well lost for the sake of a bit of cheap publicity for Zanna Modes which, I

227

understand, is on the slide again. Something to do with those new hairstyles that look like sandmartins' nests.'

For a moment all our lives were in her hands. At last, he understood what Zanna was capable of. He thought of the way the crown of her bright head fitted perfectly into his cupped hand, the warm weight of it, and steeled himself never to think of it again.

In his disordered bedroom, he opened the drawer in which he kept Zanna's letters, intending to give them back to her. It seemed to him that he was behaving like a Victorian gentleman and, much worse, that only by abiding by some starchy code of behaviour that in normal circumstances he would detest, could he stop himself from raving wildly.

Harry's gangly fingers prodded among greyish handkerchiefs and the typed-up notes for a forthcoming series of lectures he was to deliver to the Fabian Society on the Socialist Responsibility to the New Techniques of Mass Communication. But, although the drawer still smelled faintly of the lily of the valley scent that clung to everything Zanna touched, the letters had gone. Now he knew what the evidence was that Gomer had been planning to present to Acton Fordyce.

'If it can only be tea, then the Ritz. I have a Ritz mind,' Zanna said. She had come to work in her new winter coat, pale gold cashmere lined with sable that lapped over the edges of the cloth, and, after Harry's telephone call, she rummaged through the stockroom to find a Ritz-worthy hat to match it.

'Well, there's a thing,' said Mrs Harris, coming in from the salon for her mid-afternoon sandwich and a quick read of the *Daily Sketch*. The floor of the stockroom was a sea of hats, tried on and discarded, and Zanna stood in the middle of them, tapping her foot as though she wanted to kick her entire collection into the hereafter.

'No pleasing some people today,' Mrs Harris said, easing off her shoes and putting on her reading glasses. 'If you're going out in that fur-lined coat, there's a hat in the window, the one that looks like a snake uncoiling – the fur's an exact match.'

'Yikes,' Zanna said. 'I'd forgotten that one. It's called All Of It, All Of It. What inspired the name was an old Irish poem Daisy Fitzhaven taught me. Listen:

> There is one
> On whom I should gladly gaze,
> For whom I would give the bright world,
> All of it, all of it, though it be an unequal bargain.'

'Very nice,' said Mrs Harris, chewing on corned beef and piccalilli, 'but I find Patience Strong more of a comfort.'

Zanna lifted the sable hat off its stand. The fur had been stitched to millinery wire and then coiled into a writhing spiral. It curved glossily over her head, like an uncontrolled halo.

As she scurried down Bond Street, taking long strides in her buttery kid boots, people turned to look at her in her extraordinary hat that seemed to be made of air as much as fur.

Harry had his back to her; he was examining the marble fountain in the foyer. In the slubby tweed overcoat he'd worn for years, his shoulders looked slumped.

'Har-ree,' Zanna shouted as she came through the revolving door, then wished she had approached him quietly, put her hand on his arm and murmured his name, hardly audibly. From some dark, forgotten place, Gomer's hateful warning slunk inside her head: 'As far as Harry's concerned, you're a throw-away woman. You're a fool if you think he'll hang onto you after he's had enough of your vulgarity.' Of course, Gomer had been completely crackers; even so, she knew in her bones that something was wrong.

This was the first time that Harry felt like an adulterer. He sat on the edge of a small, gilt chair, at an odd, perched angle, as though about to swivel himself off it and flee.

'So you've heard,' Zanna said calmly, her squirrel's paws busy with teapot, milk jug, sugar-tongs.

'How could you?' Harry's voice was anguished, like a saw working its way through wood. 'You would have ruined my career, caused your family God knows how much anguish, and for what? To get your picture in the paper, to entice a few more rich, silly women through the door of your shop?'

'And to get you,' Zanna said with her usual unsettling candour. 'You know that's what I've always wanted.'

If she had looked up then, he might have fallen into her strange lilac eyes, but she was staring at her own pin-pricked fingers, rubbing the bowl of a silver tea-spoon over and over.

'But you'd have just walked away without a care for all the mess you left behind,' Harry persisted. He felt as though he had stepped onto a nightmarish carousel of despair.

'I've always done that, Tom Thumb. I told you years and years ago that I only really cared about the person I was in love with. And for a very long time, that's been you.'

She looked at him then. The blue vein in her temple throbbed, and her red mouth glistened. He might die of needing her. For twelve years, he had not made a speech or written an article without hearing her low, mocking growl inside his head. She forced him to look at the real, imperfect world, challenging him, arguing against him, but loving him with a happy ardour, entangling him in passion, laughter, danger and complicated excitement. How could he live without all those involving evenings they had shared down all the years?

He got up, his bulky old coat grazing the tiered cake stand with its glossy éclairs. 'I love you, and hate your guts,' he said, hearing himself sounding like a man being strangled. He pushed his shoulder at the revolving door of the hotel, so hard that the bruise lasted for weeks.

It's like there's a draught through my heart, Zanna thought, watching the door spin. Years of fondness scraped away in a sentence. I can't believe it; I thought that Harry and I were immovably tied, and yet here is love already fading into cold dust.

The lobby was filling up with people. All around her, voices boomed and blustered with false conviviality. It was New Year's Eve. Tomorrow, a new decade would begin. She couldn't just sit here, feeling that the world was going the wrong way, she had far too much to do. She reached for her gloves.

'I adore your hat.' An American woman stood over her chair, gushing at her and showing too many white, well-cared-for teeth. Zanna got to her feet. Wordlessly, she took off the spiralling sable hat and put it on the woman's neatly brushed hair. Then, bare-headed, she made her way into the festive street.

PART THREE

1960 – 1962

Chapter Nineteen

'What a time for this to happen,' Zanna complained to Natalie Mançeur, who was visiting her, a week after Raymond's funeral.

'It is so sad, coming so soon after your mother's death,' Natalie murmured.

'So inconvenient, you mean.' Zanna sighed in exasperation. 'Raymond's business turned out to be in a shocking mess; worse than mine, and that takes some doing.'

'Perhaps that was because he devoted so much time to helping you,' Natalie suggested.

'Yes, you're right. Raymond was so genuinely good. I didn't deserve him, and that always made me feel trapped.'

Zanna had been surprised at the hundreds of people who had written to express their sympathy when Raymond died. Letters from former clients, some of them writing from prison; from saddened colleagues, and old Army comrades she had never even heard of but whom Raymond had evidently been in touch with for years. She'd had no idea that he had been so loved and admired, by everyone except her, it now seemed.

When she thought of him, it was with specks of rain on his glasses, making a fuss about some dicey venture she was considering. He'd never been able to see that life was worthless if you couldn't take dizzying risks now and again. Poor old Raymond, he'd had the backbone of a soufflé. But she didn't often think about him. It was Harry who occupied her mind, even though she had not seen him in almost a year. Without him, her days stretched crazily, like a hall of mirrors. The pain under her heart was unbearable, a tight, burning pain that never got better, and she walked mazedly, in a black daydream. For the first time in her life, darkness seemed undispelled, life an infinite emptiness. She knew that to begin living again, she must go on forgetting Harry for ever, and that was the worst thing she could think of.

Nobody, not even Suzette, noticed Zanna's despair. How could they when she kept up a pretence of defiant lightheartedness, so that anyone observing her white china mask of a face would have thought her to be as untouched and indifferent as ice?

Zanna held out her long arms to Natalie's Christabel, a grave-eyed child, beautifully dressed in a navy-blue woollen frock with a sailor collar. 'Come here, sweetie-pie, and show me your new shoes.' To Natalie, she said, 'Some people have all the luck. Christabel was *born* chic. Here is a child who knows how to wear clothes.'

'There are more important things,' Natalie said. She was pregnant again, miraculously, it seemed to her doctor, who had thought that she would never be able to bear children after all she had been through in the camps. Jean-Louis had refused to believe this. 'You have not taken my virility into account,' he had insisted. 'I am hung like a donkey.' And here was Christabel, living proof of that virility, and another baby on the way. A boy this time, Jean-Louis said confidently. He liked the idea of sending a son to Eton, which turned out charming, eccentric young men who were rather better diplomats, in Jean-Louis's opinion, than the products of dreary, conformist French schools.

'More important things than fashion?' Zanna raised her fine eyebrows and retied the bow on Christabel's sailor collar. 'I disagree with you, Natalie. The idea of a universal elegance in which one can express one's individuality, I'd say that was pretty crucial to any civilized society. But try telling Aurora that.'

'Aurora has bad taste?'

'If only. Aurora has no taste at all.'

'I'm sorry you have lost so much, Zanna,' Natalie said. She wished she could comfort this woman who was too proud to accept comfort.

'My mistake,' Zanna said, in her raspy voice. 'I thought there might be a limit as to how much I could lose, but there wasn't. Everything I had was up for grabs, only I didn't know it.'

'Someone's been busy,' Mrs Harris said, coming into Zanna's workroom with a cup of sugarless black coffee and the aspirin Zanna had asked for. A tilted shelf covered with corkboard ran all the way round the room and Zanna's latest sketches were pinned to the cork along with swatches of fabric and snippets of trimming.

'I hate the lot,' Zanna said. 'They look like stuff you'd find in a museum, not like hats you'd expect to see on women's heads next spring.' She swallowed the coffee in great, thirsty gulps, although it was almost too hot to drink. 'I'm going for a walk,' she said. 'If you want me, I'll call you.'

She flounced down the steep stairs. Mrs Harris followed her, the curl on her forehead bouncing up and down and a worried expression on her exhausted face.

Zanna had always liked prowling around London, but now the shining city had turned into a cemetery without walls, every paving-stone a reminder of Harry, even though she avoided the places where they had once sought each other, bound by their bruising needs.

She stomped along Regent Street, hardly noticing the window displays, aware only of the crust of grime on the curved stone façades. Turning into Carnaby Street, she saw that John Stephen had opened another new shop, that would make it his fourth. Teenagers. That was where the money was. The boys spent their wages at John Stephen's on suede jackets and trousers so tight they could do themselves an injury. The girls built up collections of winklepicker shoes and Helen Shapiro records. Zanna looked around her. She saw young women with elaborately teased beehives, pony-tails, and long straight hair with a fringe, a style considered arty. None of these girls was wearing a hat. She walked back towards Bond Street. What is the point of keeping myself so meaninglessly on the go? she thought. Why not face it, I'm in the deep nowhere; every day is a nothing day. Because I have to, she answered herself. It's in my nature to battle on. And, God knows, fashion is a war; no point in being in this business if you're not ready to fight. In the back room of the shop, she sprayed scent on her wrists, then moved into the salon in her rich and cloudy perfume, needing all her tattered courage to face her dwindling clientele.

Harry Welliver: a name that didn't matter any more. That was the opinion of the Labour Party Conference at Scarborough. Of course, the delegates applauded him warmly when he began his platform speech, but when he thundered, 'I warn you not to take up the planks of the floor upon which the future must walk,' Charlie Belling wasn't the only one to shift his buttocks on his seat and squinny at his watch, longing for a beer. Harry was stuck in the day before yesterday, riddled with uncomfortable idealism and banging on in that adamant voice of his, that made him sound like someone sentencing the damned.

Welliver won't be among history's winners, that's a cert, Charlie Belling thought, shifting irritably in his seat again, as annoyed by Harry's refusal to take the world as he found it as the late and forgotten Tory politician Leonard Riddick had been, during the years of the Attlee government. Charlie Belling wanted to stand up and bawl at Harry, 'You think winning is all about standing up for your principles and making brilliant speeches. Perhaps it was in nineteen forty-five, perhaps it was. But the world's changed, chum. Chaps like you wouldn't know what to do with power if you got it now. That's why chaps like me are kicking the statues of all your old heroes, useless gits that they were.'

Charlie's skull hummed with energy; he could hardly wait to get things moving. Harry came to the end of his speech and Charlie was on his feet, part of the standing ovation, before scuttling off to a meeting with some like-minded men, who were plotting to get Harry off the National Executive; men who realized that politics was a game where nobody got kissed.

Harry was perfectly miserable. He had always rather enjoyed the annual conference, but, this year, there was a whiff of the ridiculous in the way the Labour Party was hellbent on destroying itself. The blundering delegates, confused about where they stood on the issue of nuclear disarmament, bored him to tears by the hopeless monotony of their speeches. Yet the atmosphere in the conference hall was so treacherous that the floor might have been rippled with snakes, and this kept Harry on edge. He considered going back to London, but the Great Windmill Street flat was so unwelcoming. Reminders of Zanna were everywhere: her hairgrips in a cheap, glass bowl, a packet of the bitter, Algerian coffee she loved in the slovenly kitchen and, on the smeary glass shelf above the bathroom basin, her lily of the valley bath essence and a new cake of soap still in its cellophane wrapping. Harry found the sight of these unendurable. He had meant to donate them to the Labour Party jumble sale in Chipperton, but found that he could not bear to part with them.

It was raining in Scarborough. Drizzle smudged the banners proclaiming Ban the Bomb and Gaitskell Must Go, which disgruntled socialists were parading through the town's damp streets. Harry thought of the log fire at Utley Lodge and bacon and eggs for breakfast. Unable to sleep, he got into his unreliable old car and drove through the night to Shropshire.

Suzette and Dominick were giving the new Daimler a run by driving to Brighton for a weekend at the Metropole. They had tickets for a revival of *Private Lives* at the Theatre Royal and were going to nose around the antiques shops in The Lanes. Dominick switched on the car radio and caught a recorded version of Harry's speech to the Labour Party Conference. 'Because we can, we *should*,' they heard him declaim to loud, insincere applause.

'That man is becoming a legend in his own mind,' Suzette said. 'See if you can get Radio Luxembourg, will you, angel-drawers? And there's a nice-looking pub coming up. Let's have a drink, then we won't care about Harry any more.'

'That's enough for tonight, my dear,' Daisy said to Aurora. 'You drive yourself much too hard. Go and say good night to Mother and then, I think, it's bedtime. I've put the new Muriel Spark on the bedside table and I'll bring you your Horlicks shortly.'

'You look after me too well, Daisy,' Aurora said, trying to rub the ink off her fingers with the edge of the old shirt she was wearing.

'You mean I'm becoming a fusspot, like Mother. We all become our mothers in the end, you know.'

'I'm going to be the exception that proves the rule,' Aurora said. She drove her knuckles into her tired eyes, and managed to smear ink on her face.

Daisy looked at her fondly: the chestnut hair was in need of a wash and her shirt and corduroy trousers looked as though she'd slept in them. 'There's a fair chance of that, I'd say,' she said, going towards the kitchen to heat the milk.

Daisy felt guilty at having, more or less, snatched Aurora away from Zanna after Raymond died. Although Zanna and Aurora had never got on, it occurred to Daisy that Zanna might need her daughter now, even though she complained that the girl was a dowdy prig and that studying for a degree in Sociology was just Aurora's way of wilfully messing about. My need is as great as Zanna's, Daisy reassured herself, lighting the gas under the milk pan. With Mother growing so frail, and Otto far away and Harry so mutely unhappy, I should find life quite joyless if I didn't have Aurora to cosset. She is such a worthwhile girl and Zanna would undoubtedly be a bad influence on her; she would suck Aurora into the millinery business, where there would be the danger of the girl's head being turned by a lot of bird-brained women with spangled names. Daisy put the mug of Horlicks on a tray and a plate of the iced biscuits that Aurora liked. She sighed as she carried the tray upstairs. For all Zanna's wicked ways, Daisy missed her dreadfully, the way one would miss the light from a fire. Aurora had a far more noble nature, that went without saying, but never once had she made Daisy laugh.

Aurora was alone in the house when Harry arrived the next morning; Daisy had driven Leonora to church. Aurora was eating toast and marmalade in the kitchen and reading Willmott and Young's *Family and Kinship in East London* when Harry came through the back door in that hurtling way of his, longing for cupfuls of strong tea after a nasty drive through the rain in his rattly car. 'It's a beast of a road from Scarborough,' he said, eyeing the teapot.

Aurora moved towards the kettle in a neat, straight-forward way, like a nurse. Even so, her tapering fingers were clumsy; she dropped the breadknife and then hacked crooked slices off the loaf, splashed boiling water on the floor as she filled the teapot. Harry thought of Zanna's hot, frantic little hands, the way they pawed his body, bringing it to life. This serious, slow-moving girl had none of her mother's wild grace.

'I'm sorry about your father,' he said, making himself look into Aurora's deep-set eyes. 'It must have been a shock.'

'Not really,' Aurora said, holding his gaze. 'Daddy's heart was starved, so it died, that's all.'

'And your mother?'

Aurora considered the question. 'Perhaps a little lustreless. Not so much of the witty insolence. I can't say I mind that.'

The thought of Zanna listlessly subdued made Harry want to weep; Zanna, whose gleaming lilac eyes had always suggested danger and possibility.

'You have every right to blame me,' he muttered.

'What would be the point?' Aurora refilled his cup. 'You were the perfect dish to feed her hungry heart; I think the war had given her a taste for everything that was dashing and shameless. In any case, Mummy will prevail; hasn't she always?'

When Aurora smiled, Harry noticed her wide mouth and the familiar, beloved stretch of her jutting lips. 'You are so very like your mother, after all,' he said.

'I'm sure you mean that as a compliment, Harry, so I forgive you,' Aurora said. She thought that he looked thin and musty, the very picture of a shabby, genteel aristocrat, for all his leftward leanings. He reached out for the book she had been studying. 'I could tell you something about those times, if you'd care to listen,' he suggested in his plummy voice.

When Leonora and Daisy came back, they found Aurora sitting with her nice, firm legs stretched out towards the Aga, while Harry, rumpled and unreasonably tall, stood in front of it, warming his shanks and gesturing with his cup and saucer as he talked about the hopeful years just after the war, when he had set about putting his worn-out country to rights.

Leonora held onto the kitchen table, the skin on her old hands like the skin on custard, and lowered her stiff body very slowly into a chair. It was a shock to find Harry there; she hadn't been expecting him that weekend and was angry with him for surprising her when she was long past the age when surprises were enjoyable. And that rubbish he was telling Aurora about equality of opportunity and fair shares for all. An equal opportunity for everyone to be miserable was how Leonora remembered the late nineteen-forties.

That dreadful winter of 1947, the filthy trains frozen on the tracks, the lack of fuel and decent food, and bedraggled queues of people with cavernous coughs gripping their ration books outside the butcher's shop. And then, in the middle of all that misery, the meeting with Zanna. Leonora remembered going through the pink door of Zanna Modes, almost fainting from cold and tiredness, and Zanna reviving her with contraband champagne in a Bakelite beaker, twirling around her in a beautiful costume with lavish, swirling skirts, brightening her life for years to come.

'We need to go back to those times,' Harry was saying. What Leonora found intolerable was the moral earnestness with which her nephew refused to recognize his own failings. Aurora was giving him her serious attention though. She was such a solemn little thing, although quite lovely.

'They were sad and bitter times; I am quite certain that nobody would wish them back,' Leonora interrupted Harry who, startled, shut his mouth with a snap.

'Furthermore,' said Leonora, 'whenever I hear the word "community" coming from your lips, Harry, I am reminded that you are the loneliest man in the world.'

Harry gave his aunt a stiff little bow and left the room, wondering what had put her in such a foul mood.

'You're being rather hard on Harry,' Daisy said.

'Well, he was haranguing Aurora and haranguing is not allowed under my roof. I said as much to the Irish MPs who came to dine with us at Lisnagreve before the Great War. They had only to mention the words Home Rule and they knew they would be shown the door. Those were different days. Everyone was able to sing or

243

tell stories or be amusing in some way.' Leonora's old, soft face began to crumple. 'I'm so homesick,' she said.

'But you *are* at home, Mother,' Daisy said. 'I think a rest before lunch would be the best idea.'

'I'm beautiful, damn it,' Suzette convinced herself, squinting into the mirror in the ladies' powder-room of the Colony nightclub in Berkeley Square. As she got older, she applied her make-up with less restraint. Tonight, her eyelids shone with a turquoise gloss and streaks of crimson rouge winged across her cheek-bones. From a distance, she seemed girlish, with her fluffed blond curls and narrow waist, but, close up, her painted lids looked pouchy over her kittenish eyes, her neck bumpy and lined above the enormous diamonds. Suzette took an eyelash curler out of her evening bag and clamped it over her stiff, bright blue lashes. 'Sometimes I think that being a woman is a performance we put on to entertain men,' she said.

'Let's hope they find it amusing then,' Zanna said, fastening the pearl button on her long, satin glove. 'It's hard enough work trying to look like hot stuff, heaven knows.'

Zanna didn't look as though elegance came anything but naturally to her. Her blazing hair was back in a chignon, a protest against the puffy, fussy new hair-styles she disapproved of. She was wearing a narrow, velvet sheath dress, the colour of ripe blackberries, in which she looked slender and insouciant.

'I wish I were free to be myself,' Suzette complained, putting away the eyelash curler that looked like some instrument of torture.

'No you don't, Suze. You know as well as I do that it's a greater freedom to be allowed to be someone else. If we'd been forced into being ourselves, you'd be selling candyfloss at funfairs and I'd be going to coffee-meetings at Minetta's. Here's to artifice every time. Now let's join the gentlemen, you should pardon the expression.'

244

They were being squired by Dominick and his friend Marty for an evening of dinner, dancing and Julie Wilson in cabaret. Zanna and Suzette reached their table just as the singer walked onto the tiny stage, her hair in a sleek bun with a gardenia tucked behind one ear. Under the spotlight, her skin had an ice-blue sheen and the sequins on her dress fizzed with light. She began to sing 'Let's Do It', her voice smooth, rich and light, like good coffee. It was a voice that made you feel you could lie in wait for surprises, and be certain of getting them.

But tonight Zanna was jumpy and on edge, not in the mood for Cole Porter or Marty's and Dominick's campy banter. Life, as Suzette might have put it, had become just too believable. She had just sacked half her work-room staff and the salon itself was going to have to go next; she hadn't a hope in hell of paying the next quarter's rent. Hats were heading for oblivion, soon they'd be part of fashion history, along with far-thingales and swordsticks. *Vogue* had ignored her last collection. Instead, it had devoted fourteen pages to the opening of Woollands new 21 Shop. The stately Knightsbridge department store had given over a whole floor to what fashion buyers referred to as 'the youth-quake'. The dresses in Woollands new department were vibrant, amusing and, above all, casual, not at all the kind of frocks that needed a hat from Bond Street to make their point. She would have to look for smaller premises; maybe a shop in Brook Street, so that the middle-aged women who came up from the country to lunch at Claridge's would be ensnared by a hat in the window, as they stumbled out of the hotel, slightly tipsy and in a shopping mood. There were still a few women in the world who believed that if they changed their hat, their heart would follow, and Zanna intended to hang onto their custom.

So far, the nightclub where she was not enjoying herself had survived the youthquake. It catered for a well-heeled clientele that wished to dine lavishly from a lengthy French menu, which included several dishes that could be flamboyantly set aflame at the table by waiters deftly juggling chafing dishes and trying not to singe their eyebrows. But, it seemed to Zanna, that the women resting their solid backs against the quilted walls of the nightclub, listening to Julie Wilson singing 'What Is This Thing Called Love', looked lumpy and gross, their arms slabby with fat. She wanted to stomp around the tables, yanking off an ugly brooch here, an unnecessary ruffle there, hissing, 'Decoration betrays.'

'Dance with me, my tauntress supreme,' Dominick said, as though he could read the thoughts in Zanna's hard, doll's eyes. He was a flashy dancer, leading her into fancy, complicated steps while, over her head, he smirked at Marty, who was propping Suzette into a rumba.

Zanna left early, pleading an early-morning appointment. Although the doorman handed her tenderly into a taxi, she felt like a woman who was no longer cherished. As she let herself into the empty flat, she told herself not to be so ridiculous. It was not as though Harry had ever cherished her; any cherishing had been done by Raymond, and it was not Raymond that she missed. She knew she was on the verge of ruin, but in a detached way, as though it were some other woman who was going to see the silk sofas and ceramic tigers carried out of the salon, some other woman who was going to have to live without love and sleep empty-armed for the rest of her life. She thought: I feel like I'm living without really doing it, and closed her eyes without much hope of sleep.

Chapter Twenty

That's the girl I'm putting on the top of my wish-list, Howard Sutch told himself, as he watched Aurora Gringrich out of the corner of his narrow eye. She was at the far end of Chipperton's community centre, where a few school desks with bumpy, tilted lids and crusted inkwells had been set up. Behind them sat desperate-eyed Bengalis, staring blankly at Aurora as she held up reading cards: SEE, JANE, DOG, meaningless words which the Bengali men, shivering in their thin, white cotton tunics, understood they must learn if they were not to perish in cold, mean Britain.

At the other end of the hall, Howard was helping some equally bewildered immigrants fill in mud-coloured forms so that they could secure a flat in one of the seeping concrete tower blocks which stood squatly on what had, a few years ago, been bomb-damaged wasteland, bright with dandelions. Howard worked quickly, guiding the men's hands as they wrote shaky, unfamiliar signatures, then witnessing these with his own name and occupation: Howard Joseph Sutch, Managing Director Daydream Dresses Ltd.

Howard Sutch was born in Chipperton in the August of 1939. A month later, every Londoner was issued with a gas mask and trenches were being dug in the flower-beds of Hyde Park. Howard was evacuated to Wales with his mother, Ida, who, until his birth, had worked in a dress shop in the Whitechapel Road. Ida had hated the soft green hillsides and, more terrified of cows than bombs, had brought her baby back to Chipperton. A year later, she was one of the four hundred and thirty civilians killed during the first night of the Blitz, that night when the docks blazed into a livid wall of flames and London's East End collapsed into smoky rubble.

Ida's husband, Clifford, had disappeared by then. He hadn't been around much since the baby was born, claiming that Howard's crying got on his nerves. Clifford was a professional gambler who hung around the racetracks by day and the illegal gaming tables in the basements of West End drinking clubs by night. After Ida's death, Howard had been brought up in the Norwood Jewish Orphanage and, on his sixteenth birthday, apprenticed to a tailor in the Marylebone Road. A year after that, the police notified him of the death of the father he couldn't even remember. Clifford had had a massive heart attack watching the races at Newbury. Everything he possessed was now Howard's: his drip-dry shirts, two cheap suits, back-numbers of *Men Only* magazine and a plastic wallet containing a betting-slip. Some instinct made Howard go to the racetrack where Clifford had died. An impassive bookmaker glanced at the betting-slip and handed over three thousand pounds. The horse his late father had successfully backed had been called Daydream. Howard didn't wait to finish his apprenticeship. He'd never been happy hovering over bank managers and solicitors as they paddled their hands along bolts of uninspired worsteds; he'd never liked the heavy smell of wadding in his nostrils. He leased an old warehouse in Chipperton and began turning out inexpensive clothes for young women. By the spring of 1961, when Aurora Gringrich caught his eye, Daydream Dresses was thriving. Howard had a talent for knowing what young girls, joyfully pocketing their first pay-packets, wanted to wear. He studied *Vogue* and *Harper's Bazaar*, spent a lot of time in the King's Road seeing what Mary Quant was up to, riffled through the Jane and Jane range designed by Jean Muir and on sale in Liberty's. He usually bought something for himself in Carnaby Street – a pair of Cuban-heeled boots or a roll-necked silk polo shirt – before going into Fuller's for a cup of tea, which he drank while making sketches of the dresses he'd liked most and which he could reproduce in a cheaper fabric and minus one or two pricey details.

Howard had a good eye, and a good ear. He listened to his machinists as they chattered above the whir of their Singers, and realized that young women in London were putting up a fight against living their mothers' lives all over again, and that included wearing the sort of clothes their mothers wore.

These happily rebellious girls didn't want clothes to last; they'd had enough of that when they were kids, their clothing restricted by the hated coupons long after the end of the war. Everything had been bought two or more sizes too big, so that by the time it fitted, it looked shabby. Now they wanted something new every few weeks, something provocative and frivolous that their mothers wouldn't like. They didn't mind if the skimpy shift they helped to make and then bought from Howard at the wholesale price began to unravel after a few months. They'd be tired of it by then, ready for the next outfit: a sheath with a dropped waistband, a jersey-knit two-piece with contrast binding. The tailor who had taught Howard to be an expert cutter had taken pride in oversewn buttonholes and silk linings. Howard knew that classy touches like that didn't matter any more. Class was dead as mud in 1961.

Luck wasn't though. The luck of his three-thousand-pound legacy from his disgrace of a father had got Howard's feet on the ladder. It was to show his appreciation of this to a God he robustly believed in that made Howard spend every Wednesday evening at the community centre, helping men, some of them as young as he was, to wangle every state benefit Howard thought they were entitled to. He wanted to clear difficulties from their path, just as some fleet-footed racehorse had cleared difficulties from his own.

And now he was being rewarded again, Howard decided, unobtrusively keeping his eyes on Aurora. Gorgeous tits, perfect as two peaches on a plate, fab hair, shiny as apples; he could eat her up with a spoon. Shocking the way she was dressed though: a cotton madras skirt with the hem hanging down and a blouse that could have belonged to her gran (he was to find out later that it had). She ought to be wearing one of his favourite Daydream Dresses, a black cotton shift, tight in the bodice to show off those terrific breasts, with whirls of black braid around the hemline which was in the new, shorter length, only two inches below the kneecap. Howard dealt with the last of the anxious claimants and busied himself filing unnecessary bits of paper into dog-eared folders until he heard the clatter of stacking chairs as Aurora's sad-eyed students left the building.

He was only feet away from her when she dropped a pile of reading cards. LOOK, PAT, BALL, cascaded to the floor and were retrieved by Howard, deft as a conjuror.

'Thank you.' Aurora smiled at the young man with curly black hair, narrow, fast-moving eyes and a smooth, thin nose like a duck's bill. As she took the cards from him, she had the sudden sense of being reached for and found. Rain began to drum on the tin roof of the community centre, another of Howard's prayers efficiently answered.

'My car's outside,' he said. 'Want a lift home?'

Lilian had left the house in Golders Green to her only granddaughter. Aurora rented the upper floor to two student friends who took down Lilian's bevelled mirrors and stuck up posters of Picasso's *Child With a Dove*, and kept the ground floor for herself, sleeping in the little end bedroom she had had as a child. Howard followed her into the kitchen where she made tea and took almond biscuits out of a tin, arranging them on a square plate with a pattern of autumn leaves on it. Then she steamed down the hallway ahead of him, carrying the tray. Her deliberate walk and the way her chestnut hair slid around her shoulders filled him with strange flarings of lust. He sipped his tea politely.

'Are you a social worker?' Aurora asked doubtfully. He seemed an unlikely one in that shiny suit with narrow lapels and those chisel-toed shoes, even though she had noticed how caringly he had treated the men at the community centre, clamouring anxiously for his attention.

'Nope. I'm in the rag trade.'

'Oh no,' Aurora said. 'I don't believe it.'

'It's not a crime,' Howard said. 'These are the best biscuits I've ever tasted. Home-made, aren't they?'

'My grandmother's secret recipe. Sorry if I sounded rude, only my mother's a milliner. She made such a carry-on about clothes; if she discovered a new shade of navy blue, it was like she'd found a cure for cancer. It was a bit overpowering, all that absorption with what people put on their backs.'

'That's not the way it is with me.' Howard looked at Aurora out of his clever, narrow eyes. 'I work to live, not the other way around. But fashion's a good living all the same. England's going to be the fashion centre of the world, bound to be. We've got this knack of turning out clothes that make people look different but the same as everyone else.'

'What my mother calls releasing floods of trash onto the market.'

'You agree with that?'

'Howard, look at the way I'm dressed. I never think about clothes.'

'What do you think about then?'

Aurora blushed. 'About being a good person, I suppose. Like my father was. Have another biscuit.'

251

She got up to draw thick curtains and switch on table-lamps with pleated silk shades. Howard loved being in this house. Everything in it was pacifying: the net curtains in the kitchen window, that shivered slightly, like sails; the sitting-room carpet with its faded primroses, the heavy armchairs, sugar lumps in a silver bowl with bevelled edges. Birds in the garden trilled mildly. After the uproar of his childhood, Howard Sutch had a passion for mildness.

It was the sort of house where children would come running to meet you as you turned the key in the lock after a day's work, where the smell of a roasting chicken would mingle with the scent of wallflowers in a vase, where two people could turn themselves into a family. You could light Chanukah candles in this house and observe the Jewish festivals in such a way that afterwards everyone would remember them as solemn and thrilling. Howard felt no bitterness at being orphaned. Thousands of London children had lost their parents during the bombing, from the Blitz in 1940 right up to the doodlebugs and V-2 rockets that had smashed the exhausted city after the triumphs of the D-Day landings in France, killing ten thousand people. Howard counted himself lucky not to have been shipped out to Australia which, one of his machinists had told him, was what had happened to most of the boys in Chipperton whose parents had been killed. 'Taken away without so much as a by your leave,' Doreen had said, fitting a new spool of thread, 'it wasn't right.'

God had spared him that terrible exile but hadn't yet provided him with a family. The time had come to help matters along. 'I'd like to see you again,' he said. 'Saturday night?'

Aurora nodded and smiled. 'You're dying to do something with me, aren't you?' she accused Howard gently, shocking him. She put a hand on his arm. 'Not that, don't be silly. You want to do something about my clothes; you're looking at me just the way my mother does when she's itching to get me to doll myself up.'

Howard mopped his forehead. 'As long as you don't take it as an insult,' he said, 'only there's this showroom sample, black cotton with braiding detail, could have been made for you. Thought you could try it on.'

'After my tutorial on Thursday,' Aurora said. 'Then you won't have to worry about me looking unsuitable on Saturday.'

'Zip-A-Dee-Doo-Dah,' Howard said out loud as he drove home in his two-tone Ford Zodiac. 'Don't move too fast, boy. This is still in the dreaming stage.'

The ecstasy of achievement was what had kept Zanna spinning. Now she felt used up. She changed the window-display in her new shop – poky little premises with a workroom that always smelled of the rancid oil that wafted in from the pub on the corner that offered egg and chips at lunch-time – sometimes as often as three times a week. But still the young women who passed by, clicking along to Fenwick's in their pointed-toe shoes, hardly glanced at it. For a quarter of the price of one of Zanna's extravagant hats they could buy a flippy little dress and a matching pair of spike-heeled shoes, the perfect outfit for dancing the cha-cha-cha or going out to supper at one of the new Italian restaurants that were springing up all over the West End.

These trattorias had tilted floors and walls that flicked noise back into the room, intensifying the jabber. The waiters wore stripy T-shirts and tight black trousers; fishing-nets were slung across the walls, candles were stuck inside straw-covered Chianti flasks; strange things like risotto, packets of breadsticks and tiny cups of espresso coffee appeared on the starched pink table-cloths. In this atmosphere of casual bustle, a hat would have looked as odd as a ballgown.

'I can't see why this place is ballyhooed to the skies,' Zanna grumbled to Suzette as they chewed tough calimari at a fashionable trattoria in Mayfair. 'You can't hear yourself speak, there's a serious risk of getting tomato sauce slopped down the back of your neck; it's

253

like a restaurant for people who don't know what a restaurant is supposed to be like.'

'That's why people like it,' Suzette said. She was having a lovely time. The head waiter had called her '*la bella signora*' and kissed her hand and now he was giving her the eye from across the room as he made thrusting movements with an enormous wooden pepper mill. 'We don't see ear to ear on this one,' Suzette said, snapping a breadstick dramatically as she returned the head waiter's gaze. 'By the way, I met Aurora's new piece of work the other night. He impressed me no end, a very high-grade individual. Trust Aurora to get the goods. She's always had both hands on the ground.'

Zanna pushed her plate away. Her eyes darkened. 'Wherever did you meet Howard Sutch?'

'At the Sunday Times Fashion Awards. The last place I expected to see Miss Prissy. I thought Aurora's idea of a nice night out was doing the washing-up in a Salvation Army soup-kitchen. But there she was, looking an absolute dish I must say. That Vidal Sassoon haircut is too sublime. I'm going right over there after lunch. Just think, no more pin-curls, no more sitting under a drier with plastic what's-its in your ears, feeling like a wally, *and* looking ten years younger. Aurora had on this sweet little frock, one of Howard's own designs, he told me. That's why they were there, because of him; he'd won some export award. Just the sort of chap Aurora needs, and good-looking as well — that fine, rather crafty face and solid chin. A real hotshot. And the way he looked at Aurora, you'd have thought he'd won the pools.'

Zanna scowled. She hadn't been invited to the Fashion Awards this year, another sign of slipping esteem, as though she needed one. 'I hate to see Aurora flop into love with nothing worked out,' she said snappishly. 'She's going backward with Howard, back to the rough ground. If she marries a man like that, she'll just dwindle into being a wife.' She blew spirals of white smoke towards the ceiling.

'Pish and posh, Zanna. It takes all sorts to make a bag of liquorice, and Aurora's not the dwindling type.'

Outside the restaurant, Suzette put on her sunglasses as the sudden light pecked at her eyes. 'You ought to keep on the right side of Aurora,' she said. 'She may look as though you could melt butter in her mouth but it wouldn't surprise me if she turned out to have a temper as big as the Ritz.'

Aurora sat on the window-sill in Howard's cutting-room, watching him pin pieces of fabric into the shape of a dress. She liked the silky motion of his wrists as he pinned the cloth; his hands darted around the hemline, pins falling out of them and landing in exactly the right place. The October sun warmed the back of her head as she leant against the window, and she closed her eyes, thinking that you could divide men into two groups, protectors and exploiters, without them even knowing which they were. Howard was a protector like Daddy. All the time she'd been studying for her finals, he'd taken over all the small nuisances of her life. He'd collected the rent from her lodgers, kept the house in repair, was always waiting for her in his car, when she stumbled out of the university library, her shoulders heavy from a long day's swotting. 'Leave it to me,' he would say, whenever she had a problem getting hold of a book or opening a tin, as though he'd been put on this earth to care for her. Like Daddy, unlike Harry Welli-ver. Aurora couldn't imagine *him* ever suggesting that Zanna left things to him. The way he banged around, his hair flopping importantly over his brow, implied that he was able to attend only to serious, impersonal things. You'd be frightened of asking him to put the kettle on or to take a pair of shoes to be heeled. That's what made him an exploiter, someone from whom you could never have any expectations, someone who didn't notice what was going on, someone who wore his self-advertised worthiness like a shield. Her eyes still closed, she felt Howard's kiss, sudden and tender, on her mouth. He lifted her down from the window-sill and buried his nose in her throat, as though it were a rose. 'Auroradorable,' he whispered into her neck, 'walk by the river with me.'

The light from the water was a feathery haze, the small pebbles under their feet sliding and dragging as the river tugged at the bank. Standing on the chipped, stone steps of an old rum warehouse they leaned into each other; through the cloth of Howard's shirt, Aurora felt the springy dark hairs that spread across his shoulder-blades bounce under her fingers. He had been carrying his jacket over one shoulder; now he draped it over her. A wind had come up and the sunless river was greying, opaque. Aurora put her hands into the pockets of Howard's jacket to warm them and her fingers bumped on a small, square box. 'Yes,' Howard said. 'Something to celebrate getting a first in your exams. Open it.'

The ring was a daisy made of diamonds. It glittered up at her, a promise of lifelong devotion. 'Yes, of course I will, Howard,' Aurora said. 'We should go to Chelsea and tell Mummy.'

'I would rather lie dead in a ditch, I'd rather have my head torn from my shoulders, I'd rather climb Everest in bare tootsies,' Howard said. He sensed how much Zanna loathed him, in spite of the macabre gaiety of her smiles. He wished he could do something right in her eyes for Auroradorable's sake but felt that he couldn't without being somebody other than Howard Sutch.

A few weeks before, he'd sauntered into Zanna's shop, thinking she might be glad of the company, with business so quiet. He'd bounced through the door, fizzing with enthusiasm. Zanna's strange violet eyes swept over his Carnaby suit like searchlights: the lapel-less jacket with cloth buttonholes, the tapered trousers breaking over his Cuban-heeled shoes. 'What do you reckon?' Howard asked. He thought that in spite of her blazing eyes, she seemed engulfed in shadows.

Zanna's wide lips pulled into a smile while her eyes glittered icily. 'Is this what is called gutter fashion?' she asked.

'Street fashion,' Howard corrected her breezily. He had just come back from Hamburg where he'd sold five hundred Daydream Dresses, most of them a size forty, German girls being on the meaty side. He'd wandered around the strip clubs on the Reeperbahn: the Kaiser-deller and the Top Ten, and listened to an English band called the Beatles. Nobody in the clubs looked more than twenty, and when he got back to London he'd noticed the same thing: the young had taken over the town. Even women in their thirties were shucking off ageing accessories like brooches and long gloves and (bad news for Zanna Gringrich) hats, in order to join the youthquake. Zanna ought to take that display of elbow-length gloves out of the window, talk about frumpy.

'Street fashion, eh?' Zanna said. 'Not the direction I should have chosen. So brazen and artful.'

'You've said it, Mrs Gringrich.' Howard was not the least bit wounded. Brazen and artful were just the right words to describe what was happening: the Beatles singing 'Twist and Shout,' in the Hamburg clubs; the pack of Cockney fashion photographers led by David Bailey, Terence Donovan and Brian Duffy, who had taken over *Vogue*, snapping models in uncontrolled poses, whirling happily across the pages, instead of standing, stalk-straight, with their necks tensely arched; the sexy new dance, the Twist, which had come slinking in from France that summer. Artful and brazen, Aurora's mother had got it in one.

'All right, I'll go and tell Mummy by myself,' Aurora said, as they walked away from the darkening river.

'Come into my arms then.' Howard held her close to his heart and propped his solid chin on her head.

'You're doing this to pay me back for killing your father,' Zanna said. She'd spent a gloomy afternoon with her

257

accountant and had a splintering headache. 'Well, it's your own life you're ruining; it's too late to ruin mine.'

Aurora considered this and shook her head. Her short, shiny hair flew about her cheeks and then settled perfectly in place. 'It wouldn't be fair to blame you for Daddy's death. You've enough to be guilty about without that. And we don't have the same ideas about how lives get to be ruined.' There was a tender contempt in her daughter's voice that Zanna didn't care for.

'To see you rolling gently downhill makes me very angry,' she snapped. 'That young man's a step in the wrong direction.'

'Why?' Aurora bellowed. Zanna's anger was catching. Aurora followed her mother from room to room as Zanna stalked about the flat, rearranging a bowl of flowers, brushing her hair with her tatty old hairbrush, rummaging through the kitchen cupboards for a fresh pack of cigarettes.

'Why?' Aurora shrieked again. 'Is it because Howard is someone who will always take care of me, watch over me, just like Daddy wanted to take care of you? You punished him by not letting him look after you – that was your way. You think I'm settling for too little, but you settled for *nothing*.'

Zanna stared hard at her, the way she used to when Aurora had been a plain, clumsy little girl. It was a stare that had always made Aurora feel that Zanna was trying to come to terms with the undeniable and unwelcome fact that this disappointing child was what she had given birth to.

'I settled for being in love,' Zanna said.

'Groundless love,' Aurora yelled. 'Stolen afternoons and secrets. Don't think I didn't know what was going on; so did Mrs Harris.'

'Mrs Harris worshipped Harry,' Zanna said. 'I can't see Howard being anybody's hero. All he wants to do is fill the chain stores with his lousy dresses. I may not have been the best mother in the world, but I brought you up to expect passion and poetry in your life. Is that

258

what Howard will provide?' She shook the flame out of a match. 'Not likely. He'll drag you back to everything I tried to escape from: an unexceptional life spent with uninspiring people, doing smarmy good deeds. You've already started on that path; it's morbid the way the two of you hang around Chipperton. Bloody patronizing too, all your fanatic sympathy for other people, reminds me of that goody-goody inscription over the fountain at Utley:

> God bless the poor!
> Teach them true liberty.
> Make them from strong drink free.
> Let their homes happy be.
> God bless the poor!

What stinking self-righteousness *that* is.'

The first time she had read that inscription had been just moments before Harry appeared, looking casually god-like in old corduroys, and driven her much too fast down the pot-holed track to Utley Lodge, impatient to make love to her. Aurora would never have memories like that, didn't deserve to. 'Do what you want,' Zanna said. 'That's what most people do in the end.' She closed her eyes, as though Aurora's commonplace plans had glutted her with boredom. Her clamped eyelids were a reproach.

Aurora was maddened by the dismissive gesture. 'I can't ever be right,' she shouted at Zanna's shuttered face. 'Everything I am, everything I do, is so hateful to you that if you were to approve of me, everything that *you* stand for would be seen to be wrong. You won't ever allow us to be proud of each other.'

Zanna's eyelids shot back into their sockets. 'When have you ever been proud of me?'

'I'm proud of you now. I know you're having a bleak time – Howard showed me an article in the *Draper's Record* about the crisis in the millinery business – but you never complain. You go around with your wide red smile, not letting anyone feel sorry for you.

Remember when some newspaper christened you "La Desirous"?'

"You bet I remember," Zanna said. "Nineteen fifty-three. The year I made you that pink dress with the musical petticoat. Coronation year. What a time for hats that was; I felt rich beyond the dreams of need.' Her eyes darkened; she got up and looked through the vast windows at the bobbing lights of the Albert Bridge. 'One goes on going on,' she said. 'In the end it's just a matter of lasting.'

Chapter Twenty-One

'Things aren't as bad as you think,' Daisy told Harry. She had just come back from Ireland, freckled and sturdy and determinedly optimistic. 'Hugh Gaitskell's looking more like a prime minister in waiting with every day that passes.'

'And what a victory for socialism when the waiting's over,' Harry said sarcastically. He looked disconsolate, tired out. It had been an eventful autumn; he'd been arrested at the ban-the-bomb march in Trafalgar Square and, in consequence, dropped from the television programme which he'd presented for seven years. The word had got around that he was unreliable, a bit of a ranter. He'd been replaced on the programme by Charlie Belling, a new image-conscious Charlie Belling whose double-cuffed shirts and side-parted haircut were copied from President Kennedy. Charlie had also adopted the Kennedy handshake: a firm grasp, with the left hand moving to the other person's wrist, as though to stop him escaping.

Mrs Belling was fighting a losing battle trying to emulate the *soignée* First Lady. Unlike Jacqueline Bouvier Kennedy, Beryl Belling was a primary-school teacher from Telford who wore long, slack skirts and flat, puffy-looking shoes with laces. There would be a new Mrs Belling before very long, an ash-blond researcher in the House of Commons library who'd had her eye on Charlie for years.

'I don't know why socialism is so universally derided,' Harry said mournfully.

'You've been chewing over that one for ever,' Daisy snapped at him. 'It's high time you found the courage to admit that there are some questions that don't have answers, like the rest of us. The first thing is to win an election on a manifesto that doesn't make the voters take to the hills. Why can't you *see* that?' Daisy riffled impatiently through the morning post. 'Letter from Otto,' she said, throwing her glasses neatly over her nose.

Harry's mouth started to droop as Daisy read his nephew's letter aloud. The boy wrote with relish of his grandparents' many-bedroomed bungalow, the black servants in their white jackets and red sashes, the sports car he'd been given on becoming twenty-one, the jeroboams of champagne which had foamed onto the starlit lawn during the birthday party. Daisy stopped reading as she heard Harry's shuddering sigh of despair. 'I know what you're thinking, Harry. You're upset that Otto hasn't mentioned what is happening in South Africa. People who have suffered too much themselves fail to notice the misfortunes of others; I've seen that happen time and time again. Now, will you help me set up the folding bed in the old day nursery? Aurora's coming to visit with this young man she's going to marry.' It was Daisy's turn to sigh. 'There's no need to cock your eyebrow at *me*, Harry. *Obviously*, they will have separate rooms. We're talking about Aurora, not her naughty mother.'

Harry ran downstairs quickly, as soon as Daisy called him, not looking down at his feet once. Leonora was lying on the floor, grey with pain; she had tripped and, although she'd landed on the hall rug, could have snapped one of her brittle old bones. As Daisy went to phone for an ambulance, a car drew up and Aurora and Howard came into the hall.

The speed of their organization was remarkable, Harry thought later when Leonora was settled in a private room in Shrewsbury hospital, woozy with pain-killers, her fractured hip examined by a visiting consultant that Howard had rustled up from somewhere.

'An ambulance will take too long to get here,' Howard had decided, and he and Aurora had made some kind of stretcher out of an ironing-board and driven Leonora to Shrewsbury.

'Silly to take her to Utley hospital, she'd only have to be moved later and Leonora would hate being in a ward with all those *old* people,' Aurora had insisted, smiling down at Leonora, who was getting on for ninety, as she strapped her to the ironing-board with the belt of her raincoat.

Afterwards, she and Howard had put themselves in charge of getting supper. Cutlets, sauté potatoes and a tomato salad appeared in no time at all, Aurora and Howard briskly passing plates in a way that made Daisy and Harry feel slow and useless.

These two are Beveridge babies, Harry thought. Living advertisements for the tentative beginnings of the welfare state. Strong limbs and white teeth courtesy of free orange juice and cod-liver oil. Courtesy of the war too, I suppose, which denied them ice-cream and sweeties while they were growing up. They'd been born in the Blitz. He wondered what effect that dangerous wartime infancy had had on their generation. Evacuations, day nurseries, fathers who were no more than a blurry memory of rough khaki and noisy boots, and, after that, a photograph on a mantelpiece, a posthumous medal kept in a drawer of a sideboard. Hadn't there been some story about Howard being orphaned during the Blitz? You would not take him for someone with a background of suffering. He sat with his arm around the back of Aurora's chair, a cheerful glint in his narrow eyes. He talked about his clothing factory in Chipperton, the jokes the women told as they inched fabric under their sewing-machines, the pins like tiny silver haystacks in their pale blue boxes, the excitement of being at the leading edge of the fashion youthquake. Harry saw that Daisy had taken to him immediately; she had always liked sprightly men. He exhausted Harry though; the energy that seemed to bristle in Howard's black curls made him feel like a tired old dog plagued by a playsome puppy.

'Harry's been the MP for Chipperton for ages,' Aurora said, leaning her head on Howard's arm. Howard was talking as though the East End belonged to him and she could see that Harry was put out. He'd done a lot of good there in his day, trying to save the docks, although that was futile once there was enough petrol to shift goods by lorry instead of sluggish cargo boats.

'Now this will interest you then, Harry.' Howard was quite unabashed. 'We're worried about some of the Asian kids. Their mums won't leave the house, so the children have to do all the shopping, fetch a doctor when someone's sick. Terrible to see them scuttling about, the weight of the world on their shoulders. So what we want to do is take a team of language teachers into their homes, teach the women English, see if they'll put their noses outside the door afterwards. Think you could wangle a grant for us?'

'I'll do my best,' Harry said wearily. 'This seems a very admirable concern of yours. Have you ever thought of going into politics?'

Aurora put her hand over Howard's and wrinkled her high-bridged nose. 'Howard and I aren't interested in politics, only people,' she said. The weight of her disapproval crushed Harry like a falling oak. He sloped off to bed, leaving Howard to telephone the hospital and make an appointment with the consultant, who had been planning to play golf the following morning but who was persuaded by Howard's cheery insistence to change his mind. 'Don't say yes until I finish talking,' Harry heard Howard say. He shut his bedroom door and took a deep breath, trying to smell a trace of Zanna's lily of the valley scent, which had evaporated months ago.

It was a rare thing to find Minetta Fadge and Natalie Mançeur in perfect agreement with one another but both of them thought that Zanna should find herself another husband. 'While you're still attractive,' Minetta added.

'*Still* attractive. What poisonous words *those* are. Like there's a good chance I could wake up tomorrow morning and discover that I'm a horrid sight or, worse still, well preserved, which always makes me think of a pickle. And don't say you wouldn't be delighted to see it happen, because I wouldn't believe you,' Zanna growled.

A born match-maker (hadn't she, after all, introduced Zanna to poor Raymond, considered such a catch at the time?), Minetta organized a dinner party so that Zanna could meet a chartered accountant, Jack Conrad, a magistrate like Minetta herself, a thoroughly upright character. A shortish man with thinning hair, he was disconcerted by Zanna's hard-edged glamour; it seemed shallow, too sleek by half. He liked women to have soft bodies, soft hands, to be younger versions of his widowed mother, with whom he shared a large house in St John's Wood.

The man seated on Zanna's right was a stockbroker called Victor Rockman. Whenever his wife's attention was elsewhere, he stared long and hard at Zanna's bony shoulders, longing to hold them. Her scrabbling squirrel's paws, lighting endless cigarettes, or pulling at a sprig of grapes, excited him madly. The next day he visited the Brook Street shop; at the weekend, telling his wife he had to visit a client in Brussels, he took Zanna to Bruges.

'I'm hoping he might give me a hot tip that will make me millions, otherwise I probably wouldn't bother,' Zanna told Suzette. 'But so far, no dice. What he *does* do is buy up a lot of my stock for his wife. She now has enough handbags to carry away the Bank of England. He thinks that he'll stop feeling guilty about *me* if he loads *her* up with presents. Some hopes. The poor sod sits on the edge of my bed in his underpants showing me pictures of his grandchildren and wiping tears from his eyes. As soon as I've conned him into buying all those elbow-length gloves I paid too much for in Rome and can't even give away, I think I'll jack it in.'

At about the same time, she met Ellis Coote, an English diplomat. That was at one of Jean-Louis and Natalie Mançeur's Sunday lunches, at their Regency house in Richmond. The Mançeur lunch parties were arranged in what Jean-Louis called '*le style Anglais*': roast beef and Yorkshire pudding, even on scorching summer days, cider in pewter tankards, sherry trifle. On Sundays, Jean-Louis wore sports jackets in glaring over-checked tweeds, so new that Zanna was certain she could hear the sleeves creak. Jean-Louis took his guests to inspect his hybrid tea roses, not nearly as pretty as Leonora's old, scented damasks, in Zanna's opinion, and she would never have dreamed, in the old days, that Jean-Louis would be capable of droning on endlessly on the subject of black spot and aphids.

It was laughable what Jean-Louis and Natalie imagined to be English style. They should take a stroll down Oxford Street, see how the department stores were stuffed with Bri-nylon and Acrilan. They should follow the crowds to Carnaby Street, see the boutiques full of the shoddy flim-flam that Howard Sutch insisted was fab gear. If you wanted cashmere with a soft bloom on it, subtle tweed suiting or, come to think of it, disease-free roses that smelled like the winds of paradise, you'd be better off living in France, which Jean-Louis refused to do on account of his country's shameful collaboration with the Germans during the war.

Zanna turned away from the dull roses and examined Ellis Coote. Wavy grey hair, startlingly white fingernails, very handsome pink jade cuff-links. Probably a queer. She was surprised when he invited her to the opera and, a week later, to the private view of an exhibition of Japanese woodblock prints. She fidgeted during the opera, a production of *La Bohème*, with a Mimi whose supposedly tiny hand was pink and hammy, attached to a sturdy wrist. She thought that the Japanese prints were revolting. Some of them were of copulating couples, the men with colossal organs that looked as thick and heavy as rolling-pins and, in Zanna's view, about as erotic.

One of the things she had loved most about Harry Welliver was that he had no interests or hobbies that had to be accommodated. Only two things absorbed him: socialism and her. Being in the company of other men meant missing Harry more than ever, something she hadn't thought possible. The smell of their breath, their bodies, racked her with longing for Harry's strange, particular odour of warm skin, tobacco, and slightly mildewed wool. Other men could be lumped together into a group called Not-Harry, indistinguishable from each other, undesirable and tiresome. The words that seeped politely out of their mouths were pale, weak opinions compared to Harry's turbulent views. The Not-Harrys led tidy lives and ate regular meals. Listening to them in restaurants, requesting lightly cooked vegetables, or discussing a particular Chablis with the wine-waiter, made Zanna ache for Harry, who never noticed what he was eating. She sighed for the cracked and hardened wedge of cheese and the baked beans spooned straight from the tin which they had shared in bed in the Great Windmill Street flat at three in the morning.

When Ellis Coote invited her to a season of Swedish films showing at the Academy cinema she invented an overseas buying trip. To keep Harry out of her thoughts, she tried to remember the words of every popular song she had ever heard. 'Love Me Or Leave Me And Let Me Be Lonely,' she sang in her coarse growl. 'Da da da da da.' The song suggested that loneliness was preferable to happiness with a new lover. That was frigging nonsense. That wasn't the choice. It was impossible to be happy with somebody else, not on the cards. You could only be *unhappy* with somebody else. Everything they said and did made you sick with misery for no reason at all, except that they *were* somebody else. When Victor Rockman adjusted the knot in his tie, when Ellis Coote jiggled the loose change in his trouser-pocket, Zanna eyed them murderously. Men you didn't love made you lonely, lonelier than being alone.

'Your mum's put a Jacqueline Kennedy pillbox in the window,' Howard said to Aurora. His sharp eyes could see the tiny, stone-coloured hat from the other side of Brook Street. He steered Aurora across the road and into Zanna's shop.

'Really?' Aurora wasn't very interested in the news. 'Does this mean she's doing the right thing at last?'

'Nope. Nobody's going to pay Mayfair prices for a pillbox when they can get the same thing at Dickins & Jones. Makes the window-display look more with it, that's all.'

Zanna was at the counter, a smile blazoned on her face. A worried-looking middle-aged man wearing a Crombie overcoat was looking doubtfully at some elbow-length gloves that Zanna had fanned out on the counter-top.

'Mr Rockman is about to deluge his wife with gifts,' Zanna said brightly. She fished a pair of ice-blue gloves out of the arrangement. 'These are the exact match with the handbag you gave her last week. What about it?' Howard entered into the spirit of salesmanship. He plucked out a glacé kid pair, the same colour as the pillbox in the window, which he lifted from its stand and flipped onto Aurora's shiny hair. 'What about *that*?' he asked admiringly. 'Fab or what? And great with the gloves, although Mrs Kennedy wears short ones.' The pillbox sat prettily on Aurora's head, suiting the simplicity of her stripey dress with its crochet collar, one of Daydream's best-selling lines, shoplifted by the dozen, Howard boasted, from Woollands dazzling new 21 Shop, that had been designed by Terence Conran.

'That's beautiful,' Victor Rockman said. 'I'll take the hat *and* the gloves. I think I already bought a handbag in the same colour.'

'No,' Zanna said. She clawed the hat off Aurora's head and put it back on the stand. Victor's wife had dyed black hair, lacquered into swollen, sticky curves. Zanna wasn't going to allow her exquisitely made pillbox to sit on top of that horrible mess of hair, like a pimple on St Paul's.

'It's not Gloria's style,' she said in a decided voice. 'I'll wrap the gloves for you.'

I don't get it, Howard thought. The way things are, she needed that sale. Anyone can see this business is going down the chute. There was a lot about his future mother-in-law that Howard didn't get: the way she looked at Auroradorable for a start, her eyes poking at the girl, making Aurora hunch her shoulders, trying to conceal her perfect breasts, not doing herself any favours.

Zanna was scary, shimmery, in a way women weren't supposed to be any more. Her tailored dresses were models of elegant restraint, but, for all their subtlety, shouted 'Only look at me,' and that didn't look right either. A few days ago, Howard had opened a cupboard in Zanna's lavish bathroom and discovered messy explosions of powders and creams, greasy wads of cottonwool. In the drawing-room, every surface glittered, the only ornament a Japanese flower arrangement composed of a twig, a stone and a single peony. The hidden disorder and the outward display of harmony symbolized Zanna, Howard thought, and felt that he had stumbled across some important secret. She lived a life between worlds, a lover of poetry with a fishwife's tongue.

'Can we go now?' Aurora asked impatiently. 'The casserole's on the automatic timer.' They were driving Zanna to Golders Green but she seemed reluctant to leave. She had started to reblock a hat over a jet of steam and then flicked through a pile of bills in a drawer, her face like stone. At last, she shut the drawer with a bang.

269

'Everyone pushes a falling fence,' she said gaily. 'I'm being killed off by hairspray and cheap copies of Mrs Kennedy's pillboxes. Well, you can't stop the music. By the way, Aurora, don't tell your aunt that Mr Rockman was in the shop, she gets upset by things like that.'

'Things like what?'

'Never you mind.'

'I hope you're not making a mistake,' Aurora said reprovingly.

'I only wish I were. My mistakes made me very happy. If I had my time over again, I'd make exactly the same ones, only sooner.'

Howard nosed his roomy, inelegant car into the traffic heading north. This was the route Raymond used to take, when he'd collected Zanna from her shop and driven her to Golders Green, to be given an uneasy welcome by Sidney and Lilian and her small daughter who hated being torn away from her grandparents every evening. How tiresome it had been, Zanna thought, to leave the West End, to pretend to be glad to see her stolid, plain little girl, to pretend not to notice Lilian's subdued resentment.

What a misbegotten motherhood this was. Aurora, although grown into a beauty, still caused her nothing but fatigue and irritation; she just couldn't get in harness with her. Zanna vibrated with annoyance at Aurora's priggish ways, and now this insufferable choice of husband, self-importance in a pop star's suit. As he drove, he talked about the changes he was going to make to the house now that the lodgers had gone: smarten up the panelled doors by making them flush with chipboard, a G-plan shelving unit for his collection of singles, take out the tiled fireplaces, put in mixer taps, scatter candy-pink cushions on Lilian's sombre settee. Aurora responded to this with banal joyfulness.

Listening to the two of them, Zanna felt as though they were walking on her eyelids. She shivered as they left Baker Street behind and moved into the red-brick and privet world that lay beyond Swiss Cottage, a world that never failed to lower her spirits. She shivered again and pulled the collar of her coat up to her chin as Howard parked the car beside the hedge, silvered with damp, outside Aurora's ugly house.

'The last of Daisy's potatoes,' Aurora announced, serving them up with the chicken casserole she had made that morning and left successfully in the self-timing oven. Zanna reluctantly held up her plate. 'See if you can find me a small one,' she said. While Aurora was spooning the potatoes around in the Pyrex dish, Zanna lit a cigarette. Aurora was behaving with brutal inconsiderateness, bringing up the subject of Utley Lodge. Well, she wasn't going to give her the satisfaction of seeming wounded.

'How are they all then, Leonora, Daisy,' – a short but stagy pause – 'Harry?'

'Leonora's spry as a cricket again after her fall. Daisy and Harry just the same, bickering about the shape of the New Jerusalem instead of starting to build it.'

Zanna *was* wounded now. Aurora had no business condescending to Harry as if he were some bumbling old has-been. The vein in Zanna's forehead began to bump under her white skin. 'This is delightful, darling,' she said, pushing away her plate with most of the food still on it. 'If only your grandmother were here to see how much you take after her.'

Aurora understood this for the insult it was intended to be and Zanna was rewarded by a ripple of annoyance in her daughter's high-bridged nose.

Something's going on here, Howard thought uneasily. Something to do with Utley Lodge. There was something fishy about the way Daisy and Leonora always asked after Zanna, their voices curdled and their eyes flicking away from Aurora's face. And Aurora mentioned Daisy's name tonight as though she were issuing a threat. She was in a punishing mood, his Auroradorable, offering her mother three different kinds of pudding when it was clear that all Zanna wanted was a light for her cigarette.

271

After supper, Aurora insisted on giving Zanna a tour of the redecorated house and the new breakfast nook in the kitchen. Zanna looked blankly at the projecting Formica shelf and padded chromium stools. It was beyond her that anyone would think of sitting down to breakfast. She, herself, started the day with a cup of instant coffee made with hot water from the bath tap and stirred with her big toe.

The wedding was six months away but Howard had already moved in some of his belongings. In Lilian's and Sidney's old bedroom, his lapel-less jackets hung on plastic hangers, his alligator shoes rested on the built-in shoe racks that had once held Sidney's sombre black Oxfords. He had not moved in himself, Zanna noted. The double bed was stripped and Aurora still slept in her small childhood bedroom on the ground floor. Zanna refused Howard's offer of a lift to Chelsea, getting into that trashy Ford was more than she could bear, and ordered a taxi. Wedding-presents, still in their boxes, were starting to pile up in the hall. Zanna knew what they would be: Venetian glass vases, rose-pink towels, an electric blender, all the glum comforts of suburban life. 'Lawdie-Gawdie, Harry,' she moaned, huddled in the back of the taxi. 'How I miss you. You wouldn't know what an electric blender was if one came up and bit you on the leg.'

'What's going on, Auroradorable?' Howard asked. He was helping Aurora do the washing-up, his supple, delicate wrists flipping plates into cupboards. 'I almost forgot you were a sociology graduate this evening, you were acting like you'd have a hard time keeping up in kindergarten. What's the deal, taking your mum over every inch of the house when you know it's not her scene?'

'Yes, I do know. It brings back unhappy memories of everyone she'd like to forget: me, Daddy, Nana and Papa, the life she wanted to leave behind.' Aurora's tears plopped into the washing-up bowl. 'She's never forgiven me for being born. I'm the one mistake she wouldn't choose to make again.'

Howard sat down on one of the chromium stools that Zanna had disliked so much and pulled Aurora uncomfortably onto his lap.

'Do you think anybody of our age wasn't a mistake?' he asked gently, his duck's bill nose in her hair. 'Can't you imagine what it must have been like, falling for a baby once the war began? It's a cert that poor Ida never wanted me; all credit to her that she didn't dump me in a nursery and push off. There were plenty who did. You know Michelle at Daydream? Tall girl, does the accounts? Her mum took her and her brother to the nursery one morning and that was the last they saw of her. Michelle says she can remember waiting, wouldn't take off her hat and coat or put down her gas mask, long after she knew her mother wasn't ever going to come back. Latest thing is a letter from San Antonio, Texas. Somehow, her mum became a GI bride to some rancher without anyone knowing. Says she'll pay for Michelle and her kids to fly out. So Michelle's decided to forgive her; says you can't blame the poor cow for what she did, there was a war on. Catch my drift, lovey?'

'Yes. I've no business to moan when you had it much worse than I did and never complain. I just wish Mummy would appreciate what we're able to give her.' Aurora waved a washing-up brush, glittery with bubbles, to indicate the gleaming kitchen, the rumbling refrigerator, stacked with food, signs of plentiful succour wherever you looked. 'You'd think with Zanna Modes on the rocks, she'd want to be cared for.'

'But it's something else she wants, isn't it?' Howard's narrow eyes were alert. 'I'm not an expert on families, not having had one, but I can tell when a secret needs a good airing. You going to tell me about it, doll?'

'It's about Harry Welliver,' Aurora said. 'Let's go inside and I'll switch the fire on; it's a long story.'

She told Howard about the Coronation Day party, when she'd caught Zanna watching Harry Welliver on television and knew instantly that he meant more to her than anyone else in the world. 'I was scared; I thought if Daddy or I interfered with her feelings for Harry, she might harm us in some way. I wanted to lock her up in the room with the television like a wicked fairy. Then we'd all be allowed to go on being ordinary people. I'll never forget the look in her eyes; she looked absolutely ravenous. I knew what was going on right away, although I couldn't have put it into words, I was only eleven. I knew that I had to protect Daddy, stop him finding out. What a laugh. He knew all the time. He and I looked after each other without ever mentioning it. We never admitted that we were frightened that Mummy might destroy us. If we had talked about it, she might not have despised us as much as she did.'

Aurora switched on the lower bar of the electric fire set in an ornate pewter surround that was decorated with miniature urns. 'Poor Daddy. He was wretchedly complaisant. All the time he was in the Army, he'd dreamed of this perfect homecoming, the wonderful life he'd have with his pretty wife and the little daughter he'd only seen in photographs. Mummy was making hats for film studios when he'd been called up. No-one had any idea that she was going to be a famous milliner. By the time Daddy was demobbed she had her own shop – and her own life. Daddy was nothing to her, except a bit of a hindrance, always wanting us to act like a family, go to the zoo, have picnics in the park, all the things that bored her. He stuck it out, though; it would have broken his heart to have to leave us again, not that it didn't break his heart to stay.'

'But Harry, of all people,' Howard marvelled, thinking of the unattractive way Harry blinked as he explained some tedious bit of Labour Party doctrine, his melancholy face drooping between his wide shoulders.

'Harry was different then. Rumpled but quite a dazzler. Daisy told me that quite soon after the war, he'd been thought of as a future prime minister.'

'Come off it, puss. I wouldn't leave Harry in charge of his own shoelaces. I wouldn't leave him in charge of putting on a tea-dance. I wouldn't leave him in charge of escaping from a brown paper bag. How long did it go on for?'

'The grand passion? Oh, years and years. They all knew, Daisy, Leonora, even Harry's peculiar brother, Gomer, the one that got killed in the fire at Utley Manor. Nobody put their foot down. All the world loves a lover, they say. Too bad if the love affair hurts people who don't make a romantic splash of their lives.'

'Your mum didn't run off with Harry, though?'

'Never had a chance. Harry had his career to think about. Having an affair with someone else's wife is one thing, marrying a divorced woman is another story. He turned Mummy into some kind of perverse legend – the woman Harry Welliver refused to marry. It was humiliating for all of us, Daddy especially, curiously enough.'

'What's to stop them marrying now, though?'

'It all came to an end about two years ago. I don't know why; nothing was ever said, as usual. It was a peculiar time: the Welliver ancestral home burnt down, Gomer dead. Then his wife and children went away.' Aurora flushed, thinking of Otto and his lunatic love of her. 'Mummy went around with what I call her china-doll face, expressionless as a mask, so I knew something had happened. Then she started staying at home in the evenings. It made Daddy feel twitchy; he'd got used to watching television on his own, nursing his ulcer with toast and hot milk.' Aurora scowled at the urns on the fire surround. 'He'd got used to being overlooked and discarded as well. She'd always treated him with pitiless indifference, made him feel pigeon-hearted. Suddenly, she was asking his advice about her business problems which were getting to be beyond a joke. Not that he was much help, didn't have your organizational flair, poor darling.'

'So he was just beginning to have her to himself when he died.' Howard could see the romance in this.

Aurora pressed her lips together. 'A bit late in the day for marital bliss. It was a sham of a marriage and he lived

275

with it for my sake. I want a real marriage for him, as much as anything else.'

'You sure?' Howard's quick eyes fixed themselves on her set face. 'You sure you're not marrying me to get even with Zanna?' His voice shook a little. All the plans they had made: three children, a swing at the far end of the garden, regular attendance at synagogue. Did Aurora want them just to set herself up as a living reproof to Zanna and her pagan ways? His hands felt clammy. He loved Aurora but she was behaving like someone whose emotional circuit wasn't fixed up properly, obsessed by her parents' marriage, which showed that she wasn't ready to start her own. He kept his eyes on the orange bars of the fire. 'Maybe it wouldn't hurt to think things over,' he said sadly.

Aurora's fingertips stiffened with panic. She couldn't lose Howard. Not now, when the pattern of her life depended on his alert tenderness, the way his black curls shook with light.

She got up and stood over his chair. She bent over him so that his sloping nose was nudged into the perfect space between her perfect breasts. 'Stay with me tonight, Howard,' she said, and her voice was lower than usual, almost a coarse growl.

Chapter Twenty-Two

'Never? Really? Aurora's letting Howard dip the pink candle before the wedding day? I'm hugely surprised.' Suzette was still in bed at three in the afternoon. She had been boozing moodily under the blankets but now sat up, listening to Zanna who was sizzling with news.

'Isn't it astounding?' Zanna said. 'Aurora's such a prig, you'd have thought shagging her fiancé was out of the question, an act of the vilest depravity. Lilian will be spinning in her grave,' she added gleefully. 'Mind you, there must be a reason for it; Aurora never does anything without a reason.'

'Maybe she just couldn't wait,' Suzette said. 'Howard's a real hunk of meat, absolutely *swoonsome*, the cat's bollocks. He's the merchandise, all right.'

'You finished, Suze? Nice looking, I grant you, but absolutely no depths. Talking to him is like exploring a basin. The conversation flows like glue. Why are you still in bed? Are you ill?'

'Nah. Just cross.' Suzette swung her feet out of bed and into a pair of velvet-and-swansdown mules and reached for her négligé. 'It's Dominick. Some old trout he bought antiques for kicked the bucket and left him enough Swiss bank accounts to buy up a continent.'

'So is he going to?'

'Even more ambitious. He's going to set up home with Marty, and you'll never guess where.'

'A *bijou* mews house behind Peter Jones,' Zanna suggested. 'A too, too terribly sweet Georgian conversion in Hampstead, next to this divine hand laundry that doesn't ruin sleeves.'

'That's where you're wrong. Dominick says he's tired of London; he thinks it's artificial.' Suzette squeezed a worm of gum onto a pair of false eyelashes and stuck them on her lids. 'He's gone and bought Croston Lacey.' She turned her anguished face towards Zanna. 'If he'd told me how much it meant to him, I would never have sold it. I don't like the way the world is, Zanna, the way everything can be flaunted, like that book by Lawrence of Arabia.'

Zanna looked puzzled. '*You* know. The one that trial was about,' Suzette said.

'That was a different Lawrence, blossom. I don't think he went to Arabia much. *Lady Chatterley's Lover*, the book was.'

'That's what I'm saying. Every kind of filthiness is right out in the open. Such a shame. There's something wonderful about a secret.'

Minetta was fuming. She shot venomous glances out of her round, ugly eyes and there was a bitterness around her mouth. 'It's a disgrace,' she snarled. 'It makes a mockery out of a white wedding.' She thumped her handbag onto the table.

'Nice handbag,' said Zanna smoothly, pouring Minetta a cup of tea.

'Gloria Rockman gave it to me,' Minetta said. 'And stop changing the subject.'

'Just the kind I should have chosen myself,' Zanna burbled on, flicking her hands over the bag which Victor Rockman had bought from her a few weeks before. 'Oh, OK, Min; I know you're upset about Aurora and Howard jumping the gun, the twang of the mattress spring has never been music to your ears. But you *must* let Geoffrey

278

give the bride away.' Zanna put her hand on her sister's cushiony shoulder. 'You owe it to Raymond's memory,' she wheedled.

'Aurora's the last girl I'd have imagined taking up with free love.' Minetta grumbled on relentlessly. She was a good woman, who had never learnt how to display her good nature.

'I'm not so sure about the free,' Zanna pondered aloud. 'I think it's more like a down payment Aurora is making, although what the whys and wherefores are, I couldn't say. But nothing could make a mockery out of the white wedding dress I'm getting her; not even if she rogers the English football team on her way up the aisle. Balenciaga. What a genius. He understands that allure depends on mystery, privacy, understatement. And I've got a surprise for you, Min. I want you to come to Paris with us when we go for the fittings. I'm going to buy you a suit for the wedding, to go with your new handbag.'

'How come you're so flush?' Minetta asked suspiciously.

'I've sold this place. An American fashion photographer. Paying an absolutely outrageous price for it too. Chelsea is so *à la page*, these days. It's not the easiest time for me to move, but with the money from the flat, this wedding can be *epic*. And, meanwhile, I can always move into the Connaught for a few weeks.'

'Very economical,' Minetta said sourly. She had a list of grievances as high as the moon. It was so unfair that Zanna, her heathen sister, was able to give her child an Orthodox Jewish wedding, when she, a pillar of her synagogue, had been denied the opportunity.

A year ago, her eldest son, Ivan, on a miserable, cloud-swaddled day, had married Clemency Hubin-Jones. There had been a brief ceremony at Winchester Registry Office, followed by a muted lunch for the immediate family – Geoffrey and Minetta and the Hubin-Joneses: a faded wife and fierce-eyed father – in the private room of a phoney-looking Hampshire pub. Everything about it was an imitation, from the cream on the strawberry tartlets, to the fake beams, winking with brass horse-shoes, that had been stuck onto the low ceiling.

Both sets of parents, silently convinced that their children were ruining their lives, gave each other pained smiles that stretched their lips but didn't reach their accusing eyes. They had all agreed on what Mrs Hubin-Jones called just a nice, quiet family wedding, as though the marriage was something shameful.

Oblivious of their saddened parents and the stringy roast chicken, Ivan and Clemency rubbed their shoulders against each other like nuzzling lion cubs and held hands tightly when Major Hubin-Jones refilled the glasses with tepid champagne and stood up to toast the bride and groom. He spoke of 'the challenges that lay ahead', making it clear that, in his view, this union could not fail to be calamitous. There was universal relief when Clemency and Ivan roared off on Ivan's Harley Davison, bound for the Dover–Calais ferry and a honeymoon on the Riviera. They slept in the pillowy beds of cheap hotels and, inspired by the Mediterranean food they ate – bouillabaisse, salade niçoise, *achhoïade* – on their return, they spent Geoffrey's wedding cheque on a down payment on a bistro at the lower end of the King's Road. The menu strangely but successfully combined the daintiness of Clemency's cordon bleu training with the pungent earthiness of a waterfront café in Marseilles.

Small potatoes, according to Geoffrey. Ivan was just mucking about with his life, giving photographers and models free meals because he liked their company, the boy had no business sense whatsoever. Unlike Howard Sutch, whom, Geoffrey had hinted heavily, he would welcome into his own firm at any time. His high regard for Howard made Minetta feel that she had brought up her own boys wrongly, in such a way that they weren't up to scratch. She felt that Geoffrey blamed her for not having produced a son like Howard, who was thin and eager with a breezy self-assurance. Howard, who had never known a mother's ruinous love, had turned out better than her own mollycoddled sons, or so Geoffrey suggested by the respectful way he grasped Howard's hand.

Minetta should have been consoled that Aurora, whom she had always loved as much as her own children, was making such a suitable marriage, but this wedding had stopped being a consolation weeks ago, ever since she had found out that Aurora and Howard were sleeping together. It had shocked Minetta deeply to see Howard's shirts dancing on the washing-line in what had been her mother's back garden. She had called round one day, knowing Howard and Aurora to be at Chipperton, to tidy up the flower-beds a bit; something she had always done in Lilian's time and which had become a habit. Another shock: the Mançeur children were to be Aurora's bridesmaid and page. Zanna had mentioned it airily just the other day, as though it were of no significance, making Minetta quiver with rage. She felt humiliated by her own lack of sophistication; she should have got over that unimportant fling of Geoffrey's by now, she knew that. What rankled as much was the way Zanna got on so well with Rabbi Solomon, an old friend of the Fadges, whose synagogue, one of the oldest in Chipperton, was where Howard and Aurora had chosen to be married.

'A jewel, your sister,' the rabbi had beamed at Minetta, when she saw him at the Bar Mitzvah of Victor and Gloria Rockman's oldest grandson. 'Such eyes I never saw. Purple light streams out of them.'

'Don't tell me she's joining your congregation.' Minetta was astonished. Zanna, sitting respectably in the women's gallery on Saturday mornings? Impossible to imagine.

'Most unlikely.' The rabbi was quick to reassure her. 'She says she thinks so little of God, she won't give Him the satisfaction of believing in Him. Such candour. I'll miss our little talks once the wedding is over.' He toddled off to congratulate the Rockmans.

Minetta knew perfectly well why Zanna was offering to take her to Paris and buy her an expensive outfit: she was trying to make amends for everything that she had taken away from Minetta in the past. It was because of Zanna that Geoffrey had met Natalie, Ivan had clapped eyes on Clemency. Whenever Minetta had lost someone she loved, there was Zanna, always Zanna. A bit late in the day for concern, Minetta thought grimly. And that solicitous look in the violet eyes, so admired by Rabbi Solomon, didn't help. The one thing she would have liked from her younger sister was envy. She had thought after Raymond's death that her own circumstances, that of a solidly married matron with no financial worries and a sumptuously furnished house, might nettle Zanna just a bit. But it was obvious that Zanna, although widowed, her business in decline, found Minetta slightly ridiculous, as she had always done. She'd accept Zanna's offer of a trip to Paris though. Zanna wouldn't be able to scoff at what she was wearing, if she'd chosen and paid for it.

Howard insisted on paying for the wedding, even though Zanna had sold the Chelsea flat and had some cash in hand. 'You should be saving that for your old age,' he said tactlessly.

'Why not say what you really mean, that you're on the up and up and I'm going downhill?' Zanna snapped at him.

Howard shrugged his shoulders. 'So as not to offend you, but since I've put my foot in it anyway, that *is* what I meant. Look, you'll bounce back, no doubt about it, then you'll need a bit of dosh,' Howard went on, more kindly. 'Meanwhile, let me take care of the bills. Have whatever you like. Money no object.'

How smug and bumptious he sounded, just like Geoffrey Fadge. No wonder Geoffrey thought the sun shone out of Howard's arse. 'It's not the thing at all,' she said. Then, thinking that she'd be able to settle with her blockmaker, who had threatened legal proceedings, 'But if you insist.'

'I do. And here's what Aurora insists on: invites to everyone at Utley Lodge, and she means everyone.'

'Why Harry?' Zanna asked Aurora that evening, as they studied the menus submitted by six Kosher catering firms. 'You've never liked him.'

'It would upset Leonora and Daisy if I left him out, and I'd never do that. They loved Daddy so much.'

'Don't borrow trouble,' Zanna said warningly.

'I already have. I sent out the invitations yesterday.'

'You're becoming rather charmingly ruthless,' Zanna said admiringly.

'It runs in the family, on the maternal side.' Mother and daughter shone identical, wide-mouthed smiles onto each other's faces.

The reception was to be held on the terrace of Suzette's flat with everything, down to the last teaspoon, supplied by a Kosher caterer.

'These menus are so insipid,' Zanna said. 'Melon and chicken, chicken and melon. I wish Clemency and Ivan could do it.'

'Out of the question and you know it. Clemency's lobster bisque and *médaillons de porc* will have to wait for another celebration,' Aurora said meaningfully.

The vein in Zanna's forehead started to bump. 'Aurora, I know what you're playing at,' she said. 'But you can't manipulate us all like this. We're not characters in a novel.'

Right up until the end of the war, there had been a dozen or more weddings in Chipperton every Sunday afternoon. Even though The Great Synagogue, built in 1772, gorgeously gilded, its walls swagged with plaster garlands, was destroyed in a bombing raid in May 1941, other synagogues survived the bombs, and wartime brides flocked to them, wearing dresses made from stolen parachute silk or a satin curtain. Between the ceremony and the reception, the brides raced across the street, holding up their skirts above the grimy pavements, new husbands in tow, to have their wedding day immortalized by one of the great East End photographers: J. Suss, Henry Shaw of the Rembrandt Studio and, most famous of them all, Boris Bennett, whose premises were fronted by a uniformed doorman and whose backdrops were equal to any in Hollywood.

Weddings were Sunday entertainments for the people of Chipperton, who lined the streets to appraise the bride, as the wedding party moved from the steps of the synagogue towards the hubbub of the Whitechapel Road, past old women selling bagels from deep baskets, past the delicatessens and soup kitchens, the furriers and the last surviving blacksmith.

There were fewer weddings in Chipperton in 1962. The Jewish population of the East End had prospered and moved out to placid suburban villas in Ilford, Edgware and Stanmore. Pantiled prisons, according to Zanna Gringrich, who found the quiet avenues, lined with cherry-trees, far more loathsome than Chipperton's tenements, since she had never understood the attraction of tranquillity.

Zanna was on her way to Rabbi Solomon's synagogue to make some sketches to give to the florist she had booked for Aurora's wedding. She planned to drape very fine muslin over the windows so that the light inside the synagogue would be softly filtered. At the end of every row of seating there would be a white rose-bush in a tub, wreathed with a white organza bow. Leaf-covered trellises would form three archways along the central aisle and guests would be given baskets of real rose petals to scatter in the bride and groom's path. Afterwards, the flowers would be given to the London Jewish Hospital.

At least there's a bit of life in this old dump, Zanna thought, as she walked with her light step along Chipperton's filthy streets. She stopped to watch a street entertainer, an escapologist, grunt his way out of his bounds of old sacking and rusted chains, and threw half-a-crown into the cap he held out. In Fashion Street, she could hear the gnat-like whir of sewing-machines

284

through the open windows of clothing factories. In them, furs were stretched, braid was embroidered and hats were blocked and steamed as they had been for four centuries. In her Mayfair workroom, Zanna had a photograph of two Edwardian milliners, neighbours of her grandparents, standing outside the sweatshop where they worked, wearing stiffened straw hats piled with improbable silk roses. The photograph reminded her of how far she had come, with her West End showroom, titled clients and Chelsea flat. Recently, it seemed more like a warning of how far she could fall if her luck didn't change. She could be put out of business at the drop of a hat.

Rabbi Solomon watched Zanna measure the synagogue's windows. She moved briskly with no sense of awe. It saddened him that she saw his synagogue as just a space to be prettified for a day, and that, after that day, he wouldn't see her again. He cleared his throat and Zanna whirled round. From her handbag, she produced a box of Schimmelpenninck, the Dutch cigarillos that the rabbi loved.

'That such an ungodly woman should be so generous.' The rabbi shook his head but smiled into Zanna's eyes.

'You're trying to wear me down,' she said. 'It won't do any good. Here, take the other end of this tape-measure.'

Rabbi Solomon, like Natalie Mançeur, had spent part of the war in a concentration camp. He had survived because, although a young boy, he had been able to do a man's work – digging the graves of those with less strength than he had. He looked over Zanna's shoulder as she made quick sketches, admiring the drawings that caught the staid, pleasing atmosphere of the Victorian interior. 'How do you live without faith?' he asked her gently. 'Believe me, this is not a criticism. I'm interested. It is not something I could sustain.'

'Sure you could,' Zanna said, closing her sketchpad. 'You just go on going on. Nothing to it.'

'You endure?'

'That's not the word I would use. It implies something serious, which I have learnt never to be. I refuse to walk into a world of grief.'

'So you never think about what happened to those like me?'

'No. That would make me feel as though I'd been dead many times over and learnt every secret of the grave.' Zanna hitched her soft leather bag of drawing materials over her shoulder. 'I try never to remember anything unpleasant,' she said. Then, because the rabbi looked stricken, she added, 'Who are we all anyway? Only stories we tell ourselves, and I want mine to have a happy ending. Let's decide on the music, shall we? I want this wedding to be right off the charts, as my future son-in-law would put it.'

One warm Wednesday morning, Daisy Fitzhaven walked clompily into Zanna's shop, inappropriately dressed for Mayfair in a mannish shirt made of thick cotton and her old denim skirt, her glasses glittering on her nose. She gave Zanna a shamefaced smile. 'Aurora insisted I came here to buy a hat for her wedding. And, even if she hadn't, I shouldn't have known where else to look.'

'Aurora has become a world-class manipulator,' Zanna said. 'Still, it's lovely to see you, Daisy. What are you going to be wearing?'

'The Hartnell dress and coat that you helped me choose when Acton Fordyce took me to a garden party at Buckingham Palace.' Zanna looks just the same, Daisy thought, sleek and expensive and a little high-hat. But something's changed. She has an unused look that wasn't there before, and there's an icy melancholy in her smile.

'Lawdie-Gawdie, Daisy,' Zanna said, laughing in her old, coarse way, 'you bought that dress in the early nineteen-fifties. Frocks aren't like antique furniture, you know. You're not supposed to preserve them. Every so often, it's considered the right thing to go out and buy a new one.'

'I shouldn't dream of it,' Daisy protested. 'I've only just begun to feel comfortable in the Hartnell.'

'Wait till I tell Norman that his frocks have to be broken in like horses.'

'They wouldn't have to be if they had elasticized waistbands,' Daisy said amiably. 'Mother wants me to get her a hat too. She's going to wear her good Mattli coat with the diamond brooch.'

'It must be a *very* good Mattli coat; Leonora was wearing it in 1947, the first time I met her, and it wasn't new then. Well, I've the perfect hat for her. Hang on here a minute, Daisy. Have a browse through this copy of *Vogue*. There's an article on how to put on eyeliner that you'll find absolutely spellbinding, I don't think.'

Zanna disappeared into the back of the shop and came back, a few minutes later, carrying one of her own hatboxes, not new, the bright pink faded by time and sunlight.

'I want Leonora to have this.' She lifted out a dramatic cartwheel of a hat; the brim a swirl of ostrich feathers, each quill spangled with a *diamanté* drop. 'It's Hope Is The Thing With Feathers; this is what drew Leonora into Zanna Modes that year when I had to wash the windows in champagne because of the water shortage. It's part of the story: the hat that launched a hundred heartaches. S'only right that Leonora should give it an airing at last. Go on, Daisy, take it, it's a present.' Zanna blew the quills into shape with her shiny red lips. 'That hat brought me a lot of happiness one way and another.'

'Oh Zanna.' Daisy subsided onto a stiff little sofa and began to snivel. 'You still hang the moon on Harry, don't you?'

'Sad but true. How is he?'

'Not right at all. There's a dangerous sort of loneliness about him. The flow of power is so very far away from where he is.'

They didn't speak for a while, both of them remembering a younger Harry, rakish and dishevelled, making speeches on the future of socialism in a voice that was

287

both poised and inflamed. They sighed in unison and then laughed at themselves.

'Do you know what Harry reminds me of now?' Daisy asked in a miserable voice. 'A bored god who the fates have obscurely thwarted. He *will* keep on remembering the Attlee years as a golden time, instead of a dreary seediness that has no appeal today.'

'Oh, it had its moments,' Zanna said. She remembered climbing the stairs to Harry's flat, carrying a brown paper bag of overpriced peaches, Harry behind her, his hands lightly slapping her thighs. She must stop this, yanking her memories to the surface. It was seeing Daisy again that had got her going. Not that she needed an excuse.

She skimmed about the shop, opening cupboards and drawers, and hooked out a length of tangerine silk, exactly the same colour as Daisy's ancient Hartnell. 'You could do with a bit of streamlining,' she said, her squirrel's paws raking through Daisy's rough, untidy hair. 'And don't even think about keeping your glasses on when you're wearing this.' She draped the piece of silk over Daisy's head, her scratched hands scraping Daisy's cheeks as she turned and twisted it into a turban shape that rose into a pleated cockade. There was a wild, satisfied look on her face as she worked, the way there had been that day at Utley Lodge, when Zanna had raided Leonora's old finery with her ragpicker's fingers and made Daisy a hat from a pair of torn lace gloves.

'Yes, that's the right shape, definitely,' Zanna said, taking the silk off Daisy's head, where it slithered magically into a length of material again. 'I'll get it made up for you.'

'Where's Mrs Harris?' Daisy asked. It had always been Mrs Harris who had presided over the order book, her eyebrows swooping in improbable arcs and her permed hair as hard as varnish.

'Mrs Harris has gone to a far, far better place,' Zanna said. 'Daydream Dresses. Your pal Howard has made her a supervisor, to strike terror in the hearts of all his cheeky little machinists. I couldn't afford her any more; business is rather slack, to put it mildly. To tell the truth, Daisy, I'm going nowhere slowly, but keep it under your hat, there's a dear.' She smiled at Daisy and shrugged her beautiful shoulders. 'Have you ever seen a bigger mess – La Desirous not knowing where to turn? I just can't see the signs.'

'Zanna, I can't believe that. You've always had something to say about the way people should look.' Daisy felt uncomfortable. She hadn't foreseen this: Zanna brought down so low. Harry had been the one she'd feared for, once that strange love affair had ended; he had been so in need of Zanna's love, love that was like an act of war. She hadn't thought that a woman as unprincipled as Zanna could be broken. Perhaps she wouldn't have acted so harshly if she had known. She and Mother had always said that the key to Zanna's character was that she was spectacularly untouched by guilt, that was part of her sunny allure. We assumed too readily that nothing could break her heart, Daisy thought, full of remorse.

'Don't look at me in that pitying way, Daisy,' Zanna said. 'I'll pull something out of the hat one of these days. Never underestimate the stubbornness of hope.'

Chapter Twenty-Three

Suzette decided that she'd go to Paris too; she'd heard of a
wonderful cosmetic surgeon who practised on l'Avenue
Foch. 'At our age, you have to buy into beauty, don't
you?' she confided to Minetta over a Pernod. They were
sitting at an outdoor café in Montparnasse, pigeons
rumbling around on the cobblestones at their feet.

'I never had it as a gift, at any age,' Minetta sighed. The
Pernod had gone to her head. It tasted delicious, like the
speckly aniseed balls she had sucked as a child, but
she'd had too many glasses; Suzette's silvery-blond
head was moving across her eyes like a fuzzy comet.

'A holiday from reality,' Zanna had called this trip but
Minetta was unnerved by the city's beauty; it was like
walking into a dream. They had gone to Balmain, where
she had sat on a satin chair while the house mannequins, thin girls with brittle, undirected eyes,
swished exotically across the floor in clothes that
Minetta thought could not possibly be adapted to fit
her own lumpy body. She shrank inside her polyester
dress that had a squiggly pattern and too many darts.
Zanna had chosen a suit for her in a soft rose-pink wool
and what Zanna called easy lines. 'This'll sit lightly, Min,
skim over the bulges,' she decided, delivering her sister to
an unsmiling *vendeuse* who made Minetta feel as though

290

she were being prepared for her own execution. She had drawn in her stomach as the tape-measure was guided around her hips, in an agony that the two metal-capped ends might not meet. Sweat had trickled down the insides of her punishing corset. Afterwards, she'd agreed to go to Montparnasse with Suzette just to get away from Zanna's glinty-eyed amusement.

Suzette wished she hadn't brought up the subject of beauty. She took one of Minetta's hands in her own. 'You've beautiful hands,' she said consolingly, 'smooth as a baby's bum.'

It was true. Minetta's hands were pink and dimpled, her nails rosy. 'My mother gave me a little manicure case when Zanna was born – a present, so I wouldn't be jealous of the new baby. I suppose that was the reason. I loved that little case. Real pigskin with a nail file and a thing to push down your cuticles, and a shammy buffer, all with pearlized handles and special leather loops to fit them into. I used to spend hours filing and buffing with all the gee-gaws.'

'So that stopped you feeling jealous?'

'Course not. From the day she was born she made me feel like an onion growing next to an orchid. I'd have murdered her with my own hands, only I didn't want to spoil them. I gave the manicure set to Robbie, once I knew I wasn't going to have a daughter of my own.' Minetta waggled her pretty fingers, pleased with Suzette's wide-eyed scrutiny of the diamond eternity ring that Geoffrey had bought her when she'd been a bit down in the dumps after Ivan's wedding. 'Robbie's made good use of it too. Her hands always look immaculate, even though she's a bit of a scruff, or was until Howard got *his* hands on her.' She gave a short, rather brutal laugh and babbled on tipsily. 'Robbie doesn't care what she looks like because Zanna always made too much fuss about clothes.' She imitated Zanna's coarse, low growl. ' "Do take that sodding bow off, darling, decoration betrays. We *are* what we wear, sweetie-pie." Never could keep her hands nice though. Robbie made a point of looking after hers, just to prove how different she was.' Minetta drained the last of her Pernod. 'Not that she is,' she said bitterly. 'Like mother, like daughter.'

Blimey, Suzette thought. Something's eating poor old Min. I don't know why she resents Zanna so much – all she did was invent another world for herself because she didn't like the one she lived in. Len and I did that too. Time to change the subject, I think. She prodded Minetta's arm. 'Look at those guys in the leather trousers, they must have needed a shoehorn to get them on. They certainly let you know what a man is thinking, no mistake about that.'

Back in the Hotel George V, Minetta sobered up. She decided to have a bath before dinner and spent an hour in the bathroom that glinted with crystal and had piles of towels as big as carpets. She was backcombing her hair, the way that her hairdresser, Monsieur Ricky of Hendon, had shown her, when Zanna rang from the next room, saying that the wedding dress had arrived and did she want to see Aurora try it on.

It was the colour of heavy cream; rich silk, unembellished. No sleeves to speak of and a narrow, square-cut train falling away from the straight skirt. It was perfect, or would have been, had Aurora not been standing so slackly that she looked like a dejected doll, the look in her eyes dull and far away. Zanna prodded her impatiently in the back to make her straighten up but, instead, Aurora bent forward, her shiny bell of hair drooping over her face which she covered with her hands. 'I'm pregnant,' she wailed through her long fingers.

Zanna gave the train a yank. 'What a nuisance,' she growled. 'I could cut your head off and pee in your skull. This means we're going to have to ask Balenciaga to take the whole skirt apart again to give it some extra ease.'

Mother and daughter glared at each other until distracted by the sound of an outraged Minetta gulping in air. 'What's the matter with *you*, Min?' Zanna asked roughly. 'The world's not going to stop turning just because your niece got herself knocked up.'

'It's a saving really,' Suzette said. 'It's so big, I won't have to replace the wallpaper for ages.'

Suzette and Zanna were in a small but very serious art gallery near the Faubourg St Honoré, where Suzette was about to buy a large portrait of a naked woman by Pierre Bonnard. The nude had long, full thighs and small, slack breasts. Her head was modestly bowed and she slumped against a tiled wall in a dozy attitude. To Zanna, the painting lacked energy; she preferred the Toulouse-Lautrec next to it: a café scene full of prostitutes and dancers with sly, mocking eyes and taut shoulders. But she agreed with Suzette that the sunlit colours of the Bonnard would add a cheerful note to the Grosvenor Square flat, which was looking a bit neglected since Dominick's departure. The rosy brocades on the sofas had slit and some of the Meissen monkeys had got chipped by the cleaning-woman who, freed from Dominick's quivering supervision, had grown careless, doing the dusting in a desultory way, a cigarette wedged in the corner of her mouth, which Dominick would never have allowed.

'Madame may like a little time to think it over,' the gallery owner said silkily. 'It is an important purchase.'

'No. I'll take it,' Suzette said. 'I loathe thinking things over. Strike while the ice is cold is what I say.'

In the street, heads dipped against the tearing wind which had unexpectedly got up and was shredding the corners of paper cloths on café tables, Zanna asked, 'Where are you going to hang it?'

'Smack over the arch opposite the front door. Nice and welcoming.'

'Do me a favour and don't put it up until after the wedding. If Minetta gets an eyeful of pubic hair the minute she steps through the door, she won't forgive me until the crack of doom.'

Suzette clamped a hand to her jaw. 'Heavens. The wedding reception. Minetta and Geoffrey. The rabbi. Howard's *bank* manager. I wasn't thinking about it at the time, the way you don't. So what we do is tell Mr Fancy-Pansy to hang on to his Bonnard for a month. Then I'll borrow a couple of Constables from Dominick and Marty for the big day. Cows, clouds, not a pussy in sight. You'll see how seemly I can be, Zanna, when I really push the ship out.'

The day before her wedding, Aurora Gringrich brought a suitcase with her going-away clothes in it to Suzette Riddick's flat in Grosvenor Square. It was raining and Suzette was on the telephone to Dominick, in Shropshire, begging him to come to London right away and put up the complicated glass roof that could be cranked out over the terrace in bad weather. Suzette was wearing dark glasses and sipped from a glass of what looked like neat whisky, not her usual drink. 'Please, angel-drawers. You're the only person on this earth who knows how to work it. How the hell can you be sure it won't rain tomorrow? Well, if you say so, but, if you're wrong, I'll give you a sock on the moosh, and I'm not joking.'

She put down the receiver, turned towards Aurora and whipped off her glasses. 'How do I look?' she asked.

The lines under her eyes and around her mouth had been smoothed away and her skin had a gloss on it, like the skin of a ripe plum. The French cosmetic surgeon had lived up to his reputation, although it had to be admitted that a certain tightness about the chin gave the impression that Suzette's six-stranded pearl necklace was choking her.

'Expensive,' Aurora decided.

'That'll do,' Suzette said. 'The problem is that I have to stop drinking, or my costly new face will get pickled.' She waved her glass. 'Iced tea,' she said. 'Like actors drink on the stage. Doesn't do a thing for me.' She squinted out of the window. 'A dreadful evening but

Dominick predicts sunshine tomorrow, so we can all rest easy in our chairs. He's a gentleman farmer now, you know. What he doesn't know about rotation crops you could write on your toenail.' She gave a yawn that ended in a yowl, like a cat's. 'Hope he's right. Happy the bride the sun shines on, and all that.'

'That's not what's important, Suzette,' Aurora said in that priggish way of hers that always made Suzette want to pull faces. 'It's not the wedding that counts but the marriage.'

'Aurora, if you weren't the daughter of my very best friend, I'd say you were insufferable. Any other girl would be thrilled to have a Balenciaga wedding dress and her photograph taken by Cecil Beaton. But, oh no, not Miss Po-Face.'

'The wedding is for Mummy; she's the party-goer of the family.' Aurora pressed her lips together.

'Oh, you silly tart,' Suzette said, exasperated. She felt sick, a symptom of alcohol withdrawal. 'You've set yourself an agenda to be all the things that Zanna isn't. She fills the world with colour, so you reduce it to sludge. Why are you so frightened of fun?'

'Fun's dangerous,' Aurora said. 'Leads to chaos. You must have found that out, Suzette.' She took her going-away suit out of the case. It had been designed by Howard and made up at the Daydream factory, a present to Aurora from all the staff. Apricot linen hopsack with a loose jacket, pleats falling from a V-shaped yoke at the back.

'Unusual cut,' Suzette conceded.

'Unusual circumstances,' Aurora said with a mysterious smile, going to hang it up in what had once been Leonard's dressing-room.

Suzette followed her in and sat down on Leonard's buttoned-leather swivel-chair. 'Zanna said that it was your idea to invite Harry Welliver,' she said. 'What's your game?'

'You've always been a fun-lover, Suzette. I thought I'd give you some.'

Aurora went on unpacking in her plodding way that Suzette found irksome. She watched the girl move between suitcase and wardrobe, a heavy patience in every step, just like Raymond, who had irked her too, poor soul, except when he danced, whirling gracefully on the tips of his heels.

Aurora arranged her underwear on the narrow day-bed: white broderie anglaise bra, suspender belt and rather substantial knickers, seamless nylons. Surely she'd put on a bit of weight, Suzette thought, no doubt just to annoy Zanna as the invitation to Harry must have done. 'My guess is, you've invited Harry just to rattle your mother,' she said nastily.

Aurora put her going-away shoes tidily beside the bed. 'You've got the plot wrong,' she said. 'I want them back together again. Both their careers are falling into ruin; their only chance of happiness in old age is to prop each other up. They'll always be stars to each other even if the world forgets them, which it might. I really resent these accusations, Suzette; you were much nicer to me when you drank.'

'I was nicer to everyone when I drank,' Suzette said.

Labour Party supporters shuffled into the Guildhall, smelling of wet Pak-a-Macs and shaking out their umbrellas. They were in sparkling mood in spite of the weather which the voters seemed inclined to blame on the Conservative government. Supermac hadn't delivered the goods. It had been a thoroughly nasty summer of flooded fields and rising unemployment, just the sort of conditions that put people in the mood for a change, or so Daisy Fitzhaven assured Harry as she folded up her plastic rain bonnet and slid it back in its wallet.

Daisy was in high good humour. She had insisted on Harry coming to this event, a lecture by Charlie Belling called 'What's Wrong With Britain', sponsored by one of the commercial television companies. 'Everyone will be there,' she said. 'Even Acton is making the effort.'

It seemed to Harry as he walked to his seat, looking battered and distinguished, that Daisy was becoming skittish in her excited anticipation of a Labour Party victory at the next general election. After Charlie Belling's lecture – the usual anti-Establishment clichés about the ineptitude of the knickerbockered squires who supposedly misruled the country, but forcefully put; Harry had to admit, for a man who had nothing to say, Belling knew how to say it – Daisy scuttled along rows of gilt chairs to shake hands with Charlie's new wife.

A dubious woman, Lucille Belling, Harry thought. Her naked ambition was channelled through Charlie. You could almost feel sorry for the brute; if he failed in his bid to become the next but one party leader, Lucille would soon switch off that swoony gaze of hers.

'You are acting in the most unprincipled way,' he grumbled to Daisy when she returned to his side.

She gave him a stern look. 'There was a time when you didn't complain about a lack of principles.'

'If you're referring to Zanna, she was shady, shifty and an adventuress. You are insincere, which is much worse.'

Acton Fordyce approached, grinning at them with his curved yellow teeth. A slight nod of his head caused the immediate approach of a white-gloved waiter balancing a tray of champagne glasses on the palm of his hand.

'Belling's the coming man, eh, eh, Daisy?' Acton prodded her in his teasing way. 'All set to take the country by the throat. A cool cat, isn't that what they call chaps like him?'

'People of our age, Acton, use perfectly good words such as dynamic and alert, so as not to make asses of themselves.'

Acton's slatted eyes gleamed in their rolls of fat. 'You'd never allow that to happen on your patch, would you, Daisy?' he honked at her. He jerked his head towards Harry, who had wandered towards the back of the hall. 'No-one's allowed to make an ass of himself in your family. They all have to toe the line, eh, eh?'

Daisy flushed. 'Not at all, Acton. I believe very much in personal freedom.'

'So does Charlie Belling. Not a qualm about trading that poor face-ache Beryl for Lucille. Smart lad.' Acton gave a short, hard laugh and dropped the butt of his cigar in the dregs of his champagne, where it made a wet hiss. 'Here's the way I look at it: a good-looking wife is a top political asset, look at Jack Profumo.' He made smacking noises with his lips to indicate his appreciation of the War Minister's elegant wife. 'Harry got any plans then? Thinking of writing his memoirs? I could be interested in the serialization rights.'

'You don't think that Charlie Belling's divorce will hold him back?' Daisy asked, ignoring Acton's last question as he knew she would.

'Nah, nah, not these days. Proves he's a spunky sod. And the Press is all over Lucille. My features editor would sell his skin for her. See that photo of her in a bowling alley in the *Sunday Times* colour supplement? Very contemporary kind of chick, know what I'm saying?'

'Only too well, Acton.' He was saying – Daisy could tell by the malicious smile in his slatted eyes – that her own moral practices no longer applied in these easygoing times. Acton had guessed that she had had something to do with Harry giving up Zanna and was gloating over her.

To calm herself, Daisy thought of the west of Ireland and the way a particular cow loomed around in the field beside the cottage that Daisy returned to every summer.

'Why don't we go on to the Establishment Club?' Acton suggested as Harry rejoined them. 'Have a bit of fun.'

Harry blinked and swayed on his heels, pulled at his cheek. The idea of having fun always left him at a loss. The truth was he didn't know how to without Zanna to guide him. He sloped off again, wide shoulders hunched, a sad, horsy look on his face.

'No thank you, Acton,' Daisy said. 'I loathe satirical cabaret; too much like Berlin in the Thirties.'

Acton hooked another glass of champagne from a passing tray. 'Harry's looking a bit musty. Completely heartbroken is what I've heard.'

'Such a silly expression, completely heartbroken,' Daisy said witheringly. 'No-one's heart breaks just a little.'

'I can see you're in one of your clever moods, Daisy. Maybe the Bellings would like to go on somewhere once Charlie has done the rounds here. What a mover. Did you hear about the time, during an election campaign, when he left his footprints all over a wet cement path? He went right up to the front door, rang the bell, said, "Good evening, I'm your Tory candidate," then ran for his life. The question one has to ask is: is the Labour Party ready for someone so professional and dynamic?'

'Does one? Well, someone else will have to answer it. Good night, Acton.'

Howard was finding dinner at the Fadges' heavy going. He was suffering from what he supposed were pre-wedding nerves: a jittery, detached feeling that he was not quite in his own mind and body. He didn't have much of an appetite and Minetta's roast lamb was winding round his teeth. He couldn't admit this without giving offence. Minetta was a good cook but she served food as though she had made unendurable sacrifices to bring it to the table.

'Howard, another slice?' she pleaded, taking deep breaths as she held the platter towards him.

'Yes, go on, boy, eat up, put some lead in your pencil,' Jonathan jeered coarsely.

Jonathan was jealous of him, Howard knew that. He was a big, awkward boy, high-shouldered like his mother with the same thrust-forward head, like that of a pull-along toy. His clumsiness drove his father nuts, that and the fact that Jonathan had already failed his accountancy exams twice. Tony, a sulky fifteen-year-old, was in the Lake District on a school trip and had refused to come home for his cousin's wedding. Quick to cause arguments, forever feeling hurt and unappreciated, he was equally unsatisfactory in his father's eyes.

Howard reluctantly picked up his knife and fork, the crisp, dark hairs on the top of his hands glinting under the overbright light from the chandelier. Geoffrey beamed at him proudly, as though he and not the unreliable dead gambler, Clifford Sutch, were Howard's father.

Howard was what Lilian would have described as zippy-zappy, Geoffrey thought. The bright glance in his narrow eyes suggested that there was nothing this boy couldn't handle, no problem he couldn't get fixed. Even when he was eating, he squared his shoulders in a purposeful way.

One day Geoffrey would get Howard into his firm. Together they'd dream up new lines – dried fruits, ready-peeled vegetables. Now that more women were going out to work there was a growing demand for convenience foods. Howard had the flair to invent packaged products that would walk off the supermarket shelf straight into the kitchen freezer. So far, he'd resisted Geoffrey's offers, told him the rag trade was in his blood. But fashion was a dicey game. Geoffrey knew more than one manufacturer who'd been caught out with a stockroom full of frocks that had gone out of style before they'd even left the warehouse.

Put it this way, once Howard was married, he'd see that he couldn't afford fancy ideas and that ready-to-cook was more reliable than ready-to-wear. Geoffrey gave Minetta a light slap on the rump as she collected the plates, forgetting, as he contemplated the rosy future of Fadge & Sutch, that she didn't much care for that sort of thing.

There were no convenience foods in Minetta's kitchen. Minetta believed with all her heart that women who

300

used cake mixes didn't really love their families. She rearranged a crystallized violet on top of the whipped cream that covered her homemade fruit trifle. The lemon meringue pie was homemade too, from her own recipe that called for nine egg yolks and double the usual amount of butter in the pastry. Where was the harm? With good food, the more of it the better.

Howard hadn't eaten much though, Minetta thought, licking cream from her fingers. Perhaps he was feeling uneasy about going through this farce of a white wedding. Not that he was to blame. Men were animals, it was in their nature. It was up to women not to give in to their demands unless there was absolutely no way out of it, and certainly not before the wedding day. Minetta was still shocked by Aurora's pregnancy but her disapproval was mixed with glee that the result of it would be to make Zanna a grandmother. She had taken to showing Zanna knitting patterns for bonnets and bootees and asking her which 'granny' preferred. She had suggested that maybe 'granny' should sell the Alfa Romeo, the white BAT 7, designed by Franco Scaglione, that was Zanna's pride and joy, and get an estate car that would be safer for 'baby'. Zanna had said that if 'baby' objected to the Alfa, 'baby' could sodding well stay home. Furthermore, if Minetta breathed a word to anyone, Zanna would kick the tripes out of her; not even Suzette had been told. But her wide mouth had looked pinched, her eyes too glittery. Placidly, Minetta wheeled in the dessert trolley; the ribbing on her jumper stretched and flattened out over her hips as she leant over to slice the pie.

Howard looked at the glossy whorls of meringue on his plate and ran his tongue over his teeth nervously. After he'd got through the slice of pie, which seemed to be about the same size as a section of a cartwheel, he'd be expected to try the trifle. In this brightly lit house, squatting behind gilt-tipped railings, he felt weighed down by more than the food. The place was a graceless hole. Was this what family life was all about? An atmosphere of resentment and boredom smothered by an excess of material comforts which couldn't disguise the dreadful frailty of marriage? Would the day come when he and Auroradorable sat at the table talkative but cagey, in an orgy of dislike? Would their baby become another Jonathan, an insolent deadbeat? Howard pushed away the thought and his plate, shaking his head apologetically at Minetta.

No, he'd never make the same mistake as Geoffrey. There was a guy who hadn't put by enough time to love his wife, and it had wiped the glow off her. Howard was going to keep Aurora glowing. He'd made a good start; in bed, she stretched out her body for him as though it were labelled 'ready-to-enjoy', like a box of Geoffrey's raisins. She was a generous lover, sometimes so generous that Howard felt like a spoilt little boy being indulged by a doting nursemaid.

Every night, he plunged and tore ecstatically at Aurora's warm body with its sweet, biscuity smell and, after his climax, would see her face swim into view, her smile calm and gentle as she reached up to stroke his hair. She was a solemn, serious girl; that was why he had fallen in love with her. So what if she didn't get carried away? He would love her into a state of rapture, however long it took.

Refusing Jonathan's offer of a night on the town, he retired to the Fadges' guest-room, uncomfortably over-fed, the backs of his eyes burning. He nosed into the pile of fat pillows and, in his uneasy sleep, put out his hand to touch Aurora's shiny hair, whimpering when he felt its absence. Across the corridor, Minetta had wound her hair on spiked rubber rollers, so that Geoffrey could not have come anywhere near her, even had he wanted to.

Aurora let herself into the Golders Green house where Zanna was going to spend the night with her and help her dress in the morning. From the living-room came the heart-tugging sound of Frank Sinatra singing 'My One and Only Love'.

Zanna was sitting cross-legged on the floor, the vein on her temple bumping under her skin, her squirrel's paws scrabbling among wild grasses, silk poppies and wired spirals of satin.

'Here I am, labouring in the salt-mines of technique,' she called out. 'Come here and try it on.'

She laid the delicate wreath on her daughter's hair.

'Oh, this is lovely,' Aurora said, fingering one of the cream poppies. 'It's like something out of a story.'

'Yup. Inspiration decided to pay me a visit, finally,' Zanna said. 'The story must be the one about Demeter and Persephone; there's a hint of the fertility goddess in this head-dress, don't you think?' They both snickered delightedly.

Aurora took off the head-dress carefully and her face clouded. 'Just as long as Rabbi Solomon won't feel we've been deceiving him all along.'

'After what he's been through? I think it's safe to say that he'll be able to take your expansive morals in his stride.' Zanna began to tidy away her materials. 'I'm the one who's shocked to the core. First of all you anticipate marriage, as they put it so nicely in *Woman's Own*. Then you throw in a bit of unprotected nookie as well. I keep hearing that we're moving into a more permissive age but I never thought *you* would. I thought you'd be the last holy-arse left on earth.'

Aurora said, 'I had this feeling that Howard wanted to leave me. I just had to bind him to me; I didn't think I could manage to go on living without him. I started the baby on purpose.'

Zanna took Aurora's head between her hands and kissed her hair. 'You were quite right then,' she said comfortingly. 'When it comes to holding on to the man you love, no trick is too mean. Not that he would ever have walked out on you. You stand first in his heart, believe me, I know the signs.'

She disengaged herself and smoothed her skirt over her hips. 'I brought round a hamper from Fortnum's, full of things we can eat with our fingers. Put another record on, not anything about girls called Peggy Sue, if you don't mind. And no electric guitars.'

As they were eating brandied cherries straight from the jar with teaspoons, Aurora said, 'The story of Persephone was all about a mother losing her daughter.'

'She got her back for half the year,' Zanna said, licking her spoon. 'That was probably long enough.'

'Another story,' Christabel Mançeur begged her father. She was too excited to sleep. Tomorrow she was going to be a bridesmaid. She was going to put on a pink dress that had two petticoats underneath. She was going to wear a straw hat with streamers. She was going to carry a basket full of rose petals and she was going to be allowed to keep the basket afterwards for ever and ever. She was going to hold her brother Bruno's hand very tightly and they were going to walk behind Aurora who was going to be a bride. Left foot. Feet together. Right foot. Feet together. If Bruno made a mistake, she was going to squeeze his hand until his knuckles clicked.

Beside her on the pillow was her bridesmaid's present from Howard: a doll dressed in a tiny version of Christabel's bridesmaid's dress, with the same stiff petticoats, a straw hat and even a tiny basket filled with rose petals, made from scraps of silk, each one hand-hemmed.

'Read me *The Little Wooden Horse Goes To A Wedding*,' she wheedled. Jean-Louis settled his weighty body on his child's bed, inhaled her bedtime smell of Vinolia talcum powder and ironed Liberty lawn and began to read. Christabel was asleep before her father brought the Little Wooden Horse to the end of his journey, lulled by the chugging rhythm inside her head. Left foot. Feet together. Right foot. Feet together. Left foot . . . 'For I am a quiet little horse and for ever after I shall be rather a dull one,' Jean-Louis read the last sentence to himself. He tiptoed out of the room, looking forward to a quiet, dull dinner with his wife.

When Harry and Daisy left the Guildhall, they went back to Great Windmill Street, not wanting to disturb Leonora, who would have already gone to bed in Daisy's flat in Victoria.

Harry's sitting-room looked more neglected than ever: books with cracked, ribbed spines lay face downwards on the dusty rug like piles of dead birds, and an island of mould floated on the top of a mug of cold coffee on the mantelpiece. Daisy wrinkled her nose. 'Let's get a bite of supper at the Dudley. We could still get a table.'

Harry pulled at his cheek so hard that he left scarlet thumb-prints on it. 'No, not there,' he said curtly. It was over a year since he'd been to the restaurant in Conduit Street, where he'd been a regular customer since before the war. He'd found that he couldn't look at the table-cloth without recalling Zanna's long, ruched gloves lying on it or, even though the banquettes had long since been recovered in a Regency-striped brocade, get out of his mind her head under its shiny straw hat leaning against the scuffed post-war Rexine, or the way she had squinted expectantly at him through the smoky veil she blew from her cigarette.

'If you don't want to eat out, I'll see what I can rummage up here,' Daisy said. She found a brown paper bag of eggs in the fridge, brought back from Utley Lodge the weekend before and none of them eaten in the meantime, and a tin of ham.

'The way you live, Harry,' she complained, shouting to him from the kitchen. 'No bread, no butter. The eggs will have to be poached, which won't be nearly as nice as having them fried. There's something snivelly about a poached egg. Ah, here's an interesting find.' Daisy was rootling around the back of the shelves which were covered in scummy oilcloth held down with rusted tacks. 'A jar of potted rillettes of pork, probably perfectly good underneath all this black muck on the lid. This will jazz things up a bit.'

Harry loped into the kitchen and peered at the jar. 'Zanna brought that back from France, years ago, when meat was rationed. Probably smuggled it past customs. We were never in the mood to eat it, somehow; what we really liked were cold baked beans straight from the tin.'

'You've never fallen out of love with her,' Daisy accused him miserably. Harry began to attack the ham with an almost useless tin-opener. 'Zanna could make a dead man fall in love with her and stay that way. She's preposterous, I know, you don't have to remind me.'

'I wasn't going to.'

'I should never have listened to you when you did, you know.'

'No. You shouldn't have. It was a sign of your weakness.'

'Zanna is my under-history,' Harry said, as though explaining this to himself.

He ate the watery ham and poached eggs unenthusiastically. Daisy had put the jar of rillettes back on the shelf. Although she was quite hungry, they had suddenly become the least appetizing thing in the world.

Outside, they could hear the rain slosh into the guttering. 'Drive me home, Harry, would you?' Daisy asked as soon as they had drunk some vile coffee. 'I won't find a taxi in this weather.'

Harry saw her up to the tiny lobby of her flat. Almost filling it, perched on a coathook, was the black cartwheel hat, spangled with *diamanté* drops. Harry screwed up his eyes. He knew about this hat, had seen it before, but where? When? It had to do with something important that had happened to him.

'Gilly's hat,' Daisy whispered, although Leonora was too deaf to have been woken up even if Daisy had shouted to the rooftops. 'Hope Is The Thing With Feathers. The hat Gomer made her relinquish, as I made you relinquish Zanna. My dear, my dear, I was wrong. Start again with her. Take a chance.'

'The time for taking chances has passed,' Harry said. He always spoke in a politician's platitudes when he was at his most uncertain.

'Nonsense. There's life in the old boy yet.' Daisy kissed him on his thin cheek-bone and didn't move from the lobby until she heard the rattling engine of his car start up in the street below.

Zanna took the photograph of Raymond out of her dressing-case. It showed him in his army uniform, his khaki cap at quite a rakish angle but his eyes, as always, bulgy with worry.

'Poor old worryguts,' she murmured. 'You really missed out on this one. Aurora's going to be just the sort of wife you wished I'd been but were too scared to say so, or maybe just too nice. Wish you could have made it, sweets; you would have enjoyed tomorrow more than I think I'm going to.'

Then she thought about seeing Harry again, and her face took on a frozen whiteness. She knew she wasn't going to get any sleep that night. She put the photograph back in her case, collected up her cigarettes and the poetry book she was reading, *The Colossus* by Sylvia Plath. She didn't think she'd find much inspiration in it for naming hats but the few poems she had read so far had intrigued her, they'd be good company to be in as she spent the night in her daughter's old bedroom, waiting for the dawn to lighten the red rooftops of Golders Green.

Chapter Twenty-Four

Dominick had been right about the weather. The early-morning sun shone down on the streets of London, making the pavements glitter. By seven o'clock, Minetta was on the telephone, but Zanna had been up for hours, watching the sun rise, hard and white in the sky.

'It's going to be a shatteringly hot day,' Minetta complained, as though this extraordinary change in the weather was one of Zanna's malicious teases. 'I'll have to leave off the jacket or I'll suffocate.'

'Don't you dare,' Zanna ordered.'The jacket is the whole *point*. It's light as gossamer in any case, unlike those horrid, sweaty, man-made, drip-dry bits of rubbish you usually wear. Leave off your roll-on, instead. The Balmain's so well-cut, you'll be able to free your flab for one glorious day, without anyone knowing.'

She hung up and wandered into the garden in her bare feet. This wasn't what she had wanted at all. She'd had plans; she had been going to float upwards into a different world from this crushing suburbia, a world that was thrilling and buoyant. Now here she was, watching her daughter settle for a life that she, Zanna, La Desirous, had done everything to try and escape from. Well, she had escaped for a while. But to make a lasting getaway you had to have something to escape *to*, not just an empty space where love and work used to be. The future yawned before her, containing nothing but small, dull obligations.

Tranquillity was the enemy always, Zanna thought, as she stalked up and down the hot stone slabs of the garden paths, smoking furiously. 'To live is to do things,' she muttered. 'The thing is to catch the future offguard; it's the only way. I'll think of something.'

Behind the bay windows, hooded in ugly red tiles, Aurora was still asleep. This time tomorrow, she'll wake up as Mrs Howard Sutch, Zanna thought grimly. Hardly the brilliant marriage I had in mind for her; my own fault for parking her with Lilian and Sidney during the war. Do what you like, you can't wipe out early influences. Zanna screwed up her eyes and frowned at the sludgy pebble-dash of this house that she detested. The place had always been a threat to her liberty. It was filling up with clutter again: a hostess trolley, an electric floor polisher. You couldn't move without bumping into yet another sign of Aurora's deplorable domesticity. Aurora, like Lilian, had a knack of creating an intolerable, cosy atmosphere that made Zanna feel congealed.

Zanna herself was living rather rootlessly at the Connaught until she found another flat. All her possessions were in store, her couture dresses packed in cedar chests, to be donated to the costume department of the Victoria and Albert Museum. One day, but not just yet. Even though so many years had gone by, some Nosy Parker might start asking questions about how she had managed to acquire a dozen Christian Dior outfits during the ruthless restrictions of 1947.

Living in a hotel room reminded her of wartime, those wonderful years when she never had to go home. She frowned at the house again. If she had stayed in it, or one just like it, during all those dangerous years, and looked after her daughter, perhaps she and Aurora would have more in common now. But what a price to have paid: no Zanna Modes, no passionate assignments, no Harry. Impossible to regret the choices she'd made. Although

309

I was asking for it, Zanna reflected. Fate must have been just itching to slap me down. Designing hats is one thing; trying to design reality was going over the imit. Still, when you hit rock bottom, you bounce.

Aurora, opening her bedroom window and holding up her face to the sun, saw her mother giving springy little jumps on the square of tidy lawn.

'What are you doing, Mummy?'

'Bouncing back, my darling. Go back to bed for a bit. I'm going to the synagogue to check that the flowers are the way they're meant to be.'

Howard's being an orphan complicated the wedding arrangements. Geoffrey, who was giving the bride away, also felt a responsibility towards the bridegroom. Jonathan, Howard's best man, was supposed to be in charge but you'd have to be daft to think an idler like him could get things sorted out. Geoffrey had had to remind him three times to put the wedding ring somewhere where he wouldn't forget it. Jonathan had yawned, beating his hand in front of his mouth before lumbering off, still in his pyjamas, to rootle through his pockets.

There were too many people, both dead and living, who were absent from the proceedings and this put Geoffrey in a glowering mood. Raymond should have been there, would have been if he hadn't worried himself to death. If he'd had money worries, Geoffrey would have helped out and been glad to do it, but Raymond's problems had been worse than financial, sure to have been brought on by Zanna's shadowy carryings-on. If Raymond had found out that she'd been on the fiddle, as Geoffrey had always suspected she had, it would have been more than enough to kill him. The poor bastard had literally scared himself to death. Dead from anxiety, whatever the coroner said about a weak heart.

The trouble with Zanna was that she thought she could leave all her sins behind her; she fiercely believed that the world would toss up something new all the time. Geoffrey hoped she wouldn't try and influence Howard with her crazy ideas although, if she did, Aurora would soon put her foot down. She wasn't a sap like her father; there was no chance of Howard being lured into building castles in the sky.

Stupid to feel angry with Raymond for not being here. Tony was another matter. Things had never gone right between father and son after Geoffrey had come back home after that insane business with Natalie. Tony had got used to having things all his own way during the months that Geoffrey hadn't been around. Minetta had been in a bad way, not up to disciplining the boy. The little scamp had been allowed to stay up watching television as late as he liked; no wonder his school reports had been shocking.

Geoffrey still felt bruised with shame and guilt when he remembered those dreadful weekends when he'd showered Tony with gifts before wretchedly driving him back to the house that Minetta refused to let Geoffrey set foot in. Well, he'd left Natalie, hadn't he? He'd done his duty and had kept on doing it. And still his youngest son refused to forgive him. Family life wasn't like a television set, Geoffrey thought, brushing his black shoes to a glinty shine. When there was a temporary breakdown, you couldn't stick up a notice that said, Normal Service Will Be Resumed As Soon As Possible, and hope that all previous lapses would be quickly forgotten. Once he'd come back to his wife and children, Geoffrey had expected to be allowed to carry on with his Saturday-morning round of golf and his Sunday-afternoon snoozes. Hopeless. Tony had followed him around the house demanding to be taken to the zoo, the waxworks, the Changing of the Guard at Buckingham Palace. When Geoffrey said he was busy, Tony screamed at him that he wanted Geoffrey to go away again so that he'd give him treats at the weekend. Geoffrey bought him Lego sets, jigsaw puzzles, a book-case of Arthur Mee's encyclopaedias, but Tony craved the entertainments offered by philandering fathers. One of the saddest results of Geoffrey's love affair was that it had left his son with a hatred of quiet, solitary pursuits.

'Look, Tony, old son,' Geoffrey would say, 'Daddy's tired. He's had a busy day at the office. How about a bit of peace?' He sounded, he thought, just like Minetta when she was trying to wheedle her way out of sexual intercourse.

Somehow or other, he and Minetta had managed to muddle through, silently accepting each other's short-comings. Tony was less merciful. He'd turned his back on his family, wouldn't even come home for Aurora's wedding, using his absence as one more way to punish his parents. Conceited little git, Geoffrey thought angrily. Him with his spots and his sulkiness; his presence wouldn't have put a song in anyone's heart. Still, it was horrible, the way this family was unravelling. It made him feel powerless and at odds with the world. If Tony had walked through the door at that moment, Geoffrey wouldn't have trusted himself not to have hit him across the mouth.

Minetta put on her rose-pink suit and looked at herself in the full-length mirror. The soft wool skimmed her body so artfully, she felt almost attractive, confident enough to face a world of strangers, even including Natalie Mançeur. She smiled at her reflection as she put on her hat, a swooping disc of pink silk with a cluster of loops on the crown.

Crossing the hall, pleased with herself, her step springy in spite of her new, spindle-heeled shoes, she ran into Geoffrey who passed her, unnoticing, as he shot into his study to ring the car-hire firm for the fifth time that morning. In a moment, her confidence drained away and she was at the mercy of harsh, helpless emotions. Geoffrey hadn't even looked at her pretty suit because he was thinking of Natalie. He had never stopped thinking of her.

There were two Geoffreys: the one who showed himself to his family, aggressively cheerful, impatient,

312

smelling of cigar smoke and polished shoes, and his hidden twin, who yearned for the long-vanished Natalie Bertoud with her light, eager eyes and blue-black hair. Natalie had been his real life; the one he lived with Minetta was only a stilted and unconvincing performance. It was no comfort that Natalie Bertoud was no more, transformed into Natalie Mançeur, wife and mother. Minetta had no idea what Natalie looked like these days – perhaps she had become as hefty as Minetta herself, an unromantic figure, tugging her children's hands on the way to school, loading cornflakes and packets of fish fingers into the boot of her car. Minetta would find out soon enough, the wedding was only hours away, but she knew that the Natalie that used to be lived on in Geoffrey's heart, leaving no room for her. Tears of self-pity ran down Minetta's cheeks and trickled inside the collar of her chiffon blouse.

Geoffrey came in as she was dabbing her wet face with her hanky. 'You know,' he said in a sad voice, 'I've been thinking about Raymond all morning, can't get him out of my mind. Typical of his lousy luck that I'm the one giving his daughter away, and not him.'

Minetta brightened. 'It's Raymond who's been on your mind?'

'Him and the cars. If I've asked Jonathan once, I've asked him a thousand times if he confirmed the journey times and he just scratches his head and looks even more goofy than usual, if that were possible. Unreliable doesn't begin to describe him. Never known such a slacker.' His voice softened. 'By the way, Min, you look like a million dollars. Come over here, you gorgeous great slice of cheesecake, and give your old man a kiss.'

Inside the synagogue, the florists bustled and sweated to carry out Zanna's orders. They moved the trellised archways three times before she was satisfied. Then she insisted on rehanging the swagged muslin that roofed the huppah, the bridal canopy, and tweaked with her squirrel's paws the roses twined around the supporting pillars.

Rabbi Solomon appeared, his beard freshly trimmed for the wedding. 'Beautiful,' he said. 'But enough now, Zanna. Everything is as perfect as it's going to get. You give yourself too tall orders. Go back and rest for an hour or two, you look tired.'

'I didn't sleep last night, must have been the heat.'

'More than the heat, I think. Your hands are trembling. You look on the brink of collapse.'

'So what else is new?' Zanna asked flatly. 'I wrench myself back from the brink on a daily basis. It's a career in itself.'

'Survival often is,' the rabbi said, walking Zanna towards her car. He watched her anxiously as she settled herself on the hot leather seat. 'May God bless you,' he said.

Zanna shook her head. 'God doesn't owe me anything, and vice versa. Don't trouble heaven with prayers for me; I'm not worth it.'

She drove off. Rabbi Solomon looked at the departing Alfa Romeo until it slid around the corner. That's the first time she didn't deny God's existence, he thought. I think we might be getting somewhere.

Zanna was suddenly hungry; she'd been up for hours and hadn't eaten anything. She stopped at a café in Brick Lane and ordered a bagel and a strong black coffee. The café was quiet and dim, almost empty so early in the morning, apart from a few old men reading the newspapers and drinking lemon tea through a cube of sugar held between their teeth. It was a few moments before her eyes adjusted to the shadowy room and she saw Howard sitting at a table and stirring the cup of coffee in front of him in an exhausted way. He was wearing a white shirt with the sleeves rolled up, tight jeans and black cowboy boots, peppered with studs.

She took her cup and plate and went to sit beside him. There were greyish smudges below his narrow eyes and his skin looked waxy. 'You look like a corpse in waiting,' Zanna said cheerfully. 'What's the matter? Didn't you sleep either?'

Howard rubbed his head. 'If I did, I don't remember. I came here just for the silence. There's pandemonium at Minetta's. She and Geoffrey are already in their wedding gear and yelling at Jonathan because he's still in his pyjamas.' He looked at Zanna guardedly. 'Families are difficult, aren't they?'

'Bloody impossible,' she agreed. 'You're lucky to have escaped one for so long. When I was a kid, someone once asked me what I most wanted to be and I said an orphan. About the only time my mother belted me one. It wasn't because I didn't love her though; I just wanted to be able to do things without anyone else thinking that they could interfere. Family life is a bit like a committee meeting that goes on for ever. I never learnt to walk in its field of rules.'

Howard looked at her sternly. 'It's not going to be like that with Aurora and me. We're on the same side.'

He zipped a match into flame on his fingernail to light Zanna's cigarette. He thought that the way that she sat, poker-backed, proclaimed her aloneness. It was the first time he had seen her without make-up and, without her red lipstick, her hair tied in a scarf, she looked unprotected somehow, not the least bit scary.

'I'm sorry,' he said, putting his hand over hers, not quite knowing what he was sorry about.

Zanna's face shut like a door. 'Don't be. I don't see myself as a brave, tragic widow, so why should you? Actually, I've had a much better relationship with Raymond since he died. I think that's true of every wife.'

'I wasn't thinking of Raymond.'

Zanna looked at him with stabbing eyes. He had needle-sharp instincts, this kid. He'd dived behind her words and pulled her thoughts into the air. Aurora would have to be careful, but she probably knew that already. 'Oh sure, *Harry*,' she said jauntily. 'What's between Harry and me is there. I don't suppose it will ever go away.'

'You feel nervous about seeing him again?'

'It's going to be one of those days when I'm going to find it difficult to pretend to be myself. But that's true of all of us, isn't it? We're all putting on an act.' She stood up. 'Time to go, buster. Time to get ready for a date with the rest of our lives.'

The mosaic floor of Suzette's terrace bounced with sunlight as Marty stood back to admire the entwined gilded branches on which stuffed white doves perched. The décor had been his idea and it had turned out just too gorgeously for words. Move over, Oliver Messel.

'You sure about those stuffed birds?' Suzette asked doubtfully, shielding her eyes from the cutting light as she looked out from the french windows.

'Too too truly convinced, petal. Every wedding needs a soupçon of kitsch, even Aurora's. *Especially* Aurora's.' He turned to look at Suzette and gave a low whistle. 'That', he said, impressed, 'is a number.'

Suzette was wearing a Quaker-grey dress and jacket by Givenchy, severely cut to show off her emerald brooch in its whorled gold mount. Zanna had designed the coolie hat made of bands of silky corded ribbon, its brim wide enough to keep the sun off Suzette's expensively renovated face. Suzette stepped out onto the terrace and twirled around on the mosaic squares in which her own and Leonard's intertwined initials had been set at intervals, picked out in bright blue and gold.

'Dee-vine,' Marty said. 'It says I don't care how I look, although as it happens I look perfect. Which you do.'

Dominick joined them, fastening his cuff-links. 'What did I tell you, hot enough to boil a lobster,' he said triumphantly.

'Go and wash your mouth out with soap,' Suzette said. 'Everything is strictly Kosher today. The caterer is going to put little cards on the tables to say so. To keep Minetta happy. She hasn't forgiven me for Clemency's oyster surprise yet – it turned out to be more of a surprise than I thought it would be – and that was yonks and yonks ago.'

'*Gesundheit*,' Marty said. '*Mazel tov*. I wish you long life.'

Suzette flapped her hands at him in agitation. 'Lordy, don't say *that*. You only wish Jewish people long life when you see them at funerals. Zanna told me that when we buried poor old Raymond. She said that she thought wishing people a long life was batty in any case because all the extra years come at the end, just when you don't want them.'

'This wedding seems to be baited with traps,' Marty sighed. 'There's a risk of my making a real clot of myself.'

Dominick rumpled Marty's hair, a gesture full of affection. 'Just react to events like a finely trained tiger and you can't go wrong,' he said fondly. 'What I forgot to tell you, Suze, is that Marty and I have been having business dealings with one of Aurora's rejected suitors, Otto Welliver.'

'Otto? I thought he was in South Africa. I don't know what happened between him and Aurora but in the end it didn't. Good thing, too. That boy had all the makings of an ugly failure.'

Suzette remembered the small boy that Otto had been when she first knew him. You could see the bones move in his skull, under his cropped hair, a sight both horrible and heart-breaking. He'd grown up to be quite a dish in a wolfish sort of way, but he seemed to smile with cold teeth. Suzette shivered slightly, recalling that smile.

'He is in South Africa,' Dominick said. 'It's his solicitor at Utley we're dealing with. Otto's too busy making his grandfather's money disappear into fast cars and faster women, well, that's the story anyway. Sounds like the boy is trouble's closest friend, subject to rages and black depressions. Probably bonkers like his mad old dad. Now *there* was violence in disguise, if ever I saw it.'

'The point is,' Marty interrupted, 'Otto's selling us Utley Manor, or what's left of it, which are a few scorched stones. Dominick's indulging me in a little foray into the restaurant business. The plan is to bring a bit of chichi to Shropshire. I'm thinking of calling the restaurant Lucullus. There'll be a series of dining-rooms in different colours, each one with a differently priced menu. Don't you think that will be rather charming, Suze?'

'Another of Marty's flights of fancy, I'm afraid,' Dominick said in a proprietorial way. 'Like his idea of growing tomatoes outdoors. I admit they tasted like mouthfuls of sunshine, but they were so ridged and humpy none of the supermarkets would touch them. Plus, I got a bollocking from the Min. of Ag. Money-makers, eight to the pound and grown under plastic, that's what everybody wants.'

'Moneymakers. They look like billiard balls and are about as tasty. The Min. of Ag. couldn't tell the differ-ence between an Elizabeth David ratatouille and a TV dinner.' Marty's voice sounded childish and petulant and he gave Dominick a sly, hurt look. Not a trace left of the rough, cocky film projectionist he'd been not so very long ago; a sturdy, muscular boy, hanging around Old Compton Street in a cracked-leather jacket, letting lecherous old publishers buy him double gins.

Today, Marty was wearing pearl-grey morning dress, the coat straining a bit over his strong shoulders. He smelled rather headily of some tangy cologne and his face had acquired the smooth sheen brought about by the complete lack of any responsibility.

And Dominick, what on earth had happened to him? Suzette wondered. He had put on weight, become quite jowly, in fact, like a yeoman in a comic opera. Could he be the same man who had been notable for the fluttery movements of his wrists as he moved among the over-priced antiques of his London shop, waving his feather duster like a wand? These days, Dominick's tread was so heavy, you felt he might make the floor crack up under his feet. He was losing his wavy hair, showing a strawberry-pink scalp dotted with freckles, and there was a thin line of dirt under his fingernails. Marty noticed Suzette's critical expression and a protective look floated across his face.

'Don't give him a lecture, dear. He's a horny-handed son of toil these days, simply can't be faffed with manicures any more. If it's impeccable you want, I'm sure we can count on Howard looking very natty.'

Suzette, sensing the first signs of what might turn out to be a lengthy bout of huffiness, took Marty's arm. 'Dominick looks peachy creamy, peachy creamy,' she said soothingly. 'Did I ever tell you about the first and only time Len and Zanna and I were invited to dinner at Utley Manor? Cold enough to freeze the arse off a stoker and then we were supposed to eat these teensy-weensy little birds that were all splinters and gristle and had this strange pong. I think it was the only time in her life that Zanna noticed what was on her plate; the bones and the smell were *that* memorable. There were creepy-crawlies in the veg too.'

Suzette was suddenly overcome with laughter. She held onto Marty's shoulder, spluttering through her giggles. 'A restaurant at Utley Manor, of all places. Dining-rooms in different colours; cream in the soup and wine waiters poncing about. O joy, O bliss. Better watch out though, boys, or Gomer will come back and haunt the joint, putting bones in the gravy and slugs in the pancakes.' She laughed so much, she had to completely redo her eye make-up.

Daisy could tell how nervous Harry was by his pomposity. He arrived at her flat hours too early – at breakfast-time while she was still in her dressing-gown – clutching a brown paper parcel, Aurora's and Howard's wedding present, which it hadn't occurred to him to post.

Daisy was reading a report in the *Irish Times* which stated that the Taoiseach, Sean Lemass, had expressed the hope that future EEC membership of his country would make a nonsense of its partition.

Still holding the parcel to his chest, Harry peered over her shoulder and said, 'I don't think you'll find that to be a particularly widely held perception,' in a plummy voice that made Daisy bristle.

He did look undeniably handsome though in his old morning coat, probably inherited from Robert, like much of Harry's mouldering wardrobe. The coat sat well on his wide shoulders and tapered in to the waist most elegantly. Looking as he did, there was really no need for Harry to be so nerve-racked or to try and hide his jitters by talking as though he were made out of granite and barbed wire. His imposing presence would always see him through.

'Harry, you are quite hopeless,' Daisy scolded him. 'You can't take a brown paper parcel into a synagogue; you would look like a perfect loon. Put it down and I'll have it delivered to the house when Aurora and Howard come back from their honeymoon. What have you bought them, anyway?' she asked curiously. Harry was renowned for his hopelessness at buying presents. His habit was to buy curious wooden or woven objects made by the peasants of the Eastern European countries he visited on Labour Party delegations, and then present them to his family and friends on their birthdays. Zanna called these strange offerings conversation pieces because, she said, 'When you put one out on display, someone is sure to ask what the hell it is, and that starts a conversation.'

'I'll show you.' Harry wrenched at the frayed string. He took out three chased and gilded wooden letters: 'A', '&' and 'H'. 'There was this shop being demolished in Great Garden Street in Chipperton,' he said. 'These were part of the old shop-front. The builders were just about to smash it up as I was passing, on my way to address a meeting at the Tailors & Garment Workers Union, so I made them sell it to me. Do you think these are acceptable? One never knows with Aurora. She dismisses so many things as being what she calls mere whimsy.'

'Perfectly acceptable,' Daisy assured him, fingering the gilded grooves of the letters. 'Far more original than guest-towels and very romantic to boot. They will look very nice on that massive shelving thing that Howard has put up for his record collection. The ampersand was a particularly thoughtful purchase.' She placed it between the A and the H on the breakfast table. 'See? It yokes them together. Long may they be ampersanded.' She raised her teacup in a toast, making Harry fidget. 'What shop was being pulled down?' Daisy asked, drinking the rest of her tea.

'A hatter's, strangely enough,' Harry said uncomfortably.

'Hmm. Not the best of times for hatters,' Daisy said, shooting him a meaningful look.

Leonora came into the kitchen, walking very slowly and wearing her beautiful old coat and the spangled cartwheel hat that Zanna had given her. Her deafness made her china-blue eyes look permanently startled as she gazed out from underneath the glossy feathers.

'Aunt Leonora, you look quite marvellous,' Harry bawled at her. 'I'm delighted that hat has made its way back to our family.'

'My fervent desire is that its creator will do the same thing,' Daisy said, making Harry pull hard at his cheek.

While they waited for Daisy to get ready, Leonora said, 'I am so terribly looking forward to seeing Zanna again. The very sight of her is like drinking your first glass of champagne. It seems such an age since we last met. I do hope there hasn't been any unpleasantness.'

Harry felt a strong desire to tell Leonora everything. She was so old that nothing would shock her: Gomer's attempts at blackmail, Zanna's treachery, Daisy's harsh censoriousness, his own craven behaviour. He cleared his throat, pushed back the lock of hair over his forehead and edged his chair nearer to hers. Leonora laid her webby old hand over his. 'No point in telling me anything, dearest boy,' she said. 'I'm deaf as a post.'

321

Daisy came back, tucking the ends of her hair under the cockaded turban which, by some sophisticated magic, made her raw-boned, untidy face look sleekly cared-for. 'We'll have to go in your car, Harry,' she said. 'Zanna has forbidden me to wear my glasses with this hat.'

Leonora had no idea what Daisy was saying, noticed only how nice she looked with her straggly hair smoothed away under her new hat. She swung her head slightly, pleased when the black plumes on her brow tipped their *diamanté* droplets into a dance. 'As a milliner, Zanna is better than perfect,' she announced, as Harry guided her towards the cage of the lift.

The smell of Chipperton on a hot summer's day never changes, Harry thought, as he parked his car outside the synagogue and helped Leonora onto the baking pavement. Drains, escaping dribbles of gas, rotting veg etables. Whenever he'd driven here with Zanna, she had dabbed some lily of the valley scent on the underside of her white wrist and held it beneath his nose. What was it that she had accused him of on one such journey? 'You like to draw people's breath for them,' that had been it, and probably true at the time too. No longer. Without Zanna, he had begun to fear the future, the worst thing that can happen to a politician. Sometimes, he felt it was almost too much of an effort to draw his own breath.

A crowd had gathered in front of the synagogue, drawn by half a dozen press photographers who had been sent out to take pictures of Aurora in her Balenciaga wedding dress and head-dress designed by Zanna Modes.

'Snap a few of the bride's mother, while you're about it,' the man from *Vogue* had been instructed by his editor. 'Zanna Gringrich. The best-dressed woman in London in her day. A bit before your time,' she added tolerantly, smiling at the photographer who had a pudding-basin haircut and wore a jacket cut like a bullfighter's bolero.

'Old bird is she then?' he asked.

'Present at the Creation,' the editor agreed. 'I doubt if she'll see forty again.'

'Where did you get that hat? Where did you get that tile?' a fat woman in the crowd began to sing as Leonora, holding onto Harry's arm, walked slowly towards the porch of the synagogue. Others in the crowd joined in, happy, on this hot day, to have something to do that didn't require much effort. Leonora couldn't hear what the crowd was singing but, encouraged by the way people smiled and waved at her, smiled and waved back.

'And that's what's-his-face,' another woman said. She wore a brightly flowered dress, the size of a tent, and wound the reins of a straying toddler around her hand. 'Didn't he used to be Harry Welliver?'

Daisy was glad to get out of the raw sunlight into the synagogue's cool, filtered shade. Mrs Harris appeared out of the shadows and led her and Leonora to the side of the room where the women sat, while David Letvin, Howard's right-hand man at Daydream Dresses, took Harry towards a cardboard box full of yarmulkes, the black skullcaps which men were required to wear, and put one on top of his floppy hair.

It suited Harry, Daisy thought, peering across the aisle at him, made him look rather scholarly. Beside her, Leonora was giving little trumpeting sounds of pleasure, breathing in the spicy scent of the roses, freshly watered in their beribboned tubs. Daisy shut her eyes and listened to the deep, mournful rumbling of the organ. Silly of her to have felt uneasy about this wedding. Now she was here she felt soaked in peace. Nothing could go wrong.

'My hat, but you're a beauty and I take all the credit for it,' Zanna crowed, straightening Aurora's train in front of Lilian's elaborate triple mirror. 'And it's about time that bloody car showed up.'

As she looked at her watch, the telephone rang. It was the driver of the Rolls-Royce that Geoffrey had ordered to collect the bride and her mother. The engine had overheated and the car had stalled on the narrowest part of the road, in front of Jack Straw's Castle, the pub from where the driver was now frantically telephoning. Behind his gibbering apologies, Zanna could hear the blare of a hundred car horns, squeezed by the fingers of a hundred furious motorists, stuck beside Hampstead Heath on the hottest day of the year, not able to budge until the Rolls with its white streamers could be hoisted away. She almost danced across the room, her wide smile triumphant. 'Your Uncle Geoffrey's loused things up again,' she said. 'He's brought the whole of North London to a standstill. He'll never be invited to fork suppers in the Bishop's Avenue for the rest of his life. So we'll just have to zoom along in the Alfa. Lucky your dress isn't a crinoline style.'

Geoffrey, waiting just inside the synagogue for his niece to arrive, watched Natalie Mançeur as she brushed her small daughter's blue-black hair. Natalie's own hair had turned strikingly grey, pinned up in a heavy bun under the blue-grey pillbox that matched her full-skirted dress.

That particular shade of blue-grey, the colour of cigar smoke, had always been Natalie's favourite colour. Geoffrey felt a stabbing pain under his ribs as he looked at her, crouched over her child, and turned away. Introductions had gone smoothly enough, thanks to Natalie's husband. Jean-Louis had complimented Minetta on her hat and then rocked her hand gently up and down in his own before planting a kiss on it, causing Minetta's soft cheeks to turn as rosy as her jacket.

Now they were all waiting rather anxiously for the bride. Natalie settled the little sailor hats on her children's smooth heads. They looked adorable – Christabel in her smocked dress and Bruno in long cream shorts and a pink-and-cream striped shirt. Even Minetta forgot her old jealousies and accepted a rose petal from Christabel's basket.

Natalie smoothed out the floating streamers on the little sailor hats one last time, as tenderly and ravenously absorbed by her children as she had once been by Geoffrey Fadge. Geoffrey stood on the porch and looked gloomily up and down the street. Aurora should have been here by now. He hated this waiting around, without even a cigar to chomp on. He stretched his neck inside the chafing starched collar of his shirt, his jaw working away, reminding Christabel of a nervous horse. Then, from the street outside, they heard the cheering begin.

By the time Zanna's Alfa Romeo turned up, the crowd on the pavement had got bigger. Word had spread that this was Aurora Gringrich's wedding: Aurora, that lovely, determined girl who sent teams of volunteers to teach Pakistani women English in their own homes, when they were too shy and frightened to leave them; Aurora who chivvied the local council into providing a play-centre here, a roof on a bus-shelter there. And she was marrying that fine piece of work, Howard Sutch. He was a bit of all right, as well, taking on more and more staff at Daydream; never too busy to explain to the bewildered and disgruntled Chipperton residents how they could winnow their way through the complicated business of living in London, a city partitioned by money. This was a wedding not to be missed. People in the nearby houses made themselves cups of strong tea and sat on their gritty front steps, munching biscuits beside the cloudy milk bottles and old newspapers, waiting for the bride to arrive.

Zanna parked the car expertly and slid out of her seat. Women, hot and sweaty in halter-topped sundresses, leaned over the brick-walled balconies of their cramped flats to drink in the sight of her. She was dressed head to toe in pale yellow, from her hat – a tilted saucer in waxy straw, each strand of which was edged in a narrow band of yellow-pink satin – to her strappy, high-heeled shoes.

In between, was a tight-sleeved coat over a matching dress, austere but fresh and brilliant. Zanna struck her model-girl pose: one foot at right angles to the other, happy to be in her natural element, which was limelight. The crowd clucked with approval. A very old woman, now totally blind, who had once been the best bead embroiderer in Chipperton, called out to her neighbour on the adjoining balcony, 'Who's this now? Who's come?'

The neighbour, a tired-looking girl with the beginning of a bad sunburn, called back, 'Must be the bride's mum from the get-up. Driving the bride in a sports car. Nice-looking tart. Skinny though; she could slip down the back of a radiator without any problem. Looks as though she's doing the whole world a favour by being here.'

She leaned her reddening arms on the balcony wall and stared hard at Zanna in the street below. 'Never seen eyes like that in my life. Like two amethysts stuck in her face.'

'Purple eyes?' The blind woman knew who the cheers were for now.

'Betcha, that's Lilian Spetner's girl. I know everything there is to be knowed about her. A real terror to work for. Always going farther than she was able to go and taking you along with her. She can't be doing so well if her daughter's getting married round here, and not even a proper wedding car. This would have broken Lilian's heart; her granddaughter back here, after she and Sidney worked like slaves to get away. *They* would have insisted on St John's Wood, God rest their souls.'

Leon Rubinstein, on his way home from his own, more Orthodox synagogue in Black Lion Yard, looked sourly at the noisy crowd. What kind of a wedding was this? Zanna's shiny sports car, the general air of high spirits in the street, the blazing sunshine itself could all be laid at Rabbi Solomon's door. Men like him, so-called enlightened men, had shredded away the old beliefs. Leon recalled his own wedding to poor Rachel. Leon and the two fathers had worn fur-trimmed hats and black frock-coats. Rachel was led towards him by their two mothers, carrying candles, and she had circled around him seven times, thus entering the seven spheres of his soul. After the ceremony, Leon and Rachel had retired to a side room to drink golden chicken soup together, this fast-breaking a symbolic consummation of their marriage, the glinting broth a symbol of the richness and warmth of their future.

Afterwards, they had joined their guests, the women in one banquet room, the men in another, the bride and groom being carried aloft on chairs to join each other for a few moments. There had been a whole week of feasting. Leon shook his head. To Rabbi Solomon and his kind, such rituals would seem out-of-date. It wouldn't tear Rabbi Solomon's heart out that the women in his congregation no longer covered their heads with the traditional wigs or that the men dared to carry umbrellas on wet sabbaths. Leon wanted to raise his fist against such godless conduct, but knew he would be ridiculed. He recognized the woman the crowd was admiring. Zanna Gringrich. Almost the last words his Rachel had spoken were to ask God to bless Zanna. And God had listened. He had given Zanna this cloudless day, after weeks of teeming rain, for her daughter's wedding day.

Leon stumbled on towards the meal his youngest daughter, Ruthie, would have prepared for him. She was the only one of his sons and daughters still at home with him in Chipperton, a timid girl, grey and noiseless as a snail. The others had left to live in the suburbs of outer London and Leon knew that they were urging Ruthie to leave too. His children thought him a tyrannical father, and shunned him. He offered up his loneliness to God as a sacrifice and gave the women sitting on the steps, thirstily drinking mugs of tea as they waited for the bride to step out of the car, a look like thunder before he turned the corner.

Aurora started to get out of the car but Zanna had seen the photographers waiting in the street. 'There are loads of girls hanging out of the windows of that factory over there,' she said. 'Seems like they know who you are,

327

chickadee. Why don't you stand up on the back seat and give them a wave?'

Aurora clambered up on the seat and shook the bouquet of cream roses and white sweet peas at a group of machinists who were yelling 'Good luck' to her, shouldering themselves into the windows and swishing banners of artificial silk, which they'd torn from the bolts of lining material piled up in the corner of their stifling workroom.

A photograph of Aurora, precariously poised, her arms outstretched in greeting, appeared on the front page of both London's evening papers. The caption in the *Daily News*, underneath the heading Wild About the Boy, read: 'Aurora Gringrich waves to admiring crowds before her marriage to Howard Sutch, head of Daydream Dresses. Aurora's head-dress of wild grasses and silk flowers, was designed by her mother, Zanna, one of London's most exclusive milliners.' Exclusive had come to mean something that hardly anyone wanted.

At last, Zanna and Aurora walked into the synagogue. 'Afraid you screwed up with the car, old bean,' Zanna greeted Geoffrey with a malevolent smile. 'Should have left it to Jonathan to organize.'

Ivan appeared at Zanna's elbow to escort her up the aisle. He had rushed here straight from the lunch-time shift at the bistro and smelled faintly of fried onions and olive oil.

Harry turned around in his seat to watch Zanna make her graceful progress to where Howard and Jonathan stood under the canopy. How beautiful she was still; that strange, sharp-edged beauty that seemed to make the light brim around her. As she passed by, her lily of the valley scent drifted from her skin. It made him want to kiss the face off her and then succumb to her own red, red kisses.

Zanna looked straight ahead, her face as blank as a doll's, but Harry knew that she must be suffering. This wasn't at all what she would have chosen for Aurora. Howard was a decent enough chap but his zeal to preserve the solid traditions and plodding duties of suburban life – everything that Zanna had tried to escape from – must be making her wince. Harry had a hunch that Aurora was using this marriage to thwart Zanna in some way, although he couldn't say how. It wasn't as though they weren't deeply in love, Howard and Aurora, in their rather funless way. It was just that they behaved as though they had passed some examination in worthiness that Zanna had failed.

Right now, Zanna was losing her daughter as surely as she had lost everything else: Raymond, her career and Harry himself. Deeply ashamed, Harry began to pull at his cheek, until a crunching look from Daisy, sitting across the aisle, made him bring his hand away from his face. What a coward he had been. His failure to protect Zanna from all the things that had made her unhappy had been unforgivable. He had stood uncaringly by as his refusal to marry her had made them both rather ridiculous figures. He had purposely ignored the misery that Zanna kept so fiercely private that only he had known it was there. There is such harm in love, he thought; you could spend a lifetime trying to undo it. He looked at the unyielding set of Zanna's straight, tailored shoulders as she retreated further down the aisle. He hoped it was not too late; he felt ripe for a second chance.

Zanna didn't dare flick her eyes around the room to search out Harry; the sight of him could have her in pieces. She kept her purple gaze on the rabbi and cantor as she approached them. In their black robes, fringed white scarves and tall black hats, they had the stately symmetry of penguins. Dropping her gaze, it fastened on Minetta's hat. Zanna frowned. The stupid cow had put it on at completely the wrong angle. After all those rehearsals in front of the mirror too, when Zanna had shown her exactly how the thing should be balanced on her head. Impossible to teach Minetta what style was; you'd be better off trying to hem a blancmange. She shuddered with rage and Ivan, thinking that the shudder

329

expressed a tremulous joy, squeezed her arm affectionately as they took their places under the canopy beside
the bridegroom.

The organist began to play the wedding music, composed by the synagogue's cantor and inspired by the
'Song of Songs'. Exultant chords unfolded and quivered
above the congregation's heads as Aurora made her
entrance on her uncle's arm.

One look at her, and Howard felt that he had reached
home after an exhausting and dangerous journey. This
luscious girl, walking towards him, her bouquet resting
on her silky arms, was his dearest upon this earth. His
old fear that he and Aurora would some day find
themselves locked in a heavy pretence of love, slithered away for ever. This wedding was entirely appro-
priate. Besides which, Auroradorable was beautiful
enough to hang on a wall.

The cantor sang a welcome; deep, velvety music
poured out of his throat, making Suzette think of
brandy in a warmed glass. She licked her lips and
decided to start drinking again. Why not? she
thought. One day, we'll all be dead, pushing up the
dahlias. As soon as I get home, I'm going to get lit up like
a chandelier. Yes, I will. Indeedy-doody.

Rabbi Solomon passed a goblet of wine to the bridegroom and recited a blessing.

'You're supposed to lift my veil, now,' Aurora whispered to Zanna out of the corner of her mouth. Zanna
did so and, dissatisfied by the way the veiling settled
over Aurora's head-dress, spent several moments rearranging it while the rabbi waited patiently.

'It doesn't have to be perfect,' Aurora hissed.

'Everything has to be perfect,' Zanna hissed back, but
stepped aside so that the goblet of wine could be passed
to the bride who, with a sigh of impatience that only
Zanna could hear, sipped from it and yanked her veil
over her face again.

The gold ring slid over Aurora's finger. *'Harey at
mekuddeshet li b'taba'at zo k'dat Moshe v'Yisrael.'*

Howard spoke his marriage vow in a clear and joyful voice and repeated it in English: 'Behold thou art consecrated unto me with this ring according to the law of Moses and of Israel.'

Rabbi Solomon began the sermon. He spoke of the honour paid to him by this gifted family celebrating a marriage in this particular synagogue, in the heart of one of the poorest areas of London: Chipperton, in whose peeling tenements the bride's grandparents had grown up and from where, because of their hard work and strong heads, they had escaped, to prosper else-where. But it was to Chipperton that Sidney and Lilian's granddaughter had returned to celebrate the most important day of her life, to share it with those less fortunate than herself, as she shared everything that was given to her. 'Never', the rabbi said, in a reverential way, 'have I been made aware of such deep kindness in a human soul. If evidence were needed of Aurora's gleaming heart, I can inform you that she has donated her magnificent bridal gown, the work, I understand, of a distinguished dress designer in Paris, to a poor girl, a factory worker in this neigh-bourhood, who is getting married tomorrow to a young man as penniless as she is herself.'

Zanna gave a start. This was the first she had heard of this inconvenient act of generosity. Unknown to Aurora, Zanna had come to a lucrative arrangement with a bridal-wear manufacturer: she would rent him the Balenciaga creation for a few days so that he could examine it seam by seam and then bring out a far cheaper copy that would go on sale in department stores all over the country.

'Howard and Aurora have lit a light in each other's hearts, and each of us is touched by the brightness,' the rabbi intoned, but Zanna had stopped listening by then, her attention skittering. Her eyes flew around the room, her gloved fingers itching to fold themselves around a pencil and make quick sketches of the hats and suits and dresses she liked the look of.

Not that there was a lot to admire; most female heads were topped with an insignificant pillbox, totally devoid of drama. And what a wriggly lot these women are, Zanna thought, tugging at their skirts all the time. Why is that? Because of skirts getting shorter, I suppose. Difficult when you have to be seated for any length of time. Skirts had been this length – about two inches below the knee – during the war, but the cut had been different, looser on the hip so more inclined to stay put, unlike these wrinkly sheaths that she saw the rows of women in front of her fidgeting with, obviously worried about their skirts riding up to reveal an inelegant display of stocking-top. This was a problem that wasn't going to go away; all the signs were that hemlines were going to rise even higher. If they did, stockings would be worse than useless, but what could women wear instead? They'd need something that reached to the top of their thighs and didn't require suspenders, the sort of thing that ballet dancers wore. Could she get in on this, transform the British hosiery industry? There would be huge money in it.

The vein in Zanna's temple went bump bump bump, as it did when she was excited. This was going to be a big thing. What a risk though, but she had to do it. The thing to fear is the thing to do, she told herself. She'd need some help. One thing she'd learnt, painfully too, was that she lacked the sort of steadiness that was crucial if you wanted to stay in business. She was useless at strategy, always had been.

She was jolted out of her reverie by the snap of breaking glass and cries of 'Mazel tov.' Howard had crushed a glass under his right foot, marking the end of the wedding ceremony.

Howard, Zanna thought. Shrewd, patient Howard with his clever, narrow eyes. He shared her energy and indestructible ambition, but harnessed both to a sound and quiet common sense. And he knew about clothes, understood the quick, tense swings of fashion better than she did. He'd do. She would take him into partnership. That would be one in the eye for Geoffrey, who'd been trying to lure Howard into his own firm and have him spend his days working out new methods of giving sliced carrots crinkly edges.

Zanna took Ivan's arm and followed Aurora's narrow train down the aisle, feeling that the earth was rolling again. Her new business plans had slammed the door on dismay; she felt composed enough to seek out Harry. There he was, at the end of the row, his long legs painfully wedged and the sunlight glinting on his gold cuff-link shaped into the head of St Jude, the patron saint of lost causes.

Zanna turned her eyes on him, those purple eyes that shone with the knowledge of disreputable and exciting secrets, and Harry met her gaze with a smile on his narrow mouth that was so wide it seemed to disappear around the back of his head. He felt weak with pride in her. One look from those beloved eyes and he knew his ruined spirit was on the mend.

Don't buy it, don't believe it, Zanna told herself sternly as she passed by but, knowing that Harry's smile was lingering on the back of her head, muttered, 'It's love, in case you don't know it,' and began to cry.

I don't know why we always thought Zanna was such a hard-bitten case, Ivan thought. Seems to me that she's touched to the core that Robbie and Howard are so in love. He squeezed Zanna's hand and gave her his handkerchief, pungent with the smell of garlic, to dry her tears.

The wedding guests tumbled into the sunshine. They felt heady, heightened somehow. Something in the air put them in a jumpy, happy mood and expectation whirled them around. They hugged each other and made explosive little kisses into the air – mmwah, mmwah – swaying slightly on the cracked and sunken pavement in a non-existent breeze, before getting into their cars and driving to Grosvenor Square for the wedding reception.

'This orange juice is too orangey,' Suzette said and ordered a waiter to put some gin in it.

Marty stretched his arm towards her and traced the fine scar behind her ear with the tip of his finger. 'Remember the new face, my dear old thing,' he warned unpleasantly.

'Oh shut up, do,' Suzette said. 'I'm going to *coast* through gins today. I want to feel abandoned enough to dance the Twist.' She cocked her head towards the four mop-headed musicians who were attacking their drums and guitars at the far end of the terrace. 'That music isn't as bad as it sounds,' she said, and began to jiggle her shoulders to the beat, while Marty headed towards the bedroom balcony to see if Cecil Beaton needed any assistance arranging Aurora against a background of clematis and honeysuckle.

By the time Aurora and Howard appeared on the terrace, Aurora turning her wedding ring around her finger over and over again, the atmosphere was hospitable and flowing and Suzette was in the state she most liked to be in: hazy and lucid at the same time.

'Darlingest ones, I hope you'll both be as happy as whales in clover,' she greeted them wildly. She tripped over someone's foot which turned out to be Jonathan's, so she led him through the gilded branches which Marty had decorated so exotically, to where people were dancing to 'Bei Mir Bist Du Shane'. Jonathan's thick, dull body lightened as her hand settled on his shoulder,

'What a surprisingly good dancer you are, Jonathan,' Suzette said. 'Although I shouldn't be surprised. Rayond was too, although he was just as clumsy as you when it came to real life.'

Clemency was stretched out on Suzette's bed, her eyes closed and her enormous belly rising in the taut curve of late pregnancy. Minetta was holding a damp, cool cloth to the girl's forehead, while Zanna was massaging her swollen ankles.

'The heat and noise were too much for her, poor lamb,' Minetta said, her voice soft with love. Already, the milky smell of her unborn grandchild sailed up her

334

nostrils. She loved babies, the way they looked at you out of their grave, navy-blue, new-born eyes and loved you, unconditionally, just because you loved them.

She had behaved very nastily towards Zanna – all that viciously undertaken knitting and taunting – but she had been goaded by jealousy. It had seemed so unfair that Zanna, who had no interest in babies at all, would be the first to be a grandmother.

That was over now. She forgave Clemency everything: her cruel, unpleasant parents, her limp yellow hair clamped in an Alice band, her failing to tell herself and Geoffrey that a baby was on the way. 'It wasn't Clemency's fault, Mum,' Ivan had explained sheepishly, as he'd helped to lower his enormous, drooping wife onto the bed. 'She was the one who said we ought to tell you, but I thought the news might send you into one of your states.'

As though it would. Minetta wrung out the cloth in a bowl of cold water and pressed it tenderly on Clemency's curved pink brow.

'I'm really thrilled for you, Min.' Zanna looked at her sister over the mound of Clemency's belly. 'And to prove it, I'm going to give you back the bobbly yellow matinée jacket you knitted for Aurora's baby. Clemency's first in the queue for a layette.' She gave Clemency's ankle a final pat and left the room.

Harry watched Zanna come out onto the terrace. He got up from his chair, setting it rocking on its back legs and startling Mrs Harris who was gossiping with Daisy and Leonora. He shouldered his way towards Zanna through the noisy crowd. He brushed against fashion editors with lacquered faces; wan young women who had been to university with Aurora and had since become social workers; the machinists from Daydream Dresses, with flowers stuck into their piled-up hair and bracelets slipping up and down their arms as they danced; sharply dressed young men who were business associates of Howard's, wearing shirts with rounded collars and Italian suits; Zanna's clients, gamely ageing women with thin legs and exquisite shoes.

Harry went whooshing past and they all moved out of the way of his bruising shoulders as he tunnelled his way towards Zanna, who was standing in front of the french windows.

He took her hand in his and found that both their hands were trembling. They stood together in the last of the light of the sun, shivering with desire.

'I miss you,' Harry said awkwardly. 'Come back to me.'

Zanna shook her head. 'I've learnt something in the last year; what Diana Vreeland called the necessity of refusal. It's what makes a good designer pare down the original conception.'

Harry groaned with exasperation. 'Why are you talking about fashion, when I'm asking you to marry me?'

'I'm not talking about fashion. I'm talking about life,' Zanna said.

Daisy, peering at them over the swirling feathers of Leonora's hat, saw that they were both glaring, locked in each other's eyes as they moved their faces and bodies closer and closer together.

Heavens, Daisy thought. How right Mother was. From the very beginning she said that this love affair was a battlefield. Those two fighting spirits had better stay ardent; it's certainly not in their natures to be amenable.

'Conjuring wildfire up, that was it,' Suzette said, pleased with herself for remembering the words Zanna used to explain the way that she and Harry loved each other. She looked at them reaching out for each other's arms. They seemed to be dissolved in light, or was that just the effect of the gin?

'Sometimes the long way round is the best way home,' Harry murmured convincingly, his narrow lips against Zanna's neck, holding her close, neither of them hearing the first gentle clap of rain on the windows.

THE END